The Growing Years

by Bernard Doove
in collaboration with
Christopher Barry

THE GROWING YEARS

This is a work of fiction. All characters and events portrayed within are fictitious.

Story copyright © 2016 Bernard Doove
Some characters and the *My Little Pony: Friendship is Magic* universe are the property of Hasbro.

A production of *The Chakat's Den* – www.chakatsden.com
All rights reserved, including the right to reproduce this book, or any portions thereof, in any form.

Cover art by *GrayPaint* © 2016

Printed by CreateSpace
ISBN-10: 1532898851
ISBN-13: 978-1532898853

Other books by Bernard Doove:

<u>MLP:FiM:</u>
  Change of Life
  Growing Up Dandy
  Conversations in a Canterlot Café
  A Different Perspective

<u>Chakat Universe:</u>
  Forest Tales
  Transformations
  More Terrible than Chains
  Other Trails Taken
  Tales from the Chakat Universe
  Life's Dream
  Flight of the Star Phoenix

<u>Other:</u>
  Jazmyn's World

Contents

Foreword 4
Chapter 1: Renaissance 5
Chapter 2: Fly Day 14
Chapter 3: Treasured 18
Chapter 4: Nightmare Nights 52
Chapter 5: Foalsitting 68
Chapter 6: Divine Introspections 82
Chapter 7: Tag! 87
Chapter 8: Spring Break 92
Chapter 9: Blue's Field Trip 131
Chapter 10: It's About Time! 145
Chapter 11: The Test 153
Chapter 12: Clandestine Conversation 159
Chapter 13: The Fall 166
Chapter 14: The Epiphany Gambit 197
Chapter 15: Meetings 225
Chapter 16: The Calm Before The Storm 242
Art Credits 256

Foreword

This story is a fan-fiction set in the *My Little Pony: Friendship is Magic* universe. The story builds on material that can be found in my previous stories: *Change of Life, The Best Present,* and *Conversations in a Canterlot Café,* and is a **direct sequel** to *A Different Perspective*. I strongly recommend that you read those books to learn about the characters and background material before you read this one.

Christopher Barry had a lot of input into this book, and wrote a lot of material for it. I massaged it into shape and blended it with my own, so if you notice a bit of a difference in style in places, that's probably Christopher's work.

A huge thank-you for all of Jeff Hartt's editing work!

And as a reminder to my American readers – Yes, I am still using British/Australian spelling for my paperback books. I hope you can forgive me! =^_^=

Bernard "Goldfur" Doove

Chapter 1:
Renaissance

Nopony took much notice of the green unicorn mare with blue mane and tail, but that was the general idea. One did not infiltrate hostile territory by attracting attention, and it was her intention to quietly slip through the passers-by without getting more than an incurious glance. An impassive expression was also a must, but she was having a hard time holding it whenever she saw the Blue Changelings occasionally among the population, and for every undisguised changeling, she was sure there were several more going about their business unrecognised in their pony guises, out of range of her ability to sense. It was imperative that she avoided undue attention from them for as long as possible, even though their hive was her ultimate goal. She had a task to fulfil, and no one – changeling or pony – was going to make her fail.

The information that the mare had procured earlier, guided her swiftly and accurately to the outskirts of Ponyville where an impressive structure of steel and glass was being built close to the crystalline castle that was the Equestrian residence of Princess Twilight Sparkle and her mate, the so-called Prince Firetail a.k.a. Free Agent a.k.a. Gossamer, Queen of the Blue Hive. She was impressed in spite of herself. The disgusting open relationship that the Blues had with the local ponies nevertheless was producing some unlikely cooperative efforts. The new Queen certainly seemed to be ensuring that she made an impression, and that was as it should be. Nevertheless, it was not her goal today.

The unicorn made her way to the castle. She had not been able to believe the initial reports that the castle was normally unguarded, and the common citizens regularly visited for various reasons to see either of the royal couple, or their important associates. It turned out to be true though, and she felt contempt for their naiveté, but it worked to her advantage. She entered the castle as nonchalantly as possible, passing through the huge entry hall into what seemed to be a bizarre throne room. Why there were six thrones all arranged about a huge round table though, utterly mystified her. How did a Queen exert her authority over her subjects in such a strange manner? She rolled her eyes in disbelief, and then pushed it out of her mind. She was not here to sightsee nor solve silly puzzles. From this point though, she knew that further progress was going to be tricky, and she needed her wits about her.

The only obvious way that she found to continue onwards was a large staircase leading further up into the castle. This was flanked by two guards, both of whom were Blue Changelings, although one wore a pegasus guise. The mare smiled to herself. That would normally have been an excellent choice, but it would backfire in her case. She observed several other Blues going about their assigned tasks, passing the guards without any concern. She assumed a purposeful air, and marched past them and up the stairs, but while they did glance at her, she received the same lack of reaction. She reached the next floor and looked around. Much of the area seemed given to temporary work stations where ponies and changelings were engrossed in various tasks. A cautious survey seemed to indicate that they were primarily engaged in the hive-building project, although some were also working on House Path projects. None had any direct bearing on her mission though.

She found another stairway, but while it was not guarded, only an occasional servant was making use of it, indicating that it most likely led to a non-public area of the castle. While the mare had been able to bluff her way here by posing as one of the regular workforce, the same would not be true of the more private sectors of the castle. She was going to have to be very careful from now onwards. She had to find one particular room among a castle full of them without attracting the attention of the staff. Some doors were open, and allowed her to dismiss those rooms quickly. The rest required stealthy looks after pausing at each door to listen for any possible occupants first. Several times she hid behind statuary, drapes, or any other convenient concealment to avoid the gaze of various people. She kept her cool despite all of the encounters up until she was almost spotted by a familiar purple alicorn. Fortunately she was in deep discussion with a small dragon, and completely ignored the unicorn mare in the maid outfit. The dragon cast a curious glance at her, but had his attention drawn back to Twilight Sparkle.

With a sigh of relief, the mare continued her searching until at last she came to a small bedroom. One cautious look inside told her that she had found her goal, and she slipped inside and closed the door behind her. She walked over to the cot and spotted the occupant fast asleep. It was a very young changeling, perhaps only a few weeks past the nymph stage, but no mere drone was this! It was the new Queen's daughter, a princess and future leader of the hive.

The mare's form was suddenly surrounded by magic green fire, and Chrysalis stepped forward with a broad grin on her face. "So I have found you at last, Epiphany."

Chrysalis watched warily as her traitorous child powered up her horn. Although Gossamer wore the form of an alicorn stallion, there was no way that her daughter could yet match her power, and yet she had withstood every attack of hers and kept coming back stronger each time. How she managed that was a mystery to Chrysalis, and the changeling queen was treating the situation much more seriously than when she had started the battle with Gossamer. Her progeny's latest actions were puzzling nevertheless. While the massive power that the pseudo-alicorn was building up was undoubtedly very dangerous, the relative slowness of the forthcoming attack would be laughably easy to dodge, or even counter. She decided to be cautious and try to anticipate the plan of attack, preparing a defence in the meantime. After what seemed an interminable length of time in this furiously-paced battle, she judged that Gossamer was about to release her attack, only to be shocked when the pseudo-alicorn disappeared. Chrysalis desperately tried to seek out her foe, but realised far too late that her enemy had reappeared behind and above her. Before Chrysalis could react, the gigantic accumulation of power was released, and a shaft of energy tore through her body. With a cry of agony, Chrysalis plummeted to the ground, and the aura of power around her started dying.

"VICTORY!" she heard her child scream, and knew that she was right. Her body was trying to heal itself as it had done so many times during their battle, but this was no mere wound. Her body was far too damaged to possibly recover, and she knew death awaited her. Yet, in these final moments of her life, she felt pride – her daughter had surpassed her! How glorious it would have been to rule Equestria together, but maybe she could give her child the chance to do so without her. She managed to watch as Gossamer landed and walked up to her. She tried to talk, but only hacked up blood. She tried again, and Gossamer moved closer to try to hear what she was saying.

"H…how?" she managed to whisper, hoping to solve that mystery before she died.

With an almost pitying look, Gossamer replied, "I told you already – True Love and the Magic of Friendship. You should have tried it."

Chrysalis managed a ghost of a smile. Such foolishness actually had some merit; she was hardly in a position to deny the results. "At last… a worthy … … heir." With the final dregs of her strength, she reached out and touched the pseudo-alicorn's nearest hoof. Upon physical contact, she was able to enact the transfer of control of the hive-mind to Gossamer, and then she collapsed, utterly spent. She had no strength left to move, or even blink, and only the enormous reservoir of love energy that still suffused her body was keeping her barely alive and conscious for the moment. She could not even react as Gossamer realised what she had done and started cursing and kicking her insensate body.

"Celestia damn you to Tartarus, you bucking bitch. You miserable excuse for a mother! Just had to get the last laugh, didn't you? I hope there's a hell and you burn in it forever!"

Such ingratitude! Still, give her time, and blood would tell. Such a daughter was destined for greatness, and she comforted herself with that thought even as the abuse continued. Eventually though, some of Gossamer's compatriots came and informed her that one of her allies was dying, and she departed hastily. Chrysalis found a small measure of satisfaction in the knowledge that she was taking one of her enemies with her. It was almost the last coherent thought that she had as her body was slowly losing the fight to stay alive.

Night finally fell, but Chrysalis could not tell how long she lay there before some drones passed in front of narrow field of vision. She barely realised that they were picking up the changeling corpses that littered the battlefield when one walked past her, brushing her body. The brief contact was enough for her to connect with the soldier though, and her mind rushed to fill the void that was the drone's consciousness, pushing it aside and leaving her in control. She gasped with the shock of the unexpected transition, and realised that she had inadvertently accomplished something no other queen had ever done before, and all because she had raised a horde of soldiers that were virtually mindless. That had left her a host for her essence, and she lived once more! She carefully broke the connection to the hive-mind so that her resurrection would remain undetected, and then she threw back her head and laughed long and loud.

"Oh, Gossamer, you had best be truly worthy of the gift that I gave you, because I will test you when I have regained my full power."

The other drones continued picking up the dead and carrying them away, but obviously avoiding her former body.

Chrysalis frowned. "So, it seems you want to keep my corpse. Do you want to parade it in front of your allies? Or maybe you just want to see what a queen's body is like after it's ripped apart by magic? Either way, you're not getting the satisfaction!"

She lit up her horn and lifted her old body. Immediately she realised the difference in power that her new smaller body had compared to the old larger one, and lifting it was proving to be a challenge. Nevertheless, she had no intention of leaving it behind, and she slowly carried it away from the city. Only the constant flow of ambient love energy let her accomplish the task long enough for her to find somewhere to conceal it and herself. There she rested and let the energy build up within her until she sensed that it was going to overwhelm her new body. Then she released it all in one surge to immolate her corpse. What remained afterwards was unrecognisable, and she was satisfied with the result. She rested a while to build up a store of energy once more before she took off and flew away. She had a promise to keep to herself, and that would begin immediately!

It took days to make her way back to her old hive, although it was keeping a low profile that slowed her up more than anything else. Eventually though, she came to a landing just short of the concealed entrance to the hive. She had congratulated herself on the foresight of leaving a skeleton staff behind to maintain the hive in her absence in case of any problems at the Crystal Empire hive, but she had never anticipated returning under these circumstances. Unlike the soldier drones that had been hastily bred for the invasion, the ones guarding this hive were fully developed and intelligent. Moreover, they were still connected to the hive-mind that was now in the control of her daughter. However, Gossamer was unlikely to have made sufficient progress with sorting through the myriad of details to even begin considering needing to update it, and the link was very tenuous at this distance. Nevertheless, the alarm could still be raised if she did not tread carefully.

From concealment, she looked for and found the sentry. She nodded in satisfaction after recognising the soldier as one particularly fanatical to her, hence why she had trusted him to be in charge of the hive's security. If she was careful, she should have little problem gaining access. She used her shape-changing ability to reform her drone body into an imitation of her queen form, although she could only manage about two thirds of her proper size due to the limited mass of this body. She would have enhanced it with illusion, but that was not one of the skills that a soldier drone's body was capable of doing. Nevertheless, it should do the job, and she took off again to approach the sentry slowly enough to be spotted and recognised.

The sentry was startled to see his queen approaching. His senses told him that it was a Blue Changeling, and she certainly looked right, even if she was smaller than she should be. He was alert but not alarmed as she approached him.

"Hail, Breezon!" Chrysalis said. "I see that you still stand duty as faithfully as ever."

The familiar words and attitude made Breezon relax a bit. "Hail, Chrysalis! Are you alright? Has something happened at the Crystal Empire?"

"Something has indeed happened at the Crystal Empire and to me. The invasion did no go well. Let me share with you." Chrysalis reached out a hoof to touch Breezon. Before the sentry could react, her powerful mind broke the link to the hive-mind and reforged one to her.

Breezon staggered as memories flooded into his mind, and then it took him some time to realise the implications. "Your Majesty! How could this have happened? What are we to do?"

"I don't fully understand how I was defeated, but I will study my enemies and I will have my revenge. But first, I need to resume control of this hive, and I will need your help to do so."

"I am yours to command as ever, Your Majesty."

"Then let us begin. Just like you, the guards inside won't be seeking a link to the hive-mind at first, so we should be able to bind them to me easily. I will act through my link to you, so just touch them so that I can make contact."

Chrysalis resumed the natural soldier drone form and they headed inside. Positioned at a strategic point in the tunnel, two guards patiently stood watch. At the approach of Breezon and Chrysalis, one of them routinely challenged him.

"Who is this, Commander?"

"A messenger from Queen Chrysalis with important news."

"What news?"

"She has returned!"

Both Breezon and Chrysalis reached out to touch a guard each simultaneously. It was trickier to do two at once, especially acting through an intermediary, but Chrysalis successfully broke the link of both and joined them to her. Both guards were stunned much as Breezon had been, but once they had recovered, they joined their queen and commander in proceeding further into the hive. From that point on, it was a simple matter of repeating the process until the last of the changelings in the hive had been converted.

"How many drones are outside of the hive at the moment, Commander?"

"Two foragers and both harvesters, Your Majesty."

See that I am alerted the moment that they return so that we can convert those also. Now, I want everyling in my throne room immediately."

The crowd that gathered in Chrysalis' throne room was pathetically small, but it was after all just the minimum required to maintain the hive in her absence. That would have to change as soon as possible. She resumed her imitation queen form.

"First priority – the breeders have to make a new body for me. This soldier drone form is completely unacceptable! Make the most powerful nymph that you can, but do not link it to us. Keep it totally uneducated. My mind will complete it. Next priority is breeding more soldiers."

Breezon frowned in puzzlement. "Your Majesty – won't we need more harvesters first to feed the new drones?"

Chrysalis regarded him carefully. "I like you, Breezon, because you aren't merely loyal, but you can think. Yes, we will need to increase our stores of love energy, but the harvester drones are weak and disloyal. When our last two are no longer needed, they will be terminated. Instead, the new soldier drones will be modified to increase their emotion gathering ability. Perhaps they will not fail me as so many of the harvesters did when I invaded Canterlot."

"A wise move, My Queen."

Chrysalis turned back to the rest. "Maximum effort will be put into regrowing this hive. Our time is limited because sooner or later, my daughter will recall its location and feel the need to visit it. By then, we should have scouted out another location and moved. While we are rebuilding though, we will need to learn as much as we can about Queen Gossamer and her allies. I will learn their secrets and eventually I will have my revenge."

It had taken a frustratingly long time for Chrysalis' new body to be ready, and when it was, it was necessary to transfer her mind into it as soon as possible to prevent it developing a mind of its own. That had made her practically helpless for a while until she grew enough to regain some of her physical power. Despite the forced growth techniques of the breeders, that meant months of being physically unable to do much, but her mind was as powerful as ever, and she directed activities with the aid of the mind-links.

Gradually, her soldier scouts brought back news that both puzzled and amazed her. What Gossamer was doing was almost incomprehensible, and completely unknown to changelings throughout history. Nevertheless, she could see the power base that was growing through Gossamer's association with House Path, and was impressed in spite of herself. It made her hate her foes even more though because they had so perverted the course that she had planned for her daughter before she had disappeared for so long.

Then she learned that Gossamer had borne a child whom she had named Epiphany. Chrysalis smiled to herself. Now she knew what she would do. When the time was right, she would be paying House Path a visit!

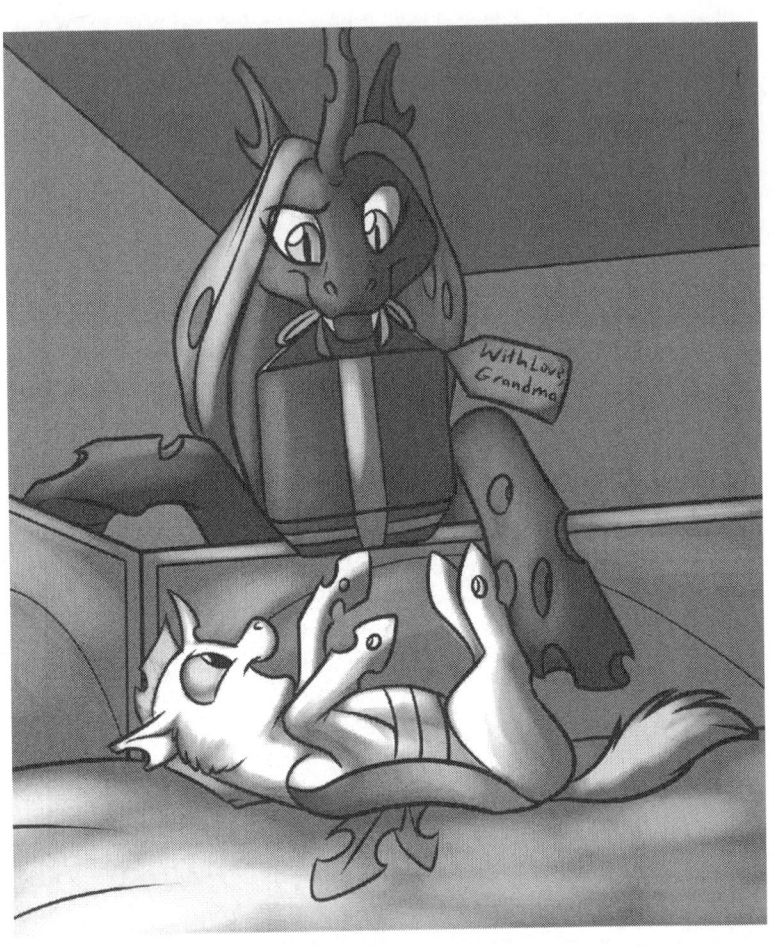

Chrysalis' smile grew wider as she leaned over the crib. She reached in and nudged the sleeping child until she opened her eyes.

Epiphany rolled over and blinked a bit, focusing on the person who had woken her. Her face lit up with a smile as she seemingly recognised Chrysalis, and she clicked and whirred in the changeling tongue, "*Who are you?*"

Chrysalis replied in the same language, "*Someone who has taken very great interest in you, little one. I have something for you.*"

Chrysalis then took the ribbons in her mouth of the box that she had been carrying all this time, and held it over Epiphany. The child reached for it, unable to read the tag on it that read: '*With love, Grandma*', but knowing that it was something wonderful anyway.

Chrysalis left the present beside Epiphany and then leaned in further to kiss the child on her cheek. "I expect great things of you, Granddaughter. Don't disappoint me." She took one last long look at Epiphany before saying, "Goodbye... Pif. You *will* be seeing me again, I hope."

Chrysalis then left the room to make her way out of the castle as stealthily as she had entered, all the while imagining with glee the uproar that would happen when Epiphany's family finally figured out who had had left the plush toy laced with love. It would be far too late though. The move to the new hive was complete, and its future was assured. Now it was just a matter of patience, and Chrysalis had plenty of that.

Chapter 2:
Fly Day

The alarm barely went off before Pif and Lucida sprang out of their beds, squealing in excitement. Lucida was six and Pif only four, so both their voices were loud and piercing as only young children seem to be, but the adults of the house were still nowhere near being awake yet. The hippogriff and ponyling scampered into their parents' room and looked at the oversized bed. It seemed to be mostly a pile of blankets, but there was a grey muzzle sticking out of one side, and a beak out of the other. Pif wrapped her mouth around the beak and blew as hard as she could, while Lucida let out a screech that no living thing should ever make. Two pair of eyes flew open as Free coughed and flailed a bit. Path sprung out of the bed and looked around still shaking.

"What?! Are we under attack?!" Path frantically looked around before he was tackled by his daughter who was giggling. Path let out a tired groan as the two other bodies stirred. Twilight and Rose woke up and yawned softly.

"They always seem to attack you two first," Rose said.

"At least it gives us more time to wake up," Twilight mumbled as she slowly stood up and opened her wings wide, flapping them a few times to settle her ruffled feathers before she folded them back up.

Path and Free had slumped back onto the bed and almost managed to go back to sleep before the two little ones started up again.

"IT'S FLY DAY! FLY DAY! FLY DAY!" The two raced around the tired husbands, making the bed bounce annoyingly.

"Nngh!" Free groaned and dragged himself out of bed. "Come on, let's get some breakfast. Then we can talk about Fly Day."

"Rainbow Dash should be arriving before noon," Path said as he joined Free. "The air becomes perfect for training as the afternoon wind moves up over the land, making a steady breeze that's perfect for lessons."

The rest of the morning was very trying for Free and Path. They kept trying to get work done, but the two who were eagerly awaiting flying lessons made it their day to get under their skin. The afternoon could not come soon enough.

They were outside when a loud rainboom signalled the approach of their instructor. The kids had finally calmed down, but they erupted in squealing and cheers as they ran out onto the middle of the lawn to greet the pegasus who circled around the castle's grounds and came in for a landing. Lucida was already running around in circles, her wings flapping randomly. Pif however was still running around in her normal earth pony form.

"Okay – so who are the two that are going to learn how to fly awesomely today?" Rainbow asked with a grin as she lifted the goggles off of her face.

Rainbow may have been expecting a verbal answer, but what she got instead was excited screaming and two small bodies tackling her to the ground. The pegasus started laughing as she moved back up into the sitting position.

"Okay, let's go to the training hill!"

Rose walked over to the excitement. "Path and Free will join us shortly, as well as Blue."

Lucida was already at the top of the hill with her wings open to their maximum extent. Pif was also on top of the hill, but she was having trouble figuring out what form to be in. She kept shifting, but the form was not coming out right. Blue and Path arrived shortly after, both of them outfitted with magitek wings.

"Why are wings so hard?" Pif whined as she shifted again and again. Each time the wings were coming out wrong.

"Pif, why don't you shift into somebody you know really well who has wings?" Path suggested.

The changeling's eyes widened and she laughed as she exploded in green fire. When it cleared, Luna was standing there, or rather a Luna scaled down by more than half. Her wings flared open as she giggled.

Free, Roseclaw and Twilight arrived in time to see the transformation. Free broke down laughing while Twilight and Rose rolled their eyes.

Rainbow Dash just grinned and walked up to the top of the hill. "Okay, let's start with the basics before we get onto the main lesson. Step one: open your wings as far open as they will go, and feel the wind moving over and under them, like this." Rainbow demonstrated for them.

Pif and Lucida opened their wings. However, Pif was way too light for how big the wings were, so she was already starting to lift off the ground as she squealed.

Rainbow went over and grabbed her front hooves as she floated in the air. "Okay, now tilt your wings down *slowly* to drop down and speed up. And up to soar up and slow down."

Pif pivoted her wings as instructed, and Rainbow slowly let go of the changeling. She wasn't very steady in the air, but soon she was hovering about ten feet in the air, the lift and drag in near perfect balance. She slowly moved forward and then backward as she tested how the air moved and how it affected her wings.

Rainbow went over to Lucida and smiled. "You won't lift off the ground with your wings angled that far down. Come on – tilt them up for me." Rainbow smiled encouragingly as she opened up her wings and tilted them up. She only lifted up a few inches before she angled them back down as nerves got the better of her, and she landed again.

"I can do this. I *can* do this." Lucida took a few deep breaths as she tilted her wings up and slowly rose into the air. She giggled as she floated in the air, although not quite as high up as Pif.

"Hah! If they can do that, then I can do so much better!" Blue boasted. He crouched down low as his magitek wings flared open rather aggressively. Twilight looked at Blue with a little concern as he drew magic from the ground as earth ponies do, but he held it in his body and in his wings without using any of it. A kind of self-amplifying feedback began to form as mana sparks jumped from the feather tips. All of the micro capacitors started to glow from being overcharged. Blue laughed; he was going to show them all!

"Blue – what are you doing? Release the magic!" Twilight shouted before she put her hoof to her mouth, realizing she phrased it wrong.

"BLUE STREAK ONE IS READY FOR LIFT OFF!" Blue yelled as he released all the magic into the wings in one hard push. He launched himself off the ground and angled himself into a steep climb, screaming in joy. The violent wind wake caused from his lift-off sent his younger sisters flying, and Rose and Twilight dived in to catch them.

Rainbow blinked in surprise with her jaw dropped as she watched Blue climb higher and higher, his voice diminishing with the rapidly growing altitude until a sonic boom thundered down to the watchers. "No way..." she said with awe.

Path went up to Rainbow and said urgently, "You need to go up and get him. He's rapidly burning up all the mana with no way of replenishing it. By the time he reaches the stall point, he won't have the magic in him to power the wings until it's too late!"

"What?! Why would you even design those wings like that?!" Rainbow screamed incredulously.

"They're only prototypes!" Path yelled as Rainbow shot up into the air. "He wasn't supposed to do that!"

Blue Streak yelled with joy as he hurtled higher and higher, clouds whipping by him until he burst into the clear air above to view the vista of sunlit clouds. He kept gaining altitude, but unlike a pegasus that was adapted to breathe the rarefied air at that height, Blue Streak was rapidly losing consciousness. The last thing that he remembered before he blacked out from the lack of oxygen was the beauty of the landscape beneath him, and a rainbow-colored streak headed his way.

"Told you...."

Chapter 3: Treasured

Long Path was surprised by the unexpected visit from Griffonia's highest ranking soldier. While they had more than a passing acquaintance, General Mara Windshear was not in the habit of making personal visits to House Path. The golden eagle/tiger griffon was an imposing figure standing in front of Path's desk, flanked by her aides.

Path was not flustered by the display of power, having had many years' experience dealing with the top political and military echelons by now. "What can I do for you, General Windshear?"

"His Majesty, King Glimfeather, commands your presence at the court, Lord Path," she replied curtly.

Path's eyebrows raised in surprise. It was unusual for Argent to make commands like that, and even more so to send such a high-ranking messenger. "May I ask what is so important that the king would send his top officer to fetch me?"

"Dragons," she replied succinctly.

"That could be bad," Path admitted. "However, I would have thought that the Griffonian military was capable of dealing with an invasion force. Do you really require the help of House Path?"

"No, we don't. There are only four of them, some obviously too young to be fighters, although one does not underestimate dragon-kind. The reason that your presence is required is that they are asking about *you*."

Path's jaw dropped in startlement. "Oh." He turned to Goldenquill who had had been patiently waiting by the doorway after ushering in the general. "'Quill, please find Free, Twilight, and Rose, and ask them to join us immediately."

"At once, milord," Goldenquill replied with a small bow before departing.

Windshear frowned. "His Majesty only sent for you."

Path smiled benignly at her. "Argent knows that for matters like this, he would expect Herd Path to turn up. I may be Lord of this House, but we four act as one."

Windshear scowled some more, annoyed at the familiarity that Path had with the king's name, but also aware of the good relationship that the kingdom's ruler had with the pony lord. She forced herself to wait patiently until the others arrived. Fortunately they did not hold up things any further, apparently having been informed of the nature of the call by Goldenquill.

Due to the urgency of the call, Path decided to put on his magitek wings which he kept handy in his office. He finished buckling them on as the last of the four arrived. "Let's go," he told General Windshear, heading for the balcony doors.

The group took off from his office's balcony and made quick time to the king's castle. The guards flanking the huge doorway admitted them to the throne room without a word, evidently expecting them. Despite the size of the room, it was impossible to miss the cause of their summons.

Four dragons – two adults and two youths – were waiting, some more patiently than others. The sheer size of the adults made Path wonder how they managed to get into the throne room despite the size of the doorway, although their more serpentine build seemed to be a clue. They were obviously of a breed slightly different from the ones that he was more familiar with back in Equestria. He watched them move with both grace and power as their attention turned to him and his company, while they were also watched closely by the retinue of griffon warriors half-filling the room.

The herd first paid their respects to King Glimfeather who thanked them for coming so promptly. Path then turned to the dragons, focusing on the larger adult who seemed to be in charge, a ruby-scaled female. "I am Long Path, Lord of the House of Path, and this is my wife, Lady Roseclaw. This is Princess Twilight Sparkle of House Path, and her husband, Lord Free Agent of House Path. I believe that you wanted to meet us?"

The dragon bobbed her head respectfully. "I am Elan Firestone, envoy from the Dragon Lands for my clan. This is my mate, Kiroc Blueshard, and our son, Alac. Also, this is Shaikhan-Gal, daughter of our Matriarch, Incendia."

"A pleasure to meet you. May I ask why you wanted us here?"

"We have heard rumours of griffons, ponies, and changelings interacting with each other, both here and in Equestria. This is unprecedented and nigh unbelievable, but the tales are myriad and many centre upon you. We have been tasked to ascertain the truth of these rumours, and how they might affect the Dragon Lands."

"And Shaikhan-Gal...?" Path asked with an inclination of his head towards the young golden female.

"Her mother wishes that she broaden her horizons. If she is ever to succeed the Matriarch one day, her education is important."

The young dragoness spoke up a little sullenly. *"If Alac wasn't with you, I wouldn't give a curse about this so-called educational visit to this barbaric country,"* she said in the draconic tongue.

"I think you might be pleasantly surprised by what you might learn here, Cinder," Path told her in the same language. It was not one of his most fluent, but he had never stopped loving learning languages.

Cinder was startled to realize that Path not only understood her, but could also translate her name, and she began to blush in embarrassment at being caught out.

Firestone's face had the hint of a smile. "As I said, she is here to learn, but so are we." She turned to King Glimfeather. "Your Majesty, our peoples have clashed in the past, but times have changed. Dragons are a long-lived race and we are loathe to change in a hurry, but the wiser among us know that the world won't wait for us. The Matriarch desires that we investigate what paths are open to us that will stop us from sliding into irrelevancy while retaining our traditional values. From what we have heard, the Griffonian House of Path seems to be an ideal means to do this, and so we wish to petition you to open formal relationships with the Western Dragon Lands."

Glimfeather nodded gravely. "You have come at a good time in our history, Elan Firestone. Griffonia is opening up to other nations in ways that we never have before. If your heart is truly in your cause, then we may indeed become allies. Your petition is accepted." He indicated the griff patiently waiting to his left. "This is Ambassador Far Scream. He will be responsible for negotiations between our peoples. Those can begin tomorrow, though. For tonight, I invite you to banquet with us to celebrate."

Firestone bowed. "We are honoured, Your Majesty." She turned back to Path. "Now that our petition is accepted, I would ask if there might be a place in your school for dragons?"

Path grinned. "House Path is always open to any suitable candidate, irrespective of political relationships or race. We would be delighted to add dragons to the list of species that have come to learn our ways."

"Excellent. Alac and Shaikhan-Gal shall be your new students, should you accept."

"What?!" screeched Cinder. "This was supposed to be a short field trip, not banishment to this... *place!*" The tone she used on the last word conveyed volumes regarding what she thought of Griffonia so far.

Firestone scowled. "Your attitude is unbecoming of the daughter of the Matriarch. It is your mother's wish that you enrol at House Path's school and learn to be a warrior-scholar, both for your benefit and the benefit of our tribe. Alac will do the same, so you will not lack for company of another dragon."

Cinder folded her arms, hunched her shoulders and looked away sullenly. "You tricked me into coming here, but you can't make me like it."

Twilight stepped over to the sulking dragon girl and said, "Trust me when I say that if you let yourself open up to the experience, you can not only enjoy it, but you can make good friends, and your life will be so much better for it."

"Hmmph! What would a mere pony know?" Cinder said contemptuously.

"Shaikhan-Gal! Do not shame us in front of the king and his lords!" Firestone reprimanded.

Twilight merely smiled and said to Cinder's guardians, "I would like to show her what mere ponies can be. May I borrow her for a few minutes?"

"You have our permission, Princess Sparkle."

"Thank you." She turned back Cinder as her horn lit up. A moment later, both disappeared in a soft bang of teleportation.

Path smiled and said, "While we're waiting for them to return, shall we discuss your son's enrolment?"

Twilight and Cinder reappeared at high altitude above the city. The young dragoness squawked and flared her wings to stop herself from falling.

"How did you *do* that?!" she demanded when she recovered.

Twilight calmly kept level with Cinder and replied, "Magical teleportation. Very useful for travelling fast to either get to places quickly or get out of trouble. Not bad for a mere pony, hey?"

"Did you expect me to be impressed with a mere magic trick?"

"Just this? No, but I've only just begun. Look down at the city. What do you see?"

"Lots of buildings, lots of griffons, some ponies... so what? I come from a nomadic tribe that lives in yurts that can be transported. I *like* it that way."

"The point is that the griffons have built themselves a civilization from cooperation, but in the past few years after opening up relationships with Equestria, that city has grown greatly. Again, mere ponies have done this." She neglected to mention that enslaved ponies had helped build much of the city in the first place. There was a time and a place to learn that, and it wasn't here and now.

"So you like to work a lot; still not impressed."

"Okay. Would you pick a fight with a griffon warrior?"

"I'm too young to be a warrior yet."

"If I am judging your age correctly, and I do know a lot about dragons, I would say that you are significantly physically older than my son, Blue Streak, although perhaps psychologically much the same. He is already a warrior-scholar, and has fought in bouts with griffons many times. The average griffon is significantly larger than the average pony too, so how do you think mere ponies fare against them?"

"Ha! You probably teleport away!" Cinder scoffed.

"My son can't teleport. Neither can the majority of ponies who fought wars with the griffons in the past. Guess who won though?"

"You're going to tell me that ponies defeated griffons?"

"Every time. However, our greatest achievement wasn't winning wars, but making them our friends. You know who managed to do that? Lord Path! While we helped and supported him, it was Path who had the vision and the drive to open up relationships with the griffons. A mere pony. We are strong in all the ways that matter, even those that you hold the most dear. You are different from us in many ways, but it's the ways that we are the same that we embrace. That's the way of House Path, and that is the word that has been spreading over Equus these past years. That is what has led your Matriarch to look into relationships with us. She understands that ponies are not so mere as you think. She understands that we ponies might change her world, and she does not wish her kind to be left behind."

Cinder was silent, not able to think of a suitable retort.

"Follow me," Twilight said as she angled her wings in the direction of House Path.

Dragon and alicorn flew swiftly until they were above the House's grounds. At that moment, there happened to be a sports event occurring, with the students playing a ball game that had been adapted to be played by multiple species.

"There are some of your future classmates. Besides griffons, there are ponies of all types, thestrals, zebras, deer, and others. In a few short years, House Path has already grown to be a much respected and powerful institute of learning as well as training for some of the best young warriors on Equus. In a few more years, we expect to achieve even more. It's been an exciting and wonderful time, and you can share in this too. So do you think you might be able to learn from mere ponies?"

Cinder pouted. "I suppose so," she mumbled. "My mom could still beat you in a real fight though."

Twilight caught the snarking though, and she grinned. "Remind me to show you someday the mountain that I levelled in my fight with Tirek." No need to tell her that she was amped up with the power of three other alicorns that day.

Cinder gulped. Right. Don't piss off the princess. "Can we go back now?"

"Are you prepared to give this a fair go?"

"Do I have a choice?"

"Everyone always has a choice. Seeing as your mother is determined that you learn something from us, you can choose to defy her, choose to obey but do nothing to cooperate, or choose to dive in and try to make the best of it. I recommend the latter."

Cinder sighed. "Okay, I'll do it. Don't expect me to like it, but I'll try."

"That's good enough for now," Twilight said with satisfaction. She powered up her horn, and a moment later they had re-joined the others.

"Shaikhan-Gal has decided to give House Path a try," Twilight announced happily.

The young dragoness rolled her eyes and sighed. "Just call me Cinder. If I have to fit in here, you might as well start with my name."

Path said, "Welcome, Cinder."

Free grinned and put a friendly wing about Cinder. "If you're feeling a bit down over the next few days, come see me. I'm in charge of morale, and I like to see our students happy."

Cinder looked askance at the overly cheerful griffon. "Okay," she said placatingly.

"First things first," Roseclaw said, brushing Free's wing off Cinder. "I will settle you and Alac into dorm rooms, after which we will arrange your study schedules. You will begin tomorrow."

Both Alac and Cinder groaned at that.

Path concealed a smile before turning to Firestone and Blueshard. "While Roseclaw is dealing with the new students, I would like to invite you to look over the House Path facilities before you need to return here."

"We would like that," Firestone replied.

Path then faced King Glimfeather. "By your leave, Your Majesty?"

Argent nodded and said, "You are dismissed, Lord Path."

The herd bowed and started to leave the throne room. The dragons followed suit, the sinuous bodies of the adults smoothly but barely squeezing through the doorway, and soon they were outside. Path activated his magitek wings and took off, to the surprise of the dragons who had taken it to be some sort of ceremonial outfit. Nevertheless they quickly took off after him and they all made their way back to the House.

A little over a week later, Cinder flew up to meet Alac at the top of the ridge overlooking the House's estate. She settled down beside him without a word, just observing the students below engaged in various activities.

Alac put up with the silence only briefly before asking, "So why did you want to meet me?"

"When do you think our parents will stop this stupid joke and let us come home?" she replied.

"Are you still complaining about that? This *isn't* a joke. We're supposed to be learning stuff here, especially you. I admit that I wasn't happy with the idea at first either, but they've got some pretty interesting things going on here, and I'm kind of liking it."

"Are you kidding me? What's so great about this? How is any of this going to make me a clan leader someday? All I need to learn is back in the Dragon Lands!"

Alac rolled his eyes. "Have you even paid any attention to the lessons we've learned this week? The world is changing, and dragons have got to learn how to change with it. The Matriarch knows this, and she also knows that it's us young dragons who need to learn how."

Cinder sighed in resignation, remembering what Twilight had said to her. "It wouldn't be so bad if things were more exciting around here."

"You're looking for excitement? Why aren't you going to this afternoon's tournament?"

"What tournament?"

Alac gave her a look of disbelief. "The exhibition tournament which is why we have this afternoon free, dummy! Aren't you paying attention to *anything*?"

"Oh, that," Cinder replied, although she barely recalled hearing it mentioned. "What's so interesting about that tournament?"

"Some of the more advanced students will be having duels with some of the professional fighters. The students get to show or test their skills, and get more practice. The pros get to prove that they're worthy fighters. Apparently the House Path students have been getting a reputation for toughness, so there's a good deal of friendly rivalry between them."

"Sounds vaguely interesting," Cinder said in a semi-bored tone, when in actuality she was quite excited at the prospect of seeing some good fights. She was hardly going to admit it to Alac though. "When do they start?"

"Very soon," Alac replied, getting to his feet. "In fact I was going to leave without you if you weren't interested. Come on, we have to hustle if we're going to get a decent place to watch from."

Cinder let Alac lead the way, matching his fast pace. They encountered some resistance from the griffs controlling entry because they were dragons, but displaying their House Path student cards near magically cleared the way. They were directed to a section of the arena seating where other students were already gathered, and they found themselves suitable places to sit.

"Hey, Goldie – down in front!" came a voice from immediately behind Cinder.

The dragoness turned around and scowled at the pegasus who had spoken. "My name is Cinder, not Goldie."

"Whatever! Just get your wings out of the view."

Cinder growled but tightly furled her leathery wings close to her body, and then turned her attention back to the arena. If the fights had not been about to start, she might have let the smart-flank know just what she thought of him.

Cinder had forgotten about the pegasus by the time several matches had been fought, so caught up in the excitement that she barely noticed when a blue earth pony trotted out onto the arena floor. Up until then, the fights had all been griffon versus griffon. This looked like it was going to be the first pony fight. Cinder fully expected another pony to be matched up against the first, but was startled when two large griffons flew down into the arena.

The master of ceremonies started making his announcement to the crowd. "Today we have a treat for you. In the first of three exhibition matches with Blue Streak, he has accepted Starscream and Badaxe's challenge to a duel. I hope you are as excited as I am. Will we see the young pony make them eat dirt, or will our doughty warriors finally teach this upstart colt a lesson? Are you ready for this?"

The crowd yelled in excitement, but Cinder started laughing uproariously.

"What's so funny?" the pegasus asked her with a look of puzzled annoyance.

"Funny? Look at him! He's half the size of those griffons, and you expect me to take this comedy act seriously?"

The pegasus started chuckling. "You haven't been here long, have you? That's Blue Streak, Master Warfist's favourite student."

"Who's Warfist?"

The pegasus looked at her as if she had grown two extra heads. "Seriously? Haven't you had any combat classes with him yet?"

"Next week, I think? So what?"

"Heh! You're in for a shock. The point is: the fight isn't a joke. Those griffs are in for a real fight."

"Ha! He won't last a minute."

"I'll make a bet with you that he not only lasts, but he'll win."

"I'll take that bet. What's the stakes?"

"If he wins, you have to ask him out on a date."

Cinder blinked in surprise before she started smirking. "I'll not only ask him out on a date, but if he wins all three of these matches they mentioned, I'll pay for it all out of my hoard!"

Their talk had attracted the attention of the other students around them, and there was quite a stir when she said that. A dragon parting with even a small portion of her hoard meant she was very serious.

"Umm, Cinder," Alac said, poking her with a claw to try to get her attention. "I wouldn't do that if I were you." While Cinder was talking with the pegasus, he had been watching the combatants. They had taken up positions at the sides of the arena about equidistant from each other, and he saw how appraisingly they had been assessing their opponents. Those griffs were taking the fight *very* seriously.

Cinder ignored Alac though, and continued saying, "However, if the pony loses, *you* have to ask him for a date while I'm there watching. Once for each time he loses."

The pegasus colt gave her a funny look before laughing. "Okay, that's weird, but I'll accept that bet, and everyone here is our witness. The same goes for you, too - three wins, three dates! Now turn around; the match is about to start!"

The duel drum boomed out at that moment, and the griffons shot towards their foe. The pony waited for them until they were two thirds of the way before taking off. Before Cinder could blink, Blue Streak had circled behind one of the griffs and launched into a flying kick. The professional duellist was not so easily fooled though, and a wing flick sent the pony flying away... straight into the other griff's flank.

"Ooh! That's gotta smart," the pegasus said. "Blue tricked the first griff into catapulting him into the second griff."

Cinder's eyes were practically bulging out of their sockets in shock. "What the...? How can anypony move so fast? That's impossible!"

The pegasus tore his eyes from the fight long enough to give her a gloating glance. "That's Blue's special talent. Nopony in history has ever moved as fast as him. When he first started doing these exhibition matches, he lost a few, but under Master Warfist's guidance, his combat skills have grown so much that no challenger has beaten him in over a year. The pros keep lining up to challenge him though because any griff who manages to beat Blue is going to be a big shot in the leagues for a long time."

"He's just a colt!" Cinder feebly protested.

"He's a colt who has fought in the Crystal Kingdom War. Goldie, you've made the biggest mistake of your life betting against him."

With growing horror, Cinder was beginning to agree with him. She watched as the fight continued, but even when the griffons worked in tandem, the best that they managed was the occasional glancing blow that Blue Streak barely noticed. He, on the other hoof, kept dancing around the slower griffons, darting through their defences before they could react, and pulling back out of reach again. It became evident that he was toying with them, but eventually he stopped playing and backed far away while both were off balance. He lined them up and took off like a shot before dropping and skidding through their legs, throwing them both to the ground. Before they could get to their feet, Blue returned to tap them on their heads, symbolically 'killing' them. The duel drum signalled the end of the bout, and the crowd erupted in cheers while the vanquished griffons got to their feet, chagrined by their loss. They paused to congratulate Blue before exiting the arena.

Alac said, "Careful, Cinder – you're drooling."

Cinder snapped her jaws shut, but she was still overwhelmed by the fight. "That was... impressive," she admitted.

"One date down, two to go," the pegasus couldn't help but rub it in.

"He hasn't won those fights yet!" she protested.

She might as well have not bothered. The second bout was against a single griffon, but one with even greater skill in unarmed combat, and with very fast reflexes. It did not matter to Blue though – no one could match his speed and reaction time. The third bout was against a visiting minotaur wrestler. Ironically this bout lasted longest because even though he was knocked down frequently, the tough bull kept bouncing back up with a roar or a laugh, or a roaring laugh. He was enjoying himself, and the crowd was entertained too. Eventually the minotaur was actually knocked out, and the match was finally over.

Cinder tried making a quick exit from the arena, but the pegasus' outstretched wing blocked her way.

"You can ask for the first of those dates right now," he said with a smug grin.

She looked about and saw that all the other students who had been within earshot all looking at her with smiles on their faces. She sighed as she realized that she had no way out, and she surrendered to the inevitable. She turned around and headed towards the edge of the arena where Blue Streak was moving toward an exit. Before he could disappear down the tunnel, she called out to him.

"Blue Streak! Could I talk to you for a moment?"

Blue turned towards her voice and smiled in recognition. "Hey, you're one of the new dragon students, aren't you? Alac, is it?"

The misidentification annoyed Cinder, but she was keenly aware of the many eyes upon her. "No, that's the *male* student. My name is Cinder."

Blue caught the emphasis on the 'male' and he grinned. "What can I do for you, Cinder?"

Gritting her teeth, she took a deep breath and said, "I was wondering if you'd like to go on a date with me?"

Blue looked amused. "A dragoness wants a date with a pony? Now why would you want that?"

"Let's just say that I was overwhelmed by your battle skills."

"Lost a bet, then?" he said with a smirk.

Cinder cringed but refused to acknowledge his correct guess. "Well, how about it? My treat."

Blue's smirk just got broader. "Well, if you put it like that, how can I refuse? Sure, I'll go on a date with you. When would you like to do that?"

Cinder thought the sooner the better to get it over with. "How about tonight?"

Blue shook his head. "It's Friday – can't miss the usual social night."

"What social night?" Cinder asked with a puzzled look.

Blue was surprised. "You've been here over a week, so you were here for last Friday. *That* social."

"Oh. I... wasn't there." The last thing that she wanted then was to rub shoulders with so many ponies and griffons, so she had gone off to the woods to hunt up some small prey instead.

"So you don't know what you missed? Tell you what – you turn up there tonight and I'll tell you when and where we'll go on the date so you can pay off your bet."

Cinder was trapped, so she nodded. "Okay," she replied with a total lack of enthusiasm.

Blue chuckled and waved. "Seeya!"

Cinder watched him trot off so confident and energetic. She sighed. '*At least I'm not stuck dating a wimp.*' She turned around to see Alac laughing his head off. She glared at him and said, "It's *your* fault this happened. If you hadn't brought me here, I would never have seen that damn pony!"

Alac managed to contain his laughter long enough to reply. "Stop being so sulky and pay attention to what's happening, or else it's going to happen again. Maybe if you learn something tonight, the date might be enjoyable. And the two more after that!" He started chuckling again.

Cinder growled and left just as quickly as she could.

After the organization and quiet discipline of the normal student meal times, the Friday night social was something of a shock to Cinder. She just stopped and stared in disbelief as students, teachers, and nobles seemed to be interacting with a total blatant disregard for proper status and dignity. Her eyes nearly bulged out of their sockets when she recognized King Glimfeather joking with the pegasus student who had made the bet with her. She wondered if he was telling the griffon monarch about the bet, and she decided to try to avoid him to spare herself some humiliation. She spotted Alac chatting with a group of ponies, and wondered if she should join him, but before she could do so, she was approached by another familiar face.

"I heard that you aren't interested in my art classes," Free said with a disappointed expression.

Cinder bowed her head and said, "I'm afraid I'm not the artistic type, Lord Free."

"Whoa! Hasn't anyone told you that there's no rank at these events? It's just Free, okay? And anyway, how do you know if you're not artistic if you don't at least give it a try?"

Cinder shrugged. "I never felt the inclination."

"Tell you what – try a couple of my classes and see what it's like before you give up on it."

Cinder dithered, not really wanting to, but neither wanting to insult one of the lords of House Path. Before she could work up a response though, Blue Streak walked up.

"Hi, Dad! I see you found my date."

"Hard to miss, Streak. I was just trying to persuade her to try my art class."

Cinder stared in shock. "*Dad?!*" she blurted out.

Blue grinned. "Yeah, one of them anyway. I have two moms also. House Path adopted me."

Cinder felt dizzy. She was not only dating a warrior, but a future lord of House Path?

Free poked her in the shoulder with a claw and it elicited no reaction. "I think you broke her, son."

Blue chuckled. "Just wait until we go out on the date!"

"I'll leave you two to enjoy the evening," Free replied with a broad grin. "I'm sure it'll be interesting."

Blue put a hoof on Cinder's shoulder and urged her in the direction of a mixed group of ponies and griffons who were chatting animatedly. "Come on, Goldie, I want you to meet some friends of mine."

Cinder snapped out of her daze, irritated at the nickname. "The name is Cinder, not Goldie!"

"Better tell everyone else that then. You've been so reclusive, nopony and nogriff knows much about you. Time to change that."

"But I don't want to!" she whined.

"Too bad. Now try to make a good impression," Blue replied as he firmly pushed her into the group. "Hey, guys – meet Cinder, my date for tomorrow night."

Cinder was surprised by the welcome that they all gave her, and she managed a smile in response.

One griffon hen asked, "Where are you going to take her?"

"I've made a booking at The Warrior's Feast."

"Ooh, that's not cheap."

"She's paying," Blue said smugly.

They all looked surprised. "A dragon paying for *both* of the meals? What's the catch?"

Cinder spoke up hastily, "It's a reward for his magnificent victories in the arena today."

Blue looked at her with a broad grin, but allowed her to get away with the face-saving lie.

While the others were still doubtful, they did not know enough about dragons to dispute her reason. They started asking questions about her and where she came from, and Cinder was glad to put the subject of the date aside.

It was with great surprise when dinner was announced and Cinder realized that she had been getting quite involved with the conversation. She was startled once again when everyone took up whatever table position that they felt like, and she spotted King Argent seated between two youngsters – a pony and a griffon – and having quite an animated conversation with them. She could not reconcile this with her world view, and wandered in a daze until she found the buffet table with carnivore fare. Her rumbling stomach finally brought her attention back, and she loaded up a plate. As she headed for the tables, she started smiling as she considered the pile of meat on her plate. She wondered how her pony date would react to her gorging on that? There weren't any seating spots near him though, so she decided it could wait for the date. In fact, that could be even better, and with a bit of luck, he might not want the other two dates she was obligated to ask for if she played it right. She set to eating her meal with a growing sense of wicked anticipation.

When Cinder went to bed that evening, she lay awake for a while pondering the social event. After a lifetime of dealing with strict status protocols, she thought that it would be much the same in Griffonia, and the griffons that she had initially met had done little to change that opinion. Tonight her expectations had been shattered as nobles mingled with commoners, teachers chatted and laughed with students, and royalty played with foals. What bizarre circumstances had she been dropped into? Someday she was destined to be Matriarch of her tribe and as such had to be strongly aware of the laws and customs of her people, but she had been forced to stay here and told to learn about this madness!

So why did she find herself liking it?

Cinder sighed and tried to calm her whirling thoughts. It didn't help that Blue Streak's grinning face kept popping into her mind, but she countered it with thoughts of the stunt that she planned to pull. With a satisfied smile, she finally dropped off to sleep.

Blue Streak had told Cinder to wait for him at the front door of the House mansion. Now that she knew that he lived there with his family, it wasn't such a surprise, but she still found it a bit daunting that she would be dating the son of the four Lords and Ladies of the House. Her political awareness made her realize that she couldn't afford to offend the family, but her plan should not cause that problem.

Blue turned up right on time, and he was wearing something that Cinder had seen on a few griffons before.

"What's that all about?" she asked.

"It's my status cape. It's a bit of a silly showy thing, I admit, but since we're going to a fairly fancy restaurant, I thought I'd dress up for a change."

"Does that mean I should have dressed up somehow too?" Cinder asked doubtfully. Aside from jewellery of various kinds, dragons did not usually dress up at all.

"Don't worry about it, Goldie. There's no dress code, and you look spectacular enough as it is."

"The name's Cinder, *not* Goldie," she growled through her teeth.

Blue just grinned maddeningly before he replied, "We'd better get going. Our reservation is in ten minutes."

"What?! How are we getting there in time? I don't even know where it is other than in the city, but even if I did know, I could fly there in five minutes, but I'm *not* carrying you!"

"It's a hundred yards south of the arena gate. Painted red and blue. Got crossed battle axes painted on the roof. Can't miss it. I'll wait for you there."

"*You'll* wait for me? What do you… mean…?" Cinder found herself staring in shock at a rapidly disappearing Blue Streak hurtling up the road towards the city. "By the shell – that's impossible," she whispered before shaking herself and hastily taking off in pursuit.

Finding the restaurant was as easy as Blue had said it would be, and sure enough the young stallion was there waiting for her, not even breathing hard or showing the slightest sign of sweating.

"I've let them know we're here already, so shall we get seated?"

He even had the time to spare for that before she got there? Sweet heavens, could he get any more astounding? And smug. Definitely smug. She hoped she could wipe that smile off his face soon.

They entered the restaurant and were immediately led to their table. The waiter, a rather gaudy parrot/puma griffon, passed a menu to Cinder, but merely asked Blue, "Will you be having the usual, Blue Streak?"

"You know me, Gaylord; I can't pass it up."

"Very good. Would madam want some time to consider her order?" he asked Cinder.

Cinder had already spotted what she wanted though. "Sirloin steak, your largest cut please."

"And how would you like it cooked?"

"Rare. Barely heated to body temperature."

"A popular choice. Any sides with that?"

"Any sapphire seasoned fries?"

"Alas, we have no jewel foods or condiments as we don't generally have dragon customers," Gaylord replied with genuine regret. "May I suggest our chili fries instead? They are a favourite of many of our clients."

"Those will do," Cinder conceded.

Gaylord retrieved Cinder's menu. "I will have the drinks waiter attend you soon." He then headed to the kitchen to place their orders.

Cinder said, "Gaylord, hey? You come here often enough to know the staff by name, *and* to have a meal that you always order. I didn't realize that you had that much money to spare."

Blue shrugged. "I don't actually, but this restaurant is one of my parents' faves, so I get to eat here often."

"I see. You're full of surprises, like the way you ran here in a few minutes."

"Kind of slow for me. I had to dodge too much traffic to make really good time."

Cinder wanted to bash her head on the table. Slow?! He had to be yanking her tail. "So how fast can you go without traffic? What's your top speed?"

"I don't know – I haven't reached it yet, but I've been measured at

Mach 1.3 so far."

"What in the heavens does Mach mean?"

"Oh. Mach One is the speed of sound. Once you break the sound barrier, you often measure speed as a multiple of the speed of sound for convenience," Blue replied in a matter-of-fact tone.

Cinder stared at him for a long moment before bursting into laughter. "Good one, Blue Streak. You had me going there for a while."

Blue just gave her one of those infuriating knowing smiles. "So, besides making bad bets, what else have you been doing since you came here?"

Cinder's mood soured instantly. "Trying to figure out a way to get back home, actually."

"Oh, come on! I saw you enjoying yourself at times last night. It can't all be that bad."

"You try dealing with being dumped in a strange land hundreds of miles from your family and friends."

Blue's expression got serious. "At least you have a family to go home to eventually. My birth parents were killed when I was a young colt. I had only an aunt who fed me and gave me a place to sleep, but wasn't really a parent. That's what it was like for me for years until Lord Path and his family took me in and adopted me. That's what House Path is like, Cinder. You can feel at home here too if you try."

Cinder was chagrined to be essentially chided by a pony who had not seemed to be able to take anything particularly seriously until now. She did not know how to respond to that, and there was an uncomfortable silence for a while until the drinks waiter turned up to take their orders.

After the waiter departed, Blue eventually spoke up. "You've got two more dates with me, so how about I use them to show you how to enjoy your stay here?"

She frowned and asked, "How did you know that I was going to ask you for two more dates?"

Blue's smirk returned. "Half the school knows by now that you bet against me and what the stakes were."

Cinder groaned. Her ploy to discourage him had better work.

Blue chuckled before noticing their server returning with a covered tray. "Looks like your meal is coming. That's the advantage of having your steak rare – it doesn't take long."

Cinder was dismayed; he was acting too casual about it. Gaylord placed the tray on the table and removed the lid. He then placed a plate with a huge steak on it in front of Cinder, plus a bowl of seasoned fries. She licked her lips in anticipation before thanking Gaylord who gave her a smile and small bow before leaving.

"Don't wait for me," Blue commented.

Cinder had no intention of doing so. Eschewing the cutlery, she picked up the steak in her talons and ripped off a chunk of meat. She deliberately made a production of chewing the steak, letting some of its bloody juices dribble down her chin. *'Let's see the grass-eater deal with this!'* she thought to herself smugly.

Blue just rolled his eyes at the display before his own meal turned up. Gaylord uncovered the tray and served up a large plate of food.

"Thanks, Gaylord," Blue said. "It looks great as always."

Cinder stopped eating as she stared in surprise at the tenderloin steak with mushroom gravy that was served with roasted vegetables. Her dropped even further as Blue cut off a chunk, put it in his mouth, and chewed with a blissful expression. "But... ponies can't eat meat!" she protested.

Blue waved his fork in disagreement until he swallowed his mouthful. "Correction – ponies *can* eat meat. It's just that most don't and are too repulsed to even try. As long as there isn't too much fat, it's perfectly acceptable for us. Papa Path and I have it quite often."

Cinder was too stunned by that revelation to reply. She had been counting on disgusting him with her blatant carnivorous display, but instead of being so turned off by the bloody meal that he'd call off the date and perhaps the others, he was relishing a steak of his own! Was *nothing* normal about this pony? She put down her steak and sighed.

"By the way," Blue continued, and pointed with his fork, "If you look around, you'll see several griffons eating their steaks just like you. Did you really think I was going to get turned off by a dragoness doing the same?"

Cinder looked around and finally noticed that he was right. How blind and stupid she had been! She had been too focused on her 'clever' plan that she didn't even see what was right under her muzzle. She sighed again. "Round one to you, Blue Streak."

Blue chuckled. "Finish your steak, Goldie. After all, you're paying for it."

Cinder glumly did just that, too dispirited to even correct his use of that nickname. Just two little bright spots remained – the steak was delicious, and at least she wasn't eating it with some weak-stomached grass-eater.

The meal had been completed with only a little more conversation exchanged, and the duo stepped out into the street with full stomachs. Cinder had winced a bit when paying for the meals, but while they had not been cheap, she consoled herself with the thought that at least Blue had not insisted on one of the really expensive high-class restaurants. For a member of one of the most influential Griffonian Houses, he had decidedly middle-class tastes.

"I think this qualifies as completing the first date, so I'll let you escape," Blue Streak said cheerfully. "However, I'm going to pick you up at nine tomorrow morning for the second."

"Wait... what?" Cinder asked in confusion. She had not even considered the second date as yet.

"See all the tents down the road?" Blue indicated with his hoof.

There were brightly colored tents lining the street as far as she could see. "Yes?"

"Tomorrow is Kilkarn Street Festival, and we're going to spend the day there."

"*All* day?" she asked with dread.

Blue's smile just grew wider. "I'm going to show you how to enjoy this city even if it kills me."

"I could save you that effort," she offered helpfully.

"And miss out on all the fun? Pass. Catch you tomorrow. Don't be late!"

With that, Blue Streak dashed off.

Cinder groaned. How could he run like that with such a full stomach? With no small effort, she launched herself into the air to take a more leisurely trip back to her dormitory. She didn't feel like doing anything else except sleeping off the huge meal that she had just eaten.

Cinder was annoyed with herself. She had started the day with deciding what she would do on the date while she ate her breakfast. Blue Streak had arrived promptly, and they had ridden a cart into the city. Cinder had expected him to run and she to fly like yesterday, but apparently riding a cider cart was considered one way to make a fitting entrance at this festival, and the large mug of non-alcoholic cider that they each got to drink along the way was enjoyable. It probably helped to contribute to why she was annoyed. Her ploy was to make the experience as frustrating and unpleasant as possible for Blue, but she was rapidly distracted from that goal. She was enjoying herself, damn it!

Until now, she had been content with the nomadic tribal lifestyle of her clan. Today though, the festival was opening her eyes to all the different ways to celebrate and enjoy life. The colours and the music buoyed her up. The games of skill excited her, and stage shows enthralled her. Exotic snack foods tantalized her taste buds, and wild rides almost made her throw it all up again. She totally forgot her intention to be miserable, and when the festival finally closed and they headed back to the House, she quietly walked alongside Blue with a happy smile on her face.

Eventually Blue broke the silence. "So, what's the score, Cinder?"

"Hmm? Score?"

"Yeah, you said I won the date yesterday. What about today?"

Cinder snorted in amusement. "Let's call it a tie."

Blue grinned. "Works for me."

"So what have you in mind for the third date?"

Blue shrugged. "We've got classes for the next few days. I'll think of something by Friday and let you know. Try to endure until then."

Cinder rolled her eyes and stuck her tongue out at him. "You think I can't?"

"No, I think you can. I just don't want you dying of frustration of not being on a date with me for so long," he replied with a smirk.

"WHAT?! You smug hatchling! I'll show you who's frustrated!" she said as she lunged at him.

Of course Blue easily dodged, but he stayed tantalizingly almost within reach. Cinder continued to chase him down the road while he playfully skipped away, chuckling all the while.

Cinder was exhausted by the time they reached the House dormitory and collapsed onto her bed. She thought about the day that she had spent with the infuriating pony, and a tiny smile curled the corner of her mouth.

"I was wrong, Blue Streak," she murmured. "Looks like I was today's winner after all. I look forward to seeing what you have in mind for the tie-breaker."

Cinder was so determined to prove to Blue that she could 'endure' the week that she actually stopped sulking and started paying more attention to classes. It helped that the last one on the first day was unarmed combat taught by an old griffon named Warfist. She vaguely recalled the pegasus at the stadium mentioning him as Blue's teacher, although the colt had not brought up the subject at either of their dates. Not exactly the stuff of date talk, she assumed, although this encounter might be something to share with him on their next date. Blue was not in this class, which she found curious until she recalled the part about being his special student. Probably had private lessons. Well, he wasn't the only one to have combat training from a master. Maybe she could show the old griff a thing or two.

Cinder collapsed on her bunk with a groan.

"Note to self," she mumbled. "Dear idiot – never *ever* do something that stupid again. Your battered and bruised self, Shaikhan-Gal."

Cinder groaned again, thinking of the 'encouragement' that Warfist had assigned her.

"Shards! Blue Streak is going to laugh his arse off if I'm too wrecked to make it to our date." She tried to get up off the bed to have a shower, but her body refused to cooperate. "I hate that old catbird," she murmured into her pillow before succumbing to fatigue.

Fortunately for Cinder, she did manage to recover after a good night's sleep, although she still ached a bit in the morning. She had missed dinner the previous night, so she ate an enormous breakfast to compensate. She was going to need the energy!

Between Warfist's assignments and the new studies, Cinder was kept so preoccupied that the week flew by, and before she knew it, it was Friday evening and the usual informal social was happening. She hadn't had much opportunity to do much more than exchange greetings with Blue for most of the week. He sought her out deliberately this time though.

"Hi, Cinder. You haven't made any plans for tomorrow, have you?"

"No. I figured you would want that third date. What have you planned?"

"A picnic."

"A what?" That word was not in her vocabulary.

"You know – pack food in a basket, walk out into the countryside, share the food with the ants, and talk."

"Oh. Sounds dull. I kind of thought you'd come up with something to top the festival."

Blue grinned. "Depends on what you expect to get out of it. I heard you had your first lesson with Master Warfist. I bet you didn't expect that, did you?"

Cinder shuddered. "Point taken. Okay, I'll give this picnic thing of yours a try. Not like I have a choice."

"Come on, Goldie, do you think I'd let you down by now? I've managed to surprise you on both occasions so far."

"Stop calling me Goldie!" she growled, rising to the bait as always.

"Stop making the dates sound like such a bad thing, and I will," he shot back with a smirk.

Cinder snorted, and then gave him her biggest grin, one full of sharp teeth. "I'm smiling – see!"

Blue chuckled. "Close enough. Have a good sleep-in. I'll pick you up about eleven tomorrow."

Cinder was glad to be able to sleep in and rest up from the training regimen that Warfist had assigned her. Thus she was feeling pretty fit and ready for the date when Blue turned up. She was surprised to see him carrying two large saddle packs though. He shrugged off one of them and pointed at it with a hoof.

"You get to carry that one. It has all the food and drink."

"What's in the other?" Cinder asked as she grabbed it and slung it over her back.

"That's a surprise for later."

Cinder shrugged. "Okay. Lead on."

Although she suspected that Blue would take off at his normal headlong pace, he surprised her by matching her walking gait, leading the way across the grounds of the mansion.

"You told me that you did some hunting in the forest on our grounds, but have you had the opportunity to explore anywhere else?" Blue asked.

"Not really. A bit of scouting of the area is about all I've had the time to do."

"Great! Then this will be even better. I'll take you up to the gorge."

They left the carefully tended gardens and lawn surrounding the mansion and crossed an open field after traversing a boundary fence. Blue kept them heading towards the low ranges on the far side of the fields, which is where Cinder presumed the gorge was.

"Are these fields part of House Path?" she asked.

"Yep. The House owns all the land between the mansion and the foothills of the ranges, plus the forest to the east. The forest to the west belongs to another House, so that's where the boundary is."

"What are these fields for?"

"That steak you had last week has to come from somewhere. Like the other Houses, we have herds of non-sapient animals that are grown for food."

"Oh, right. We're nomadic hunters, so herding is a bit strange to me. Actually it seems a bit odd for griffons also."

"I know what you mean, but there are still herders among the griffons, although there are a lot of earth ponies who do that job these days."

"Are we going to walk all the way across these fields?"

"I thought you just said that your tribe was nomadic?"

"We are, but everything is designed to be carried while flying. We don't walk that much."

"Considering that you're training as a warrior, you'll have to toughen up a bit, so consider this a bit of voluntary training," Blue said with a grin.

Cinder scowled. "I'm still waiting for the fun to begin."

"Sometimes you have to make an effort before the payoff."

Cinder just grumbled under her breath, but kept marching on regardless.

Eventually they reached the foothills and encountered a small river. Blue started following it uphill, and the going got more difficult. There was no path, so they had to climb over boulders and push through vegetation quite frequently. The effort required kept Cinder from noticing the walls of rock rising on either side until they started casting a shadow over them.

"Is this the gorge you mentioned?" Cinder asked.

"Yep. We have just a little further to go."

Ten minutes later, the rock walls opened out and Cinder found herself walking out onto a small meadow on one side of the stream. On the far side of the meadow, the rock walls closed in again and ended the gorge with a steep cliff over which the river poured in a waterfall. The sun reflecting off the light-coloured rock gave strong indirect lighting that made the meadow bright but cooler than the countryside that they had tramped through. Between the light, water, and temperature that stayed fairly consistent throughout the year, the gorge's floor virtually exploded with lush vegetation highlighted by a myriad of flowers.

"We're here," Blue announced. "I hope you find the location suitable."

Cinder was almost speechless as she gazed in awe. "I... approve. I admit that I would not have thought you would be so... attuned to natural beauty."

"Why? Because I'm a warrior? One of my dads is an artist; don't you think I could learn a thing or two from him also? He found this place and took the family here. It's kind of special to us."

"Then thank you. I feel privileged."

"No worries. I think you've earned a meal. Let's see what the cooks have packed for us, hey?"

Blue spread out a blanket first before they unpacked the contents of the picnic basket. The House staff had done a fine job of preparing a selection of food and drink suitable for the two of them, and both had a big appetite after the hike. It didn't take long for them to consume everything, and they both laid back on the blanket with contented sighs.

"So, this is a picnic," Cinder said. "I'm disappointed."

Blue looked at her in puzzlement. "Why?"

"You promised me ants, and I didn't see a single one."

Blue chuckled. "Nobody's perfect. I did promise you something else though, and that was some excitement afterwards. Ready for that yet?"

"Just give me a few minutes. After the hectic week, I'd like to enjoy a bit of doing absolutely nothing for a while but listening to the waterfall and the birds while lazing in the sunshine."

"I can agree with that," Blue said as he folded his forelegs behind his head, crossed his hind legs, and gazed up at the sky. There was a long moment of quiet before he spoke up again. "Cinder, why do you so dislike being here? At the House, I mean – not this spot."

Cinder considered her words. "I suppose it's not that I'm here, but that I'm *not* back home. I feel so out of place here. These lands are so different from my mine, and the customs are strange. Almost everything that your family does as normal goes against what I learned back in the Dragon Lands. But the worst thing was that I wasn't given a choice. I had to leave behind my family and friends and stay with griffons and ponies, with not another dragon around except Alac."

"Yeah, that's a bit harsh."

"My turn. Why have you been going so out of your way to make such great effort to make me enjoy these dates – dates that you weren't under any obligation to accept in the first place?"

"Some of it is because I thought it would be fun. Some of it is because one of my moms is the Princess of Friendship, and I thought you could use a friend."

"You seem to look up to your parents a lot."

"They're the best thing that happened to me after my birth parents died. One day I hope to be a great warrior like Warfist, but I'm going to take with me lessons that all my parents have taught me. Papa Path tries to teach me to see all sides of a problem. Mama Roseclaw teaches me honor and diplomacy. Papa Free teaches me to see the beauty in things. And of course Mama Twilight leads by example in making friends whenever she can. When I have to fight, I fight for them and what they represent."

"That is awesome, Blue Streak. I mean it. You are blessed."

"I know, and I want you to know that you can feel like you belong here among us also. Give House Path a chance, and I swear your life will be as fulfilling."

"I can try."

"That's all I can ask. Now, how about a change of pace?"

"What did you have in mind? Something to do with what's in your pack?"

"Yep," Blue said as he got to his hooves and walked over to his backpack. He opened it and started pulling out its contents.

Cinder quickly recognized the apparatus. "Are those artificial wings like your father wore when he met us the first day?"

"Tek-wings, and yeah they are, except these are mine. I've taken you on a ground journey to get here, so how about we take to the skies for a while?"

Cinder grinned. "I would love to stretch my wings, and my feet thank you."

"Great!" Blue said as he started shrugging on the harness. "You can help me tighten the straps so I don't add to the excitement by plummeting from the skies."

Blue Streak was soon securely fastened into his flight harness, and a mental command spread the wings.

"Ready?" Cinder asked.

"Lead the way!" Blue replied with a grin.

With a small roar, Cinder leaped into the air and thrust hard with her wings, rapidly gaining altitude. Looking back, she saw Blue virtually copy her motions, and quickly follow. He was not quite as fast nor as graceful, but the fact that an earth pony flew at all was amazing to Cinder, and she was fascinated. They climbed further into the sky, rapidly leaving the gorge below, and then they levelled out.

"What do you want to do?" Cinder asked.

Blue's smile grew, and without a word of warning, he dove at her and tapped her tail. "Tag! You're it!"

Cinder blinked in surprise before she grinned and took off after him. What followed was half an hour of diving and dodging, climbing and hiding in clouds, and laughter – laughing with all the joy and love of life of two youths despite their differences.

Eventually Blue brought them back to earth. "The mana pack was being depleted very quickly by what I was making the wings do. I don't want to run out of power up there."

"I would catch you... probably," Cinder said with a smirk.

Blue chuckled. "It's good for a few more minutes. Gather your empty pack and I'll grab mine. We'll fly out to the beginning of the fields and I'll go on by hoof from there."

Cinder groaned. "More walking."

"Nope; not for you anyway. You can fly and try to keep up with me."

"Ha! Just because you're faster than me when I'm in unfamiliar territory and trying to make altitude, doesn't mean that you're going to show me up on those level open fields."

"Have you forgotten how fast I said I can go?"

"I dismissed that as boasting right away."

Blue grinned a little evilly. "Well then, you're going to get your chance to rub it in my muzzle, aren't you?"

Cinder matched his grin with a really toothy one. "And I'll love doing it."

"Let's get going then!"

They took off and rapidly retraced their course up the gorge until they reached the bottom of the foothills where the plains opened up. They landed and Blue stowed his wings in the pack which he then started securing firmly to his back.

"Want me to carry those for you? Don't want to slow you down," Cinder said snarkily.

Blue shook his head. "You might as well head off while I finish strapping this on. You're going to need the head start."

"Still boasting. Okay, I'm not above rubbing it in a bit. See you back at the House!"

Cinder took off, but didn't waste time and energy by gaining too much altitude. Instead she concentrated on speed, and she was quickly zooming over the fields. She took a moment to glance back and saw that Blue still had not started, and she grinned. She did not slack off one bit though. The second time that she glanced back, Blue had started galloping after her, but she was now halfway back to the way to the House. No way was he going to beat her there!

She was concentrating on her goal when a boom of thunder and a shockwave made her tumble in the air. By the time she recovered control, Blue Streak was well ahead of her, and moving at a pace she could not hope to match. She chased after him at her best speed, and finally landed beside him at the door of the mansion where they had started that day.

"What *was* that thunderclap?" she demanded.

"It's called a sonic boom. That's what happens when I exceed the speed of sound. The shockwave could hurt you if I ran too close to you."

"You weren't boasting at all, were you? How can you *do* that?!"

"It's my special talent." He lifted up one foreleg. "These custom shoes help me get enough traction to break the sound barrier. I had them in my pack with the wings."

"I've underestimated you again, Blue Streak."

"Could you just call me Blue, or even Streak, but not both. You sound like my moms when you use my full name."

"As long as you never call me Goldie again."

"Deal. Well, I hope you enjoyed the third date, Cinder?"

"I did. I really did. So when do you want to go on the fourth?"

Blue gave her a quizzical look. "I thought that you only had to ask for three?"

"Is there any reason why I have to stop at just three?" she responded.

"None that I can think of."

"Then meet me here tomorrow at the same time, and I'll try to show you as much fun as you showed me today."

Blue's smile grew wide. "You're on!"

Cinder dropped her pack, gave him a wink, and took off.

Blue watched her leave and chuckled. "Well, how about that?" he murmured as he bent to grab the pack to take it inside.

Cinder lay on her bed, staring at the ceiling. Why had she asked for a *fourth date*? Why hadn't she just asked if he wanted to hang out as *friends*? She couldn't like a pony *that* much, could she? After a long moment of confused feelings, there was inevitably one other question she had to ask herself – could a *pony* like a *dragon* that much?

Moira Skytalon slammed her plate down on the dining hall table, startling her friends. They stared at the griffoness in a mixture of concern and annoyance.

"What's got your tail in a twist this time, Moira?" one asked.

"What else? That she-dragon just won't leave Blue Streak alone. What's a reptile doing monopolizing a pony's affections anyway?" Moira sulked, ignoring the food that she had just brought over from the food counter. She stared back that way at the blue earth pony and dragoness who were getting their food, laughing about something.

Gail Redfeather snorted a bit contemptuously. "I don't know why you're so obsessed with the pony anyway. Stop worrying about Cinder and start paying attention to the griffs who keep asking you for a date."

"Why should I pay any attention to them? I don't need them, but think of the status I'd gain if I could hook the son of Lord Path."

"You don't like the idea of a pony and a dragon being an item, but you have no problem with a griff and a pony?"

"Lord Path married Lady Roseclaw and had a child, so it's obvious we two species belong together. Who ever heard of a dragon-pony relationship?"

"And *that's* your problem, not the dragon," Gail replied. "House Path is all about working with other races, while all you're interested in is building status. Those two obviously don't care about their difference in species. It's evident after a few months together that they're more than just friends, but you can't accept that."

"I can be a better partner than her! Lady Roseclaw is Lord Path's strong right talon. Blue Streak should have the same. I come from one of the highest ranked Noble Houses in Griffonia; we would make a great pairing!" She scowled as she watched the two heading towards a table with their food, and she got up to her feet.

"Let it go, Moira," another griffoness urged.

"No! Fortune favours the bold! I'm going over there and asking him for a date." She started to march determinedly towards the couple.

Gail called out, "Moira! Don't be an idiot!" However, she was ignored, and the griffoness sighed in resignation. "Everygriff take cover – this isn't going to be pretty."

Blue and Cinder had just put their food on a free table when Moira marched up to them.

"Blue Streak! I, Moira Skytalon, wish to have a date with you! We're both high nobles and would make a fine couple!"

Gail faceclawed. "It's going to be worse than I thought," she groaned.

Blue just stared at Moira, stunned by her bold and totally unexpected statement.

Cinder glared balefully at the upstart griffoness. "Back off, catbird. He's not interested."

Moira ignored the dragoness and advanced on Blue. "Come on, Blue Streak, I'll make it worth your while." She reached up and pulled his face to hers to nuzzle him.

Cinder growled and pulled Moira away from Blue. She then enfolded Blue in her forearms, one clawed appendage roughly cupping his stallionhood. "I said back off! He's *my* treasure!"

Blue blushed fiercely. While their relationship had grown a lot over the past few weeks, neither had admitted to more than a strong friendship up until now, and while he could empathize with her urges, having them displayed so blatantly in front of the lunchtime crowd was more than a little embarrassing. "Quit groping me in public, will you?" he hissed urgently, but Cinder didn't appear to notice.

"He doesn't belong to you!" snarled Moira. "Let him choose a real potential mate, just like his dad."

"He already has me, hoard thief!"

"He's not gold or gems to add to your collection, lizard!"

"He's not a status-seeking spoiled noble brat like you!"

Blue just looked back and forth between the bickering rivals. He had *two* females fighting over him? What the heck?!

"I can offer him more than you can. We would make an awesome couple and bring great honour to our Houses!" Moira proclaimed.

"I am the heir to Matriarchy, and we would bring great glory with our union!" Cinder shouted.

Blue's mind was beginning to lock up. These two were getting deadly serious about what they wanted of him, but he hadn't even started thinking that far ahead yet.

"Let him go so he can choose," the griffoness said, tugging on Blue's foreleg.

"No! He's MINE!" Cinder bellowed, tightening her grip on the pony.

Blue's eyes bulged as the air was forced from his lungs. "Can't... breathe..." he gasped.

Cinder finally noticed what she was doing to him and released her grasp, but Moira's tugging made him fall away from both of them. He lay panting on the floor, mortified by all the attention caused by the ruckus. All conversation had ceased as everyone watched dumbstruck by the confrontation.

By this time though, neither of the rival females was paying any attention to those around them. Moira let out a screech of challenge, and Cinder roared in defiance. Then, before anyone could blink, they lunged at each other, talons and claws raking their rival. Then they grappled and chairs went flying. Blue hastily scrambled out of the way just before they crashed into a table, smashing it in half. Cinder threw Moira off, but the griffoness checked her momentum with her wings and leaped back at her. The crowd started cheering on their favourites as the fight progressed.

Inevitably the commotion drew the attention of the faculty, and Free Agent was one of the first to arrive on the scene. He spotted Blue staring at the battling females and went up to him.

"Why is Cinder fighting with that she-griff, Blue?"

Without taking his eyes from the battle, Blue replied in an incredulous tone, "They're fighting over *me*!"

Free Looked at Blue with pleased surprise. "Really? That's awesome!"

Blue was surprised enough to tear his eyes away from the fight.

"Awesome? You're cool with them fighting over me? I thought you'd want to try to break it up."

Free chuckled. "If there's one thing that I learned early, it's that you *never* get involved in a cat-fight. It's a great way to get maimed."

"Okay, but what's so awesome about it?"

"Oh, come on, Blue – I've known how Cinder and you really feel about each other for a while now, but neither of you have been willing to admit it out loud to each other. This finally brings it out into the open."

Blue knew it was impossible to hide emotions from his changeling dad, and yet he still was surprised that Free knew what he had not been able to even admit to himself. Despite the many nights he'd been unable to get to sleep due to his state of arousal after a date with Cinder, he had been unable to convince himself that a dragoness could feel that way about him too. Only some less-than-satisfying self-relief had let him finally relax enough to find slumber. Now Free was telling him that Cinder felt the same way?

The battle spilled out the doorway and into the grounds. That only gave the duo more room to manoeuvre, and both took to the air. They circled each other and then charged at their opponent, coming together with a crash, feathers and claws flying. They parted and grappled again several times until Cinder got some altitude on Moira. With an unholy screech, she dived on the griffoness, unleashing a torrent of dragonfire. Moira barely dodged, getting away with only a few singed feathers, and they grappled again.

"Aren't you going to do *anything* about this?" Blue asked a little desperately. They had all followed the combatants outside to continue to watch them.

Free shrugged. "I could get us some popcorn while we watch."

"Seriously, Dad?"

Just then Path arrived with Roseclaw, and he went up to Free and asked, "What's going on?"

Free replied, "Apparently that griffoness challenged Cinder for Blue. Cinder's possessive dragon instincts kicked in, and the griff's stubborn fighting instincts did too. They are currently fighting for dominance, and it's dangerous to intervene."

Blue blinked in surprise at Free's serious and concisely accurate assessment of the situation. Despite the changeling's light-hearted responses earlier, apparently he had not been taking it quite that lightly after all.

"So, Cinder has finally admitted her feelings for Blue, has she?" Roseclaw asked.

"It would seem so, and quite spectacularly," Free replied.

Blue stared at them with shock. Did *all* his parents know what he hadn't?

Path said, "While that's good, we can't have them fighting like that. Any ideas about how to break it up without either them or us getting hurt?"

"That's the tricky bit," Free admitted as Moira had her tail tuft burned off after failing to completely dodge another stream of dragonfire.

They grappled again, and after a few long moments, Cinder suddenly had Moira's limbs captured and helpless. "I HAVE YOU NOW, TREASURE-STEALER!" Cinder bellowed. She drew a deep breath in preparation for breathing fire on the terrified griffoness.

A griffon burst out of the crowd and slammed into them. Warfist reached out with his forelegs, grasping the head of each of the combatants in one of them, and slammed them together. Stunned, Cinder released her grip and both started dropping to the ground, their wings hardly slowing their fall.

Blue gasped and raced out onto the grounds and under Cinder. He reared up on his hind legs and caught the dragoness, breaking her fall. They were brought to the ground by her momentum, but they were both unscathed. Meanwhile, Moira fell into a hedge, saving her from a more painful meeting with the lawn.

"There, the dumb-arse colt picked one of them," Warfist declared. "'*Encouragement*' in ten minutes for all you slackers here who let this get out of control!"

There was a groan from everyone present as the crowd broke up.

Path walked over to the three remaining. Cinder and Moira were both recovering their wits after the mutual head-butt, and he glared at them. "You two – my office *now!*"

"Yes, sir," they both said meekly.

"Can I come with Cinder, Dad?" Blue asked.

Path considered it for a moment, and then nodded. He then headed off to the office, with Free, Roseclaw, and Warfist falling in with him. As Cinder, Blue, and Moira followed, they encountered Twilight in the hallway. After a quick, quiet word to her from Path, she fell in with them. The trio was told to wait outside the office while the others went inside and closed the door behind them. While they waited nervously, Blue reached out and put an arm around Cinder. She leaned into the hug and they quietly enjoyed being together, ignoring the angry looks from the griffoness.

After a few minutes, the office door opened and Twilight stepped out. "Moira Skytalon – please come inside."

The griffoness got up and followed the alicorn inside, and the door closed once more.

Blue took the opportunity of the moment of privacy to ask, "Why didn't you tell me how you felt about me?"

Cinder snorted deprecatingly. "Why would you want a dragon marefriend?"

Blue grimaced. "Funny – all this time I've been wondering how a dragoness could possibly want a coltfriend."

She stared at him with surprise and not a little hope. "Really? You think we could have a future together?"

Blue felt a little bit of his usual self-confidence returning now that their feelings were out in the open. "Why not? Stranger things have happened in my family. Besides, haven't you already claimed me?" he asked with a smirk.

Cinder blushed in embarrassment. "I… I'm sorry about that."

"I'm not. I think I like being treasured by you."

Cinder smiled shyly. "I think you're the most valuable item in my hoard."

Blue matched her smile. "And nobody will steal me from my dragon," he said and leaned in to kiss her.

Cinder met his lips with hers, and they kissed fervently. Eventually they parted and gazed at each other lovingly.

They were still doing so when the office door was flung open, and a weeping Moira ran out and disappeared down the hallway.

Twilight came out again and said, "Cinder, please come in now."

Blue said, "Mama – can I come in with Cinder?"

Twilight nodded. "This involves you both, so it would be a good idea."

Cinder and Blue followed Twilight into the office, and the alicorn seated herself beside the four others.

Path was seated behind his desk, with Roseclaw and Warfist to his left, and Free and Twilight to his right. He looked gravely at Cinder. "We have just expelled Moira Skytalon from the House Path school."

Cinder slumped in resignation. "I see. I'll start packing."

"No! You can't send her away!" Blue protested.

Path shook his head. "No, you're not expelled, Cinder. I'm telling you this though to impress upon you the seriousness of the situation. Whenever a candidate comes to the school, they are assessed for suitability. Not every candidate meets the requirements of House Path. Griffons especially need to let go of their desire to seek status above all. However, Moira managed to get past our weeding-out process, but she was already on our watch list for her poor attitude. The fight was just the final straw, although admittedly that was more like a *bale* of straw. Moira was expelled because she could not live up to the ideals of House Path. You, however, gained admittance under different circumstances.

Nevertheless, you are still required to live up to our ideals. For your part in the fight, you will be receiving a severe punishment. Master Warfist will be seeing to most of that. We will expect you to curb your dragon instincts better in future. However, it is our assessment that you are otherwise adapting well to our customs, and you still have a great future at House Path."

Both Cinder and Blue heaved a sigh of relief.

Free added with a grin, "Besides, I don't think our wives would forgive us if we broke you two up now that you've finally admitted your feelings for each other."

Blue and Cinder blushed fiercely, even as they hugged each happily.

Twilight did her best to look stern as she spoke up. "Now, my young stallion and dragoness, I believe you're late for your classes."

"Yes, ma'am!" they both cried as they jumped to their feet and hooves.

Warfist said, "Report to me straight after classes, Cinder."

"Yes, sir!" Cinder replied, and she and Blue hastily exited the office.

"Ah, young love!" Free declared happily when the pair had left.

"With some more discipline, she will help balance out his recklessness," Roseclaw agreed with satisfaction. "She will make a fine mate for our son one day."

Cinder wearily landed at the front door of the House Path mansion and she pressed the doorbell. Soon it was answered by Goldenquill who smiled in recognition.

"Can I come in and see Blue?" Cinder asked.

"Master Blue Streak said that he hoped to see you this evening, Miss Cinder. Please come in." He stood aside to allow Cinder inside before continuing, "I believe you know where his room is."

"Thanks, Goldenquill." Cinder headed to Blue's room where they had planned several of their outings. This time though, she had something else in mind. She tapped on his door and entered when he replied. She smiled shyly. "Hi, Blue."

"Hey, Cinder," Blue replied from where he was seated behind a desk. "I was wondering when Warfist would be finished with you."

She snorted. "He's barely started, but we're done for the night. I'm tired, but I wanted to see you again before I head back to the dorm."

"I'm glad you did," he said, coming over to her and giving her a kiss.

She kissed him back happily.

He stepped back with a smile on his muzzle. "Don't go back to the dorm tonight."

"Where am I going to sleep?" she replied coyly.

Blue inclined his head towards his large bed. "This has always been way too big for me alone. It's been feeling a bit too empty also lately. Care to help fix that?"

Cinder smiled. "I'll give it a try, my Treasure."

The next morning, Blue joined the family for breakfast, walking with a bit of a limp. Free hid a grin behind his mug of coffee when he noticed. Twilight frowned in concern.

"Is something wrong, hon?" the alicorn asked.

Blue groaned as he sat himself down at the table. "I think I strained a muscle yesterday."

"How did that happen?" Roseclaw asked.

Just then, Cinder entered the room, also walking a little oddly. "Um, good morning," she said with a little trepidation as Blue waved her over to sit next to him.

Roseclaw's brow rose a little before she said, "Never mind. I think I can guess."

Twilight's eyes widened and her mouth went into a silent 'Oh'.

Path smiled and asked, "Can we expect you for breakfast on a frequent basis from now on?"

Cinder looked down with a blush colouring her cheeks. "I really hope so, sir."

"Then welcome to House Path, my dear."

Chapter 4: Nightmare Nights

If Path had not been close to the balcony doors, he might not have heard the distinctive sound of someone arriving by teleportation. The regular House Path Friday dinner was due to start soon, and most of the staff and warrior-scholars had already gathered and were chatting loudly enough to drown out most incidental noises. Path could see Twilight on the other side of the room, so he knew that it had not been her that he had heard, and curiosity pushed him to investigate. He moved aside the drapes covering the doors and opened one. He almost bumped into the pony that stood there with her hoof raised to push the latch.

"Princess Luna? We weren't expecting you today. To what do we owe this visit?"

Luna gave him a slightly embarrassed smile. "Thy pardon, Lord Path, but I took it upon myself to drop in on thee on a whim. I regret not forewarning thee."

Path stepped out onto the balcony. He suspected that the Moon Princess had other motivations than a mere whim. "Y'know, as a member of the House of Path, you have the right to join us at any time that you desire without having to ask? What's more, after all the time that we've known you and you have participated in our activities, we would like to call you our dear friend and have you visit us more often anyway."

Luna grimaced. "'Tis not so easy, Long Path. As a princess of Equestria, I have my station to keep, and my duties to perform. My time is not my own."

"And yet here you are in Griffonia on a whim? C'mon, Luna, what's really bothering you?"

Luna looked embarrassed. "I... I miss you."

Path's eyebrows rose in surprise. "You miss us? You have a castle full of guards and servants, a city of your subjects at your doorstep, and endless opportunities to do just about anything you wish to do, and yet you come here for dinner and a chat?"

"'Tis not the repast that draws me here. 'Tis what happens afterwards that lingers in my memory and makes me long for more."

Path nodded in understanding. "You mean the quiet family time that we have each night. You miss having a family, don't you? Is

Celestia aware of this?"

"My sister knows, and she tries hard to make its absence bearable, for which I love her. But she is a princess too, and her time is limited, not to mention that we are seldom awake at the same time. I do not fault her for that, but I feel the need for more. My times spent with thy family have helped fill that void, and yet I do not wish to foist myself upon you..."

"Whoa! Stop right there!" Path commanded. "First of all, you have *never* foisted yourself upon us. We've always enjoyed your company. Second of all, I for one would like to have you visit more often. It seems that we and you have always gotten along together exceptionally well, especially once we started the Village Ponies gig. You were so into it that it made my heart glad to see you enjoying yourself so much, and it's been that way every time since. Luna, if you're looking for a surrogate family, I most sincerely offer ours, or even if you just want friends to hang out with, that's okay too. Look around you – this is Griffonia, not Equestria. Feel free to leave your crown back there and just be Luna the mare if you want."

Luna was surprised at Path's speech, and she looked thoughtful for a long moment. Then her horn glowed and her tiara lifted from her head and floated in front of her face. "It is strange – I seldom take off this symbol of my status, and yet I still wear it when all I wish is to be anything but a princess for a while. Perhaps thou art right – if Luna the mare is to find happiness, Luna the princess must stay back in Equestria." With a pop, the tiara disappeared.

Path smiled. "I think I heard the dinner bell. Care to join us, Luna?"

"My pleasure, Path."

Destined Path lay asleep between Luna's forelegs. The infant alicorn had tired himself out playing with the much older alicorn mare, and he had fallen asleep right there. Luna was careful not to disturb him while she chatted with the adults. Lucida was yawning prodigiously while insisting that she was not tired. Her younger brother, Flix, a hippogriff like his sister but with red feathers and chestnut fur instead, had succumbed a short time ago. Only Epiphany was still quite active, although that was pretty typical for a Friday night. The earth pony changeling always got hyped up on all the emotional energy she took in, and it took a while for her to work it off. Just like her mother, she had assumed her sire's base form shortly after leaving nymph stage, and was a pretty normal filly otherwise, except for her remarkable eyes. She had

solid blue eyes with black slitted pupils, pointing unmistakably to her heritage, and Luna wondered if they would be the cause for concern in the child's future, or a mere curiosity.

"I had better put Destined to bed," Twilight said, her horn's glow gently enveloping the blue-coated colt and levitating him without disturbing his slumber.

"Sounds like a plan," Path replied. "Let's get these chicks to bed too."

"But, D-a-d!" Lucida whined.

"Don't 'but Dad' me, young lady! You need your sleep just as much as your brother."

"Mind your father," Roseclaw said as she placed Flix upon Path's back. "Now climb up and we'll tuck you in."

Lucida reluctantly climbed onto her mother's back, and the four headed off to the bedrooms.

"And then there was one!" Free pronounced, eyeing his progeny with determination.

The mischievous ponyling squealed and took off at a gallop. While she was very young, she had the huge advantage of being extensively educated as a nymph connected to the hive-mind, and she understood exactly what was happening. She was *not* going to be put to bed!

A chase ensued between mother and child. Free frequently took mare form when spending time in intimate family moments with the children, and eight hooves thundered around the room for several minutes as the small child ducked and weaved through places her parent could not. Eventually she was cornered though, and Free embraced her and gave her a long kiss on the cheek. Pif's eyelids drooped, and she ceased struggling. Free winked at Luna. "Path wishes he could do that."

"What didst thou do?" Luna asked curiously.

"I used my changeling queen ability to draw the excess emotional energy out of her. Now that she's no longer overcharged, she'll sleep normally."

"Very convenient," Luna admitted.

"I'll be back soon."

Luna was left to herself for the moment, and she contemplated the time that had just passed. She had greatly enjoyed playing 'Auntie Lulu' to the children. True, they could be a hoof-full occasionally, but their childish innocence and sheer sense of fun more than made up for that. It was also part of the whole family experience that she craved, and she was feeling quite content. Aside from excusing herself for a brief few minutes to raise the moon on schedule, she had pushed aside all her cares and concerns for the evening, and just let herself go with the flow.

Luna considered the children. When she first heard that Path had gotten all three of his herd-mates pregnant, she had been more than a little surprised, especially when it came to Twilight. That paled to the shock everyone experienced when Twilight's foal had been born. Wagers had been made on whether it would be an earth pony or a unicorn, but very few had even considered that it would be an alicorn despite her brother, Shining Armor and Cadance's daughter, Flurry Heart. To Luna's knowledge, there had never been a male alicorn before Shining Armor had ascended, nor a natural-born alicorn before Flurry Heart, and now there was a foal who was both! She wondered if it might portend great things for his future. Small wonder that Twilight Sparkle and Long Path had named him Destined.

Luna got up and stretched her limbs; the alicorn colt had been so cute curled up between her legs, but it had left her a little cramped. She headed to the balcony to take in the night air while she awaited the return of the adults. She took in deep breaths of the cool night air, while admiring the scenery under the glow of her moon. It was a picturesque sight that she was beginning to like more and more, mostly for the association with the Path herd though. Her night vision was superb, of course, and she could appreciate details that few besides the thestrals could match. It did not escape her attention therefore when she spotted an unusual sight a few balconies away.

A small dragon laboured to carry an object to the balcony, wings flapping furiously to cope with the uncooperative load. Luna realised that it was a pony, and for a moment she was concerned about what was happening. Dragons of any kind, no matter what size, were reason to be concerned. Then she overheard them talking.

"Stop squirming or else I might drop you!" the dragon hissed urgently in what seemed to Luna to be a female voice.

"Look at me though – I'm flying!" the pony replied, flailing his legs like he was trying to flap wings.

Luna recognised the voice of Blue Streak, and the colt was very evidently not in distress. Drunk as a skunk perhaps, but not in any real danger, except perhaps of being dropped if he kept up his attempts to fly. Just then, Twilight returned and walked out onto the balcony to join Luna.

"What are you up to, Luna?" Twilight asked curiously.

"Tell me, Twilight, is it common for your son to be flown to his room by dragon?"

"What?" Twilight looked in the direction Luna was facing. "That's Streak's marefriend, Cinder. What in Equestria are they up to?"

"Perhaps his state of inebriation has something to do with it?"

"He's *drunk*?! He's still a teenager and too young to be getting drunk!" Twilight stormed away, heading to Streak's room. She passed Path along the way, and said, "Follow me. We have a little discipline problem to deal with."

Path blinked in surprise, but dutifully followed.

They arrived at Streak's room and entered without knocking. They found Cinder placing Streak on his bed, and the golden dragoness turned and grinned sheepishly at having been caught.

"Hello, Lady Twilight, Lord Path."

"Hi, Mom! Hi, Dad!" Streak said with a giggle.

Twilight frowned. "Care to explain, Cinder? Blue Streak has only just turned old enough to be allowed alcohol, but he's only supposed to have one or two drinks, if any. It's quite obvious that he's very drunk though."

Cinder looked very embarrassed. "It's my fault. Blue complained that his hyper-metabolism burned off the alcohol faster than it could affect him, so I challenged him to drink a bottle of Eyrish Whiskey and prove it."

Path face-hoofed. Worst thing that you could do to a teenage colt was something like that. He sighed. "How big a bottle?"

"Um… a Griffonian quart…"

Both Path and Twilight boggled at that.

"And he's still conscious?" Twilight asked.

Cinder shrugged. "Well, he did prove his point – he was perfectly sober until nearly three quarters of the way through the bottle. Then it suddenly hit him and… well… he's been like this since."

Path said, "Sounds to me that there's a limit to how much his fast metabolism can cope with, and he found it tonight. He should be okay if the rest of what Cinder said is true. He'll probably get the traditional hangover and regret ever touching the stuff. Right now though, he's in no state to lecture."

Twilight scowled. "The same can't be said for you though, young lady! I am very disappointed in you, Cinder. When you started dating our son, I thought you would be a moderating influence on his recklessness. Instead you do this!"

"I'm really sorry, Lady Twilight. It won't happen again."

Path said, "You better go to your room, Cinder. We'll talk about this more later."

"Yes, sir. Good night." Cinder hastened to depart through the window through which she had arrived.

"Are you just going to just let Streak get away with this?" Twilight demanded of Path, indicating their giggling foster son.

"I seem to recall both of us getting pretty blotto soon after we arrived in Griffonia the first time. Drinking to excess happens to us all sooner or later, especially in Griffonia."

"He's still too young to do that though!"

"Yes, he is, but it will serve as a valuable lesson, and we've learned a little bit more about him at the same time. We can scold him in the morning, but our son is growing up, and we have to balance our concerns against reality."

Twilight slumped in defeat. "I suppose you're right. None of the books that I've read about raising colts has really prepared me for the real thing."

Path put an arm around Twilight's shoulders and gently guided her out of the room. "Believe me, I understand completely, and I *was* a teenage colt once!"

They left Blue Streak to sleep off his binge, and went to rejoin with Luna, Roseclaw and Free.

Free had shifted back to his preferred griffon form, and he looked curiously at Twilight and Path as they entered the family room. "Luna tells me that she saw Cinder carrying Streak to his room."

Path replied, "Short version – our son got drunk and Cinder was trying to sneak him into his room. We'll deal with it in the morning when he's sobered up."

"In the middle of his hangover, of course," Free said with a grin.

"Naturally," Path replied with a matching smile.

"It's things like these that show me how much time has passed since we first met," Luna said. "To me, it seems like just yesterday that you adopted the colt, and now he's growing into a stallion."

Roseclaw replied, "I think the perception changes if you spend every day with your family, especially when you need to tend to children. Your occasional visits capture highlights only."

"'Tis true. I think that I might be missing some important moments."

Path said, "As I said earlier today, you are more than welcome to visit more often. Come again tomorrow if you like. It's Saturday and we try to do family things together."

"Nay, I cannot. Tomorrow night is Nightmare Night, and I need take care of matters early and prepare for it."

Twilight looked surprised and a little annoyed. "That's right! I had forgotten all about Nightmare Night. I've missed it for the past couple of years because I've been over here each time."

"What is this Nightmare Night?" Roseclaw asked.

It was Path's turn to be surprised. "I've never mentioned it before? It's an annual festival with a spooky theme where ponies dress up in costumes and play special games, and foals go door to door begging for candy."

"And you just give them candy for no reason?"

Path grinned. "Oh no, it's important that they have lots of candy so that they can offer a portion of it to Nightmare Moon when she comes to the village. Otherwise how else would they turn her away each year?"

Roseclaw blinked in non-comprehension. "I know little of the legend of Nightmare Moon, but wasn't she defeated and... well..." Roseclaw looked at Luna.

"Yes, Roseclaw, Nightmare Moon was defeated and I was freed from the curse of envy and bitterness that created her. The lesson was learned, and my sister forgave me, as I forgave her for the neglect that led to my curse. Eventually I even forgave myself. The legend lives on though, and each year I visit Ponyville, the first town to accept me back into their hearts, and I reprise the role of Nightmare Moon for the purposes of entertainment only."

Twilight added, "Ponyville has become quite famous for its Nightmare Night pageant, and it attracts a growing number of visitors each year. It's great for tourism, and I think it's safe to say that Luna enjoys her interactions with the foals."

Luna smiled fondly in remembrance. "Aye. That is why I will not forsake the event."

"What does this pageant entail?" Roseclaw asked.

Twilight explained, "Basically it starts with a retelling of the story of Nightmare Moon and how she tried to take over Equestria, was banished to the moon for a thousand years, escaped and banished Celestia to the sun, and then tried to make night eternal. Then we thrill the foals with scary tales of the trials that my friends and I went through before we found the Elements of Harmony, defeated Nightmare Moon, and returned Luna to her sister. After that, Nightmare Moon makes her return to demand her tribute, and the foals give her some of their candy. If they give her enough, she is satisfied and leaves them alone for another year. It's all done in a spooky manner that we try to keep at a manageable level for young foals."

Roseclaw scoffed. "You would not get much candy from griffon chicks. They would not scare as easily as pony foals."

Luna lifted a sceptical eyebrow. "Wouldst thou think it impossible to scare griffon chicks if we chose?"

"In a pageant? Probably."

Luna looked at Twilight. "I sense a challenge. How quickly couldst thou arrange a similar pageant here?"

Twilight was startled. "Well, I know everything that needs to be done from having arranged so many before Amethyst Star took it over. Hmm… I think the House theatre group would be able to throw something together pretty quickly. They'll complain about the short notice, but I know that they've been eager to try something new. I'll need to spread the word as soon as possible to attract as many children as we can." A quill and sheaf of papers floated over to her and she started madly writing down notes, totally oblivious to everyone else in the room.

Free chuckled. "Princess Twilight has left the room! Luna, I think you can safely say that you have yourself a pageant to attend and a challenge to meet. Would you like a bit of changeling help to spice it up a bit?"

He and Luna exchanged a conspiratorial glance and they both laughed.

"Sweet Celestia, what have we done?" Path sighed.

Despite the very late start, Twilight managed to pull off a miracle of organisation, and a fair of modest size was being erected. Tables and materials were brought out from the school to improvise stalls, themed decorations were created in mere hours, and the House's students threw together various street entertainment ideas. They not only informed their families of the event, but they also urged them to pass the word around as much as possible. Many students sacrificed their day off in exchange for later favours, but others were caught up in the excitement of the impromptu event. Twilight looked very pleased with how everything was working out despite being a little frazzled by all the work involved.

Roseclaw looked worriedly at the sky though. "The weather looks like it could ruin the pageant. The open-air stage is rather vulnerable. Maybe we should move it inside to the Great Hall?"

Path smiled reassuringly. "Don't worry about the weather. Twilight has called in help from Equestria. Celestia herself has teleported over a team of weather pegasi for us. They've been working all day not only to ensure that the conditions stay pleasant, but that they also have material to work with for the actual pageant tonight."

"I'm not used to having our weather manipulated like this."

"I know, but you must admit that it has its uses."

"Yes, it would be a shame if all this effort went to waste because of rain or excessive wind. It's a pity that we couldn't start the pageant sooner though. It will be very close to the children's bedtime."

"Can't be helped. Luna still has to put in her appearance in Ponyville, and then she'll stick around for a while to socialise with the foals. They're moving their pageant up the schedule to allow her to leave earlier to come here, so it's not as bad as it could be."

"She really wants this to work, doesn't she?"

Path nodded. "Luna is still gaining acceptance among some ponies, and I think she also wants to impress us."

"Us?" Roseclaw said in surprise. "Why would an alicorn princess want to impress *us*?"

"An alicorn princess doesn't, but a slightly lonely mare does. I was talking to Luna last night, and I think that more than anything else, she desires a family. Aside from her sister, she has none. She has outlived all other relationships, and now she longs for new ones. We've been her surrogate family for a while – why do you think she's found so many excuses to come to Griffonia?"

"I see – you have a point. Perhaps we should find more excuses for her to visit?"

"I think it might be better if we make it plain that she doesn't need an excuse, but I suppose it wouldn't hurt to ease her into that. While she's a very self-confident ruler, she's quite the opposite when it comes to personal relationships. Maybe she had some bad experiences when she was younger? She certainly didn't have a chance to do anything about it for ten centuries, unlike Celestia."

Just then, Twilight trotted out to meet them.

"Have you seen Streak? I didn't get the chance to scold him this morning because I was so busy getting work under way."

Path replied, "I set him to work straight after breakfast."

"You gave him a lecture, I hope?"

"Nope. Just gave him my most disappointed look while he tried to eat, and then ordered him to help building the stage."

"Why the stage? That hardly seems the best use of his abilities."

"Plenty of hammering and other loud noises," Path explained.

Twilight thought about that for a moment before she winced. "That's cruel and entirely appropriate punishment. I don't think he'll want to get another hangover for a very long time. That is if he doesn't try to shirk the work."

"I have Warfist keeping an eye on him. He has ways of *encouraging* people to do things, you know?"

Twilight did know. Warfist was infamous for dealing out various forms of *encouragement* that were very effective in making people highly desire not repeating their mistakes. "That will do for now. I might temper my scolding later, depending on how much *encouragement* he needs. Whatever else happens, he's grounded for two weeks, agreed?"

Both Path and Roseclaw nodded in agreement.

"I have to get back to work, and I bet you do too. Lots to do yet!" Twilight trotted off to her next task.

"She hasn't slowed down since she got up this morning," Roseclaw remarked. "She's going to be exhausted by the end of the day."

Path smiled. "Twilight's in her element. Far from being exhausted, I reckon she'll be energised by a successful event. And speaking of which, as she so subtly hinted, we'd better get on with doing our part."

The impromptu fair drew in more attendees than expected, allaying their fears that it would be a complete flop. It seemed that the griffon community was intrigued by the theme of the event, and because House Path was running it, it also was an excuse for mingling with the popular Griffonian House, with the possibility of adding to their status. The biggest hurdle though was keeping their interest for long enough to stay for the pageant, and professional party planner Cheese Sandwich had been tempted over to Griffonia by the challenge of entertaining a largely griffon contingent. The children, mostly young griffs but some foals too, had various games and challenges where they could win candy or jerky treats, which kept them both interested and amused. Many of the events were designed for parents to share with their children, but Twilight had made sure to provide some items of adult interest also, mostly relating to the history of Nightmare Night and its growth into popular Equestrian culture. The Herd Path members were relieved though when Luna teleported in and they were able to start the play.

Announcements were made that the play was about to begin, and attendees were ushered to the outdoor stage which was lit only with torches in sconces mounted on the stage walls, giving it an appropriate ambiance. The children were given places closer to the stage, while the adults sat at the back. When it seemed that everyone who might be coming had settled, Path signalled the weather pegasi to begin. Soon, a thick ground fog started creeping in from behind the stage, rolling over it and spilling into the audience. All illumination except for the stage torches was extinguished, and even the moon was obscured by thick clouds. Behind the walls of the stage, the House orchestra started quietly playing eerie music, setting the mood for the scene. They let the tension rise among the audience until with a sudden shriek of the strings and a flash of lightning (triggered by a waiting pegasus), Free appeared out of the mist which blew aside in a gust of wind (provided telekinetically by Twilight).

Free had enhanced his griffon form to look more sinister, and he laughed maniacally before announcing, "Welcome foolish mortals to the first celebration of Nightmare Night in Griffonia. May you live long enough to tell the tale! I have heard that some of you do not know why we celebrate this night. Some of you might have heard that it signifies the defeat of Nightmare Moon who would have made the night last forever. I'm here to tell you that you have been deceived! Nightmare Moon lives, and each year she comes demanding tribute from those who would play in her beautiful night. Yes, you are gathered here in this beautiful gloomy evening to give the Nightmare her due, or suffer the consequences!" He laughed madly once more.

This departure from the more staid retelling of the Nightmare Moon story was a calculated risk. After putting some ideas past some of the House griffons, especially those more interested in the Arts, they had elected to go for a more scary and confronting performance for the griffon audience. The Griffonian ponies tended to have a bias that way also due to their upbringing, and so they had hastily written a script to suit. Fortunately, Free was a born ham, and his deliberately over-the-top performance was selling it. The audience was hooked.

Free turned his back to the audience and raised his talons to the partially obscured full moon which was rising above the walls of the stage. "Come, Princess of the Night! Come, Dancer in Dreams and Bringer of Nightmares! Come claim your due, and punish the unbelievers!"

The weather pegasi awaiting their cue pushed aside the obscuring clouds, while others started bucking lightning out of the heavy storm clouds that they had parked to the side. Then something else shadowed the moon – a form that quickly grew in size until the shape became recognisable as an alicorn. The midnight blue form plunged to the stage and arrived in a crash of thunder and lightning. Nightmare Moon held open her huge wings threateningly as she cackled in terrible glee. Luna had refined her performance of her former alter ego over the years, and she had been told not to hold anything back for this particular audience.

"Well, well, if it isn't another lot of sun-lovers who have not learned that the night is not theirs to play in without my permission. I see that I might have to teach you all a harsh lesson… unless you mollify me with your tribute!" She leaned over the edge of the stage to grin menacingly at the children closest to the stage. "And if I don't get what I demand, perhaps I will take some of these delightfully plump little chicks." Her sinister smile widened to show off her fangs to them.

Most of the young ones squealed in fright, but one of the older children jumped forward defiantly and said, "I'm not afraid of you, Nightmare Moon!"

The possibility of one or more of the griffon youngsters standing up to Nightmare Moon had not only been considered, but it had even been counted on, and Luna was ready for it. She threw back her head and laughed again. "How delicious! I will make *thee* my first meal if thou dost wish. But first, see what happens to those who would resist me." She reared up and a burst of purple light exploded from her horn. "Come, my undead slave. Show these fools their fate if they defy me!"

While Luna had held the attention of the audience, Free had slipped offstage and shape-changed in preparation for his next role. With a loud groan, he stumbled onto the stage, almost blindly staggering to Nightmare Moon's side. The audience started muttering in dismay as they beheld the sickly green griffon with flesh melting off its bones, feathers moulting, one eye a black pit while the other glowed a sinister red. One wing dragged on the floor, while the other was a mere bloody stump. Free moaned, "What is your wish, Mistress?"

Luna was almost shaken out of her role by the sight also. She'd had a preview of the zombie form, but it was another thing entirely when the scene was set, the mood was right, and Free was performing to the hilt. Nevertheless, she continued on. "Tell me, slave, what dost thou desire most?"

Free leered at the nearby children. "Brains! I must eat brains!"

The squeals were much louder this time, and even the defiant ones were daunted this time.

Again Nightmare Moon laughed. "Such is the fate of those who defy me. Even the dead obey my commands, and they hunger! Perhaps if you give him some of your candy or jerky, he might be satisfied." She smirked evilly at the audience. "Or maybe not. Do you dare to find out?"

Twilight suddenly burst onto the stage. "Stop right there, Nightmare Moon! I won't let you harm these children!"

The Nightmare cackled contemptuously. "Dost thou think that thou can stop me, puny princess? Thou dost not have the Elements of Harmony to banish me this time!"

"I won't let that stop me from fighting you to my last breath!"

"Oh, that is so wonderfully naïve of thee to think that thou hast the slightest chance of defeating me. I think I will do something special with thee."

"You don't scare me! Leave these children alone and release your victim from his curse!"

"I think not!"

Nightmare Moon fired off a blast of energy at Twilight, who countered with a blast of her own. Although they seemed matched for a moment, gradually Nightmare Moon overcame Twilight, and with a cry of despair, the young alicorn was enveloped by dark magic... well, actually just a shadow spell. Twilight and Luna had been exchanging harmless bolts of light until then, and the shadow spell enabled Twilight a moment to cast an illusion spell on herself. She burst out of the shadow with bat wings spread, her mane a crazed mess, her coat turned blood red in colour, and fangs protruding from her mouth. She giggled crazily as she gazed at the audience with glowing green eyes.

Nightmare Moon laughed. "There! Much better! What should we do with these children now, my servant?"

Twilight hissed and bared her fangs. "Drink their blood! Please, mistress, I thirst!"

"Patience my pretty vampire. Thou shalt slake thy thirst if I do not get my tribute soon." Nightmare Moon eyed the audience. "Who will be first? Who will risk my wrath and attempt to appease me with gifts of candy and jerky? Perhaps if you quell my hunger, I shall spare you all."

Some of the braver children started to move towards the stage, but then a piercing cry came from above. Roseclaw plunged from the sky, clad in full battle armour, carrying a great sword. She hurtled to the stage and landed with a crash in front of the startled Nightmare. Roseclaw brandished the sword in her enemy's face.

"Not so fast, villain! These children are under the protection of the noble Griffonian House of Path. Not one feather nor patch of fur will be harmed!"

Nightmare Moon stared at her incredulously. "*One* griffon warrior against *me*? What dost thou think that thou can do when thy mighty alicorn princess failed so utterly?"

"You are not all-powerful, Nightmare Moon. I know your weakness! While you embody the night, your sister embodies the day, and the light will always banish the dark. This sword is called Sol Invictus, the sword of the sun, and by my will and its power, I will defeat you!"

The sword began to glow brighter and brighter, and waves of heat could also be felt coming from it. Nightmare Moon screamed in pain and staggered back from it, as did vampire Twilight and zombie Free.

"No! How didst thou get that?" Nightmare Moon cried.

Roseclaw replied, "The warriors of Griffonia have allied with those of Equestria to fight you and all your minions, whenever and wherever you should show yourself. Now begone before I send you to the grave!"

Nightmare Moon screamed in rage and snarled, "Thou hast not won yet! I shall return again and get what is due to me. Be ever vigilant because Nightmare Night is mine!"

"**Cease your threats and leave!**" Roseclaw shouted, blasting the Nightmare with a beam from the sword.

Nightmare Moon howled and fled, while Twilight and Free disappeared in a puff of smoke. Roseclaw sheathed the prop sword which had been enchanted to make a convincing light show, and turned to the audience.

"Fear not, children. Nightmare Moon will not return this night. Be brave and bold, and you will be able to defy her again when she returns next Nightmare Night. Farewell!"

She took off from the stage and disappeared into the night. Fog rolled over the stage once more and then parted to reveal Long Path.

"It seems that we have much to be thankful for tonight. Nightmare Night has come to an end, and we have all survived. Thank you for coming, and I hope you dare to come again next year."

The audience burst into applause. Lots of the griffon children surprised Path by coming up to him and begging to meet Nightmare Moon, vindicating his griffon advisors who had recommended a scarier play than was done for Equestrian foals.

"Sorry, kids, but the Nightmare has been banished. Maybe next year? She never got her candy after all. Maybe if you let her know that you want to give her some of your jerky, she'll even let you live."

By this time, Twilight, Free, and Luna joined him on stage, restored to their normal selves, and Roseclaw returned without the armour. Several of the adults who had enjoyed the show came up to express their pleasure to the actors. Luna was smiling a lot, pleased with the reaction to her performance. Free was grinning widely, enjoying all the positive emotion that flooded the stage. Twilight was mostly just relieved that she hadn't blown her lines, but she enjoyed the congratulations also.

Streak raced over to them and said, "That was awesome! Can I play a part next year?"

Path looked at Luna. "*Is* there going to be another next year?" he asked pointedly.

Luna grinned back. "Verily, there must, for now that I am doing two Nightmare Night pageants, the fun has truly been doubled!"

The children were all put to bed, even Streak who complained bitterly about getting punished enough already. The family finally got to relax with Luna once more in the living room, with hot chocolate provided by the attentive staff. They quietly sipped their drinks by the glow of the fireplace, not needing to talk for the moment, but enjoying their time of togetherness. Eventually Free broke their reverie.

"So, Luna, do you think you might drop by more often? We sure had fun today!"

Luna smiled softly and nodded. "If you all would not mind, I enjoy these times that we spend together."

"Much like a family?" Path hinted.

Luna blushed a little. "Yes."

Path looked at Free and their eyes met. Nodding in unspoken understanding, they both stood up and moved over to where Luna relaxed on the rug. They lay down next to her, one on each side, and snuggled up to her as they beckoned their mates to join them. As they quietly expressed their affection for the night alicorn, Free projected some of the love energy that he had acquired that night to her. Luna's eyes moistened with the depth of the emotions she was feeling, and she whispered, "Thank you."

After a long while, Free said, "Y'know, there's a family thing that you might like to try, if you feel up to the challenge?"

"Oh? And what would that be, Free?" Luna asked curiously.

"How would you like to foalsit for a night?" he asked with a mischievous grin.

Luna couldn't help but have suspicions, especially as it was Free Agent doing the asking, but she asked herself, '*Their children are wonderful, so how hard can it be?*' She smiled confidently. "I would be delighted!"

The snorts and chuckles that statement received were just a little disconcerting though.

Chapter 5: Foalsitting

Princess Celestia yawned in a thoroughly undignified and unprincesslike manner as she walked from the throne room to her and Luna's private dining room, but the absence of any other pony in that section of the castle allowed her to get away with it. Not that it was likely to have stopped her anyway. It had been a particularly exhausting day at court, and she was too tired to care much what other ponies thought. She perked up a bit though when she entered the dining room and realised that her sister was there.

Celestia beckoned over the servant mare who had just poured coffee for Luna, before saying, "Good evening, Lulu. Aren't you up a bit early today? You don't have to raise the moon for another hour yet."

"Hi, Tia! I'm heading over to Griffonia later, and I wanted to get my work out of the way quickly."

Celestia levitated the Royal Mug over to the maid who proceeded to fill the capacious cup with the hot, strong brew that was the princess' beverage of choice at this time of day. While the Alicorn of the Sun preferred tea during the day, she liked a good strong espresso to help perk her up a bit after Day Court. While it was being filled, Celestia continued her conversation.

"Your visits to House Path have become more frequent lately."

Luna arched an eyebrow at Celestia. "Dost thou object to this?"

Celestia shook her head with a smile. "On the contrary, I believe that the time that you have been spending with Path's herd has been doing you a lot of good. I haven't seen you so happy and full of life in a long time."

Luna blushed a little. "I... never expected that to happen. I just enjoyed being able to socialise with them without having to be a princess all the time. But they have wormed their way into my heart, especially the foals. Tia... they've as much as said that they consider me to be family." She bit her lower lip and looked at her sister a little guiltily. "I'm not trying to ignore thee, Sister..."

Celestia waved a hoof dismissively. "We still spend much time together on the weekends, and I don't believe we'll ever let anything get between us like it did a millennium ago. However, I am as busy as ever during the week, and we see little of each other then, so why not take advantage of your new family?" She paused to sip her coffee. "I like to see you happy, Lulu. It helps heal the memories of the lonely years without you."

Luna cast her eyes down and shook her head in wistful regret. "So much wasted time, and all because I thought ponies did not appreciate my beautiful night. Had I the patience, I would have seen such growth of our civilisation that would see the night become almost as popular as the day. Now, if it suits my whim, I can go to a late concert, dine at any number of all-night restaurants, or dance the night away at a nightclub...." She shrugged off the mood. "But thou art correct, Tia, I will take my opportunities now and enjoy them to the fullest."

Luna got up from the table and went over to Celestia to kiss her on the cheek. "I'll see thee on the morrow, Sister. Have a pleasant evening."

Celestia smiled and nodded. As soon as Luna departed, she yawned ferociously once more and eyed her empty mug.

"Refill, Your Highness?" the maid asked, holding up a fresh pot of coffee.

"You know me too well, Café au Lait," Celestia replied, as the maid filled her mug once more.

Free decided to give it one more try before leaving Luna to her fate. "Honestly, I was just teasing you. Snow Wing usually foalsits for us, and she can call on more help from the castle staff if necessary."

Luna was too excited at the prospect of having the foals to herself though, and was deaf to Free's earnestness. "Nonsense! I said that I would be happy to foalsit for you, and I meant it. Surely you don't think that they're too much for an alicorn to handle?" She arched an eyebrow at Free, daring him to contradict her.

Luna failed to see Roseclaw rolling her eyes or Twilight stifling a laugh behind a hoof. Only Path managed to keep a straight face... barely.

Free shrugged. "You know where to find us if you need us. It's only a social occasion, and no business will be discussed, or at least not if I have any say in it. We're all going there to relax and enjoy ourselves. We love our children to bits, but everypony needs a break now and then."

Luna smirked. "And yet you all are still here, worrying about *me*. Begone!" she commanded as she waved a hoof dismissively. "Auntie Luna is on the job!"

Roseclaw spread her wings wide to chivvy the others out. "You heard the foalsitter – let's get going and let her do her job!"

With the four adults finally gone, Luna turned to the children and smiled widely. "Who wants to hear me read a story?"

There was a chorus of positive replies, and Luna guided them to the family room. "Which story shall we read?"

"*Where's My Cow?!*" shouted Flix.

"What? 'Tis a silly book!"

However the other children started calling for the same story, and looking at Luna with pleading eyes.

Luna sighed. "Alright, we shall read *Where's My Cow?*" Then under her breath, she added, "For the hundredth time."

The foals made themselves comfortable around Luna as she settled down on the family room rug, or in Destined's case, in his favoured position on Luna's back, looking over her shoulder. Luna found it awkward but endearing, and tolerated it far more than she knew she should. She levitated the book from its all-too-familiar place on the bookshelf and opened it in front of her. She started reading aloud...

"Every day, Commander Ham Dines of the City Watch would be home at six o'clock to read to Young Bam, who was one year old. Six o'clock, no matter what... or who... or why... because some things are important." *

Luna continued on with the story of the griffon father who always read to his son every night, while doing all the silly animal noises that made the story more fun. She was sure by now that the children wanted her to read the book not so much for the story, but all the silly nonsense that she did to liven it up, but perhaps that was why she always relented when they asked for it.

The book-reading took only about twenty minutes. As always, Epiphany got charged up on the excited emotions of everyone, and started fidgeting from the extra energy. She jumped up and started bouncing around the room, repeating all the animal noises that Luna had done. By this point, Free or Path normally took charge of their daughter and helped burn off her extra energy. However, Luna had the other three foals to concern herself with. Destined was only a problem in that he had curled up to have a nap on Luna's back, and she was loathe to disturb him. Lucida and Flix got up to start playing tag with Pif. Because they had wings, it would seem that they had the advantage over the earth pony filly, but of course she was also a changeling. Diaphanous wings sprouted from her back, and soon she was buzzing around the room, chased by the two hippogriff siblings.

Luna chewed her lower lip in concern. While not a problem so far, she knew that their excitement would only grow greater, and that's when things would begin to get knocked over. She wanted them to have their

fun, but she also wanted the herd to come back to an intact family room. She was about to reach out with her telekinesis to slow them down when they solved the problem of damaging the room by themselves… they zoomed out into the rest of the castle to wreak their havoc elsewhere.

It took only seconds before an indignant shriek followed by the crash of metal trays came back to Luna. She sighed before carefully lifting Destined off her back and placing him on the rug, hopefully without disturbing him. Then she dashed out in pursuit of the other foals. She passed by one of the castle's servants still picking up the contents of two trays that he had been carrying.

"A thousand apologies!" Luna said as she galloped past in pursuit of the children. She caught a glimpse of Flix headed upstairs. He was the slowest flyer, so she presumed that the other two had to be ahead of him somewhere. She spread her wings and zoomed up the grand staircase, looking and listening for further clues as to where the foals might be. Another series of noises came from the Grand Ballroom.

"By the Moon, no!" Luna exclaimed as she burst into the room. The ballroom had been set up for a big event that would be held the following evening. She could not believe how so much damage had been done in so little time as the foals tore over and under tables, and through the decorations. Apparently the hippogriffs had still not caught Pif whose buzzing flightpath was far more erratic than their more classic flying techniques could cope with, and they constantly overshot her as she jerked away in some unexpected direction.

Luna's horn flared, and Epiphany was caught in a telekinetic field and brought back to Luna's side. Unable to escape, Lucida and Flix caught up and tagged her.

"Aw! Auntie Luna, that's cheating!" The changeling child gave her the biggest saddest eyes.

Luna immediately started feeling bad. In fact she was feeling really depressed about having to spoil their fun. It was awful! It was....
"Pif! Stop that!"

Epiphany blinked and stopped draining Luna's positive emotions. It hadn't been a malicious act – the young changeling queen did it instinctively. Free Agent was normally there to catch her at it early and prevent it from going too far though. Luna hoped that self-discipline would soon put a stop to that, and she wondered not for the first time how Free's griffon parents had coped with him during his early years.

Still carrying Epiphany, Luna led the other two foals out of the ballroom. She passed by the same castle servant who pressed himself against the wall to avoid another collision.

"Inform the staff that repairs need to be made in the ballroom as soon as possible," Luna informed him.

The elderly griffon bowed his head and said, "Yes, Milady."

"Auntie Luna, I'm hungry!" Lucida announced.

"Nonsense – dinner was but an hour ago," Luna replied.

"I'm hungry too," Flix said, following his sister's lead.

"Me three!" Epiphany added.

Luna scowled at her. "Didn't thou not just have a big snack on my emotions? Thou *cannot* be hungered!"

"Cookie?" Epiphany asked unabashed.

Luna sighed and capitulated, knowing that they would probably nag her constantly now that they had gotten the idea in their heads. She took them to the kitchen and started looking about for wherever the cookies might be.

"Can I help you, Milady?" asked one of the kitchen staff, an earth pony mare.

"Where dost thou keep the cookie jar?"

The mare led her to a shelf full of jars of various kinds of cookies, and the alicorn thanked her. Turning to the foals, she asked, "What kind of cookie would you like? Only one each!"

"Raisin!" Epiphany said.

"Peanut butter!" Lucida said emphatically.

"Chocolate!" Flix chirped.

Luna snorted. Of *course* they all wanted something different. She levitated the raisin cookies down first and passed out one to Epiphany who started munching it immediately. Next in line were the chocolate cookies, so she got out one for Flix. After looking through the jars, she found the peanut butter cookies and gave one to Lucida. Destined Path was waiting his turn, and Luna asked what he wanted.

"Raisin, please."

'Now why didn't he ask in the first place while she had that jar out?' she grumbled to herself. As she passed it out to him though, something suddenly occurred to her. Didn't Destined hate raisins? And didn't she leave him asleep in the family room? She glared at the colt. "Pif?"

The foal stuffed the cookie in his mouth and cantered away, magic fire flaring about his form to reveal Epiphany.

Luna begrudgingly gave the foal credit for fooling her, even as she made plans for creating a small spell to prevent that from happening again. She took out a chocolate chip cookie which she knew that Destined liked, and brought the other two foals back to the family room. She found Epiphany snuggled up innocently with her half-brother who yawned and woke up. He saw the cookie that floated in front of his eyes and grabbed it with his own magic.

"Thanks, Auntie Luna!" he said before starting to munch on it.

Luna nodded and said, "What do you wish to do before bedtime?"

"Ball catch!" Destined suggested excitedly.

"Read another book!" Lucida pleaded.

"Play a game!" Epiphany insisted

"Sing songs!" Flix exclaimed, and proceeded to do so.

The little hippogriff had a wonderful voice, and Luna loved to listen to him sing. Unfortunately all the other foals decided that they would do their own thing also at the same time. Lucida brought over a book that she wanted Luna to read, Destined found his training ball and hovered it near Luna's face, while Epiphany dug out her favourite board game.

"Children! I cannot do everything at once!" Luna protested to no avail, and the situation deteriorated further. For the first time, she started to doubt her ability to cope by herself. Nevertheless, she still didn't wish to call on the House's staff after adamantly denying the need for them. She dithered for a bit before realising that she had an ace in the wing.

She used her magic to pull the cord that summoned a staff member, and shortly a maid turned up.

The maid looked askance at the chaos in the room before asking, "How may I serve you, Milady?"

"Please go to Corporal Leatherwing's room and ask him to join me here as soon as possible."

"Immediately, Milady," the maid replied and hastily exited.

Leatherwing always enjoyed Luna's jaunts to visit the House Path members. When it was merely as far as the Ponyville castle, it was a pleasant break from his more boring duties. However, it was more often to the Griffonian House, and that was really enjoyable. The princess insisted that she did not need a personal guard while there, and dismissed him the moment that they arrived. He had the run of the castle, and he enjoyed the use of all the facilities there, and ate some superb meals. He also had his own permanent room now, and although it was the least opulent of all the guest rooms, it was still magnificent in comparison to his usual barracks. He was currently comfortably lounging on a huge stuffed sofa, reading a book while nibbling on a bowl of snacks. The knock on his door was unexpected though. Leatherwing got up and answered the door.

The maid waiting outside gave him a respectful nod of her head before saying, "Milady Luna requests your presence in the family room as soon as possible, sir."

Princess Luna never summoned him, and this exception surprised him. Nevertheless he responded immediately, grabbing only the harness which held his weapon. He pulled it over his head as he flew down the hallway, heading to the family room as fast as possible. If the Princess needed his services, he would not be found lacking!

The chaos and cacophony in the family room brought him to screeching halt, and he spent precious time trying to sort out what was happening. Luna's voice swiftly brought focus though.

"Leatherwing! Attend Destined and Epiphany at once!"

Leatherwing saw that they were engaged in a wild game of ball tag which involved them dodging and weaving throughout the room, while incidentally wreaking havoc on anything that got in their way. Epiphany had sprouted wings and horn to compete with Destined on an equal basis, and they were both telekinetically hurling the ball and catching it with little regard for whatever else might be in the way. For a moment he was paralysed with indecision. He had been an only child with no siblings to deal with, and he was still a bachelor inexperienced with having foals of his own. He was trained as a Royal Guard, not a foalsitter!

"*Leatherwing!*"

Luna's command tone snapped him out of it, and he took to the air to intercept the ball. If he thought that would put an end to the game though, he was sorely mistaken. Instead, he became the target, and he found himself desperately fending off two alicorn foals. Leatherwing was pulled this way and that both physically and telekinetically, and he desperately looked for an alternative. A glance at the princess showed him that Luna was quite preoccupied with the hippogriff siblings who seemed to be squabbling over something so fiercely that it was taking all of Luna's attention.

Luna was on the verge of panicking. In all her centuries, she had never learned the skill of dealing with bickering children, and all her attempts to defray the situation had instead made things worse. She tried to pull the two apart with her horn, but they were so tightly wrestling with each other that she could not separate them without unintentionally hurting them. While Lucida was much bigger than her younger brother, he was fierce and determined, and armed with razor sharp claws. Fur and feathers were flying as Luna pleaded with them to stop fighting.

At last she had an idea. A blast from her horn flung the balcony doors open, and she spread her wings and launched herself outside, with Lucida and Flix in tow. A few moments later, there was a huge splash as she flung them into the moonlit pond nearby. The hippogriffs quickly resurfaced, their fight forgotten, paddling wildly while squawking in shock. Luna let them cool off a bit more before she lifted them out of the pond. They hung in mid-air, suspended in Luna's magic field, while pond water dripped off their bedraggled forms.

Luna scowled at them and said, "Auntie Luna is *very* cross with you both."

Lucida pouted. "*He* started it!" she said as she pointed out her brother.

"Nuh uh!" Flix said emphatically, sticking his tongue out at her.

"Did too!" Lucida managed to flick her tail tuft in Flix's face.

Flix tried to lunge for her and would have succeeded if he'd actually had something to push against.

"Do you want another swim?" Luna asked as she drew them further apart.

"No, Auntie Luna," they chorused.

"Good. Now let's find some towels and dry– *OOF!*"

Luna was knocked off her hooves as Leatherwing flew out of the night gloom and collided with her shoulder. Surprise caused her to drop the telekinetic field, and the siblings dropped to the grass. Luna was not so lucky, and she toppled into the pond.

When Luna had flown outside, Leatherwing had taken the opportunity to take the mêlée out of the room. Securing the ball once more, he had dived for the doorway before one or the other of the foals could stop him. The competition was no less fierce in the open, but at least nothing was likely to be damaged, right?

The poor light conditions out in the garden did little to slow down Epiphany and Destined. In fact, it seemed to spur them to greater speeds now that they weren't confined to the living room. To Leatherwing's dismay, the game had escalated into a game of dodgeball, with him as the target. Catching the ball proved to be the wrong idea because that just became a challenge to tackle him and wrestle the ball away. Desperately afraid of hurting them, he instead took a lot of physical abuse. The Royal Guard were trained to deal with everything from troublesome protesters to potential assassins, but rambunctious foals were definitely out of his skill set.

"For Luna's sake, please stop!" he begged them, but they were so wrapped up in their competition that they were deaf to his pleas. In desperation, he intercepted the ball once more and accelerated away as fast as he could, hoping to wear them out in a protracted chase. It was a good idea, if only Destined hadn't managed to tackle him from the side before he got up to speed. While not enough to stop him, nevertheless Leatherwing was pushed off course. He only had an instant to realise that he was on a collision course with an alicorn before he impacted.

Leatherwing watched in horror as Luna plunged into the cold water of the pond, unable to prevent it in the slightest. He scrambled to his hooves and looked about to see if he could help her, but was stopped when the water exploded and the Moon Princess rose out of the pond, her normally ethereal mane plastered to her body, and her eyes glowing with power.

"**I command that all will CEASE!**" Luna thundered in the Royal Canterlot Voice. Her magic flared and all the foals and also Leatherwing were caught up in a stasis field. It finally got through to the foals that their Auntie was really angry, and perhaps they had gone too far. They cringed a little under her fierce glare, and even Leatherwing failed to get off free.

"Thou wert supposed to help, not make things worse!" she accused him.

"M-my d-deepest ap-pologies, Y-your Highness," Leatherwing stammered.

Luna glared at him for a while longer before she sighed and let him free. She had spent too much time trying to get him to loosen up around her as her personal guard to want to jeopardise their relationship with harsh criticism. "Apology accepted. I was no less successful controlling

Lucida and Flix, so I suppose it would be hypocritical of me to expect more of thee. Go to the bathroom and prepare a hot bath. We have four foals to clean off and warm up."

"*Four*, Your Highness?"

Suddenly Epiphany and Destined were hurled into the pond. The foals emerged coughing and sputtering, with Epiphany returned to her normal earth pony default form.

Leatherwing nodded. "Right – *four* foals," he confirmed with a trace of satisfaction.

Leatherwing was tasked with ensuring the four children were properly bathed and dried off while Luna went to her own room's en suite bathroom to do the same. Happily, the foals remained subdued by Luna's anger, and cooperated with him. When they were all dried off, he took them back down to the living room, but he was shocked by its state of disarray. While he had been preoccupied by Destined and Epiphany, things had evidently gotten much worse. He turned to frown at the foals, and they had the grace to look guilty.

Luna joined them just then, and after a glance inside, she snorted and said tiredly, "There will evidently be no more use of this room until it is righted. I think it best if the foals be put to bed now."

"Aw, Auntie!" Lucida complained.

"Nay, child, no protests from thee. If thou had behaved, I would have considered letting thee go to bed later, but that is a reward for well-behaved foals, not rambunctious ones."

"Can we at least have hot chocolate?"

Luna was about to deny that too, but she reconsidered it. The family always sent their foals to bed after a mug of hot chocolate, and she was loathe to break that habit. Besides, she knew from past experiences that a full stomach made for sleepy foals.

"Very well, let us go to the kitchen. Leatherwing, please ensure that none wander off."

Luna then led the way to the kitchen with the thestral bringing up the rear. The way they looked at him and giggled did not fill him with a great deal of confidence, however. Once they were there, both of them realised that they had no idea how to go about making the hot chocolate. Fortunately there was always at least one of the kitchen staff on duty to cater to the whims of the House members, and soon four mugs of hot chocolate were presented to the foals.

Destined looked up to Luna with a milk moustache that made her smile. "Cookie please, Auntie Luna?"

Luna shook her head. "Thou hast had thy cookie tonight. Finish thy chocolate."

Destined was disappointed, and the other three's hopes sank also.

When the foals were finished, Luna took them upstairs to the common room, with Leatherwing bringing up the rear once more. Amazingly, it seemed to Leatherwing that there would be no more incidents before they put them to bed. Alas, he was to be disappointed. As they placed the foals on the bed, Destined suddenly disappeared with a small flash-bang.

Leatherwing gasped. "Wha... what happened?"

Luna blinked in surprise. "By the stars! He has teleported!"

"Teleported? A foal can teleport already?" the thestral asked incredulously. "Where's he gone, Princess?"

"One moment..." Luna's horn lit up and for a moment she concentrated, only to disappear herself. A few seconds passed and she reappeared with a grumpy foal in her arms. "The scoundrel went to the kitchen and was headed for the cookie jars," she explained. "Fortunately I could trace his magic and follow. Now go to bed, child."

Destined reluctantly complied, and Luna spread a blanket over the four.

"Goodnight, children. I will guard your dreams tonight," Luna said as she and Leatherwing left the room.

Just as the door closed though, there was a faint noise.

Leatherwing looked at Luna. "Did you hear what I heard, Princess?"

Luna nodded grimly. "Hold tight, Leatherwing." Luna powered up her horn, and an instant later they teleported into the kitchen.

After a moment's disorientation, Leatherwing spotted the alicorn foal with his hooves on a cookie jar. He flapped over and grabbed the little thief, relieving him of the jar.

Destined Path pouted and shouted, "BAD BAT!" His little horn lit up, and in a flash, Leatherwing disappeared.

Luna caught the falling foal in her telekinetic field and turned him to face her. "That was extremely naughty of thee! Where hast thou sent him?"

Destined just frowned and refused to talk.

Luna sighed in resignation. She could not trace the non-magical thestral, but she doubted he would end up anywhere harmful. She also knew that the stubborn foal would be unlikely to be able to tell her anyway. She recognised the instinctual use of magic, which meant that the foal really didn't know other than somewhere not close by. She took him back to bed and tucked him back in. This time she laid a light slumber spell on him to ensure he did not try a cookie raid again. She stood there for a long moment, watching their seemingly innocent faces, and wondered how she had ever thought that foalsitting would be simple. In fact it was complex and very tiring, and she had to give credit to the herd for keeping their foals under control with such deceptive ease.

"Auntie – can I have a cuddle?" Lucida asked uncertainly.

Luna considered the hippogriff filly. Normally she was a well-behaved and inquisitive child, but this evening had shown another side of Lucida. Now that she had calmed down, Lucida realised she had been misbehaving in front of her favourite Auntie, and being older than the rest, felt the need for reassurance while the others had probably forgotten most of it by now. Luna climbed up onto the bed next to Lucida and gave her a long hug.

"No more fighting with thy brother, understand?"

"Yes, Auntie Luna."

"Good. Rest well, for tomorrow awaits thee."

Some minutes later, Lucida fell asleep in Luna's arms.

Leatherwing reappeared amidst a cacophony of noise and smells that was strangely familiar. Surprised shouts from griffons surrounding him drew the stares of even more. Then one grinned and clapped him on the back with his large wing.

"Hey, it's Batty! Where's Moonbutt? I've never seen you here before without her. Come to join us in a drink at last like you promised?"

Leatherwing blinked and recognised the griffon. "Hi, Shrill Shriek. I kind of hadn't planned on coming. Luna's back at the House."

"Then you have no excuse not to drink with us," Shrill Shriek replied jovially as he shoved Leatherwing towards the bar of Herd Path's favourite pub. The thestral had always deflected the offers of alcohol with the excuse of being on duty, but he had promised to join them for a drink one day when he wasn't, knowing full well that he had no intention of coming here without the princess. Now, as Shriek had said, he no longer had an excuse.

"Two specials," Shrill Shriek ordered. "My buddy and I have some serious drinking to do!" He looked back at Leatherwing and asked, "What's that you've got there?"

Leatherwing sighed in resignation and held up the jar that he was still holding. "Would you like a cookie?"

When the Herd Path adults arrived home, they headed directly to the family room. While it was fairly late and the foals were unlikely to be up still, nevertheless they thought that Luna might be found there.

What they did find left them all gaping in shock. The orderly alicorn was most distressed by the mess.

"What happened to our beautiful family room?" Twilight wailed.

"I sense the foals might have something to do with this," Free said.

"Where's Luna?" Path wondered.

"Where are the children?" Roseclaw asked even as she turned and headed upstairs.

The others followed close behind as they hastened to the common room, pausing only to quietly open the door. They crept inside and when they saw the occupants of the bed, they all started to grin.

Luna was fast asleep with Lucida still in her arms, but she had also gained an alicorn foal curled up on her back in his favourite position while the remaining two had snuggled up to her. The Moon Princess's mouth was open and gently snoring as she drooled on the pillow.

Free snickered and softly said, "Mares and Gentlecolts, I present to you the foalsitter!"

The moon was already well past midnight when two griffons flew down to a sloppy landing on the front porch of House Path and released the burden that they had carried between them.

Leatherwing staggered to his hooves, barely able to walk let alone fly. "Shanks, flies... I mean thanks, guys. Be seein' ya!"

Shrill Shriek grinned. "Your turn to buy next time, Batty."

"Shoor fing, Screechy. Gotta go. Prinshess Moonbutt awaits!" He took one step, stumbled, and fell flat on his face.

Shrill Shriek helped him up and pushed him towards the door while the other griffon held it open for him while giving a mocking bow.

"At eashe!" Leatherwing said as he threw him a salute, promptly losing his balance again in doing so. He did an amazing pirouette as he tried to regain his balance, all four legs going in random directions, but astoundingly he stayed upright. "Aced it!" he said proudly as he shuffled inside.

The griffons chuckled, closed the door and flew off.

Leatherwing stumbled his way to the family room, burst in the door, and loudly proclaimed, "Reduting for porty! Er... Reporting... duty..." He looked around blearily and found no one there. "All'sh well," he declared happily before slumping to the rug and passing out.

Celestia was making her way to the private dining room when she saw a familiar thestral. Although he was out of his Lunar Guard uniform, she easily recognised Luna's personal guard. However, he was hanging his head and his batlike wings were almost dragging on the ground as he slowly shuffled in the direction of his barracks.

"Good heavens, my little pony!" Celestia exclaimed, "What happened to you?"

Leatherwing stopped and shuddered at the sound of Celestia's piercing voice. He turned to her, showing his hangdog expression and bloodshot eyes. "Foalsitting," he explained and started shuffling away before he stopped once more to add, "Your Highness" with a salute. He winced as his hoof tapped his head, and then resumed walking.

Celestia watched him go for a long moment before resuming her trip to the dining room. She trotted a bit faster, hoping to catch her sister there. *'If that's an example of whatever happened last night at House Path, I'm **very** eager hear the rest of this tale!'* she thought with a huge grin.

* *Where's My Cow* is an actual book written by Terry Pratchett. I've only changed the names for the little excerpt. And yes, 'tis indeed a very silly book.

Chapter 6:
Divine Introspections

The summer solstice was almost upon them, and for Herd Path, that meant pleasantly warm evenings spent with the family while it was still light. However, it was now time for the youngsters to go to bed, although not without the obligatory whining about wanting to stay up longer. Nevertheless, they were quickly chivvied off to their rooms after giving Auntie Luna a goodnight hug. While the parents were occupied with tucking in their children for the night, Luna made her way out onto the balcony. The lowering sun was just touching the horizon, and she was ready to raise the moon in its stead.

Luna felt her sister's magic as she set the sun, and she called to her moon with her own power. Soon, a three-quarter phase moon rose as the sun disappeared, and the light faded. Luna did not need the illumination of her satellite to see the grounds of House Path's estate – it had become very familiar to her by now because of her frequent visits. She closed her eyes and felt the serenity of the gardens, even as the creatures of the night stirred and began to go about their business. She smelled the newly mown grass and the scent of the flowering shrubs that lined the path that led to the entrance of the House, and she let the ambiance imbue her with its peacefulness.

Long Path found her still there on the balcony when he went looking for her after putting the foals to bed. He was troubled when he noticed tears running down Luna's cheek, the tracks of moisture glistening in the moonlight.

"Luna, what's wrong?" Path asked with deep concern in his voice.

Luna opened her eyes to look at him. She smiled softly and replied, "Better to ask what is right."

Path cocked an eyebrow curiously. "Okay then, what's so right that has you crying?"

"Everything," she said with a broad sweep of a wing that encompassed all. "As of this moment, I believe I have never been happier in all my long life. Since my return, I have reconciled with my sister, and we have never been closer. I have made friends, and even better, I have begun relationships with people who have become so very dear to me. I have a family that cares for me and brings me joy. Even if I am a poor foalsitter," she added with a chuckle.

"Ah, then those are tears of happiness?" Path asked with some relief.

"Indeed. Today has been such perfection that I could not keep them in."

"Surely you had to have experienced times like this before?"

"Of course I have had such times, especially when Tia and I were much younger, long before my *fall*. But my family has grown, and my emotions have matured, and I can appreciate the difference between simple childhood happiness, and the joy of a rich and fulfilling adulthood. I am at last comfortable with my place in this world, and I owe it all to my friends, starting with Twilight Sparkle who went out of her way to make me feel welcome in a world that still feared Nightmare Moon, and then to my acquaintances who saw me as a mare with needs rather than just an aloof divine ruler. Herd Path has completed me in ways I had never dared dream."

"I suppose it must be tough for the average pony to see a goddess as a person whom they can relate to," Path mused.

Luna was quiet for a long moment before she replied. "What dost thou think I am, Path?" she asked placidly.

The question surprised Path, and he had to stop to think for a moment. "I don't usually think of you in those terms, but you are a divine alicorn, Goddess of the Moon and Night, and Princess of Equestria."

Luna snorted in amusement. "Divine goddess… yes, I suppose that's what many ponies tend to think of me, but consider for a moment – has either Celestia or myself ever *explicitly* claimed to be a god?"

"I… don't recall any occasions."

"That is because we do *not* claim such. While it is true that we still allow that assumption to be unchallenged in many cases where it is expeditious, it is something that we are working slowly to eliminate. It is our goal to govern entirely through wisdom and good will, but it is a long and slow process. I have several groups that I must gradually bring to the modern way of thinking, but for now I need to play the part still. Nevertheless, I will be happy when the day comes when no one thinks of me as a god."

Path frowned in puzzlement. "But if you're not a god, what are you then?"

"Is Twilight Sparkle a god?" Luna asked rather than answer directly.

Path laughed. "Twilight would look at me as if I were insane if I said she was."

"Exactly, and yet she is no less an alicorn than I despite her youth. She will grow in power as the years pass until she matches or even *exceeds* me. The same can be said of Cadance. However, if we were gods, we would have near absolute power, and yet thou dost know for a fact how many times we have failed or struggled to achieve our goals. Remember, in the end, it was neither my actions nor Celestia's that ultimately saved the Crystal Kingdom."

"Then what *is* an alicorn if not a god?"

"We are Aspects of Harmony. We are tasked with maintaining the balance between Chaos and Order. That is why Twilight and her friends were able to defeat Tirek in spite of him stealing all their magic. When I grew corrupt and became Nightmare Moon, I was disconnected from Harmony, and thus vulnerable to it also, hence why Celestia was able to banish me with the Elements of Harmony. Yes, we are very powerful in magic too, but it is not our primary tool. Harmony manifests itself in many ways, and as this world matures and the population grows, I foresee more alicorns ascending to help maintain the balance."

"So is that's why Twilight became an alicorn?"

"Yes, I believe so. Celestia has the gift of foresight, and although she did not know exactly who at the time of the vision, she foresaw that she would guide a worthy filly to fulfil that destiny." Luna chuckled wryly. "It's somewhat ironic that her first major step towards that destiny was defeating Nightmare Moon, but I consider that most fortunate for me."

"What about Destined? He was *born* an alicorn. Did Harmony decide to make him its agent even as he was conceived?"

"Destined Path… why did you name him so? I think it's because you already knew the answer to that question. Herd Path seems to have become the focus for Harmony lately, and he may yet play a large role in the fate of this world. However, there is an oddity about him. Art thou aware that alicorn foals have only ever been born of *two* alicorn parents? All other pairings with alicorns have always resulted in pony offspring of one type or another. When Flurry Heart was born, that seemed to break the rule, but Shining Armor later ascended to alicornhood, so we now believe that it is enough for the parent to have the *potential* to be an alicorn in order to have alicorn progeny."

"Well, *I'm* no alicorn," Path said with a self-deprecating chuckle, "So perhaps it's not such an iron-clad rule after all?"

Luna regarded him for a long moment, seemingly reassessing him. She shook her head. "I beg to differ. Thou art in your own way an alicorn. In fact, I have always regarded Prince Shining Armor's ascension as rather odd. While I in no way believe that he did not deserve to ascend, if for no other reason than to never have to leave the Alicorn of Love alone, I don't believe that it was his original destiny. There was one on that battlefield who was destined to be that agent of

Harmony, the Alicorn of Protection, but he died on the field in achieving it."

Path was stunned. "But... you mean... I could have been... an alicorn?"

"I believe that was thy destiny, yes."

"But you're not sure?"

Luna shrugged. "As I said, I am not a god. I am neither omniscient nor privy to all of Harmony's secrets. However, I have lived a very long life, even before my banishment, and I have observed much that supports my hypothesis."

"How about that? I could have had wings like everyone else," he said with a smirk. "Ah well, I don't know if I'd be cut out to be an alicorn anyway."

Luna smiled in amusement. "As I said, thou art already one in thine own fashion. I believe that thou dost serve Harmony in another way. After all, why did Mort send thee back?"

"Huh? He said something about being a focal point and he felt that it was not my destiny to die as yet. I don't recall exactly now."

"Even the Spirit of the Dead plays his part. He probably sensed what I do, that thou wert an agent of Harmony, and had yet to finish playing thy part."

"So that's why my son is an alicorn? Is that what I was destined to do?"

"Perhaps, but do not belittle thyself. Thou still hast much to do before thou can achieve thy lofty goals."

"I couldn't do it without my family. Still, it seems that we have succeeded in one thing."

"And what is that?" Luna asked curiously.

"Making you happy," Path said with a fond smile.

"Was my happiness *that* important to thee?"

"To *all* of us, Luna. You are family to us, and we love and support each other. You needed it and we were happy to give it, and we've all been the better for it. In fact, I think it's time that we took the next step. Look behind you, Luna."

The Alicorn of the Moon turned around to see Twilight, Free, and Roseclaw all sitting at the balcony doorway, quietly watching and listening to their conversation. They smiled happily at her.

Path continued, "We have been wondering if we even had the right to ask, but as you have just told me, you are not a god – you are a very wonderful mare, and you deserve so much. So, will you do us the honour, the privilege, and the outright joy of officially joining Herd Path?"

The tears that had dried up started flowing again. They all gathered around Luna and hugged her. She sniffled a bit and then said, "I was too hasty when I spoke earlier – *this* is the happiest moment of my life. Yes, I would be overjoyed to join your Herd."

Twilight spoke up. "I'll call Celestia and ask her to come over if she's free. She can officially pronounce our union, and I'm sure she'll want to share in your joy too, Luna."

Luna nodded. "Certainly, but as selfish as this may seem to be, that is *all* she will be getting!"

They all laughed and hugged once more.

It was a *long* time before Twilight got around to calling Celestia.

Chapter 7:
TAG!

OR

"That One Time That Destined Path Ruled Equestria For Ninety Seconds"

She should have done this a lot sooner. She had not felt so good for eons!

Luna was standing in a large classroom of about eighty griffons, ponies, diamond dogs, and even a few New World thestrals. Her hair was pulled back into a ponytail and she was wearing a pair of circular glasses. She had even dressed like a stereotypical college professor on a whim.

"This doth conclude the class for today, students. I need you all to read the chapter twelve section on stellar evolution. When we return on Friday, I want you to discuss what is your favourite phase and why it is so. After that, we will break into groups and log some observatory time cataloguing stars of thy chosen phase! Until then, class is dismissed!"

Luna spent several minutes answering questions from a few students who lagged behind before she gathered up her books, grinned, and disappeared with a pop. She reappeared in the main hall where the rest of the herd was going to meet up. Twilight came bouncing in, looking unusually happy.

"Hmmm... didst thou have a good class this morn, Twilight?" Luna asked.

"It really was! Some of the unicorn transfer students are learning about how magic can act differently in lands where there isn't a high density of magic users. Like in Griffonia, some spells are actually easier because there are less unicorns running around," Twilight said as she sat down.

Path was the next one to show up. He sighed weakly as he slumped down into his seat. Rubbing his head, he clearly had a headache and he just laid it down onto the table. "I am never teaching the changeling language again. Not for all the crowns in Griffonia!" he groaned and closed his eyes just as Free walked in, grinning.

"Poor Path! He can't handle trying to teach others the changeling language. The class was four hours long, and he was trying to explain gender qualifiers to them. The end result was them screeching at him twice, then he would blink in shock and try to correct them. This went on and on for hours! I know this because my art class was right next to his language class." Free sat down next to Twilight, his grin growing broader.

"I think that my class is the best," Luna stated with conviction. "All my students really want to be there, and they are all so excited to learn about the night sky! Everyone passed their first test, with an average of 92%! My class is the best class!" Luna set her books down with a grin before she sat down herself. "And furthermore –"

Luna was interrupted when she felt hooves wrap around her from behind. "Auntie, let's play tag!" Destined ran in circles around the table, and kept tagging Twilight and Luna. "You're it! You're it! You're it!" He skidded to a halt as Luna and Twilight looked at each other before looking back to Destined with mischievous grins.

Destined squealed and his horn powered up. He disappeared in a messily constructed but still successful teleport spell.

"You know... he's getting stronger every day," Twilight said. "This should really flex his power. I figure we could estimate his total reserves by doing this."

Luna nodded in agreement. "The chase is on!" she declared, and they both disappeared, tracking the young alicorn by his magical signature.

Path looked at Free with a fond smile of recollection. "Remember when we used to come home to our apartment after work and just split a jumbo-sized hungry-griff dinner?"

Free laughed. "Simpler times! Simpler times...."

Cinder and Blue Streak were curled up with each other on the far edge of the estate, watching the sky and relaxing during the time they had between classes, when a loud pop startled Blue into jumping up to his hooves.

"Brother! Brother! I need your help! Mom and Auntie are going to get me!" Destined begged with a laugh as he pounced upon him.

"This cannot come to be! Whatever can I do to help?!" Blue asked with comic seriousness as Cinder leaned to the side, confused as to what was happening.

"We need to play airship; I need to go *fast*!" Destined started to trot anxiously in place.

"What do you mean? Do you want to go light speed?" Blue asked with a grin.

"No, no! Light speed is too slow; I need to go so fast it's *ludicrous*!" Destined demanded as he began flying in circles around Blue, waiting for him to grab onto the two legs closest to him.

"How does an eight-year-old even know what ludicrous means?" Cinder commented.

Blue reared up and grabbed onto Destined. He started to spin on his hind legs, using one as a rotation point as the other one kept kicking the ground to speed up faster and faster. Destined pulled in his wings as he squealed in joy. Blue kept spinning until he suddenly let go of Destined, and the young alicorn shot back toward the castle with a plaid streak trailing behind him.

"EEEEeeeeeeeeeee...." Destined disappeared out of sight as Blue sat back down with a laugh.

Luna and Twilight teleported in moments later with two loud pops.

"Did you see Destined?! Was he just here?!" Twilight and Luna exclaimed.

Cinder just pointed at the contrail that was fading away. The two alicorns grinned and disappeared again in a loud twin pop.

Cinder looked at Blue Streak. "Your family is weird."

Blue grinned. "Yeah, but that's one reason why I love them."

Destined landed on Luna's balcony just in time to see the two alicorns appear on the other side.

"Gonna get you, Destined!" the two princesses chanted as Destined laughed excitedly.

He charged his horn, but this time it was a lot brighter than the last time, and his eyes started to glow a bright white. Destined was really digging deep into his magical reserves as the two princesses watched.

Destined suddenly felt something familiar and he smiled broadly. "And for my next trick...!" He abruptly disappeared, but not in a small pop like usual, but this time with enough concussive force to shove the two against the wall.

"What happened?! Where did he go?!" Twilight exclaimed as Luna laughed.

"He actually did it! I was not expecting him to understand how to find and activate an arcane thread at such a young age!" Luna smiled smugly. "My student really is the best."

"So – where is he?" Twilight asked.

"Come on, follow me." Luna replied with a smirk.

Celestia was just wrapping up Day Court. With a beneficent smile, she got up from her throne and stepped forward to dismiss the audience. When the last of the petitioners had exited, she nodded to her guards to close the doors and then turned to her scribe.

"I believe that today is officially don-mmph?!"

In the middle of her closing formalities, Destined appeared, spread-eagled in the air and moving fast. He collided with Celestia's muzzle, knocking her backwards onto the dais. The guards all blinked in shocked surprise before approaching the princess whose wings were flat out against the ground, while her legs were pointed straight up almost like a fainting goat. Her face was covered by Destined's midsection, and they were about to act to remove the offending assailant when Twilight and Luna appeared next to Celestia, halting their advance.

"Destined Path... please get off my face and let me up," came Celestia's muffled voice.

Destined did as she asked, but the princess still did not get up from her awkward position.

"Are you stuck?" Destined asked with a little concern.

"Yes, my horn is stuck in the throne, and I don't want to blast it apart to get out," Celestia replied softly.

"I will help you get free if you make me Prince of Equestria," Destined said with a mischievous grin.

Luna and Twilight looked at each other and giggled.

"What are you ta-AHAHAHAHA!" Celestia started flailing about, her four legs kicking the air as Destined blew raspberries on her stomach.

"Make me Prince!" Destined demanded again between raspberries.

"Luna!" Celestia cried out to her sister. "Help me, LunaHAHAHAHAHAHA!" She kept laughing and gasping for air. Meanwhile Luna just watched with a smirk on her muzzle.

"Do it!" Destined grinned and blew raspberries again.

"OK! OK! You win! You're the Prince of Equestria!" Celestia gasped, her legs shaking as Destined stopped and looked at the scribe.

"I have a Royal Decree!" Destined said as he floated Celestia's crown onto his head. It was too big for him though, and it settled unevenly around his shoulders instead.

The scribe blinked and picked up his quill.

"I declare that the former Princess Celestia is to get every Friday off. No court; no royal duties! I have decreed it! I... I also decree that candy is the best! And lastly, I decree that Celestia is now a Princess of Equestria again!"

Luna levitated her sister at an angle to slowly slide her horn out of

the throne without further damaging it, and Destined levitated the crown back onto Celestia's head.

Celestia chuckled and looked at Destined. "Was that really necessary?"

Destined just grinned back at Celestia. "But it was fun, wasn't it?"

Celestia could not help but match Destined's grin as she stood up. "Well it *was* fun, but now I need to sleep before I have to hold court again tomorrow."

The scribe cleared his throat to gain their attention. "Actually, Your Highness, you don't. As per the new law that was decreed into effect by Prince Destined, you have tomorrow off. No court can be held."

Destined's grin was enormous, and Luna started laughing. "It looks like thou can come spend all day with us *and* attend the Friday dinner then, hmm?"

Celestia just blinked in surprise, and then asked with great chagrin, "Did I just get outmanoeuvred by an eight-year-old colt?"

Chapter 8: Spring Break

"Mmnhh..." Blue groaned slightly, and covered himself up tighter in the blankets. Still cold, he grabbed something heavy and pulled it over his midsection before his eyes opened and he looked down and saw a golden leather wing draped over him. He snickered a bit and turned around to face Cinder... who was still passed out with her mouth wide open and her tongue lolling out.

"My girlfriend, everybody," Blue snickered.

"**Ssnnoore!**" Cinder droned.

Blue slowly closed her muzzle, took a deep breath and blew into her snout as hard as he could. The dragon's eyes shot open, and she flailed around. Blue let her muzzle go as she coughed and huffed.

"Ngh... too early..." Cinder grabbed Blue tighter and rolled over, wrapping him up with her wings as she blew a small jet of intense fire into the air to heat up the room.

Blue sighed softly and nuzzled up against her as he drifted back to sleep.

Downstairs the rest of the family were eating breakfast.

"Where is Blue?" Twilight looked around as Free started to grin.

"By the taste of things – curled up with Cinder in his room," Free said with a laugh.

Twilight rolled her eyes. "I have half a mind to go up there..."

"Oh, just let them sleep. I'll wake them up if they aren't up by lunch time. It's not like they have any classes; it's Saturday after all," Path said with a smile.

"Sigh... fine, but he better not make it a habit!" Twilight huffed. "Anyway, I need to get going; there are a few meetings I need to handle. And Free, you need to talk to the Western Hive Queen. She is thinking about letting some of her drones transfer to the Equestrian campuses."

Free rolled his eyes. "If it's not one meeting, then it's another. I'll be gone till dinner."

Rose piped up, "And then we have the dinner with the other heads of the griffon Houses."

Both Free and Path groaned.

Rose narrowed her eyes. "Do I need to get Warfist to *encourage* you two?"

The two males jumped up. "No, ma'am!"

Twilight laughed as the two guys ran out.

"Sometimes they are too easy," Rose smirked and looked at Twilight. "Come on, let's get started."

The ladies cleaned up after themselves and left the meal hall.

Blue woke up yet again with a groan. "Come on, Cinder... get up. It's nearly noon." He squirmed a bit and nibbled on her neck.

Cinder yawned and stretched, her tail uncoiling from around Blue's legs as she licked her lips and looked at him. "Mmm... morning, Blue."

"It's nearly noon, and being so late to wake up isn't going to make it easier to convince Moms and Dads to let me go with you to the Dragonlands," Blue huffed as he rolled out of bed. Cinder soon followed him, heading down to the main hall just as lunch was being served. Already Blue was starting to feel tense; he did not know how to approach this. Soon the tension was noticed by Free.

"So... gonna tell us what's going on?" Free slowly turned to Blue with a grin which made him feel another apprehensive spike when Cinder became tense.

"Hey, Dads..." Blue said in his sing-song I-want-something kind of voice.

"Oh, here it comes," Path said with a grin. "What is he going to ask for this time?"

"Last time he wanted to go to the moon." "The time before that he wanted a chrome suit of armour," Free chuckled.

"Might as well just spit it out, Bluey." Cinder looked at him as she put her head on the table with a grin.

"I'm waiting until they get here," Blue stated.

"Who?" Twilight asked.

Blue just grinned as Techbird walked in, carrying what looked like a new pair of metal wings. Azon walked in behind her holding what looked like a mask and a pill. Blue pulled out a few papers as he cleared his throat. Twilight just blinked, looking at the three of them while Free whistled.

"Looks like our son has a plan," Free commented to a grinning Path.

"I am officially submitting Form 20L and four different Form

35A's," Blue said to a confused Twilight.

"Intent to leave the grounds for a measure of time greater than three days and shorter than two weeks, and Intent to test four prototype projects," Twilight rattled off for those around her who didn't know what the form numbers meant. "You were paying attention during your high school orientation?" she said in astonishment.

Free, Path, and Rose started laughing at her last statement as they all sat down.

"Okay, Blue, where are you going for spring break?" Twilight asked with a grin.

"I want to go with Cinder to meet her parents in the Dragon Lands." Twilight was about to say something before Blue cut her off. "*And... and* I'm going to test two innovations from Techbird and Azon. They're here to present their projects that have made it past the theoretical phase and now need a practical trial."

Azon made a motion to Techbird as she started speaking. "Okay! So I have two things I want Blue to test for me. The first one is the Albatoss-1E, a pair of magitek wings that are designed to overcome the limitations of the original magitek wings. While the original prototype was good for combat situations, it cannot last for more than about two hours. These use crystal capacitors to hold a large charge and release it slowly so there is less of a drain on the user. Performance goes down though, so I created them to be soaring wings. They're much larger and slower than the Rainbow Dash style wings I modelled the first types after."

"The second innovation is something that Proper Place noticed during the Crystal Siege. When Blue ran and broke the sound barrier, as he spoke on the crystal com at speed, his voice was pitched lower. After experimenting I have come up with this!" Techbird pulled out what looked like an ear piece. "This is an undercharged version of your trottie and has a range of only about fifty miles. The pitch changes subtly depending on how it's moving in relation to its companion crystal. With this we should not only be able to track the speed of Blue, but also his direction!" Techbird was almost jumping up and down with excitement.

Azon chuckled a bit as he soaked in the ambient emotion. "My innovations are not nearly as flashy, but just as important. The first one is an enzyme supplement. It will allow a pony to eat fatty meats without the resulting... unpleasantries. However it does not give him the eleven necessary vitamins and oils needed that are found only in plants." He then held up the mask. "This is kind of a combination effort between Techbird and I. This mask is so that those used to being on the ground can breathe the thin air without passing out. However, the higher the person goes, the faster they need to be going to make sure the mask draws enough air."

The two sat down as Twilight hmmed a bit.

"I honestly wasn't expecting to be outmanoeuvred like this. I have got let you go to the Dragon Lands even though I don't want to, because we need to get the devices tested. So some ground rules – You will use the trottie to call me every day at noon. No drinking! And you have to give a report of your time in the Dragon Lands to the first-years so they might consider going there as well," Twilight stated.

"So I can go?" Blue tensed up anxiously.

"Yes, you can go. Don't make me regret this decision." Twilight grinned.

"Hey, aren't you going to ask if we say yes?!" Free pouted.

"No, because once Blue came in, you were already on board with what he wanted. You two always are." Twilight smiled and gave Free a kiss on his forehead.

Blue looked at Cinder. "Let's get ready!" Blue dashed out of the hall and outside.

"Cinder... make sure he behaves... and stays safe," Twilight sighed as the dragoness went to follow Blue.

"Don't worry, I'll make him be good." Cinder smiled as she left.

Cinder smiled a bit as she watched Blue race around the room, picking up things and then setting them down. "Bluey, you're only going to be able to bring a backpack with you... so here... let me help." Cinder walked over and picked up his trottie crystal before digging under his bed.

Blue Streak looked over to her as he panicked. "H-hey, don't dig under my bed!"

Cinder looked over at Blue with a deadpan face. "Really, Blue.... Really?" She held up a 'questionable' magazine. "Why would you even have this? I'm right freaking here!"

Blue just chuckled. "Well for what it's worth, I haven't actually used the book in a long while. Why were you digging under there?"

Cinder chuckled and pulled a silver bottle from under his bed. "I was looking for this. Now, go to the mess hall and eat. I'll be down in a bit."

Blue laughed and walked out of his room.

It was early morning, just before dawn, when they all met up at the field. Blue was wearing those large wings and he extended them a few times.

Techbird and Twilight were going over their calculations. "Okay, Streak, these are soaring wings. They aren't acrobatic style. So what we need you to do is keep them closed. Then run along the ground to your top sub-sonic speed, then slam them open. The resulting lift will thrust you up into the upper atmosphere, where Cinder tells me there is a high speed air current."

"The Seers call it '*The Breath of Equus*'. It allows us to go vast distances in a short amount of time. It's faster than even than the Skyshark." Cinder walked over to them as she smiled. "Ready to go?"

Path and Free walked over to Blue and gave him a hug each. "I want you on your best behaviour – you are an ambassador of the House, the *first* ambassador. *Please* be good," Path begged.

Then Free came up and grinned. "Don't listen to Path; be yourself! That's what he did."

Blue laughed as he walked to the far end of the field and opened the wings a few times. "Okay, Cinder, get a head start. I'll catch up with you!"

The dragoness nodded as she took to the air. She was surprisingly fast as within a few minutes she was just a dot.

Azon ran up to Blue. "Sorry I'm late! Here are the devices!" He slipped the mask over Blue, and put a bag of pills in his backpack. "Oh... and when you are in a crowded area, wear these and tell me your findings." Blue raised an eyebrow as the griffon put a pair of spectacles in his pack as well.

Techbird grinned. "Ten seconds till launch!"

Blue crouched down as he felt the energy move into his hooves.

Techbird shouted, "Go!"

Blue shot off like a rocket, accelerating faster and faster crossing the field, and at the last possible moment the magitek wings shot open and the lift carried him up into the air. His body tensed up under the acceleration as he soon caught up with Cinder as they both went higher and higher, his respirator enabling him to still gain altitude.

"Get ready, Blue, we are about to enter the *Breath*." Cinder gave one final flap as she angled her wings strangely.

Blue saw them fill with wind and she shot off like a rocket. Blue mimicked her movement and soon he was accelerated as well, flying beside Cinder as they cruised. "How long will it take to get to your clan?"

"About thirteen hours. We'll arrive just before sundown." Cinder grinned as she watched Blue loop around her.

"It doesn't even seem like we're going that fast!" Blue stated as he looked down at the ground slowly moving by.

"We're going faster than you can normally. Ask a Seer about it when we get there, but speed and air don't work the same this high up," Cinder said.

Blue Streak nodded as he kept those wings open, silently watching as they moved to the east.

The sun was low in the sky as Cinder and Blue Streak slipped out of the *Breath*. They began dropping their altitude once the settlement, a large cluster of yurts lit up by a fire in the centre, came into view.

"Ah, right where they said they would be... come on let's go!"

From the centre of the yurts, fire flared slightly. Cinder grinned and took a deep breath, blowing out a jet of fire in response. "They're waiting for us – don't fall behind!" Cinder folded her wings and fell from the sky quickly speeding up as Blue followed her. Soon the both of them were skimming along the surface, bleeding speed until they both landed at the edge of the encampment. They folded up their wings as one of the larger dragons walked over to them.

The large dragon was a deep brown in colour which contrasted well with the red runes that were covering his body. "Shaikhan-Gal , ene ni kheterkhii urt baina!" *<Beautiful Fire, It has been too long!>*

Cinder moved up to the larger dragon and nuzzled him. "Bi aav ta aldsan." *<I missed you too, Father.>*

Blue only knew a few words of Draconic. Once their pleasantries were exchanged he walked up to the dragon with a smile, and tried his best to speak. His father had always told him that it was a compliment to try to speak to another species with their own language. "Takhiany khökh öngötei ." *<The chicken is blue.>* He just stood and awaited his response with a smile.

Cinder and her father lasted all of two seconds before they burst into laughter.

Eventually the large male looked down at them both. "Come, you both must be tired from the trip. We set up a yurt for the two of you. The hunters have just come back with their haul. You can eat tonight, but tomorrow you will have to hunt with the others to earn your share."

Blue did not know how he should feel about the prospect of hunting, but then again he could just fish. Meat is meat right? They dumped their packs in their yurt, but Blue was taken off guard when Cinder curled around him in the middle of the shelter.

"You have a week, Blue. You need to impress them. I know you will, like you did me." Cinder licked his cheek before letting him go.

Blue chuckled a bit before he pulled out his trottie, activating it. After a few beeps he heard a very tired Free pick up.

"Hey Blue... did you just make it in?"

"Yeah, I don't think I have ever gone so fast so long!"

"Yeah, once Tech and Twilight got a hold of the data before you went over the horizon they went into their manic mode. Anyway, I'll let everyone know you're okay."

Blue blinked as the trottie disconnected. He looked over to Cinder who was walking around in circles. It looked like she was stomping out a depression in the ground, and by the looks of it, it was for two. He grinned a bit. "Think I should go out and do ambassador things? I mean, my dad really wanted me to do ambassador stuff, even though I have no idea what that is." He sighed a bit.

"Sure, everyone here already knows who you are and why you are here. Just try not to say things in draconic that you don't understand. I don't know if they could handle the fact that the chicken is blue." Cinder chuckled as Blue rolled his eyes and walked outside.

Blue walked over to the large fire-pit in the centre where several of the larger dragons were dancing around the roaring fire. A few of the smaller dragons were vibrating their wings, the thin air of the highlands and the strength of their wings creating a strange resonance he had never heard before. He began to move and weave with the subtle ebbs and flows of the beat. A few dragons turned to watch him and grin.

Blue seemed to be on auto pilot, the soothing rhythmic beats, the older dragons' deep growling voices, or the flickering of the fire, but soon he was dancing in the circle with the other dragons.

Cinder came up with her father and just watched Blue for a moment before she spoke. "Interesting how he picks up our dancing so easily."

"Not so easily. He's tranced by the fire, and his body is mimicking the motions of the air around him. I have known this to happen to zebras when they come for trade and talks, but for it to happen to a pony – this is interesting indeed." He watched as some of the dragons blew fire straight up into the air and was curious as to what Blue would do.

His eyes were glazed over. But he had enough of his faculties to realize in a few steps he would have to blow fire. He reached into one of his hip packs and pulled out a flint snap. He took a quick swig of his silver flask as his eyes widened. When it was his turn, the majority of the dragons not paying attention to him turned to see if he would just go through the motions or not.

His hoof sparked slightly as he blew out triple proof whiskey. He was not expecting his body to act like a conduit for the overwhelming earth magic. With no earth ponies constantly tapping into it, he was connecting to a *much* stronger source, so when the whiskey ignited with the aid of the flint snap, the magic found a way to escape to the air. The result was a massive upward plume of fire that dwarfed even the bonfire. It kept going for about five seconds before Blue fell onto his rump, closing his mouth and shutting the bridge for the magic to flow. He blinked a few times as the music stopped. One of the younger dragons was going to say something before he sat down and kneeled. One of the older dragons slowly stood and walked over to the pony.

"Eat. Then come to the Seer's tent," her dual-layered voice communicated in both Draconic and Equish.

Cinder looked over to her dad. "Is that good or bad?"

"We will find out, won't we?" her father said with a smirk.

Blue had an uneasy dinner. Thanks to Azon, he was able to stomach their mostly meat diet. He ended up giving his portion of calcite to Cinder though. It was almost midnight by the time he arrived at the Seer's hut. He didn't really know how to knock, but soon the hut opened up and the Seer called him in.

Blue looked around as he entered the hut; it was slightly bigger than the others. It had a hole in the roof in the centre of the hut, a small fire was burning in a pit underneath it, and the ground around it was lined with pelts. A large dragon was sitting there.

"The interesting pony comes in with the daughter. The Beautiful Fire knows you, but you do not know yourself." The Seer grinned slowly and motioned for him to sit down, Blue sat down and looked at her and then to the fire. The dragoness breathed out a dull violet smoke that began filling the hut. It was very thin and barely perceptible in the campfire light.

"Ponies... they rely on manipulating their environment to live – the cities to quell the land – the pegasi to tame the skies. The *Breath* no longer travels over that country; it moves to the north and sometimes the south." She looked to him as Blue nodded slowly, his eyes growing lidded as he breathed in the smoke.

"The griffons are somewhat better; they do not destroy their land as much, but still pillage it for iron and coal." She breathed out again, and the smoke got thicker.

Blue was having a hard time focusing on the dragoness as he started to swoon.

"As a Seer, I can perceive things that most living beings can't even comprehend – the threads of fate... they weave around you so densely... more so than anyone I've seen so far." Again she breathed out another breath of smoke.

"Breathe, young Blue Streak. Breathe and look within," the

dragoness hissed out slowly.

Blue was trying his best to keep his focus on the dragoness as his eyes glazed over and he fell onto his side onto the soft pelts. In his vision, he saw the dragoness start to fade away, her glowing eyes the last thing to leave his sight as the fire sparked and flared violently before it turned a bright blue. Soon a fire pony came out of the flames, its legs a blinding white and his irises a bright blue.

Blue's eyes went wide as he saw the imposing figure made out of pale blue/white fire.

"Do. Not. Fail!" its voice boomed out.

"W-who are you...?" Blue squeaked out.

"Do. Not. Yield!" The white fire pony bellowed.

"Yield to what...?" Blue whispered.

"The. Darkness. Do. Not. Give. In!" it bellowed louder.

"Give in to what?" Blue whimpered.

"What could have been," it growled before it moved in closer to Blue, so close his nose was getting hot.

Blue's consciousness faded as the being whispered one last thing in his ear before everything went black.

"Live... Win... Die..."

Blue woke up with a start. He looked around at his environment, trying to figure out where he was. His panicked motions were soon soothed as he felt a familiar wing wrapped around him, and he looked back to see Cinder looking down at him with a smile.

"Looks like I woke up first this time." Cinder nuzzled his neck.

"Mmnhh... what happened? There was a being... made of blue fi–" Blue was silenced as she wrapped her talons around his muzzle.

"What you saw was for your eyes only; you don't need to share what you have seen. But know that you are the first pony to see it. You must have impressed her with your fire display." Cinder slowly removed her claw as Blue huffed.

"She also left you this." Cinder motioned to what looked like a sealed letter. "I didn't open it, and I have no idea what it says. Whatever it is, it's not in Draconic, Griffish, or Equish," she said as she pointed out the writing on the envelope.

Blue slowly got up to his feet. He shakily stretched out before he yawned. "So what's on the agenda for today?" he asked with a grin as he looked at her.

Cinder returned the smile. "Well, today you are going with the males to hunt. This will be your chance to impress father, while most of the females are going to head to the calcite cliffs to gather some for dinner. I'll talk you up to Mom so when we have the feast tonight, she will be more apt to like you."

"Something I was wondering – why are all of the females larger than the males? It seems to be a common trait here." Blue looked over to Cinder and raised an eyebrow.

"Ah, well I guess ponies and griffons would call it reverse sexual dimorphism. The females here are larger because they need to fly further, carry more, bear eggs, and fight for territory if the need arises. Males on the other hand tend to just hunt, and gather." Cinder grinned.

"I... I kind of thought it would be the other way around. Huh, glad you told me that, or it might have led to some confusion down the road." Blue rubbed the back of his head ruefully.

"It's okay – my father is going with you, and you know he speaks Griffish, so you'll be able to speak with him. Just... are you okay with the fact that you are going to hunt? I mean I heard what happened to your dad when he went on his first hunt." Cinder wilted slightly.

"That was different; those monsters made him hunt a sapient race. As long as what we are hunting has no trace of true intelligence, I'm okay with hunting for food purposes." Blue puffed out his chest.

"I... I was not expecting you to be so okay with it... but I am certain that father won't make you actually do the killing blow. Such a thing could really do some psychological damage to a pony. We usually hunt herds of feral goats – they tend to graze as they move from mountain range to mountain range." Cinder wrapped her wings around Blue, nuzzling him.

"I'll do it, it'll be fine. Worst case scenario I freak out and I'll have to impress them some other way." Blue pulled out a pair of spectacles from his backpack and put them on.

"What are those?" Cinder asked as she looked over the glasses.

"It's just an experiment that the doc wanted me to test, unofficially of course." He stepped outside and looked around; all of the dragons had a halo around them. The females had a much larger aura than the males, but then Blue was surprised to see that the colours were generally all different shades and hues of blue or green. What he did not expect however is that that two of the dragons – one a smaller male, the other a fairly large female, had no auras around them at all. He accidentally locked eyes with the male and the dragon's eyes widened, blinked once, and then quickly looked away.

Blue put the glasses away as Cinder's father came up to him.

"So, are you ready to earn your keep tonight?" He couldn't help but grin.

"I will do that and so much more." Blue flexed the magitek wings. "Are we ready to go?"

Cinder's father looked over to the males and let out a loud booming roar, calling them to the hunt. The rest of them quickly got into line and their wings opened up. One by one, they all took to the skies. Blue had to get a running start, so he was the last to take off after getting up to take-off speed, but soon he joined the rest of the dozen males.

Back at the encampment, Cinder looked up to her mother. The young dragoness looked happy, but the Matriarch not so much.

"You could have any male you wanted, literally. I could have bent any one of them to my will and then they would be yours, but instead you pick a pony of all things. A griffon I could see, I would accept a zebra or a thestral, but an Earth Pony? What is it that you see that I do not?" The Matriarch growled slowly. "Whatever it is, the Seer has already picked up on it." She tapped her rather imposing claws on the ground in irritation. "I do not like being kept in the dark, Shaikhan-Gal."

Cinder just smiled as the males disappeared over the horizon. "Don't worry, Mom – before we leave, you will see what I do."

The sun was still low on the horizon as the pack flew in a large V-formation. Blue flew up next to the Hunt-Master as they came upon the herd. "And you are sure those are non-sapient?"

The large male dragon grinned. "You have Cinder's heart, which means if one of us was to trick you, we would face the Matriarch's wrath, which is something none of us want."

Blue circled around the small herd while the others discussed how to coordinate their strike. Looking over to Cinder's father, he asked, "How many of the herd were you wanting to take?"

The dragon just laughed. "We are lucky to get two or three. It's why we need to hunt so often."

Blue just looked at them confused. "You're dragons... can't you just swoop down and breathe fire all over everything?"

"Breathing fire tends to take a lot of out of us. Also, they are small while we are large, and they can outmanoeuvre us surprisingly easily."

Blue just looked at the herd – this one wasn't a very large, maybe about a dozen. He then had an idea, or rather a spark of inspiration. He thought back to the siege on the Crystal City castle and the role he played. He approached the Hunt-Master. "I have an idea. Can you stay up here while I fly down there? If this works, I bet we could take them all at once."

The Hunt-Master was sceptical, but nodded in permission, curious to see what the earth pony was going to try.

"Watch for my signal!" Blue started to glide away to the east, downwind of the herd.

One of the smaller males moved up to talk to Cinder's father.

"What is the pony doing?"

"I'm not sure, but let's see what he can do. Worst case scenario: we all get to laugh as the pony fails and gets head-butted by a goat. Best case scenario: we won't have to hunt for a few days."

The dragon pack soared on the thermals too high for the goats to notice while they waited.

Blue landed on the ground about six miles away, tightly folded his wings, and activated his special horse shoes. His eyes went wide as he felt the sudden surge of power. He was unaware that without earth ponies drawing constantly from the land, there was an abundance of earth mana that he'd never felt before!

High up in the sky, the Hunt-Master and the other males saw three flashes of light coming from the horizon. "That must be his signal. Let's begin a slow descent so we can see what he's about to do."

The Hunt-Master made a motion, and the dragons began to descend.

"LOOK AT THE HORIZON!" one of the younger hunters yelled out.

They stopped and watched as a huge plume of dust moving in a straight line headed toward the small herd. It accelerated, and just as it passed through the herd, a loud boom echoed across the plains, the tall grass flattening around the herd as the streak kept going.

The Hunt-Master swooped down as did the rest of the dragons.

Cinder and her mother were talking with the Seer when the ground rumbled and a low-pitched rolling boom echoed through the encampment.

"What... what was that?" A few of the males tending to the eggs started to worry as they fussed and curled around them, while two of the larger females stood tall and looked around warily.

"That's my guy," Cinder said proudly.

"The pony made that sound?" Her mother just blinked disbelievingly.

When the Hunt-Master landed, he saw that the majority of the goats had been knocked unconscious, although not killed.

Blue returned and skidded to a halt in front of them with a broad grin on his face. "Not bad for a pony, hmmm?"

Cinder's father rolled his eyes a bit and patted Blue on the head with one of his talons. "You're a good kid. I wasn't expecting you to be so... *fast*."

A few of the other males landed and started chanting at Blue. "Shuurkhai Odoi! Shuurkhai Odoi!"

Blue looked at the Hunt-Master who just grinned. "Looks like you just earned your name, Shuurkhai Odoi."

"What does that even mean?" Blue asked.

"It means Swift Pony. A name well-earned, all things considered." He chuckled a bit. "But it is not every day that somebody executes a hunt as well as this. Pick the biggest one – it is yours."

Blue walked over to the largest one, probably the male that was guiding the herd. "Can we tie this one up? I want to give it to Cinder as a gift."

The large male looked amazed before he looked to the rest of the dragons and said something which caused them to cheer. One of them roped up the largest goat as the rest then picked out their own.

"You might want to go over to that stream for a few minutes while we... prepare the goats to be brought back. We will leave yours alive for Cinder."

Blue nodded and trotted off in the direction of the water. He went quite a ways out before he found some particularly green grass next to the water, with some tasty daisies nearby. *'Well, the doc did say that I still had to eat greens to get some vitamins,'* he thought as he leaned down and started to graze, slowly moving from one patch to another.

The Hunt-Master and the others were hard at work field-dressing the goats, while one of them was readying Blue's for carrying back alive. "Does he know what it means when he gives a female the largest prey in a hunt?"

The Hunt-Master chuckled. "He isn't stupid. He might not know the details, but he knows his intent. I bet he plans on making a huge fuss about it in front of Cinder's moth–"

He was cut off when he heard a loud whinny. He didn't know what it meant, but he could hear the fear and he knew that it was in the direction that Blue had gone.

"Oh no, no, no, **no!**" The Hunt-Master took off and flew low to the ground until he saw the clearing next to the river. His eyes went wide. "Ohhh... Cinder is going to kill me." He inhaled deeply and let out a massive plume of fire into the sky. In a few moments two other dragons were with him and they flew down to the pony.

In front of them was a scene of carnage. Blue was lying down on his belly, breathing hard, one of his eyes closed. His flank was badly ripped, and red was staining his blue coat. The *beast*, also known as a smilodon, was lying motionless on his back. The Hunt-Master examined the beast. He put a talon to its chest only to feel a massive hoof indentation and broken ribs – the pony had put enough force and speed behind his buck to push the beast's sternum into his heart.

"By the birth mother... he took out a smilodon!"

The Hunt-Master called the rest of the hunting party over and they picked up the passed-out Blue Streak, his kill plus the rest of the goats, and headed back to the encampment.

"*You did **what**?!*" Everyone stopped when the Matriarch began openly yelling at her husband, the Hunt-Master. "**How could you just let him go out on his own?! There are things out there that don't exist even in their nightmares!**" The Matriarch grabbed the Hunt-Master and dragged him into the head yurt. Cinder ran past the feuding pair to see an unconscious Blue Streak being taken into the Seer's hut, along with the smilodon. She was about to walk in when she was stopped by a smaller female, the Seer's apprentice.

"I am sorry, but if you want her to save Blue Streak, you have to let her work. I will come to your yurt when he can be seen." The dragon tried to smile.

Cinder huffed and stomped off. She was clearly worried about Blue Streak, but she was also worried about what would happen when the leader of a multinational organization and his two alicorn family members found out that their son was injured.

It was a pleasant night at House Path. 'Aunt' Luna was over again and was playing with Destined. She would lightly toss a brightly coloured ball with her magic, and he would capture it in his own magic and throw it back as hard as he could. He thought it was fun, however Twilight and Luna knew what she was doing. Helping a pony practice their magic at an early age was proven to increase their strength later on in life.

Lucida was with Twilight, quietly reading a book, while Free was helping Pif practice her shape-shifting ability. Slick was scurrying around the pair, and every few moments he would flip a card up from a deck and show it to the both of them. The picture could be of any species that a changeling could shift into. Free was not okay with how easily his daughter was beating him.

"Eee!" Pif clapped as Slick moved over to a chalkboard, picked up a stick of chalk, and scrawled another line under Pif's name. The score was now Pif: 9 to Free: 1.

The trottie rang and Path got up to answer it, connecting it to a crystal headset – one of Twilight's latest innovations. Everyone stopped and looked at Path as he spoke.

"Huh…. Okay…. Okay…. Yeah… Hmmm makes sense… I see… Okay… No, no, it's okay… Yes… Okay… Tonight?... Got it… Bye, Cinder!" Path hung up the trottie and looked at Free. "Remember the time when you thought about the thing in case of the other thing with the thing?" Path hit his left hoof on the ground once… twice… then hit his right hoof once.

Twilight and Luna just looked at Path, confused by the utter nonsense he had just said. However, Free walked over to Twilight and shifted into his alicorn form. He then sat on Twilight so his belly was on her back.

"Free! Get off!" Twilight started to light up her horn, but her magic shorted out when he gave her horn a long lick. Twilight crumpled back down onto the ground with a groan. "Really – is this really necessary?" Twilight grumbled.

Path replied, "Once I tell you about my conversation, it will be. I know Luna is a lot more mature, so she's less likely to just randomly run off in a concerned rage."

Now Path had everyone's attention.

"So that was Cinder. Blue was actually doing okay for his second day there. They gave him a dragon name after the hunt pack saw him single-handedly incapacitate a herd of feral goats. They ended up getting enough food to last for about four days." Path stated.

Twilight frowned. "While I would imagine that you would think I would be mad at him for hunting, he was raised in a Griffonian environment where hunting is the norm, so as long as they were non-sapient, I'm okay with that." She let out a frustrated groan as her gradually-charging horn was again discharged when Free gave it another lick.

"Well that's not the bad part," Path continued. "The bad news is that when Blue separated from the hunting group to graze while they prepared the goats for transport back home, he was ambushed by a smilodon."

"*WHAT?!*" Twilight screeched as her horn lit up violently in preparation for a teleport spell, only to be dispelled by another lick to her horn. "Nngghh…" Twilight crumpled again.

"I expect there is more to the story, or else thou wouldst not be telling us this so calmly?" Luna said with an edge in her voice.

"You are correct. Blue was rushed back to their encampment and is currently being looked after by the Seer of the clan. She told Cinder that he will be fine in a few days, and that he's managed to impress the Matriarch. A smilodon is very hard for a dragon to take down, and even more so by an unarmed earth pony. Still though, if it's not too much trouble, Luna, could you take a look at him when you're dream-walking tonight?"

Luna nodded in agreement. "I had intended to do so anyway."

Path smiled as he sat back down. "Still, I restate again: Blue will be fine. Can I have Free get off of you without worrying about you trying to teleport away, Twilight?"

Twilight fumed but then huffed. "Fine…"

Free got up and Twilight narrowed her eyes at him. "*You* are cut off – two weeks!"

The changeling queen let out a piteous whine but Twilight turned away in a huff. Free grinned and winked at the others.

Path, Luna and Roseclaw chuckled, knowing full well that Twilight wasn't serious and would quickly relent. Little Pif laughed too, not really knowing what it all meant, but enjoying the taste of good humour.

Back at the Dragon Lands, the blue earth pony was resting in the large yurt. The Seer had been able to stop the bleeding and stabilize him. The Seer placed him on the floor in the centre of the room, still unconscious. She drew runes all along the edge of the yurt, as well as on Blue himself, and they lightly glowed before fading into the ground. She kept the yurt warm as she slowly petted the top of his head as he shivered. All of those runes were working to funnel the abundant mana in the ground towards the pony. She looked over at his flank where three large gashes were slashed through his left cutie mark. However, his body was mending the wound faster than she had expected.

"It is not your time yet. You have a greater purpose to fulfil… Shuurkhai Odoi!" she hissed.

Luna materialized into what looked like a rolling plain sprawling for as far as the eye could see. Some long grass here and there, some short grass, and every now and then there was a tree or two. It was under one of those trees that she saw Blue Streak sitting. She smiled and cantered toward him, only to slow down in surprise as she came closer.

"Blue Streak – what has happened to thee?" Luna gasped as she looked at her nephew.

The earth pony had strikingly different features: two large horns emerged behind his ears, his eyes were slit much like Cinder's were, and he had a pair of blue scaled wings coming out of his back.

"Oh... these.... I'm not exactly sure, to be honest with you. I've just been sitting here for I don't know how long, just thinking about things. Have a seat with me, Auntie?" Blue opened up a wing as Luna sat down next to him. He draped his wing around her.

Some runes flickered across his body as Luna's eyes widened. "Ah, so that's what transpires. They are using their runic magic to heal thee, and it's causing these changes. I hope they're temporary; I don't need thy mother reacting how she usually does." Luna giggled softly before turning to look up at him... Wait! *Up* at him? "Did you get taller?"

Blue looked at himself before smirking slightly. "I guess I did. Huh! Interesting!"

Luna looked back up at him. "All things considered, art thou doing okay? Thou dost not seem like thou art all there."

Blue looked up at the vibrant sunset with an odd smile. "Yeah, something seems off. Something is missing. I don't feel rested when I dream like I normally do...."

Blue's head lifted from the floor of the yurt, and he looked around with a low growl. The Seer was nowhere to be seen. With a longer growl, he slowly dragged himself out of the yurt and walked toward the sound of the greatest commotion.

The males were preparing the meal, and Cinder happened to be watching them idly, listening to their chatter. Then she noticed Blue walk up to them.

"Blue, you're okay!" She ran up to him and then skidded to a halt as she saw him lean down and start to chew on some raw meat. A few of the males clearly looked confused. Cinder was close enough to not only see his muzzle soaked in goat blood, but also his slit eyes. "Blue? **Blue?!**" She turned and screeched. "Where is the Seer?!"

Blue sighed as he watched the twilight colours form in the sky. On one side he could see the moon starting to rise, and on the other he could see the sun halfway through setting.

"I know I'm not your favourite, but could you stay a while and talk with me, Auntie?" he asked her with a weak smile.

"Oh, Blue Streak, thou dost know I love *all* of the herd. Of course I'm here to listen." Luna smiled reassuringly and nuzzled him. "Come on – tell me what's wrong."

He sighed a bit and let out a soft growl, smoke venting from his nose slightly as he took a few deep breaths and started talking. "What am I in the House, Luna? I'm not one of the founding members like Moms and Dads." He laid down on his belly as he spoke. "I'm not being groomed for anything special. I mean, look at Lucida – she's already learning languages left and right… understanding international policy… she's *four*! How does a four-year-old even do that?"

Blue opened his wings as if waving his arms in emphasis, letting Luna free. She stood up and walked in front of him, lying down so that they were eye to eye.

Blue continued to speak, although it was descending into rambling. "And you have Free, Dianthia and Clue training and grooming Pif to be a queen – a freaking queen! She's already learning faster than me, and she's not even an eighth my age! I can't connect to the hive network like she can; how can I compete with that?" He started whimpering as he laid his head on the soft grass. "How can I be a good son when I feel like they barely care if I exist?"

Everyone stared at Blue Streak, seemingly in shock as he growled at them.

The Matriarch whispered to the Seer, "Is this a side-effect of using the mana of the world to heal him?" The large dragon crooked an eyebrow and grinned.

The Seer whispered back, "I believe that most of him is still asleep, repairing itself, but his instincts, or rather the draconian tinged version of his instincts, is awake, which is why he's running around like that." The Seer coughed a bit.

"And why he has declared my daughter as his?"

"Yes, that too."

Cinder was staring dumbfounded as Blue stood in front of her, his chest puffing out at a few of the males that were starting to get close to her. Blue only said one word. "*Mine!*"

"Seer – how long is this going to last?" Cinder looked up at her somewhat worried.

"Well, I don't imagine it would last longer th–"

She was interrupted by one of the younger males, about a year younger than Cinder, who stood up and said, "And what if somebody else wants to take he–"

The teenage dragon didn't even get to finish his sentence before Blue Streak closed the distance between himself and the aggressor, and with a sickening crack, head-butted the upstart dragon with a staggering amount of force. The dragon crumpled to the ground as Blue walked back to Cinder and then growled at the others. "***Mine!***"

The Matriarch leaned over to whisper to the Seer, "I like him – he has... pep!"

The Seer just blinked before turning to the Matriarch. "Be that as it may, I think I am going to restrain him back at the yurt until his mind is whole again." She looked back to the scene. "Where did Blue and Cinder go?"

Luna sighed and looked at Blue earnestly. "I think thou art putting too much pressure on thyself. Thou dost want to serve the house that thou dost love, but thou art only considering the roles that others have. Of course Pif is going to be a queen. She was literally born for that purpose. Lucida is going to be the head of the house when Path retires, but that wasn't always the case. They figured that thee with thy love of speed and fast-paced lifestyle, would absolutely hate going to meetings for hours at a time with the same one person droning on... and on... and on ... about the same inane topic, driving it into the ground." Luna's eyes glazed over as she went on and on, proving just how bored she was getting just talking about it.

"So what's left for me? I don't want to be like that Blueblood guy. From what I've heard of him, he hasn't got any real role, and because of that, he's just become this whining pony that annoys Celestia for every little thing... wait! Am I whining now?!" Blue started to panic until Luna nuzzled him to calm him down.

"Thou art *nothing* like him; trust me on this. Thou went to war to save a kingdom thou barely even heard of. Thou dost look at every situation with a viewpoint that is the polar opposite to that one. My sister likes to call him a prince, but in reality he's just a noble riding on the coattails of an honourable pony that died years ago. Thou hast no idea how infuriating he can be." Luna narrowed her eyes for a moment and nearly hissed.

Cinder panted and groaned as she held onto one of the large support structures of her yurt, her eyes threatening to roll into the back of her head. The strain on the yurt made the normally stable structure creak and sway as if it was in a windstorm.

Blue growled loudly over her. "Mine...."

Cinder panted out. "Y-yes, I'm yours... nngghh... *y-yours!*"

Luna and Blue sighed a bit at the same time.

"Blue Streak, who says that thou must take a path that is given to thee? Why dost thou not find thine own way? Use the House's resources to do some good in the world! Dost thou know that there are lands that the House has no knowledge of yet? Lands that are so far away and so different it can boggle the mind? Maybe one of these days when thou dost visit me, I'll tell thee about them."

Blue was about to reply when a strange red rift started to form in mid-air, a few yards away.

"Oh, this *is* interesting," Luna said as they both stood up to stare at the widening rift. "It looks like thou art going to have a second visitor, Blue Streak."

Soon the Seer stepped through the rift and it closed behind her. The Dragoness flapped her wings a few times as her eyes adjusted, and she looked to the alicorn and Blue Streak, raising an eyebrow at his changes.

"Oh, this does explain a lot." The Seer grinned a bit as she sat down in front of them. "While you are here, Queen Nocturne, speaking with Blue's *Ego* and *Superego*, his *Id* has been running around outside unchecked in his waking body, causing all kinds of chaos for the clan."

Luna's eyes widened. "What is he doing?"

"Well, he ate a goat raw, head-butted an adolescent dragon that wanted to claim Cinder, made a point to claim Cinder as his own.... Now I think both of them are sleeping it off in the yurt. For what it's worth, the Matriarch really likes you now. The upstart that you head-butted had been really getting under her skin. However, instead of the Matriarch having to crack down on the drake herself, you did it for her." The Seer sighed a bit as she looked around the dreamscape. "I must say it has been a while since I have ventured into another's dream. It is nice that I was able to see you once again, Queen Nocturne, it has been far too long."

Blue looked at the Seer and then at Luna. He noticed that the dragoness was looking higher than Luna's eye level and further away. "Hmm... Luna – does she see you differently than I do?"

Luna just grinned. "Blue Streak, thou just asked a question that no being has asked in a very long time. Without going into details, yes, she sees me differently. Wouldst thou like to see me as she does?"

Blue nodded and her form began to shift and warp. Luna grew in size and shifted from an alicorn to a large queen dragon. Her size dwarfed both of them by a large margin. Her jet black scales shimmered in the twilight, and even though she did not have a mane anymore, her scales mimicked the star pattern. Her eyes were a bright white, much like the full moon.

Blue just blinked a few times. "All of a sudden, the name Queen Nocturne begins to make sense." He leaned against the scaled goddess. "Does every race see you as something different depending on their cultural beliefs?"

This time it was the Seer that spoke. "Do ponies not know that you are the embodiment of aspects? All cultures see you differently from all the others unless you exert your form upon them?"

Luna was about to say something but Blue cut her off. "I guess that makes sense. I mean, all other cultures have different cautionary legends. Ponies have Luna and Celestia. Griffons have the Golden Primary and the Pale Down. Dragons have Queen Nocturne and Diurnal. It would make more sense for it to be the same pair in different cultures than many pairs of the same thing."

Luna just grinned with her large jaws, showing off all of her teeth. "Blue, thou hast reached a level of understanding that not even Twilight or Path has yet to achieve. That is because that while they immersed themselves in the culture, their preconceptions of Celestia and I have formed a bias as they researched. Thou, on the other hoof, grew up without Equestrian influence, nor hast thou interacted with us in a way that would require us to force your conception of us upon thy psyche. So thou might be one of the few that can see our multiple projections."

Blue just sat there. "But what are you really?"

The dragoness just looked down at him, her expression turning slightly serious. "Dost thou *really* want to know?"

The Seer chuckled. "This is not for my eyes to behold. I now know that Blue Streak will be fine, so I will depart." The red rift opened up yet again, and the Seer left the pair alone.

Blue turned back to the dragoness as she started to change again, growing larger and brighter as his eyes went wide. He was only able to witness it for a split second before his entire dream universe collapsed from such an unrestrained display.

Energy.

Pure. Overwhelming. Endless.

Blue woke up with a groan. His entire body hurt, and he couldn't help but taste copper in his mouth. He licked his lips slightly and slowly opened up one eye to look up at the centre of the yurt and the stars that shone through.

"Mmph..." Blue huffed and looked around, not used to being sprawled out on his back. It took him a few moments to see Cinder lying next to him. Based on her positioning and the huge grin on her snout, he could only assume that they'd had quite the night.

Blue stood up slowly and walked out the door, carefully closing it behind him before he walked toward the ever-burning fire and sat down. He stared into it for a few moments before he looked at the trottie headset. This was not going to be a fun talk, but he figured he couldn't put it off forever. He was so distracted that he did not notice the Seer and the Matriarch approaching him until the last moment. The Seer's face had her usual knowing smile, but the Matriarch's face was unreadable.

"The Goat Destroyer awakes," the Matriarch said with a smirk.

Blue cringed a little. "Listen... I'm really sorry about what happened. I'll understand if you want me to leave. I am really sorry I caused such chaos." His ears drooped as he turned to face them, and he made his body slightly smaller.

The Matriarch laughed softly as she looked up to the sky. The stars were starting to fade as the sky brightened with the approaching dawn. "You know, when Cinder begged me to let you visit, I was halfway tempted to agree just so I could eat you. A pony suitor for my daughter? Such madness! However, Cinder, the Seer, and my mate figured it would be bad for the relationships that we sought to build." The Matriarch sighed.

Blue just blinked. "Well... I'm glad you decided not to eat me?" he responded uncertainly.

The Seer chuckled, then changed the topic. "I won't go into details, Blue Streak, but when you came to me injured from your battle, you were close to death. Your injuries were great and you weren't responding to normal treatment, so I had to open up your mana channels and take advantage of the oversaturated mana of our lands to heal you. As a side effect though, you might have picked up some of our ingrained instinctual behaviour as well as some of our physical characteristics, but I assure you it is temporary... I think."

The Matriarch just looked at the Seer with a raised eyebrow.

"What? It's not like I read a book about this; it was a dire situation and I had to improvise!"

Blue looked at the Seer somewhat confused.

She sighed and rolled her eyes. "I used earth magic to heal your body, but other stuff went in as well, so that's why your eyes are slit," she explained simplistically. "They should revert back to normal in a few days, by the way. Other things might take more time, like the urge to horde things, and the growling."

"What about breathing fire?" Blue asked. "Breathing fire was pretty cool, not going to lie."

The Seer rubbed the back of her head in puzzlement. "I don't really know how you did that. The best thing I can assume is that you acted as a conduit for the earth magic to shift phases, The 'fire' was nothing more than an arc reaction. Like a slow moving lightning maybe?" The Seer hummed thoughtfully, deciding to look into it further when she had the opportunity. "We honestly don't know if the... well, for lack of a better word... *taint* is permanent, or if it will bleed out in time. Just... until we know more, don't get too worked up, okay?"

While the Seer smiled at Blue, the Matriarch still looked neutral at best. "So... were you serious about my daughter, or was that just your inner beast?" she asked with a snarl.

That made Blue think over his answer carefully as opposed to saying the first thing that came to his head. "You know... I think I am." Blue's body language visibly brightened as he smiled up at the dragon. "That is, if it's okay with you, ma'am?" He gave her his best confident smile.

The Matriarch rolled her eyes. "It takes more than breathing fire and grabbing a goat to impress me, but you are on your way." She snickered and stood up, motioning for the Seer to follow her. "We need to talk more about your new condition. Take some time, enjoy the morning fire and contact your parents." They turned around and walked back to the Seer's hut.

Everyone was in the main hall eating dinner when the crystal comm rang. Path looked at the comm, then to Free, and then to Twilight.

"No, no, not again!" Twilight squealed and tried to cast a levitation spell on Free, but before she was able to cast it, she was beaned by a pillow. "**Who keeps a pillow in the dining room?!**" she squealed again as she felt Free move on top of her and lick her horn. "Why do you keep doing this?!" she whined helplessly.

Roseclaw and Luna were holding themselves laughing. The frustrated look on Twilight's face and the look of conquest on Free's was perfect.

"I like your initiative, Free, but this time you won't need to do that," Path said.

"What initiative? Do what?" Free said with an innocent tilt to his head as Luna and Rose fell over laughing, trying to catch their breaths.

Path pressed a button on the comm to put it into loudspeaker mode, and the entire room could hear Blue Streak on the other end.

"Hey, Moms and Dads!" Blue spoke.

At that point, Twilight and Roseclaw ran up to the comm and started yelling at him.

"How could you do something so dangerous!" Twilight screamed!

"When you get back, your hide is going to get a tanning!" Roseclaw squawked.

Path spoke up. "So before you punish and beat him, maybe you should ask if he's okay?" Path rolled his eyes and Free grinned in agreement.

Twilight and Roseclaw sighed. "Tell us what happened please, Blue," Twilight ordered firmly.

Blue Streak chuckled – it wasn't very often that the dads shut down the moms like that. "Well, it's not like I went asking for it. After I hunted, successfully I might add, I decided to go graze near the river since I remembered the doc saying that I still need to eat plants because of the vitamins or something. So while I was eating, there came a great stabbing pain in my flank along with a deep growl. It hurt so bad, but I managed to buck it off. Then it came back around. I stood on my one good leg, and when it came in range, I bucked as hard as I could. Then things went dizzy and I woke up a few hours ago."

Free blinked in awe. "Dude – our son kicks ass!"

Roseclaw and Twilight screeched at the griffon in unison, **"Don't encourage him!"**

Roseclaw went on to say in a more moderate tone, "But you're going to be okay right? Do you want us to come and get you? I bet the crew of the Skyshark would love to go visit a new land."

Blue replied, "No, no, I'm okay, and I think the Matriarch is starting to like me now! Apparently I am very dragon-like. I know you can't see me right now, but I'm puffing my chest out at nothing."

Twilight was still very wary. "Okay then, but call me if there are any other problems."

"Okay. Oh! Before I forget, later on tonight, the Seer – she's the dragon equivalent of a shaman, I guess – and the Matriarch want to speak to you! So the next time the comm chimes, it probably won't be me. Anyway, if there's nothing else, I gotta go, okay?"

All of his parents replied all at once. "Be careful!" "Call us soon!"

The crystal comm stopped glowing, indicating the closing of the connection.

Free looked at Path. "You know that Blue is pretty much following in our adventurous footsteps?"

"Yes, and you have no idea how happy that makes me." Path

picked up a radish and took a bite out of it, oblivious to the glare of his mate.

Blue walked into the Seer's hut later that day after being summoned. The Matriarch was there as well, and they both turned to him.

"So, we think we know why you had draconic traits when I was in your dream, as well as why you had draconic eyes when you were suffering the side-effects of the healing process," the Seer said as she moved to one spot in the large yurt, and indicated for Blue Streak to move to a different spot.

"You do? Lu– I mean Queen Nocturne was thinking it had to do with the energy you were using to heal me," Blue said as he sat down on the spot.

"We believe her to be correct. However, there is one way to know for certain. Tell me, how are you feeling right now?" the Matriarch asked.

"I'm feeling pretty good, actually." Blue smiled as he looked at the two dragons.

"Please take your horseshoes off and put your hooves directly on the ground," the Seer instructed as she started to draw some runes on the ground.

"Okay, so what's the test?" Blue asked as the Seer drew a few sets of runes leading from the Matriarch to Blue Streak.

"I'm going to focus some of my mana into the runes, and see how your body reacts," the Matriarch replied. "The Seer believes that this will confirm or refute her theory."

The Seer activated the runes as the Matriarch put one heavy talon into one of the circles. The effect was almost immediate. Blue stood up straighter and his eyes gradually shifted shape, his pupils turning into slits as he let out a low growl.

"Oh... oh, this is interesting." The Seer watched and made mental notes, as the Matriarch sent another pulse into the rune sets between herself and Blue Streak.

The pony snarled and smoke came out of his nostrils as he went into a crouch. Moving into a stalking position, he advanced on the Matriarch.

She raised an eyebrow. "You're kidding, right?"

The earth pony growled and began to charge at her, only to stop dead in his tracks as she opened up her wings, wrapping them along the perimeter of the yurt as she let out a threatening roar.

Blue's eyes widened as he stopped only about a foot from her and let out a whimper, crouching down and making himself look small.

The Matriarch grinned and put one of her large fore-talons on his back to keep him crouched down. "Even when you're overrun with energy that controls you, your body still follows the nature of the mana you have absorbed." The Matriarch looked at the Seer who nodded and reversed the flow.

The Seer was still quite amazed. "A Mana Synthesist... I have heard of some Zebrican mystics able to do such a thing, but an earth pony, and one so young? Blue, you keep surprising me every day you are here, although it does explain how you are able to convert that mana to speed." The Seer smiled as Blue Streak groaned weakly as the dragon-tinged energy was drawn out of him and his eyes reverted to normal.

"Ngh.... hungry..." Blue groaned.

"Good. I think it's almost time to eat anyway." The Matriarch moved her talon off of Blue. "Put your shoes back on and go wake up Cinder. The Seer and I will be out shortly."

Blue Streak left quickly as the Matriarch looked back at the Seer with a grin.

The Seer just watched the pony leave the yurt, her eyes flickering a few times before she sat down with a sigh. "Incendia... the pony does not even realize what it means. Can nobody in their land see the beginning and the end?"

The Matriarch sighed. "Not many can embrace all instances without succumbing to madness. If they did, then everyone would be a Seer and your hut would be crowded."

The Seer couldn't help but chuckle as she shook her head.

It took Blue a while to wake Cinder. She was most likely the heaviest sleeper he had ever met, even worse than Papa Path. "Oh, for the love of... COME ON!!!" He scuffed his feet along the rug and felt the static charge building up. Then he touched her nose. The resulting snap of electricity made her wake with a jerk, and she flailed around a bit.

"Okay, okay! I'm up! Nnggh... it's too early," Cinder groaned, and then began to lay back down before Blue pushed her to get her on her feet.

"No, no, no! It's mealtime and we are going. I hunted a ram, and you're going to eat it! I didn't work that hard to grab the biggest one just so you can sleep through my success!"

Blue kept fighting to get her to wake, but when he mentioned the size of the ram, her eyes sprung open and she looked at him eagerly. "Really? You kept the biggest one for me?" Her eyes started to water and Blue became uneasy.

"Yes?" Blue said more like a question than a statement.

"Come on – let's go then!" Cinder ran out of the yurt as Blue followed after her, puzzled as to her abrupt turnaround.

Later that evening, the Matriarch and the Seer borrowed the comm from Blue Streak and took it into the Seer's hut. Blue was a little worried about it in spite of knowing that he would get it back safely.

"Are you ready to break the news to them?" The Seer sighed as she tapped the crystal as she had been instructed. It glowed to indicate that it was establishing a connection to the other side. After a rather annoying but brief hum, the dragons could hear a voice as clear as day coming from the other end.

"*Hello. Is this the Seer and the Matriarch like Blue Streak said would call around this time?*" a rather perky female voice asked.

"You are speaking to the Twelfth Matriarch, Incendia, leader of the Western Clan, Fourth pledged to the Greater Matriarch Council." Incendia rumbled before glancing at the Seer.

"Ah, yes. I would be the Thirteenth Greater Seer, advisor to Incendia... and general knower of things!" The Seer could not help but chuckle slightly. Despite the gravity of her position, she had always had a wicked sense of humour.

The voice resumed. "*I am Princess Twilight Sparkle of Equestria, Lady of the House of Path, and with me is Lord Long Path, the one who created the school that Cinder attends, and his mate Lady Roseclaw. Also my mate, Free Agent and–*"

Twilight was abruptly cut off as a deep rumbling voice came across the comm. "*Queen Nocturne!*"

"Q-Queen Nocturne!" the Seer stammered. "Many apologies for disturbing you again, but the news we bring is very important as it concerns Cinder's boyfriend and your nephew!"

"*What is this news? I was told that thou wert able to heal him of his wounds, both of his spirit as well as of his body. This is what Cinder said. Incendia – was thy daughter less than completely truthful?*" Queen Nocturne ended her sentence with subtle threat in her voice.

"No, no! It wasn't that! It was that she couldn't know everything that happened to Blue Streak, or rather what our healing runes unlocked within him."

The Seer went to say more before the Matriarch cut her off. "We discussed Blue Streak's achievements with him, and it appears that he already had a slight ability as a mana synthesist before he visited our lands. That is why when he races in Equestria he could break the sound barrier, but only just. When he did it in the newly restored Crystal Kingdom, there was even more ambient energy for him to draw on. However, when he came here and interacted with the untapped mana lines of the Dragon Lands, he managed to break the sound barrier within seconds, according to the Hunt-Master."

The Seer added, "But when we had to heal him, the resulting influx of mana forced all of his channels fully open. As you know, Queen Nocturne, once they are open, they cannot be closed."

"*I'm confused; why is this a bad thing?*" Twilight asked.

Luna/Nocturne answered, "*Because... think of an opponent thou faced a few years past that was able to drain magic out of ponies, and nearly destroyed Equestria.*"

"**My son is not Tirek!**" Twilight yelled.

"He isn't, I can assure you," Incendia replied. "However, when we conducted our tests, he unconsciously attempted to pull my mana into himself. Using the earth as a conduit, he managed to get quite a large portion, and it threw him into a rage. He tried to attack, but dragon magic follows dragon rules. After a display of power, Blue Streak submitted, and I was able to draw it back into myself."

"*How do you know so much about Tirek, Matriarch Incendia?*" Path *finally* spoke up.

"Because it was the Matriarch Council that held him at bay while Queen Nocturne and Diurnal built up the spell that originally cast him into Tartarus." Incendia said simply.

"*I have heard enough!*" Luna bellowed. "*I am coming to pick up Blue Streak and Cinder myself!*"

"I understand, Queen Nocturne. However, Cinder and Blue have already managed to get two other younger dragons interested in your House – a lesser male and the Seer's apprentice."

"*It matters not! Prepare thyself for I will soon be there!*" Luna growled sternly.

"Very well, we will await your arrival."

The connection was broken, and Incendia gave the Seer a troubled look. "Should we be worried?" Despite her age and power, the grand old dragoness was shaken by the power and authority in Queen Nocturne's voice.

The Seer grimaced. "We have annoyed a goddess – what do *you* think?"

Incendia snorted. "If I had known that Blue Streak was of her family, I would have done things differently."

"I thought you said that you were considering eating her nephew?" the Seer said dryly.

Incendia shuddered. "Upon reconsideration, I lost my appetite."

"What was all that about, Luna? Or should I say *Nocturne*?" Path asked as the alicorn headed for the balcony.

Luna paused to explain. "We are known by many names, and by many cultures. To dragonkind, I am Queen Nocturne, and my dealings with them reflect their expectations. Dragons respect strength first, and all other considerations must follow." She opened the balcony doors and stepped out into the moonlight.

"They could have hardly known the consequences of Blue's actions. There's no need to strike fear into them because of what has happened."

"Nay, 'tis not fear that I desire, but dragons seldom listen if there are no consequences to their actions. To make them understand, I must command respect in a manner that dragons know well."

With that, Luna spread her wings wide and her horn glowed. Then her whole body shimmered and started to expand. As she grew, her features shifted – her eyes' pupils became slits and her snout lengthened, with long sharp fangs protruding from her mouth. Her horn seemed to divide in two and each shifted to one side of the head even as they grew thicker and gnarled. Scales began appearing on her extremities and steadily replaced her fur until she was covered in obsidian armour. Her barrel expanded, as did her limbs, both rippling with powerful muscles. Hooves turned into talons and ethereal tail became a mighty bludgeon. Her leathery wings beat strongly and she launched herself into the night sky. Moments later, the boom of teleportation rumbled across the estate.

All the herd members had been watching in awe, but it was Free who finally broke the silence.

"Whoa! Anyone else turned on like I am right now?"

Both Twilight and Roseclaw glared at him, while Path just rolled his eyes. Some things never changed.

There was no mistaking Queen Nocturne's arrival; the crack of thunder even made Incendia jump, and the monstrously huge form of a dragon eclipsed the moon and threw most of the campsite into shadow. Incendia watched as Nocturne lowered herself to the ground in a clear area that the Matriarch had ordered to be made vacant. The Queen of the

Night was at least half again as big as her, and barely fitted. Worst yet was the glare that that was fixed upon her.

"**Art thou the Matriarch?**" Luna/Nocturne thundered.

"I am, Your Majesty."

"**Then t'was thy responsibility for the welfare of my nephew!**"

Incendia nodded. "Yes, Your Majesty."

"**And yet not two days pass before he is almost killed, and still he suffers the consequences.**"

"Blue Streak is a headstrong youth, Queen Nocturne. Responsibility for his actions must at least be partially borne by him." Incendia cringed a little inside as she saw Nocturne's reaction to that.

Nocturne's glare grew more intense, and her eyes glowed with building power, but after several tense moments, both died down to normal levels. "**Indeed, he is headstrong, but as thou didst just say, he is but a youth. I believe I knew thee as a youth of a mere two centuries, and thou wert as headstrong as Blue Streak back then. He has less than two decades of experience with the harsh realities of the world, and thou should have been aware of his vulnerability.**"

Incendia hung her head. "My abject apologies for my failures, Your Majesty."

Nocturne nodded in satisfaction. "**I expect better next time. Meanwhile, it is my will that dragonkind and ponykind work toward a mutual understanding. Although their lives are unfortunately brief, ponies nevertheless have much to teach dragons, and in turn learn from dragons. For this reason, I will accept the two dragon youths who wish to travel back with us. Bring them forth now.**" Nocturne looked around. "**Where are Blue Streak and Cinder?**"

Blue Streak stepped forth from a group of dragon youths, pulling Cinder along with him. "We're here, Auntie." Although he had been a little stunned when the gigantic dragon had arrived, once Blue realized that it was actually Luna's Queen Nocturne form, he had been intrigued rather than concerned... not counting the scolding that he anticipated getting later. To the other dragons though, his confident familiarity with the dragon goddess left them awestruck.

Cinder though was just about to faint from sheer terror. Until this moment, she had not realized just who she had been treating with almost contemptuous familiarity on the few occasions that she had met Luna. She had never truly associated the pony princess with the dragon goddess, even after Blue had told her about the dreamscape. Right now, she felt less than a bug that deserved to be squished.

Blue noticed his girlfriend's reluctance and put a reassuring arm around her shoulders. "Don't let Auntie bother you too much, Cinder. I reckon you have to worry more about my Moms' tongue-lashings when we get back."

Cinder cringed a little more. "Maybe I should stay right here."

Blue chuckled sympathetically and pulled her towards Nocturne. "If I gotta take it, so do you."

Meanwhile, two young dragons broke from the crowd and stood nervously at Nocturne's feet. Blue and Cinder joined them, and the massive dragoness spread her wings and enfolded them all. Then, with a surge of magic that all present felt like a physical blow, Nocturne teleported out with a thunderous boom.

All the dragons just stayed where they were for a while, pondering their encounter with a living goddess. Eventually the Matriarch turned to the Seer and said, "Why do I feel like a hatchling scolded by her parents?"

The Seer smirked. "Probably because that is what we are to one such as she. Now if she considered us responsible adults, think how much greater her anger would have been."

Incendia gulped. "Point taken."

Nocturne arrived outside House Path with an equally impressive thunderclap, and released her passengers from her enfolding wings. Then as they watched, she drew her power within herself once more and her form shrank down and resumed pony form. Within a minute, alicorn princess Luna stood in Nocturne's place.

The new dragons had watched in awe, stunned by her eventual transformation. Although Cinder already knew Luna, her perception of the alicorn had been radically altered by the experience, and she was no less blown away. As Path approached Luna and started talking with her, none of them could comprehend how an earth pony could be so familiar with a goddess.

"You look tired, Luna. Are you alright?"

"I am fine, Path, but teleporting so far directly, and with passengers, is no easy task, not to mention my manifestation in dragon form."

"How come you didn't use that when we fought the changelings?" Path asked curiously.

Luna gave him a tired smile. "There is a price to pay for everything, some greater than others. While I am more powerful as Nocturne, my endurance is much lower. The battle of the Crystal City was one of attrition, and best fought in my normal alicorn form."

Path nodded. "Makes sense." He then peered behind Luna where he spotted Blue and Cinder trying to look inconspicuous. "Come on, you two. You're only putting off the inevitable."

By then, the other members of Herd Path had joined him. Blue was grinned meekly as he was stared down by a purple alicorn and giant griffoness. "H-Hi, Moms... I'd like you to meet my two friends who would like admission into the House if it was possible."

The Seer's apprentice walked over to join them. She was a quadrupedal dragon, slightly larger than Cinder, but instead of a rich gold colour, her hide was a mottled brown, and her eyes were a contrasting deep, rich hazel. She was wearing a strange wooden necklace and there were runes painted on her form in jet black ink.

She smiled nervously and bowed to the group. "Ah, hello. Maybe we have met? Are we meeting now? Maybe we have yet to meet? My name is Oörchlögdsön Üzmerchor... translated into a pony name, I believe that would be called Altered Seer" She bowed again.

The smaller male slinked out from behind Luna and Altered. "H-hi... my name is Ondög Ayuulaas. If you translate it like how Altered did, it means Egg Warden, which I guess makes sense since back in the clan I watch the eggs with the other lesser males while most are out hunting or gathering minerals." His eyes met Free's and widened in recognition. He made a small squeak and crouched down, making himself look smaller than he already was.

Twilight and Roseclaw were quiet just long enough for Altered Seer and Egg Warden to give their introductions before they launched themselves onto Blue. Twilight grabbed him with her magic and lifted him up.

"**You have no idea how much trouble you are in, mister!**" Twilight snarled.

"*I'm going to make sure that Warfist gives you extra encouragement!*" Rose squawked as Blue was carted off into the main house, protesting all the way. Cinder followed after them, trying to better explain what happened.

Free was glaring daggers at Egg Warden and was about to say something before Path put his hoof in the way.

"How about Altered and Luna go and talk while they get some supper. I'm sure that Luna could do with some food and rest, and she can help Altered Seer adjust to House life," Path said, giving Luna a knowing look. "While she is doing that, Free, you and I will learn more about our newest student?"

Free huffed and turned to walk toward the meeting room. "Yes. Yes we will. Let's go, Egg Warden."

Free walked off while Egg Warden slinked behind the griffon. Path rolled his eyes a bit before saying to Luna, "We'll join you a little later." Path then followed the pair.

Luna looked down to Altered Seer and smiled reassuringly as she led her toward the House cafeteria which was always open in order to cater to the needs of the House's students. "I am surprised that thou art not wondering why I look different, nor why they call me Luna instead of Queen Nocturne?"

Altered giggled. "Oh, I have been an apprentice for a while. I understand the order of the Aspects. In each culture you are represented differently based on the cultural perceptions. While this is true for the four Prime Gods – those of Light, Dark, Chaos and Order – there are lesser beings that are not subject to those rules, like Miss Twilight and I believe her name is Cadance?"

Luna was impressed that the apprentice knew so much, but then again she did have a good teacher. "Ah, so is that why thou hast adapted so quickly and act so casually with me then, Altered Seer?"

"Well, actually it's a theory that my master shared with me after she visited you in Blue's dream. She asked me something." Altered grinned a bit. "What is the difference between a good and a bad Aspect?"

"Hmm... what was thine answer?" Luna asked.

"I don't really remember to be honest, because she stopped me halfway and told me that there is no difference. The better question to ask is if the Aspect acts in its own interests, stays neutral, or in the interest of others. She said that the Aspect of Chaos acts only in his own interests, the Aspect of Order keeps neutral and watches, while the Aspects of Light and Dark act in the interests of others. True to Harmony, you and your sister, Light and Dark, are working toward the common goal of peace. Only your methods differ." Altered held open the door to the large cafeteria for Luna and then followed her in.

"By that logic, art thou calling me a dark god?" Luna asked with a smirk as she grabbed a tray telekinetically.

Altered Seer followed suit. "Well, the idea of Light and Dark is not nearly as cut and dried as most think; not even their definition is concrete. That's the confusing part about the higher order to those not on its level." Altered spotted a delicious-looking salmon and added some to her plate.

"Ah, so then what thou art doing now is mimicking how the others are acting so that thou can figure out what their cultural representation of me is?" Luna chose a table and sat down, followed by Altered Seer, and they began eating.

"Correct. I have to admit however, that I definitely was not expecting things to be so casual. It's a huge difference from the Queen that you are in the Dragon Lands, to the princess in Equestria, to the 'Auntie Luna' here in House Path. I... I think it's cute."

"Hmm..." Luna considered that as she ate some cauliflower

smothered in cheese sauce. "I do muchly like it here like this. Even a god needs family to help keep her balanced."

"Well, you know, if an Aspect lives for all eternity, then it stands to reason that there is a one hundred percent chance that you will eventually do everything, including this," Altered Seer pointed out.

"Huh... I cannot dispute that." Luna blinked a few times and she started to laugh.

Path, Free, and Egg Warden moved into Path's office, and as soon as the door shut with them inside, green fire flashed around Free as he changed into his changeling queen form, adding to his intimidation, as he moved up into Egg Warden's face.

"You can quit faking. I want to know what hive you are from and what your intentions are right now!" the Chrome Queen growled as Egg Warden squeaked and lowered himself down again, moving almost into a corner of the room before Path intervened.

"Okay, how about we decide not to go overboard with the scare tactics. He is one changeling far away from home, and no threat to you, 'Queenie'." Path grinned a bit as Free huffed and calmed down. He motioned to Warden to sit down in front of the desk and Free did the same.

"So, you already know Free Agent here, also known as Queen Gossamer of the Chrome Hive," Path said as he smiled at Free who now looked more impatient than angry. "I am Lord Long Path, a noble in pretty much every civilization that was involved in the Crystal Kingdom crisis, as well as a few that weren't." Path grinned as Free rolled his eyes. "So, Egg Warden – tell us about yourself."

"Ah... Well I'm a changeling, as you already figured out. I'm a part of a loose association of changeling hives from the Dragon Lands that calls themselves the United Changeling Council – four hives ruling the four cardinal directions. But then again, ruling is a rather broad term. It's more like loosely defined territories. We don't have hives nearly as large as yours because we need to deal with the nomadic dragons. It's honestly really hard to explain because I don't know the whole story. While you might be in a constant state of breeding, my queen doesn't do it very often, opting instead for short intense seasons rather than low intensity year round breeding. So that's why I have that role in Cinder's clan; I tend to and care for the eggs with the other actual males, because that is what my role is when my queen has her season."

Egg Warden focused a bit, and deep red flames flickered around his feet before moving up his body to reveal his changeling form. He actually didn't look a lot like any changeling that they were familiar with, and his chitin was rather blocky, obviously armour of some kind. If he had been a changeling from Equestria, he would definitely be classified as a soldier class, but judging from his submissive demeanour and his fear, it was clear he was a support-class changeling.

Path grinned. "Good. Now that you two have started talking, I'm going to go make us some love tea." He stood up and walked into the side room.

"*Love* tea?" Egg asked.

"It's when he has one of my assistants take a little bit of his love, then dilutes it into a rather sweet tea," Free explained. "If you're not used to the flavour, it's quite a treat. Even I don't get it very often."

"Oh! I look forward to it!" Egg said with a growing smile.

Free locked eyes with the dragon changeling. "Now – let's get back to our talks, shall we?"

Egg Warden shuddered.

Twilight threw open the doors and Blue sailed inside, still caught up in her magical field. Roseclaw stomped after her, followed by Cinder who ran in and interposed herself between the two and Blue Streak.

"**Wait! Wait! Before you punish him, hear me out, please!**" Cinder screamed as she opened her wings to their maximum extent. This was a sign of great aggression, so Roseclaw opened hers up as well and let out a battle screech. Twilight, however, had no such instincts, so all of her steam was lost at the sight of the two females circling each other, wings flared and claws bared.

"You have been a very bad girl, Cinder," Roseclaw spoke in a tone that she very rarely used, and the dads outright feared. "Give me one reason why I shouldn't punish you myself. Blue is our oldest son – how well do you think I would handle him nearly dying?"

"That wasn't my intention at all! Blue wanted to show the rest of the males that he was capable! He was trying to gain favour with my Hunt-Master father! He rightly earned that favour because he was able to provide food for the clan for nearly a week through his strength," Cinder said, not letting her wings down yet. Her pupils were fully dilated as she expected to be attacked at any moment.

"Go on…" Roseclaw said, her tone still unchanged.

"He wasn't attacked when he was hunting; he was attacked while he was grazing before the flight back! We patched him up the best we could, really we did!" Cinder was now very upset, her wings shaking slightly. "I didn't want to lose him!" Cinder started crying as her wings folded down. "Then when he woke up, things were weird, and nobody but the Seer and the Matriarch knew what was going on. He ended up eating half a goat raw, then knocking out one of my suitors in one hit. Then he...." She trailed off.

"Then he what?" Roseclaw asked as she took a step closer to Cinder, her muscles tensing up.

Cinder looked away briefly due to embarrassment, and it was the opening that Roseclaw needed. She was on top of Cinder in an instant, her stronger frame pinning the smaller dragon down on her back as her beak moved until it was an inch from Cinder's ear.

"I forgive you this time, Cinder, but if anything like this happens again while he is in your care, I'll be wearing a dragon skin coat. Am I clear?" Roseclaw spoke in an eerie calm voice as Cinder screamed and nodded fervently.

"HEY!" Blue yelled at Roseclaw. "**Don't threaten her like that! You leave her alone!**"

Roseclaw turned her head to rebuke Blue Streak, only to feel the tug of Twilight's telekinesis pulling her away from the terrified dragoness.

"Blue's right, Rose. Not only don't we do that in the House of Path, but you are also threatening his potential mate."

Roseclaw frowned hard. "Cinder was responsible for his safety. She should have been with the hunt pack to protect him from the unknown, but she wasn't. She needs to know that is unacceptable."

"She knows it without needing to threaten her life. She made a mistake – let her learn from it."

Roseclaw's frown eased and she nodded. She turned to Cinder and said, "Leave us now."

Cinder scrambled back up to her feet and ran out.

"That... that was intense," Blue said, drawing Twilight's attention back to him.

"Blue Streak, you're going to be punished as well, and it won't be as nice as Cinder's," Twilight told Blue as Roseclaw walked over to them.

"Why am I even being punished?! It was a sneak attack!" Blue fumed and thrashed around in the magical field.

"**Because you were careless!**" both mothers screamed.

"We are going to see Azon and Techbird for a complete examination and testing," Twilight said as they started to walk down the hall.

"That's it?" Blue asked.

"You *wish* that was it!" Twilight laughed.

They rounded the corner and Blue was face to face with fear itself

– the Warmaster.

"So glad to see you, Blue Streak, so very, very glad. I am very disappointed with you, and I'm told that I will be allowed to give you *special encouragement* – 3pm to 9pm – one month straight. We will become great friends you and I." Blue had no idea how he could grin like that with a beak, but that old bird had the ability to instil fear into anyone.

"Yaayy...?" Blue was barely able to squeak out.

"Now let's get you to the examination room!" Twilight said smugly as the three of them continued down the hall.

Warfist watched them go, a satisfied smile on his face. He had been looking for an excuse to get Blue's training back on track. The colt's hormones and youthful impetuousness had completely disrupted the training that had started so promisingly years ago. When Twilight and Roseclaw had approached him about this incident, he had suggested a month of intense coaching as 'punishment' to catch up, with special emphasis on situational awareness. If Blue wanted to be a great warrior when he grew up, by the Egg, he would make him one!

Much later at night when all of the young ones were asleep, and even Blue and Cinder were passed out in their bed, Twilight, Luna, Path, Free, Roseclaw were all down in the meeting room with Techbird and Azon.

"So... how bad is it?" Path asked, looking at the doctor with a rather concerned look on his face.

"It's not bad... it's not good... honestly I don't know what it all means. I am not a magic specialist." The disguised changeling put a few images on the table so everyone could look at them. "This is what I do know though. As you can see, his mana channels are several times larger than they should be. The ones that earth ponies usually use for their passive earth pony abilities are generally microscopic, just like the pegasi, because if their channels were open any more, you would get earth ponies draining whole tracts of land, or even other ponies, to aid in their cultivation. Or even worse, you would have pegasi flying so fast that they would break apart under the aerodynamic stresses."

Azon showed comparison pictures of Applejack and Rainbow Dash, showing their mana channels that were slightly larger than normal ponies. "Blue, on the other claw, has had his channels forced way open by the draconic healing. Once they are opened that wide, they can't be closed again. Right now the only things keeping him from draining everything around him is that he doesn't know how to activate the draw unless under duress, plus the fact that those traction-enhancing shoes are actually limiting how much he can take in."

The herd listened intently as Azon continued on.

"Also, since the eyes are the window into one's magic, or one's soul if you will, it explains why his eyes change. I heard in the report that his eyes were draconic slits while under the influence of the enhanced mana. This would make sense due to the draconic magic that pervades their lands overriding his own. I believe that if he takes in more than he has already, there may be further physical changes. This is bad because it means that after a certain point he loses control, and the magic itself is driving him. It's a slippery slope." Azon picked up the photos and reports and passed them over to Twilight so she could draw her own conclusions from the data.

Roseclaw asked, "Aside from that little problem, how is he?"

"Healthy. In fact, robustly so. Whatever the Seer did to heal him was extremely effective, although of course not without those unintended side-effects. I could scarcely even see the signs of his injuries. I suspect that it's the dragon magic that is responsible for that, so it's not exactly something that I could easily reproduce, but the results are undeniable."

"Well, that's something good at least," Roseclaw conceded.

Path nodded in agreement. "For now, let's just keep a watch on Blue to make sure that no other problems pop up. Techbird, Blue's shoes acting as limiters is something that they weren't designed to do, and that might cause them to fail somehow. I'd like you to look into making a new set for him with this specifically in mind. Maybe throw in some improvements at the same time. Blue must be encouraged to wear them at all times. I want that the first thing that he does of a morning as he climbs out of bed is to slip into his shoes."

Techbird's head was already spinning with ideas, and she nodded eagerly.

Path drew a deep breath and steadied his nerves for what he had to say next. "Twilight, Roseclaw, I know that you're not going to like this, but once we're sure that Blue's situation is stable, I want to slowly start training him to use this new power available to him."

"What?!" exclaimed Twilight.

"Absolutely not!" Roseclaw said with an angry flare of her wings.

"Nay, Long Path has the right of it," Luna said sternly. "Blue Streak must learn to control the power, or it will control him. That is a bitter lesson to learn the hard way."

Roseclaw glared at Luna for a long moment before relaxing her wings and nodding.

Twilight shook her head. "I still don't like it, but I see no alternative. History shows what happens if you ignore it." She then turned a resolute eye on Luna. "But he should learn this from someone who knows the consequences of failure."

Luna nodded gravely with a touch of shame. "Aye. Blue shall receive extra teachings from me, an apprentice if you will. Equus will never again face another like Tirek… or the Nightmare."

Chapter 9: Blue's Field Trip

"Maximo Coloniam," Luna stated as she smiled at the rest of the herd.

"What?" Path and Free both asked as they looked at her in confusion.

Twilight stared at Luna. "I've never heard of that place, and this is coming from somebody who lived in a library from the age of four to seventeen, then moved to a different library."

"Ah, well it's not very well known to Equestrian historians, especially since as far back as I could remember, the last time they had any kind of contact with ponies was somewhere around 100BB." Luna said.

"100 BB?" Free queried.

"One hundred years before banishment," Luna replied.

"So what and where is Maximo Coloniam." Path asked.

"It is a *very* old way of saying the Grand Colony, the original colony for the thestral race, but it's so far away that most times it is very difficult to reach it. However, tomorrow there will be a twelve hour period from moon-set to moon-rise that is most propitious," Luna said as she yawned slightly.

"So you want us to go with you?" Roseclaw asked.

"As much as I would like to take all of you, there are various reasons why I cannot. I wish to take just one person with me, and I would like that to be Blue Streak. If that has your blessing, I think he would enjoy the mini-vacation and learn a lot at the same time. His non-Equestrian upbringing and cultural view will make their culture easier for him to understand."

Path and Free had already started looking excited about a visit to a long-forgotten land. Path huffed and looked hurt. Free, however, just grinned.

"I think Streak is going to have a wonderful time. Does he know he's going to go?"

Blue Streak rushed up to Luna with a grin. Around his neck was what looked like a camera. He was practically vibrating with excitement. "YOU SAID YES! WOOHOOO!" He ran around Luna so fast it looked like she had a light blue halo.

The Lunar Aspect chuckled before she activated her horn and stopped the Blue Streak from running. "They said yes, and now I need you to go to bed and get plenty of sleep so you can wake up early in time for our departure."

"Okay!" Blue replied, and then dashed off.

Twilight smiled at his enthusiasm before she grew serious again and asked Luna, "Is it safe for him? He'll be visiting a people so far removed from us that they know very little about our society."

"Although it has been a long time since I've visited them, they know I will be arriving, and anyone in my company will be considered under my protection, so there is no need to worry." Luna turned to Path and Free. "I'll bring a present back for each of thee to make up for not also bringing you." Luna giggled and winked before she headed out of the meeting room. "I'm going to take a nap; powering such a teleport will be most strenuous."

It was a few minutes before sunrise when they all ran out to the field where Luna and Twilight were waiting. Blue was antsy with excitement "This is going to be so cool!"

As Luna prepared to lower the full moon prior to the sunrise, Twilight asked, "I don't understand why you will be doing this now. I would have thought that you would use the power of the full moon when you are strongest?"

Luna smiled. "Thou art correct, but that is exactly why we will be going now, for while the moon doth set here, it will rise for the Grand Colony, and I will have its power at my beck and call for the duration of our visit."

"Ah! That makes sense. I had not realized that it was quite that distant."

As Luna's horn started to glow, Twilight cast several spells onto Blue Streak.

"What was that?" Blue asked Twilight.

"Air spell, translation spell and glamor spell – you'll understand when you get there." Twilight chuckled as she took a few steps back.

Luna's horn was now glowing violently as she slowly turned and aimed at the moon. Blue went to stand next to her. "R-ready, Blue Streak?" Luna strained as the magical matrices began to visualize.

"READY!" Blue Streak screamed out in excitement.

The complicated spell executed and the two of them disappeared with a shock wave that knocked the rest of the herd over.

It was then that Pif who had been hiding in Free's folded wings, pushed her head out from behind Free's feathers and squealed, "*Big boom!*" She giggled in delight.

The pair rematerialized, but it was not a place that Blue Streak recognized. The sky was black, the ground was a stark white, and he slowly floated down and landed on ground that was soft and powdery. His eyes went wide as he looked around, and then up to the small blue marble floating above them.

"Is that...?" Blue asked, dumbstruck.

"It is," Luna said with a smile.

"Are we?" Blue looked at Luna.

"We are," Luna answered.

"Am I?" Blue squeaked out.

"Thou art." Luna grinned.

"EEEEE!" Blue screamed in delight as he started to run... only to find out that his first two launch steps pushed him far up off the ground. His legs whirred around aimlessly as he floated there in confusion before Luna grabbed him in her magic and set him back down next to her.

"Stay still – we have but a few minutes before I must activate the second part of the teleportation spell, and I need to... well... thou shalt see." She laughed softly as her form shifted in front of his eyes. She grew taller, her coat darker, her eyes turned draconic and armour appeared over most of her body. She smiled at Blue Streak with teeth that had become much sharper.

Blue Streak stared at her before bursting out, "*You. Look. Awesome!* Like you can take on a whole army and then eat an entire steak kind of awesome!"

Luna smiled happily. This was why she chose to have Blue Streak come with her. His view, devoid of other cultural bias, made him able to appreciate various cultural interpretations of herself. He had only ever seen a tamer version of this form hamming it up on stage for the Nightmare Night festivals in Griffonia, but it was a form that most ponies had feared, but her thestrals loved. The Equestrian public knew this interpretation as Nightmare Moon, the being that nearly doomed an entire civilization. However, the Thestral Colonies knew her by a different name: the Lunar Imperatrix.

Luna started to work her magic on the glamor spell that Twilight had placed on Blue Streak, making his coat and cutie mark darker. It also made his eyes a dark blue. As she worked, she asked, "Thou hast been training with Warfist, correct? When last I checked, thou hast been working with him early in the morning for the past year or so. I believe he called it '*private encouragement*'?"

"Yeah, it's been about a year and a half now. It took him a month to get me to actually take things seriously, then another two before we were able to find a weapon that didn't shatter under the forces involved with running so fast. He gave me a long sword and it broke in half in like two days. He says I have to stick to unarmed combat or small bladed weapons," Blue said as he collected some of the moon dust into a little pile.

"Good – thou must act like thou art training with Warfist whilst we are there. Take it seriously; be disciplined, prim and proper, legs squared, neck straight and the perfect personal guard. They completely embrace pomp and circumstance, so thou must also. Dost thou think that thou can do that just until the party starts?" Luna gave him her most encouraging smile.

Blue perked up his ears. "Sure! I can do that."

"Excellent! Oh! Hold a moment – I need to make thee a suitable set of armour."

Luna lit up her horn a little more and the white lunar regolith turned red hot as it was shaped and moulded. The silicon and titanium present in the rocks mixed and fused until what was left was a deep blue. She shaped it and formed it around Blue Streak making a Lunar Guard styled light armour designed not to interfere with his speed. "Ah that should work. Now let me remind thee that this society is from a different time, and I will have to be very strict. Because of that, thou cannot be familiar with me in public. Thou must always address me as 'My Empress'. Strength is shown not implied. Hast thou any questions?"

Blue Streak shook his head. "I'll remember."

"Ready for the second jump?" Luna asked.

Blue Streak nodded. "I'm ready!"

Luna's horn charged up again, although this time it didn't take nearly as long, probably due to her actually standing on her aspect and source of power. With a bright flash, they disappeared from the bleak landscape. Due to the fact they had been in a vacuum just before they teleported, a large cloud of mist condensed out of the air when they appeared and their protective shield dropped. Blue waited until it dissipated, then he looked around and was amazed.

It looked like a scene right of a history book. In the twilight, he could see that they were on top of what looked like a large altar in the sky; maybe they were on top of a building? When he looked around, he caught a last glimpse of the sun to his left as it was called to the other side of Equus to bring dawn to Equestria, while to his right the full moon was rising. The pale white marble at his hooves reflected the light of the bright orb, and when he looked hard enough, he was able to see runes etched into its surface, but he had neither the magical knowledge nor the required linguistics to understand them.

Just then, four flying formations of thestrals approached their location from what he believed to be the four cardinal directions. First seven thestrals of thin build landed, dressed in white togas with silver trim. The second group to land was another set of seven thestrals that rivalled Big Macintosh in their build, and whose togas were of a similar red hue with gold trim. The third group to land was wearing purple and black togas that hid most of their forms. The last seven to land looked rather normal, and their simple togas were tan. Once all had landed, they all bowed in one deep synchronous motion.

"Imperatrix advenit!" Luna proclaimed.

The bat ponies stood up, stomping their hooves as they cheered. Then the thestrals quieted down and waited for their Luna to continue, although a few were looking curiously at the earth pony standing impassively next to their leader.

An officer sensed the confusion over the earth pony's presence, and he stepped forward and kneeled before Luna. "My Empress, why is this earth pony here? There has not been visitor of his kind to the colonies since before the Great Betrayal."

Blue kept his expression neutral, but he intended to ask Luna about this '*Great Betrayal*' later on.

Luna locked her gaze with the thestral's until he averted his eyes. "If thou must know, Captain Night Strike, this is my apprentice, Cobalt. He is my personal guard for this visit."

The captain however was indignant. "Your apprentice? My Empress, how can this mud pony be worthy of your mentorship?!"

Luna stomped her left hoof hard and narrowed her eyes at the captain. 'Cobalt' caught her lead and narrowed his eyes, growling at the captain as well.

"If thou dost think my choice so horrible, why dost thou not challenge him, Captain?" Luna spoke with a sharp edge to her voice.

The captain did not hesitate in the slightest and he began to charge, but he barely made a hoof step before he was staring at a dark blue armoured hoof not half an inch from his snout.

Blue Streak tapped the captain on the nose, and the thestral flared his wings to take a flapping leap back with a growl. He reached for his sword only to find it missing from his scabbard, but when he looked back up again, he found himself staring at its point which was centred an inch from his eyes. Blue tapped his nose again with the sword before flipping it to present the handle back to the captain.

Night Strike was becoming frustrated. "You think you are so fast, and you may be able to handle me alone, but the Empress' Guard must be able to defend against multiple aggressors." He let out a chirp that Blue Streak could not hear, and four thestrals flew to his side.

Blue Streak turned to Luna with one eyebrow cocked enquiringly.

She considered for a moment before nodding in consent.

Blue Streak braced his legs and waited as all four of them came at him their swords drawn. They all slashed or stabbed the upstart pony... and their swords went right through him as if he was immaterial. They were startled, and only grew more confused as they all kept trying to strike him.

Blue Streak, however, was outmanoeuvring them all. To everyone watching, his form was blurring and vibrating, and it was hard to figure out where to strike, but not one of the blows landed. A fraction of a second before a weapon would touch him, Blue Streak would move extremely rapidly just far enough out of its way to miss, and then move back again, giving the illusion that he had not moved at all. After long moments of fruitless effort, the captain chirped again, and his soldiers pulled back and sheathed their weapons. Night Strike did so as well before he nodded respectfully to 'Cobalt', and then bowed deeply to Luna yet again.

"My deepest apologies for doubting your choice, Empress."

Luna nodded gravely. "I will allow thine impertinence to go unpunished this time; it is the Eclipse Festival after all. Everyone is free to go about their business. Captain Night Strike, Apprentice Cobalt, accompany me as I go to speak to the Senate." Luna started to walk off.

"Yes, My Empress," both Blue Streak and Night Strike chorused, falling in behind her.

'*Oh, this is going to be so much **fun**,*' Blue Streak thought to himself while trying to fight off a smile.

They approached a marble building surrounded by colonnades and entered. A crowd of thestrals, too many to count and all of them wearing togas the various colours of the city states that they happened to represent, occupied the amphitheatre within. The building was filled with the sound of intense debate, but once Luna entered the centre of the forum, they all quieted down and bowed.

"Exorior Patres Conscripti!" Luna announced firmly as she began to talk. "As you all know, I have been exploring, investigating, and observing since my recovery from the... proditio." Luna looked around as the senators muttered among themselves, clearly displeased with the memory of the betrayal.

"As you know, we are not ready yet to begin talks with Sol proditor... but there is a new faction arising! A faction whose only motivation is the pursuit of knowledge, as well as the improvement of one's self!" As she spoke Blue Streak could see two groups of thestrals, one wearing pure white togas while another wore red and gold, that seemed a *lot* more interested now.

"My new apprentice, Cobalt, hails from this faction. He is an earth pony born and raised in a griffon society, and he has benefited of both!"

All eyes were on Blue as he stood there, tensing up just slightly to try to look a little more muscular and impressive.

"I command that the senate bring forth one volunteer from each district who is about to enter their mandatory service. There are three hours before the festival begins. Bring me your candidates before it starts. I will look them over and choose one. He or she will participate in a cultural exchange that will determine if we are ready for the outside world... and if the world is ready for us."

Luna stopped and looked at the senators as they all began to stomp their hooves in approval.

"I will await you at the Altar of the Moon. Until then, Senators." Luna turned and walked out while Blue Streak followed her.

Once they were alone, he spoke to Luna in a hushed whisper. "That was amazing! I don't think I've ever seen anything run like that before."

"That's because the Griffon Empire is technically a militant-timocracy. Equestria is an absolutist-diarchy, but we are trying to guide it to a constitutional diarchy. Most changeling hives are an absolute monarchy due to their biological and mental make-up," Luna started lecturing.

Blue Streak rolled his eyes. "Aw, come on... don't be like Mom. Let's go explore while we wait for the festival to begin." Blue was getting antsy.

"We don't have the time to explore right now, but we will have time during the festival since it's one huge party, but for now..." Luna started to power her horn up for a short-range teleport, "we will be late to watch the honour trials. It is one of the oldest traditions here, and I need to oversee the final match as the winner gains my favour."

Blue nodded as a thought formed in the back of his mind. *'Hmmm... Warfist would be proud if I came back with a medal or a trophy from this tournament.'* He just grinned as they both disappeared in a flash of light.

Teleporting was always so disorienting. It took Blue a few moments to gather his bearings before he realized that he was standing next to Luna in the sky box of what looked like a massive arena. The cheering was almost deafening as Luna waved to the crowd. He barely heard one of the advisors murmur to Luna under the volume of the

celebration.

"My queen, the final match is ready; we have Champion Nineteen going up against the Captain's three eldest sons. If he wins this match, it will be his twentieth annual victory, and he will obtain your favour."

Blue's interest was sparked as he looked down to the champion. He was a middle-aged looking thestral, with a massive but well-balanced build. He was dressed in brilliant silver and blue, with a helmet which had a bright blue tuft of plumage. His gaze was keen, and he actually kind of reminded him of a thestral version of Warfist.

Luna stepped forward and raised a hoof. The crowd quieted and she boomed out in the Royal Canterlot Voice, "CHAMPION

NINETEEN – THIS IS THE EVE OF YOUR FINAL TRIAL. SURPASS THIS AND MY LAST TASK, AND YOU WILL ASCEND WITH ME TO THE ALTERED REALM. ARE YOU READY FOR YOUR FINAL GAUNTLET?"

The champion nodded once and put on his helmet, raised his spear in salute, and then took a combat stance with shield and spear at the ready.

"SO BE IT THEN! BRING OUT THE FINAL CHALLENGE!"

Blue's eyes went wide as he saw three blurs shoot across the arena, spiralling around the champion before they came to a landing, encircling Champion XIX. The three brothers gazed appraisingly at the champion, each of them holding dual short swords at the ready. Blue Streak couldn't help but smirk; the sons used a similar style as himself.

"BEGIN!" Luna shouted.

The three cautiously moved around the champion. When it started, the fighting was explosive in nature as all three closed in on the champion and prepared to hack and slash at him. Their swords never touched him as he ducked, weaved, and used his shield to deflect their weapons. If Blue had to describe it, he would have to say that Champion was free-flowing, using their own actions against them.

The crowd cheered as the four kept battling, and soon the champion landed the first decisive blow, when the youngest of the three left an opening, and the blunt end of the spear shot out and slammed into his chest with enough force to launch him nearly ten feet away before he crumpled on the ground, gasping for air. The judge threw a red flag down on the son indicating a kill.

Luna looked over to Blue and she started to grin. His eyes were following all that that was going on, and an idea formed in her head as she looked back to the battle just in time to see the champion's shield bash the middle son and bring his staff down against his temple, knocking him out.

The battle was now one on one, and the two circled each other warily before the oldest son charged in and started swinging ferociously. The champion dodged and deflected, but the son was only gaining more momentum and speeding up. The champion ducked under a lunge, dropped his shield and sword, and grabbed his opponent's hoof before his other hoof slammed into the eldest son's neck, causing him to collapse. The judge tossed the last flag and the crowd cheered. The champion helped up his opponents, and they bowed to each other and then to Luna.

Luna narrowed her eyes slightly and a glow covered her mouth as she spoke silently. The champion suddenly looked towards Luna with his ears swivelled in her direction. He nodded once with a grin, and he readied himself again.

"What's he getting ready for?" Blue asked.

"For thee," Luna said with a grin. "Thou art going to be his final challenge. However, thou must *not* take off thy hoof shoes."

Blue was ecstatic. "It won't be much of a challenge. I'll beat him in one punch." Blue laughed a bit as he was floated down to the arena.

"MY SUBJECTS, THE LAST ROUND IS UPON US. THE CHAMPION WILL FACE MY APPRENTICE IN BATTLE. TO WIN IS TO GAIN ASCENSION. TO LOSE IS TO BECOME THE HEAD OF THE WARRIOR GUILD. MY CHAMPION HAS FOUGHT WELL AND WILL EARN HIS JUST REWARD REGARDLESS OF THE OUTCOME!" Luna bellowed out as the crowd cheered.

Blue looked to Champion. "I'll try to make it fast, old man."

The champion just grinned as he set his spear and shield down and assumed a defensive posture.

"Oh, try and make it interesting for me," Blue said cockily.

When Luna signalled the start of the match, neither of them moved as the crowd cheered.

"Game over," Blue said as he suddenly took off at the champion.

The crowd suddenly went silent. Nobody saw Blue move – nobody but the champion. They all looked at Blue's outstretched hoof… and the thestral hoof that blocked that punch. The bat-pony was grinning while Blue looked at him with wide eyes.

"H-how? Nobody has ever blocked me!"

The champion laughed. "I am more than your common brawler, apprentice." He pulled his hoof back and punched the shocked pony *hard*.

Blue stumbled back, not yet falling over but it was clear he was going to have a black eye. Blue let out a loud growl. "NO MORE GAMES!" he screamed out, his pride hurt more than his body.

The champion kept up a defensive posture as Blue raced around him, raining blows upon him that never managed to hit their target. Unknown to the earth pony, the champion was sending out several sonic pulses a second to track him. Every time Blue moved in, he was blocked or countered each time, and the champion either punched or kicked him in a way that would not end the fight. The crowd was screaming in excitement, enthralled by the fight as Blue stopped on the opposite side of the arena.

Baring his teeth as he screamed, "I *WILL* WIN!" Blue started taking off his hoof shoes. Nobody realized what was happening, but Luna did as she watched Blue Streak stare ferociously at his foe. The champion's eyes went wide as he also realized what was about to happen. He picked up his shield and braced himself just before the arena rang out with the clang of hooves on metal. Champion was pushed halfway back to the edge of the arena, his shield dented with two hoofprints. Blue landed back where he started, hissing in rage, his eyes shining a bright gold and his now-sharp teeth bared.

The last thing that the champion noticed was Blue Streak hovering in front of him, a moment from striking the decisive blow, but he was suddenly covered in a dark blue aura and froze in place. Luna floated down to the floor of the arena and walked up to the pair.

"I am disappointed in thee, Blue Streak. Thou had but one restriction and thou couldst not follow it."

Luna turned to the crowd which was waiting in awed silence. **"Cobalt has been disqualified! Champion Nineteen is now Champion Twenty, AND HAS GAINED THE RIGHT OF ASCENSION!"**

The thestrals erupted into cheers and the crowd emptied out onto the main floor as they carried away the champion.

"THIS CELEBRATION WILL BE THE BEST IN AGES!" Luna bellowed out as everyone started to make their way toward the already set up festivities.

Blue blinked and looked towards Luna. "I... lost? I *lost*?!"

Luna looked at him and frowned. "Thou had no chance of winning in fair combat. I had hoped that this would be a lesson to thee that speed isn't everything in battle. Now thou must live with the humiliation of disqualification instead of honourable defeat. Perhaps this will serve as a more urgently needed lesson in respecting thy foes." She sighed before smiling once more. "But for now, this is supposed to be a festival, so how about enjoying thyself before we must head back to Equestria?"

Blue was not happy, but he shrugged it off as Luna passed him his shoes and he put them back on. "Yeah, a good party is just what I need."

The rest of the party was a blur. Blue managed to run into Champion XX and he apologized to the thestral, who graciously accepted. They started chatting, and actually found that they had a lot in common despite their age difference. Once they realized that, their friendship grew, and they spent the entire night drinking and partying in the traditional ancient thestral style. When Luna caught up with the pair, they were at a table with two other warriors and playing a dice game. However, as one side began to stack the dice, before they could roll them, Blue and Champion stood up and began bellowing out their war song, which by this time in their inebriated state had degenerated into a few phrases.

"Glory to the colony!"
"Honour to the Queen!"
"Long live the Imperatrix!"
"Now everybody sing!"

The two started chugging on a large glass of ale each and slammed them down next to the four dozen other mugs, knocking over the other side's dice as they laughed, winning the round. Their entourage was drunk as well, and they joined in the laughter. Luna rolled her eyes and chuckled as she went back to her duties.

Several hours later, the horizon brightened as sunrise neared, and Luna found the pair in the middle of what looked like a massive bar brawl. At least a hundred different thestrals were in the fray, and in the centre of it all there was the pair fighting together and defending each other. Luna cleared her throat and let her magic flare. The single act was enough to cut through the brawl and everyone settled down.

"Champion, Cobalt, it is time to depart." Luna said softly before turning and exiting the tavern. The two warriors followed after her and they walked back to the winding staircase that led up to the moon altar. Luna paused there and regarded the four young thestrals who were waiting in the company of the elders.

There were two females and two males, and they stood there with a mixture of excitement and nervousness. Luna did not ask anything of them, but merely observed them keenly. Under her scrutiny, both males and one of the females eventually averted their eyes, but the remaining female returned her gaze with fierce determination.

"What is thy name, filly?" Luna asked.

"Moonlight Mist, Imperatrix," she replied.

Luna considered the filly's pale fur and silver mane and felt that she was well named. "I hope that thou art prepared for great changes to thy conceptions of the world, for thou art my choice."

"I am honoured, Imperatrix, and I will not disappoint you."

Luna nodded in satisfaction before she turned to Champion. "Hast thou made thy farewells?"

"Yes, my Empress," Champion replied.

"Very good." The moon was low in the sky as Luna started to cast spells on Champion and Moonlight Mist as they stood there, girding themselves for this new adventure.

Luna rose up into the air as she made a big show for all those who had gathered. "This has been a most glorious festival, and I am well pleased. I shall return next year, but until then, my subjects, fare thee well!"

There was a bright flash, and all four of them disappeared. In an extra show, the watchers saw four stars shoot toward the moon, and just before it set, they witnessed four flashes on the moon. They cheered before they dispersed, the festival ceremonies complete for another year.

Champion and Moonlight looked around at the lunar landscape then back to Luna.

"My Imperatrix, is this your domain?" Champion asked.

Luna chuckled. "This is *part* of my domain, but not our final destination. As I told thee earlier, this is a one-way trip. Thou art unlikely to return, but thou art still my subject, and my Champion. However, it is time for thee and Moonlight Mist to start learning that the world has changed, and I have changed along with it." Luna shed the imperial form that they were familiar with, and they gasped in surprise at the princess' new look.

"My Queen... what are you saying?!" Champion asked as he stared at her.

Blue Streak moved up to him and said with a slight slur, "It means that your world is about to get a whole lot bigger, Batty."

Luna chuckled as Champion reacted to Blue's changed looks also. Then she looked up to the blue-green marble that was Equus, waiting for the right moment before her horn glowed once more.

Back on the ground, Twilight, Leatherwing, Path, Cinder, Roseclaw and Free were waiting around the courtyard. The moon was halfway on the horizon, just starting to rise.

"Is she going to make it, or did she decide to stay a few more days?" Path asked.

"No," Twilight replied, her horn aglow, "I can sense her powering up the spell. She's on the moon right now, and it feels like she's bringing back company."

"How do you know that?" Free asked.

"Because her spell is significantly stronger this time. The most likely way to account for that is extra passengers," Twilight explained with a knowing grin.

Path's eyes went wide as he saw four flashes on the moon, and a few seconds later, a dark purple vertical beam of energy speared to the ground in the middle of the spell array, and they struggled to not get blown away. After a few moments, the energy faded, and Luna stood there smiling, flanked by her companions. Blue Streak was still rather drunk and flopped over. Champion, however, stood there as sturdy as ever. Morning Mist just looked about her in bewilderment.

Leatherwing ran up to Luna, only to stop and stare at Champion who was easily two heads taller than him, had more impressive armour, and was practically all muscle. "You... you're big – bigger than the ex-captain," he gulped.

Champion looked down at Leatherwing. "I am as big as I need to be. I am the Lunar Imperatrix's Champion, Victor of the Lunar Gauntlet, worthy of the highest honour." Champion continued to stare sternly as he opened up his wings, easily dwarfing the smaller thestral.

Cinder went over to Blue and picked him up. "Had a little fun, did you?"

Blue nodded happily and was about to say something before Luna spoke up.

"Let us all go to the main hall. I believe that we all need to welcome Champion and Moonlight Mist to their new home, and begin educating them on life in Griffonia and Equestria."

They all agreed and started walking into the house with Cinder bringing up the rear as she carried her inebriated boyfriend on her back.

Warfist looked up from his desk as Blue entered his office. He nodded and asked gruffly, "I trust that your trip was educational?"

Blue Streak grimaced. "Yeah, and in more than one way. I learned a very important thing while I was there."

"And what would that be?"

"If I'm going to contend with the heavy hitters, I need to get a lot better at combat."

"That does not surprise me. What do you want to do about it?"

Blue reared up and put both his forehooves on Warfist's desk and stared at him seriously. "Stop with your silly 'encouragement' and start teaching me to be a *real* warrior."

Warfist's beak split in a huge grin of satisfaction. "It's about bloody time!"

Chapter 10:
It's About Time!

Weeks passed since the Lunar Festival, and Luna had her work more than cut out for her. Although he was trying with all the determination that earned him his title, Champion was having a hard time adjusting to life in Equestria. For starters he wouldn't give himself a different name. Champion's name was not in fact Champion Twenty; that just signified that he was the champion of the trials, and that he had won twenty times in a row. His real name was Nox Terrorem which, while true to his roots, did little to soothe the panic of the Solar Guards. Luna still shuddered every time she recalled the inauspicious moment when he had encountered her sister. Some of the Solar Guards were *still* recovering. Nox was assigned as Luna's personal guard along with Leatherwing. The ambiguous title made things worse when a few Solar Guards tried to pull rank on him.

Luna and Celestia happened to be talking during the closing moments of the Night Court, when they saw a flood of Solar Guards move down a hallway, heading toward the barracks and then down a side hallway. There was also a large movement of Lunar Guards heading in the same direction.

"Ever have a feeling that something is happening under your nose?" Celestia commented dryly to her sister.

"It has been a while since the guard rivalries were sparked; maybe Nox lit the fire? 'Tis good to have a healthy rivalry as the need to one-up each other keeps them fit, but if another brawl has broken out..." Luna rolled her eyes slightly and sighed.

Celestia grinned widely. "Well you're still on duty at the moment, so you get to take care of it!" Before Luna could protest, Celestia teleported away, most likely to her room.

Luna groaned and teleported herself to the barracks. She had been expecting a minor scuffle, but not the all-out riot that was happening. Thestrals and Solar ponies were involved in a massive brawl, and the stench of alcohol was overwhelming. In the centre of the brawl were the two who had apparently started everything – Nox and Leatherwing. Luna groaned; she would have words with them later, but first things first. She took a deep breath and bellowed out in the Royal Canterlot Voice: **"CEASE THIS AT ONCE!"**

Everyone froze in their place and looked at Luna with trepidation.

"Thestrals – all those on duty, go back to your posts. All others, go to your barracks. My sister and I will have stern words with you all in the morning! Anypony still in this room in three seconds will be on latrine cleaning duty for a month. **GO!**" Her horn lit up threateningly as the Guards of both shifts hastily departed, leaving the recreation area completely abandoned. Luna sighed and started walking back to her quarters, grumbling, "They are the best that Equestria has to offer, but sometimes they act like drunken college foals."

As she reached her room, she noticed that her crystal transceiver was chirping. She hastened over to it and picked it up. "Hello? Princess Luna speaking." She couldn't help but grin when she heard Free Agent on the line.

"Hi, Luna! Are you free for a short talk as well as a request?"

"Night Court has finished, and I have little to do aside from paperwork. I would welcome a respite."

The griffon chuckled and said, "I doubt this will be a respite, but it won't involve stuffy nobles, I can tell you that much. Twilight is fretting over it, so I told her I would ask you about what's going on."

Luna blinked a few times and started to worry. "Hast thou a problem?"

"It's Destined, actually. It's nothing bad, or at least we don't think so. It's not like he's fighting anyone or anything, but you know how he's always liked meditating after you taught him years ago? Well, he's been meditating for about a week straight now. Every now and then his horn lights up, but we don't know what's going on. He seems to be really into it."

She blinked, more startled than worried. "A week continuously? Please tell me that he hath taken breaks?"

Free chuckled nervously. "If he has, we haven't seen him take them. Twilight and Rose are currently curled around him…."

Luna cut Free off as he was about to continue talking. "This is not good. I thought that I had taught him better than that. It is possible that he has lost himself, or at the very least become so disconnected from his sense of time that he has no idea that he needs to focus back on the real world."

Free tried to soothe the worrying alicorn. "I don't think it's nearly so dire. I'm thinking he might have just lost track of time. I was thinking that if he was deep enough in a trance, could you see him in the dreamscape?"

Luna paused to think a moment before responding. "It would depend on the type of meditation he has been doing. The dreamscape is not the same thing, although it is possible that he could have crossed over as his body tired. In any event, 'tis worth a try."

Free perked up a bit. "Thanks! And also, the students are asking about when you are going to come back. The seniors especially loved your astronomy classes, and the stories about them have spread. There are people asking Path when are you going to be a guest instructor again?"

Luna smiled, flattered by the request. "My duties in Canterlot have eased up once more, so tell Path to send a suggested timetable to me so that I can work it into my schedule. As a member of House Path, I feel it's my obligation to teach again, and of course it's a good excuse to visit my herd more often."

Free replied, "I agree. We all miss you, but we know that you have your royal duties."

Luna mused to herself, "'Tis ironic – I once did wish to be the sole princess of Equestria, but now I find myself wishing more time free of the responsibilities of rule. But enough of my wishful thinking – I would like to attempt to commune with my student."

Free chuckled. "Okay! I'll call you later then, Luna?"

Luna smiled. "Agreed. Farewell, Free." She shut down the comm and headed for her bedroom after instructing the Night Guard that she wished not to be disturbed. After making herself comfortable on her bed, she easily slipped into the dream realm and searched for evidence of Destined's presence. With a sigh of relief, she found it and passed into his dreamscape.

The dreamscape was bland to say the least. The alicorn was just floating in a black void, his horn lighting up occasionally as he concentrated on something. He was currently too focused to notice Luna's entry into his dreamscape. The closer she got to Destined, the slower her perception and movement became. It was as if the dreamscape had some kind of complexity that had yet to be made known to her.

Luna studied the dreamscape for a while without interruption. It was never wise to barge in on someone without at least a partial understanding of the situation, but this one was defying her analysis. However, it did not seem to be threatening, so she eventually floated up beside Destined and quietly said, "Good evening, student."

Destined was distracted from his task, and he blinked a few times before looking at Luna with a smile, his horn still brightly lit. "Hi, Auntie! How are you doing today?"

Luna noticed that his eyes were glowing a bright white. Clearly he was channelling something. "I am fine, dear nephew. May I ask thee what thou art doing?"

Instead of answering, he replied, "Can I ask you something?"

Luna smiled encouragingly. "Of course."

"Time – what do you think of it?"

Luna considered the question. "Thou hast chosen a complex subject to discuss. 'Tis a property of the universe, and is as vast as the sky and as fleeting as a moment. We are bound to it, and yet manipulate it in many ways. So tell me, dear Destined, which of these aspects dost intrigue thee right now?"

Destined smiled as he floated at her side. "Time, space, and how we perceive it. Everyone sees time as a line, only flowing in one direction. But then I was reading Twilight's old friendship reports and a few things really interested me, especially causality and the illusion of choice. So I created a model of it to try to figure out what it might be like. It... it's very hard to explain time travel if time is a linear line, because that means that once Future Twilight went back in time, she destroyed Past Twilight's free will."

Luna watched as a single point came into being in the black featureless sky. "One dimension, no length, no height, no width, existing for the smallest determinable length of time – a quantum unit."

Luna looked toward Destined smiling approvingly, wanting to see how developed his idea was.

"Time has inertia. Attempts to make changes will frequently result in no change in the long run. When Mama Twilight attempted to warn her past self of a future problem, she in fact created that problem. That is the classic self-fulfilling prophesy syndrome, but it's also a graphic example of how temporal inertia works. When Starlight Glimmer made far more substantial changes to the time-stream, the results were far more dangerous, and yet eventually the time-stream was restored to its proper course. Temporal inertia acts in many ways, but does not preclude free will. If Mama Twilight had not chosen to fight Starlight's actions, would time have righted itself? That is a matter for debate, although I suspect that you might have some ideas of your own."

"Perhaps, but I would not dream of muddying the waters of thy theory. Go on."

Destined nodded. "I came up with a few ideas to try to explain time travel. That's why I decided to meditate on it for a few hours to try to compute it with all of my capacity. Would you like to see my latest model?"

Luna nodded but couldn't help but chuckle. "I would indeed, but I fear it might take a little longer than thou might think. Thou hast been meditating not for mere hours, but for days! Didst thou not think it strange that I am here conversing with thee? My realm is the world of dreams, not thy mind-scape."

He blinked a few times. "I've been in here for days?! I knew it would take time, but that much?!" He sighed a bit. "Mom is going to kill me!" he couldn't help but groan. "Well, would you like to see anyway before I get grounded?"

Luna snickered and nodded. "The deed is done, so thou might as well show me the fruits of thy labours."

Destined floated around her a few times as he grinned. "The best I can come up with is this: time is not linear like we all think. Instead it is instance based. In an infinitely small unit of time, all that is, was and ever will be occurred. However, we are just experiencing it slowly due to our limited cognitive ability. To ask when something occurs is meaningless as it is *every* time and *all* the time. To ask where is also meaningless because without time to determine distance, all things are both infinitely close and far away."

That one small floating point began to divide and diverge again, lines connecting to them as a rotating tesseract formed in front of them.

Luna thought for a few moments. "Hmm, thou didst mention all that was and all that will be, but what about all that could have been? Remember the alternate realities that Twilight did experience in her struggles with Starlight Glimmer? What of those?"

Destined nodded in acknowledgement and his horn glowed even brighter as he backed up quite a bit from the display. "I actually thought about that. I think that all actions were taken in an instant, creating this!"

The resulting dream construct was truly baffling and the dreamscape struggled for a moment. The infinitely dense, constantly moving... *cloud* was the best way it could described... took Luna a long while to even determine that it was entirely made up of a series of counter-rotating connected points which were always moving and always changing.

"The dekeract – a ten-dimensional theoretical M-space construct. I don't even know how the dreamverse can show this."

Luna winced, realizing that he was in fact borrowing upon her own ability to perceive higher-order magical constructs. "Methinks I know why thou hast lost track of time in the real world. Thou hast not merely envisaged the temporal matrix, but been enmeshed in it. Beware, my student! Even alicorns might get lost amidst its complexity. Thou dost dabble with disaster." The construct slowly rotated, and she could see all of the many inner workings, far more than Destined could ever see.

The alicorn colt continued his explanation. "It is my idea that everything that is, was and ever will be was created in this M-space construct. Twilight wasn't going through time; she was changing her reference point. That's what teleportation is – changing your relative observation point. Instead of shifting your physical body, you have to let the construct shift around you. I think this is why teleporting takes so

much energy and how time travel is out of the reach of almost everyone. They try to push themselves through time, when in reality they just need to change their perception. However, even this is dwarfed by what contains it, and this is the latest step in my progress so far." His horn glowed brighter and brighter as the strain started to build.

Luna gasped "Careful, child! What art thou doing?"

Several of those spheres formed, and then one monstrous form contained them all. By the time the dream construction was finished, something that could never *ever* exist in normal three dimensional space was created. The dream realm was on the verge of buckling under the mental strain being put upon the mind creating it. The sixteen dimensional construct acted like a cage to hold the many star-like points: a septendecapetadakon. Destined panted heavily as he floated in the void, that strange structure resonating and humming as the infinite number of points moved and merged with one another before splitting off once more. "This... this is the forefront of my meditation. Each star-like point is a universe, and the universes grow, form, fade and are reborn inside the overarching space. Beyond this, I cannot fathom what else there could be. This is as far out as I can go. To ask when or where is meaningless; you are everywhere, and you are everywhen. You both are and are not; any identifying relative observation point is rendered moot. You can't even say that you 'are' because there are an infinite number of points where you are, and when you are not."

Luna looked at the humming construct, finding beauty in its

complexity. "Then thou art saying that our concept of time is merely our path through those everywhens, and the inertia that I mentioned is just the most probable of those paths?"

Destined nodded. "It even gets more confusing because our consciousness is traveling along *all* paths. That's why when Twilight and Starlight had their fight, she ran into several different Rainbow Dashes; they represent the different paths she could have taken. So to say that there is Future Rainbow Dash or a Past Rainbow Dash isn't accurate. Rainbow Dash is at everywhere and everywhen and in every-state, but she can just perceive one possible path. Rainbow Dash just *is*."

Luna stared at the projection in front of her. That massive construct was hypnotizing. The more she stared, the more detail she found, and it only urged her to look deeper into it. She realized how deep that one could see was proportional to one's magical strength. Destined couldn't perceive many layers, but Luna had yet to reach her limitation.

The entire thing slowly rotated as Destined floated over, looking somewhat tired. "Are you finished yet? You have been studying it for something like an hour," he said with a smile.

Luna took it all in and stored it in one part of her vast mind to study it in detail later. She arched an eyebrow at him. "Now thou dost know how thou didst end up mired in this for days. I would suggest that if it is thy desire to study this further, thou dost not do so alone. Methinks that thou hast given the scholars much to think about. Right now though, I see that the most likely timeline has very worried parents in it. Unless thou hast something more of urgency to show me, I would suggest that thou withdraw from this dream-state and wake up to the real world." She took a deep breath. "I had best depart thy dreamscape to ease thy transition. Tell thy parents that I shall come to the House forthwith."

Destined nodded and smiled as the constructed faded away. He looked a lot less drained once it was gone. "I'll see ya in person soon, Auntie!"

Luna chuckled softly. "Farewell for the moment. I will see thee anon, and perhaps give thee lessons on the prudent amount of time spent in meditation, no matter thy perception of it!"

When Luna exited the dreamscape, the first thing she noticed was Leatherwing screaming mere inches from her face.

"PRINCESS LUNA, WAKE UP! YOU'RE GOING TO BE LATE FOR EVENING COURT!"

Champion was standing by the doorway, watching to see if Leatherwing's efforts were effective.

Luna just stared at Leatherwing. "What art thou talking about, Leatherwing? Night Court hath ended already this evening."

Leatherwing blinked in surprise. "You have been asleep since yesterday evening, and all day and into the beginning of the next night. Night Court is due to start in five minutes!"

Luna sat up with eyes wide open in shock. "The moon!" Luna looked out her window and saw that the moon was close to where it was supposed to be, but not exactly.

Champion spoke up. "Celestia came by in the morning to see why you didn't lower the moon. I said that you were dealing with a complex situation in the dreamverse, so she lowered and raised it for you, but it seems off."

Luna shook her head. "A mere couple of decades and she gets out of practice!" Her horn glowed and the heavenly body's course was corrected. She then turned back to Champion. "Prepare the court for my arrival. I will be there momentarily. Leatherwing, we shall depart for the court after I make a quick call to House Path. We will be visiting my herd when the night's proceedings are done."

Champion bowed and ran down the hall, accompanied by his retinue of thestrals. Leatherwing started the familiar task of packing some of Luna's travel things, although she didn't require much; most of what she needed was already at the House. After all, it was her home away from Canterlot.

Luna called House Path, and as soon as she heard the griffon changeling on the line, she asked, "Free? Is Destined awake and okay?"

Free laughed, and in the background she could hear Twilight and Rose yelling, most likely at Destined. "Yeah, he woke up, and ended up getting scolded not two seconds after he came to."

"Yes, I have no doubt that he's being chided, but let me just say one thing in Destined's defence – I was equally deceived by the passage of time in his dreamscape, and I had no idea that I was disassociated from my usual awareness. It's a warning for caution on the subject of his meditation, but he has accomplished much. I will be coming over after Night Court to talk about this more. I must run now. Love thee!"

"We'll be waiting here when you show up. See ya later, Hon!"

Luna shut off the crystal comm and galloped to the throne room to start her Night Court.

Chapter 11:
The Test

Lucida put her backpack on as she walked out of her classroom, and she waved goodbye to her friends as she left. Soon after she had exited the room, she saw her sire looking at her with a smile of anticipation. Falling in beside her, he walked along with her down the path.

"So, do you know why I'm here, Lucida?"

"No, Dad. Well, actually, if I had to take a guess, I would assume that it's time for one of your big tests? It's been a while since the last one." Lucida recalled that the last major test from him had been when she was twelve, and she was fifteen now, and she had passed that test easily.

"Oh, you bet, but this is a test unlike any other. You know how last time it was all paper and pencils?"

"Yes…?" Lucida stopped and looked at him suspiciously.

"The Minor Austri Island Chain. You have a week; all your other classes are postponed. Good luck!" Path started to walk off.

Lucida stared uncomprehendingly at her father. "Wait! What… what am I supposed to do with that?!" Lucida yelled, but the earth pony just shrugged and kept walking. Lucida, while not biologically related to Twilight, took after a lot of her herd-mother's mannerisms, and a few feathers tweaked out of place before she turned and ran to the library. All the while, Path just chuckled to himself.

For all of the next day and most of day two, nobody saw much of the hippogriff because she was in the capital library, researching. Eventually the family did see her at dinner on the second day after receiving the challenge, with a scroll and book fort surrounding her and her dinner plate.

"Path, why do you do this to her? She's going to start moulting at this rate." Roseclaw looked over at her daughter who was shovelling food into her beak with one claw and turning the pages of a book on the other.

"Because, these little mental stress tests keep her in top shape, and this test actually matters." Path grinned. "Besides, it's not like Celestia didn't do it to Twilight when she was learning." The earth pony watched Lucida for a while before going back to eating. A few moments later the teen hippogriff's eyes widened.

"Moms!" Lucida yelled out.

"Yes?" Twilight and Roseclaw echoed.

Lucida pointed at Roseclaw. "Can I go to Equestria for a few days?" She then pointed at Twilight "Can you teleport me to Canterlot? I need to talk to Celestia."

Path just grinned even wider as the two females nodded. Roseclaw got up and fetched the comm to contact Celestia. She talked on it for a few moments before giving the claw-up sign to Twilight. Fifteen years of practice had enabled Twilight to greatly stretch her teleportation range, and since she had a large magical signature to lock onto, teleporting something the vast distance was fairly straightforward. With a gradual build-up of power and then a loud pop, the hippogriff was gone.

Free finally piped up, "For the future leader of the House, you're sure putting a lot of pressure on her early on."

Path looked at Free. "I have to get her used to it; tough decisions require tough training. She has to learn to think without me, or any of us for that matter."

Lucida arrived with a huge pop in Twilight's old chambers in the castle where Celestia was sitting waiting for her.

"It is always good to see my former student's daughter. How are you tod-*ack!*"

Celestia was stopped mid-sentence when the hippogriff hugged her tightly, nuzzling into her soft fur slightly. Celestia had always been Lucida's favourite. Epiphany favoured Techbird, Flix and Discord got on together like best buddies, Blue adored Shining, and Destined favoured Luna. It was interesting how their talents and abilities mirrored them all somehow.

"Auntie! I need help! Dad gave me a test but the test is so confusing. It's about the Minor Austri Island Chain. I don't know what the questions are – I just know it's about that!" Lucida looked up with her *huge* eyes.

Celestia realized what was going on in only a few moments, and she smiled. "I shall give you access to the Canterlot geographical archives. It has all that we know about that area."

Lucida squeed, thanked the alicorn, and ran off… the strange sound of both talons and hooves clattering on the floor was amusing to Celestia.

"Oh, Path, you're going to have her do that, are you? You really believe in throwing her in the deep end," Celestia murmured as she walked back to the royal chambers with a knowing smile on her face.

Day three and four passed. Celestia saw Lucida every now and then, and she made sure that the hippogriff was actually eating while in her scroll book fort. It was at lunch during the fourth day that Lucida just huffed, climbed out of her book fort, and looked at Celestia at the other side of the table.

"I've checked all the major records, but I can find nothing significant dated more recently than 150 years ago, and that was a geological survey of the island. I found a similar report in the Griffonian archives. But it's like nobody has been there since!" Lucida exclaimed.

Celestia nodded. "That's probably because nobody has. The Islands were for a short time a topic of a territorial dispute between Equestria and Griffonia, but that died out a long while ago."

"Can we go there to see what's changed since then?" Lucida asked.

"Well I can't. I have things that I need to get done here – you know a princess' work is never done – but I can give you a locator crystal and send you there. Then after, say, twelve hours, I'll lock onto the crystal and teleport you back?" Celestia grinned.

"Yes! Let's do that. Just let me get my things!" She ran off to Twilight's old room, and once she returned, Celestia passed the crystal to the hippogriff girl, and sent her on her way.

Day Seven…

At nine in the morning, Path was waiting at the entrance to the meeting room. Lucida ran up, trying to catch her breath.

"I was wondering if you would show up," Path said with a smile. "Let's go inside, shall we?"

When the two walked in, she could see two ambassadors on opposite sides of the conference table. Based on how everything was set up, this was an official mediation. She had sat in on a few of them when different nations came to House Path to settle deadlocked disputes.

The Griffonian ambassador looked at her with a smile and a nod, as did the Equestrian ambassador.

Path said, "After considering their options, the ambassadors have decided to have their case deliberated by you. The matter of dispute is this: Does the Minor Austri Island chain belong to the Equestrian or Griffonian Nation? In the past week, you have gathered information about both sides without influence from either. Now you get to hear both of them make their cases. You then have an hour to think it all over. Then you give your ruling – your first official, *binding* ruling."

The next two hours were filled with Lucida listening to the two ambassadors give their speeches and the reasoning behind why they thought their nation should have authority over the island chain, and making rebuttals to their counterpart. When they were done, Lucida left to deliberate on it for an hour. When she came back, she was smiling softly.

"I have reached a decision, but first I want to ask you both a question," Lucida stated. "When was the last time your respective countries visited these isles?" Both of the ambassadors paled slightly. "I thought as much. I have somebody with me who has been there his whole life. Please come in, Chief Scruffy."

All three of the other participants looked on as a moderately sized Diamond Dog walked in. He was dressed cleanly and simply. He bowed to both of the ambassadors, and they just blinked in surprise before giving a slight bow back. Lucida handed a gem etched with runes to Scruffy. He put it to his throat and started to speak, and the gem glowed as his words were shifted into a language that they could all understand.

"You came here to ask what the fate of my land would be. I am here to tell you that it is not in *your* power to decide. My people have lived on those islands for many generations. I have heard your words, and why you desire it. Some bird-cats and some ponies came by three generations ago, dug around without permission, and then left, and now you act on their reports. The Canis City State will not be subject to annexation by either the griffons or the ponies. However, despite all of this I have a counter-offer for the both of you."

The diamond dog sat down and waited for the others to do the same. "Lucida tells me she is to be a mediator between all of us. I can tell you this: I will not give up any part of the Canis Islands. However, I am open to the idea of opening up trade ports. You want the mineral goods we possess, and we want trade goods that both of you can offer. Let us deal."

Scruffy nodded to Lucida and she took over.

"Based on the evidence as well as your own testimonials, my ruling is this: Neither the Equestrian Nation or the Griffonian Nation has a claim to the Islands because they are already their own sovereign city state. We are instead ruling that trade agreements be opened with the Canis People so that all three parties can get what they need."

Both the Griffonian and Equestrian ambassador stood up.

"Surely you can't be suggesting we deal with them?" the griffon ambassador demanded.

"They barely even count as a civilization!" the Equestrian ambassador protested.

Lucida slammed her claws down onto the table, hard enough to cause deep gashes as her feathers and fur *poofed* out and her wings opened up in a very aggressive posture. She let out a deafening screech to get everyone to go silent.

"**You will *not* insult the Canis people!**" She said intensely with a glare at the griffon ambassador "**You dishonour yourself and your House!**" She then turned her glare to the pony ambassador. "**Celestia will be displeased that her representative insulted another race.**" She looked to them all and then to her dad. "**My ruling is final. Go back to your leaders and begin drafting trade agreements!**" She slammed the gavel down hard enough to almost break it. All three representatives left the room before Lucida allowed herself to collapse into her chair.

Path rubbed his ear with a hoof and smirked. "You did good, and you passed your test. But next time, please warn me that you're bringing in a third party; I didn't think you were going to take it that far."

Lucida, however, was still slightly shaking in her chair. "I... I wasn't expecting to start yelling at them. I just... is this what you have to deal with all the time when you are in your talks?"

Path sat down next to her. "Sometimes it's worse, sometimes it's easier, but I'm glad you looked at all sides before making a ruling."

Lucida just smiled a bit, her feathers and fur smoothing out. "Did you know about the diamond dogs, Dad?"

Path smiled knowingly. "You don't think that absolutely no one ever visited those islands in a century and a half, do you? It's visited regularly by some crafty merchant sailors who have kept it mostly secret because it was in their best interest to do so. I learned of that when the House was approached for mediation on the matter, and I looked into it closer. The diamond dogs were being cheated, but with the claim pushing everything out into the open, they'll be treated more fairly from now on. Now – how did *you* find out that the diamond dogs were on the island?"

Lucida smiled. "While I was in Equestria, I asked Celestia to send me there so I could look at the place myself. I never thought of asking the sailors."

"Ah, I see. Let's not tell Mom about that part. I don't think she would be happy with the idea of you being teleported halfway around the world blindly." Path pushed Lucida up to her feet. "Come on, let's go. We need to give Scruffy a proper welcome before he goes back to his people."

As they walked out of the conference room, Lucida asked, "Dad, what if I hadn't learned about them, and made the wrong decision? You said that it would be binding."

Path nodded. "I had confidence that you would learn the truth somehow, but in the event that you didn't... well, the ruling isn't final until the meeting is adjourned. I would have offered an advisory before you banged the gavel. I would not let you make a mistake due to lack of relevant information, but I had to give you every opportunity to do everything yourself. I'm very proud of you, Lucy. You're going to make a fine House leader when I retire."

Lucida smiled and leaned into her father's flank. "Thanks, Dad. Do that to me again and I'll pluck your mane bald!"

Path guffawed and nuzzled her. "Deal!"

Chapter 12:
Clandestine Conversation

This was one of Epiphany's favourite times of the week – shortly after school had let out on Friday afternoon, and the population of Ponyville was winding down from a week of honest toil. One of the preferred places to do so was the Java 'n Jazz Cafeteria where many ponies, changelings, and even a couple of griffons could be found quietly talking to each other in small groups while enjoying the shop's fare. The Cafeteria served an excellent range of hot and cold drinks, and a variety of foods from cake to light meals. Some were hanging around just enjoying the positive emotions in the air, the overall calm vibe being enhanced by the smooth jazz being played by the house band.

During a pause in the music, the oboe player said, "Hello, I am Smooth Beats, with Resonant Thorax on the drums, and on the piano is Tickling Ivory. We are *Catch the Relax*, and we're just going to keep on playing for your pleasure for the next two hours. To all the students who have joined us this night, try to keep calm during the difficult finals ahead." The band then eased into another quiet tune.

The sixteen-year-old filly in her guise of a unicorn with tan fur and pink mane walked toward her usual sunken-in booth where she relaxed on the plush seats and set most of her books down gently on the table and the seats surrounding her. She reserved this anonymous identity to escape the recognition and fuss that normally accompanied the princess of the Chrome Hive, and while other changelings could recognize that she was a changeling, as long as she didn't utilize the hive-mind, they were unable to distinguish her from any other Chrome Changeling. She took a deep relaxing breath before sipping carefully on her steaming hot tea. Pif sighed in satisfaction before regarding the books that she had brought with her. High-level mathematics, astronomy, resource management and big business administration were a few of the subjects on her plate today – not everyone's idea of fun, but like one of her mothers, she never could get enough of book-learning. She closed her eyes for a few moments to take in the atmosphere. "Mmm... this is nice."

A middle-aged unicorn mare with a blue-gray coat and green mane approached the booth carrying a cup of espresso coffee and a bag of cakes. She observed the teenage unicorn for a long moment with a sly smile before finally speaking up. "Pardon me, it's quite busy tonight, and all the booths and tables are occupied. May I join you at yours?"

Epiphany looked up at the unicorn, smiled and nodded. Her senses told her that this was another changeling, but that was hardly unusual in Ponyville, and even though she was princess of the hive, she certainly did not personally know every single one of them. A quick peek into the hive-mind would have informed her, but it would also give herself away, and she simply was not that curious anyway. She levitated all of the books that she had piled up on one side to stack on those on the other side, leaving room for the mare to put down her cup and the bag of cakes that she was carrying. "The more the merrier," she said rather lazily, the calming emotions of the room getting to her and making her more relaxed than normal. "My name is Vibrant Ledger, what's yours?"

The mare put her coffee and cake on the cleared area and sat down. She gave Epiphany a wide smile and said, "Oh, I've been called many things, my dear, but right now why don't you just call me *Grandma*?"

The filly blinked in surprise as she was shaken out of her calm by the mare's tone and sly smile. She started to piece things together. '*Grandma...? No way!*' She almost squealed in delight, but she restrained herself and said in a hushed tone, "GramGram? How are you here? *Why* are you here? Moms and Dads want your head on a pike!"

Chrysalis raised an eyebrow questioningly. "What? Can't a grandmother pay a social visit to her granddaughter?" She looked around approvingly, blithely ignoring the frantic tone in Pif's voice. "And such a tasty atmosphere to meet you too. Seems like the perfect place to me."

Epiphany was stunned that Chrysalis would take such a risk to visit. "You hardly look any different from your colouration in your natural form – aren't you worried that you'll be recognised?"

"Pfft! Ponies *look*, but they don't *see*!" Chrysalis scoffed. "I've been using this disguise for a long while, and no one ever picks up on that."

"I'm still worried, but I'm glad you decided to pay me a visit. One of my first memories was of you looking down at me and giving me that doll. I still have Mr. ClickClick somewhere. Anyway, have you been well?" She was now letting the atmosphere soak back into her as she calmed down with a smile.

Chrysalis chuckled softly. "Ah yes, I remember that day well – I rather enjoyed bringing that gift to you. My agents reported that you were seldom seen without it. I was a little surprised that they let you keep it though. The aftermath was quite a hoot." She took a sip of the hot coffee and nodded approvingly. "They still serve the best coffee in Ponyville here. Anyway, to answer your question, I have indeed been well, and getting better every year."

Pif giggled a bit. "Oh, they were *so* mad, but after they scanned it

about a million times, they gave it back to me. Mr. Clickclick went everywhere with me." She let out a happy sigh before she smiled and looked back at Chrysalis, raising an eyebrow inquiringly. "I'm glad that you're well, but what do you mean you're getting better? You seem fine right now?" She took a sip of her tea and waited for an answer.

Chrysalis gave her a melodramatic sigh. "After the rather rude setback that your mother gave me, I've had to do a lot of rebuilding. It's not easy starting all over again, but at least I had the benefit of experience, while my daughter... well, I sometimes despair for what she's done with her legacy. So I've been slowly laying plans to correct that, and I'd love it if you would be part of them."

Pif let out a sad sigh. "While I don't completely agree with how they went about the Crystal Empire situation, I don't particularly agree with your part either." She crossed her arms. "You both could have done things differently, and that would have saved a lot of bloodshed. The Blue Hive has been getting a lot better though since being reborn as the Chrome Hive. Actually, Dad is trying really hard to push the hive onto me so that he can go off adventuring again. I already know what direction I want to take it. Dad doesn't realise it, but I have a few citizens directly linked to me. By the way, I don't call them drones; I call them citizens because it's less demeaning. Anyway, they are researching in libraries as we speak." She waved her hooves expansively. "Lately I have been consumed with this desire to know *everything*."

Chrysalis nibbled on a cake as Pif talked, and she licked a few crumbs from her lips. "If you want to know everything, perhaps you should spend some time with me and learn what it is to be a *true* queen? Gossamer certainly doesn't! Maybe you would understand my motivations better then. It's been my dream for a long time to unite this world under my leadership, and pass that on to... well... *you* now. The very fact that you have some dron... ah, citizens... under your control shows that you take a lot after me. You know what you want, and you act accordingly."

Epiphany smiled. "But see, here's the thing. As civilisations become more and more advanced, they are also more and more resistant to absolute monarchy, which is what you are suggesting. The only way to maintain a hold on the entire world would be to keep the entire world in the dark. I think that you as well as a few other changeling queens that are up there in age are old-style changelings, traditionalists with a strict hierarchy. I might go so far as to say that you are a changeling supremacist. If truth be told, Dad is a pretty bad queen because he didn't want to be one in the first place, but he still has everyone's best interests at heart. That being said, your end goal to unite the world is a goal that I share. I just think our ways of doing it are completely different." She took a sip of her tea. "I'm not saying that your way is totally wrong, or right; neither is mine, but my way is a one that has yet to be tried. So yes, I have eleven currently working for me, three of whom are reading in the Griffon Kingdom, four in the Crystal Empire, and four are hounding the princesses to give me access to the restricted Canterlot Library wing."

Chrysalis pondered those words while sipping her coffee. Eventually she replied, "I admire your proactive approach – seeking knowledge has ever been the Blue Changelings' hallmark, and knowledge is power. You talk about absolute monarchy as if it's a bad thing, and yet it has worked very well for centuries. I do not see a reason to change that now. Just because I have failed to do so yet only means that I have yet to find the right approach. With my experience and your resources once you take over control of your hive, we can achieve that goal of uniting the world under us."

Epiphany let out another sad sigh. "But as education and technology improve, it becomes increasingly difficult to control a world population and renders an absolute monarchy obsolete. Even the princesses are attempting to move away from it, one resolution at a time. An empire's stability decreases in proportion to its size, which leaves only two options: it either becomes a dictatorship where you need an increasingly large police force to keep the masses in check, or you give more and more concessions to keep things stable until you are nothing more than a figurehead." She smiled. "My route is to become more of a technocracy. Explore several key markets, monopolize them, then use that monopoly to exert pressure on foreign powers. It's not enough to outright control them, but if they want the newest and most efficient thing, they will listen to what I have to say, using their own greed to get what I want." She grinned a bit before she shook her head. "I'm really not that dark, I promise! I just want to begin a massive technological revolution once I'm in charge."

Chrysalis beamed proudly. "Don't put yourself down, granddaughter – those sound like perfectly wonderful plans of domination. However, I feel that they would be so much easier to implement if you start from a position of power. First establish your leadership, *then* make your approaches with the illusion of freedom. Working in the background is a true changeling trait and one that you should use to your advantage. One does not have to sit on a gleaming throne in a showy castle on a mountaintop to be the undisputed power in the land." She smirked as she finished off her coffee. "Just ask the citizens of Saddle Arabia if they are free. They will give you a hearty affirmation… and do exactly as I want them to."

Pif blinked in surprise. "*Your* hive controls Saddle Arabia?" She stared at Chrysalis for a long moment before she finally realized what was going on. "I think we have a fundamental breakdown in understanding. This is why we start off on the same page, but then we diverge." She rubbed her temples with her hooves. "See... I want ponies, and griffons, and even my own citizens to *actually* be free to do as they wish, as opposed to the illusion of freedom. I'm concerned that you have already taken over a country that Path and Free are currently in negotiations with." She sighed again and sipped her tea. "I don't want to *dominate*, I want to *thrive*, and to do that requires a *lot* of math. So much math!" she added with a groan and rubbed her eyes. "Anyway, I feel that I can reduce our divergent trains of thought with one question."

Chrysalis frowned. "We have always thrived *by* dominating, so that is meaningless to me, but let me hear your question anyway."

Pif snorted. "According to the other five queens, your statement is false. Generally in science, when six independent sources come up with answers, and five have the same answer while one has a different one, the different answer is considered an error and discarded. Anyway, my question is this: What are ponies?"

Chrysalis was perplexed. Knowing her granddaughter, the obvious answer was not what she was looking for, but it seemed like the only correct one. "They are food."

Pif grinned and decided to see if she could outmanoeuvre her grandma. "I agree. Surprised?"

Chrysalis blinked uncomprehendingly. "Then what was the point of your question?"

She picked up her cup and set it on the table between herself and Chrysalis. "This is a pony. This pony is full of love." She moved the cup around. "La, la, la.... Here comes a changeling." She sipped some of the tea from the cup and set it back down. "Now – would you say that this cup pony has less love than before?"

"Obviously."

"So now you come along." She took another sip. "And a lot more changelings come around." She took a longer long sip. "She can't explore, she can't grow as a person." She took more and more sips, naming off consequences each time that Chrysalis would cause by taking over. She set the empty cup down. "Would you agree that this cup pony is empty, there is no love, there is no tea?"

Chrysalis smirked. "But ponies are not cups of tea." She picked up an apple from the bowl of fruit on the table. "They are like an apple tree – harvest all the apples and they just grow more the next season."

Pif's pupils dilated as she grinned. Chrysalis had fallen for it! "And you are correct... unless you harvest so many apples that you harm the tree to the point it stops bearing any more fruit." She leaned in with a grin. Chrysalis might remember this look from a report from one of her drones; it's the look Epiphany got when she thinks she's winning. "You can break a pony to the point where they cease to function and become just husks. No love; no foals; just a shell going through the motions until they die. The last 'season', to use your analogy. What will you do then, GramGram, with your barren orchard? Move on to peaches?" She made a griffon crooning sound. "Pears?" She made a dragon growl. "With your method, eventually you will have the world, but a world of nothing, and the last hunger will set in."

Chrysalis' temper was fraying. This conversation was not achieving what she had hoped when she had walked in. "Plant more trees then!" she snarled.

Pif shrugged. "But you have eaten all the apples, pears, and peaches. Where will you get the seeds to begin again? Will you try to raid the other hives? It won't matter because with the planet barren, there will be no redemption, and all will eventually die. That is why I believe my way is more efficient in the long run. We don't dominate, but we will have monopolized the things they think they need for everyday life. Monetize love; create a changeling trading market; make it so that the ponies pay love for goods and services. Their lives improve, the cup overfills, and the hive profits." Her tone changed; she actually really liked Chrysalis and the old queen could sense it. "I guess I'm the middle ground between you and Gossamer. She doesn't like my ideas either. It's why I'm not sharing them over the hive-mind anymore."

Chrysalis just stared at Epiphany for a long while before she started chuckling, then breaking out into outright laughter. A few of the other patrons turned and stared at her for a moment before rolling their eyes at the weird mare. When Chrysalis calmed down, she said, "I love your deviousness, but you will find that that enough is *never* enough. I would share my power with you, granddaughter, but that's as far as I would go." She picked up her coffee and swigged it one gulp. She put the cup down and continued. "I will sip or I will gulp at my will because unless I have it all, I have nothing." She stood up. "I have enjoyed our little conversation. We must do so again sometime. I really want some more of that… coffee."

Pif gave her a happy smile and got up. "You always know where I like to hang out, GramGram. You should visit me more if you feel like it." Still grinning, she decided to take one more blatantly playful jab at her grandmother before she left. "I do hope that later on you decide to pay *my* hive a visit." She gave Chrysalis a warm hug. After all that had been said, she still regarded her rather favourably; maybe even more so than before.

Chrysalis smirked. "Now that will be the day! Farewell, Granddaughter. Make me proud." She turned to leave, but paused and looked over her shoulder. "But don't get in my way." She then exited the cafeteria, her bag of cakes floating in her magic after her.

Pif turned back to her books and murmured, "I'll try, GramGram, but I suggest you don't get in *mine*!"

Chapter 13:
The Fall

The Need

It had started slowly at first – the need to know! Nobody understood it, not even when Epiphany tried to explain it to others. Her mind was a mini-nexus, capable of being the next hub in the new Chrome Hive, and she craved to make full use of it. To this end, she had pursued many avenues of inquiry, often with the assistance of Techbird, but all with the same goal – knowledge!

Pif had been working on her latest experiment, delving into the nature of the hives and how their limited-range communication worked. For months she had been devising various theories with Techbird, and hours upon hours were spent in their lab. The prototype device had ended up being nearly half the size of the large room, and merely describing what it was could easily take several pages if it was publicized. Basically though, it was an arcano-harmonic resonator, able to mimic a new kind of wave that Techbird had been exploring. More testing was needed though; a *lot* more testing. It looked like the she was going to be putting in long nights from here on out.

Chrysalis was going about her business and generally feeling the condition of the hive as she worked. She had the Saddle Arabian royal family under her hoof, but it needed her attention occasionally to ensure it stayed that way. Her hive got to enjoy the tribute it received from them, and she was happy with the satisfaction level of her drones, a far cry from the nearly mindless hordes that she had previously raised.

So what was distracting her right now? From the fringe of her hive network, Chrysalis could feel… *something*. Given the distance that Saddle Arabia was from Griffonia, it was much too far to get anything but an impression of feelings.

The queen narrowed her eyes as she contemplated from her throne room. "What is happening over there that pricks on my consciousness so?" In the end, what else could she do but dispatch agents to investigate the cause?

Today was the day; Pif knew it! She just had to tune it... come on... almost there... **got it**! Her eyes went wide as the device seemed to resonate with her mini-network, and it suddenly expanded hugely, strengthening all of the links until she could hear the minds of some of her hive's furthest members. She clearly sensed one reading a book on old Crystal Kingdom history in Canterlot before the system's power breaker tripped, and the network lost all of its artificial intensity. What she didn't realize was that her mini-network wasn't the only one affected.

Back in the Blue Hive, far away from the western world, Chrysalis was meeting with her Griffonian agents, and one had a smile of satisfaction on his muzzle. He told Chrysalis how Pif was currently working on an experiment, toying with the nature of the hive network, as well as trying to boost transmission strength. The strange sensations that Chrysalis had felt were the result of those experiments. It was apparently a black project, so finding out about it had been extremely difficult, and the agent had been justifiably proud of his success.

Just then the old queen felt it, but just for a brief moment. If it had been anybody else, or if she had been distracted, she would have missed it, but there was a flicker and for a brief moment one of her furthest drones on her network dimmed and faded out of existence, only to appear again stronger than usual before reducing back to normal. Chrysalis smiled as she realized the implications of those experiments. Communications was a powerful tool, and in her hooves, it could advance her plans immensely.

The next breakthrough came a week later when, for some reason, she actually *heard* the thoughts of one of her agents on the House Path team. From the fog of distance, the one drone lit up like a star, causing confusion from the rest of the much closer hive. It only lasted for a few seconds, but the words Chrysalis heard were: "...the nymph is starting her..."

So many questions unanswered! Chrysalis was concerned. What was her granddaughter doing? How was she making this happen? If Epiphany was experimenting with Chrome Changelings, how was it that Chrysalis' Blue agent's connection was suddenly amplified enough for her to hear its thoughts briefly?

A few days later, one of her drones on the fringe of the network started dimming and brightening, never fading away but never becoming as bright as before. A few days after that, one of her 'lings from the House Path mole taskforce ran into her throne room.

"My Queen! I bring news about your granddaughter!"

The infiltrator seemed to be extremely well fed, far more than was normal for one of her new breed of soldier-harvesters. This aroused Chrysalis' suspicions. "Well? Don't keep me waiting!"

"Her experiments! She's been uncovering the underlying properties of how a hive-link and the network works, and we believe she's made a breakthrough! She somehow found out about us, perhaps through those same experiments, but she didn't out us or hurt us... well, not intentionally."

Chrysalis frowned. "You are supposedly my best infiltrators, and yet '*somehow*' you were discovered and used. This information that you bring had better be very useful, or else I might have to replace you... permanently!" she said with a hiss. Then she smiled benevolently. "So, my granddaughter has apparently achieved something thought impossible. Tell me more."

The drone looked up at Chrysalis, locking eyes with her, somewhat afraid. "She told me to say, '*Hello, GramGram. I see you.*' " The drone's eyes went wide as green magic flames started climbing up his legs, beginning a transformation, and its position on the hive network lit up light a blinding star. Several other changelings had lit up as well, each further from the hive than the next, strung out along a line that led towards the griffon kingdom. It looked like a link of five changelings, each burning up love energy at a prodigious rate. The drone in front of her was gradually transforming, but it was taking longer than normal and was burning a lot more love than it should.

Chrysalis smiled broadly. She had already suspected that her agent might not be fully hers anymore, and it seemed her suspicions were about to be vindicated. "Hello, Granddaughter."

The drone fully shifted into Pif's hybrid form which occasionally blurred a bit as she grinned up at Chrysalis. It looked like she was talking, maybe to one of the drones in the link. "Maximum communication duration... 91 seconds. Signal variance... within expectations." Her grin widened. "I would say something witty, but this is the first time this has fully worked. Are you wondering how I was able to do this?" The form blurred and reformed.

"Of course, dear child. You have done something very new, and potentially very helpful to my plans. Which begs the question – why are you showing it to me?"

The form shifted and shimmered a few times. "Because I wanted to see you, GramGram." She started to walk around the larger queen as she smiled. "I also wanted to let you know what I've been up to."

There was a lot more activity on the hive network, far more than there should be, the entire network was confused and chaos was starting to erupt.

"As your agent probably has told you by now, I have been looking into the nature of the hive network, figuring out how it works at its most basic level, trying to find out why communication diminishes with distance and whether it could be amplified... questions like these!"

"And you obviously made a breakthrough." Chrysalis smiled slyly. "Perhaps something that I can glean from my agent once you're done with him."

Pif chuckled. "Oh, he's just the end point, but I'll tell you what I'm doing anyway, GramGram. I've amplified your drone's communication signal while I'm using your other agents as relays to him so I can gain access via the remaining drone that I still have here in my laboratory. They are still yours – I won't steal from you, GramGram. I'm just *borrowing* them. I figure it's only fair, right?" Pif's grin grew wider. "After all, you have been spying on me, so it's reasonable that I return the favour. You might get things from this drone, but right now I'm copying everything that's on your hive network from the point you rebuilt it onward."

The reason for the chaos and the nearly maxed-out network activity was explained as Pif's grin darkened. "I know where you are. I know the numbers you command. I know your strengths and your weak points. I know your plans. *I know it all!* However, it's not enough, GramGram. I need to know *more*, and now that I know this works with a similar network, I need to see if I can do this with the others. I *will* know *everything!*" The form flickered again as Pif reached up and gave Chrysalis a hug. "But I won't do anything to harm you with what I know. You're my GramGram!"

Chrysalis stiffened at Pif's boast. Suddenly it all made sense. Her agent was now the relay that not only let Pif communicate with her, but to also draw upon the hive-mind while Pif distracted her with the chat. At first she was furious at the invasion, but then she suddenly broke into loud laughter. "Well done, Epiphany. I knew that you would achieve great things, but even I had no idea that you would do something like this. You are indeed the granddaughter I deserve. Contact me again when you wish to ally yourself with me to advance your plans."

Pif smiled as her form flickered again. "Poke into this one's mind for your Hearth's Warming gift once the network has stabilized. Only five seconds left. See you later, GramGram." Pif's form suddenly burned off and the drone collapsed to the ground, panting like it had just run a marathon. Chrysalis watched the link break apart, and the drones that made the link up were very dim after having burned up so much love to maintain the connection. None of her drones had been destroyed, nor removed from her control, so it appeared that Pif could 'ride' on the network but could not grab and take the members of it.

The drone looked up at her weakly. "My Queen... what happened?"

Chrysalis frowned at the drone. "What happened? You compromised my entire hive and gave away all its secrets. There is only one reason why I won't kill you right now."

The drone looked shocked and horrified. It tried to speak, but terror locked him up. Eventually he managed to squeak, "Why?"

"Because you still have something I want!" Chrysalis' force of will knocked the drone to its knees, and its mind opened up to her.

The drone began to scream as his mind was forcefully stripped of its memories. It looked like there was one especially strong memory. He was looking at a chalkboard with Pif talking to one of her supervisor drones. "Now if we had a reliable source of pure sand of this type, we could use this process to create a new kind of glass. Without getting too technical, it's a multifaceted lattice that allows love to be stored in a solid form with a density several times greater than that of even the most advanced amorphous love gels." She tapped the board a few times. "I need that sand! Go and figure out where I can find it!"

All of the formulas and tables were on the board, and the supervisor rubbed his head with concern. "That's going to take a lot of sand, and a lot of energy to fuse it; how would we get so much without raising flags with Free and Iridia?"

"I'm not sure yet. Just find me a source and I'll worry about it later."

Chrysalis chuckled. If there was anything that Saddle Arabia had in abundance, it was many varieties of sand. "Thank you, Granddaughter," she murmured to herself.

When she had finished securing every last bit of the drone's knowledge, she released it, and it collapsed to the floor in a groaning heap. "Thank you for you services, but they will no longer be required." She then powered up her horn and blasted it to ashes. "And you shall not be of service to my granddaughter ever again either." She turned to an attendant. "Recall all my other spies. They are going to be 'retired' also."

As the attendant hastened to do Chrysalis' bidding, she smiled to herself. "My dear Epiphany, you aren't the only queen to withhold critical information from the hive-mind." She then burst out into maniacal laughter that went on for far too long.

The Disagreement

Free passed a tray of cookies to Path as they enjoyed their favorite drinks. "By the way, Pif's up to twelve drones now." He might not like being a queen, but he was not a fool either.

Path looked over at Free as he set his newspaper down. "She's not being the very stealthy about it, is she? I mean a blocked-off section of the hive mind – I imagine it would have been the equivalent of me putting a tape line in the bedroom."

Free chuckled. "She's good, but not experienced at subterfuge yet."

Path rolled his eyes. "Can you figure out what the twelve are up to? I don't imagine they would be spies, but I am rather curious."

Free grinned knowingly. "When I have thousands of eyes everywhere that are all connected to me, I don't need to assign any one drone to watch. They *all* do, and what they don't see directly, can be deduced. Anyway, it looks like she's trying to accumulate knowledge and manipulate that to build a power base that's separate from the Hive and the House, so when she takes over, she can leverage it to her advantage. However, as far as I can see, she's doing it in a way that doesn't hurt others, so I'm just watching for now to see how it plays out."

Path raised an eyebrow "Why is that? I mean when she's old enough, you're just going to pass the hive to her anyway... Oh... she wants to get a power base that Princess Iridia doesn't know about." He brought his hoof to his chin and thought for a few moments. "You know she has been talking about technology and the like – maybe she's planning a massive innovation boom once she's in control, and she doesn't want the Green Hive to steal her thunder?"

Free nodded. "Sounds very likely. She's very pragmatic, and strong in her beliefs that she has the right answers. She wouldn't want any others distorting her plans. Iridia would try to make her see a more traditional point of view, so she side-steps that possibility. However, she's trying to do the same with us, and she needs some balancing viewpoints, otherwise she could eventually become a tyrant. A benevolent one, perhaps, but still a tyrant."

"Well, when you think about it, it kind of makes sense right? I mean she seems to take more after Techbird and Warfist than us. I try to guide her, but she doesn't need me to help her with languages; she just takes it off the hive network and *bam* – she knows more languages than me. She gets frustrated with you because she can feel that you don't want to be queen; Luna is busy with Destined, while Twilight and Rose are always busy with Lucida." He sighed. "We need to spend time with her to get her to even out a bit. At the rate she's going, all she's going to see is numbers and figures. Less of a Queen and more of an administrator, you know?"

"Exactly. I think she's going to be a little bit shocked when I *don't* hand over the Hive to her." Free smirked when he saw Path's expression. "Don't look at me like that! I might not like being the queen of the hive, but despite what Pif might think otherwise, I'm not going to drop it into her lap until I'm sure she's ready. As you pointed out, she's obsessed with Techbird, and the other kids have their favorites also. I propose we switch things about. Pif will have to spend time with Luna and you, and the others will have to switch around also. I don't expect them to be converted to other ways of thinking, but hopefully they'll find some balance to theirs."

Path chuckled a bit. "I'm worried though; if she's already calculating that Iridia might be an issue, I don't know how much she's factored you and me into things. She might not take it well if she doesn't get control of the hive when she turns eighteen. It might cause the entire thing to blow up in our faces." He folded the newspaper and shook his head. "I don't see Pif enjoying time with Luna and myself."

"I never promised Pif the hive at any age. I've only ever said that I wanted her to have it when she was ready. She's the one who has been assuming that she'd get it when she came of age. Anyway, liking the switch-around is not an obligation of her education. Some things we all need to learn the hard way. We sure did, remember? Luna especially, and that's why I reckon she's the best one to get Pif to understand that she has to be able to see things from different perspectives. Until then, Pif could be as big a problem as Nightmare Moon in her own way. I dunno - I'm not omniscient. I do worry a lot though."

"There is another thing I noticed, Free. Are you keeping track of all of your tunnellers? Normally they are all below ground extending the hive, but I saw two of them wandering to the eastern part of Ponyville a few days ago. Are you building something over there?"

Free narrowed his eyes as he looked at Path and smirked. "What do you think I'm up to?"

Path rolled his eyes. "I don't think it's you. I'm thinking that maybe Pif is trying to set something up, and she's banking on the fact that you can't zoom in on every drone you have unless something big happens. The twelve she has might be functioning as decoys."

Free looked thoughtful. "Hmm... She's right that I can't be checking on all my drones all the time, but I do have supervisor drones for that purpose. I can have them look into that discreetly."

Path shrugged. "I was figuring we could just go for a walk and check it out ourselves."

Free pondered that suggestion. "It might be a bit suspicious if she sees both of us there." Magic fire flared and Free was replaced by a teenage earth pony mare. "But if you're showing around a new student perhaps?"

Path looked Free over. "Yeah, that could work. I could be showing you the local sights since it was near the library?"

"Lead on, Teacher!" Free said in a cute filly voice.

Path rolled his eyes slightly as he walked out of the main hall and into the outdoors. He walked alongside the filly as they crossed through the quad. As they passed by a group of ponies, Path said, "So as you can see, Star Flower, the grounds that we have allocated for agri-science are among the biggest in Equestria. Since this branch is in an area where there are primarily herbivores, we catered our programs primarily toward them. Likewise if you decide to transfer to our main campus in Griffonia, you would have the option to take animal husbandry or hunting classes, non-sapient species of course." Path kept walking with her toward one side of the campus, the side that wasn't very developed yet.

Free trotted around looking about like an eager schoolfilly. "Ooh! I love it! But what's that new structure going up over there? More classrooms?"

Path chuckled as he walked toward the structure with the filly. Free saw a burrower changeling go inside and shut the door. However it failed to latch properly and the door creaked open again. "Hmm. Well, as you can see, this is one of our maintenance rooms. There are times when we need to set these up..." Path trailed off as he opened the door and waited for Free to come in with him.

Free hesitated, knowing that if she got too close, the burrowers would detect that she's a changeling too. "Is it safe to go on a work site? They might not like us going in there." She hoped that Path got the hint.

Path nodded. "Ah, you're correct. Well, let me just tell you that usually what's going on in there is that they are just working on the grounds and what-not." He closed the door and started to walk back toward the castle.

However, Free did not follow. She closed her eyes to concentrate on the hive-mind and detect how many changelings were nearby, and what type. She could tell that there were about thirty burrowers and three supervisor drones directly below them. Exactly how far below them was still an unknown. However, as she pinged the hive-mind, she could feel the state of Pif's signature change, from focused to extremely agitated. She broke off and hastened after Path who remained unaware that any of this was going on, and continued giving a fake speech about the campus' agri-science program. They walked back into the main room where they started, only to find a very angry Pif waiting for them.

Free came to an abrupt halt as she saw Pif too late, and she knew the jig was up. Free changed back to his normal griffon self and asked, "Something bothering you, Daughter?"

Pif was in her normal earth pony form, ears folded back against her head. "There was a 91.8 percent chance you would have just accepted the twelve that we both knew I sectioned off from the hive, and would leave it at that. Why won't you let me have any privacy to work? This is important!" She stomped her front hooves on the ground in frustration.

Free shrugged. "An 8.2% chance of non-acceptance is a serious risk. It's not that you want to keep things from me that bothers me, because all teenagers do that. It's part of growing up, even if you're a changeling, or maybe especially if you're a changeling queen brought up in a herd. No, it's because you're running a double blind that made your actions suspicious. That's not mere teen angst but deliberate subterfuge. At this point, I suggest you start being more honest with us, or we might just get genuinely annoyed instead of merely concerned."

Pif was a teen, and to make matters worse, she was a teen changeling queen, which meant her emotions were reeling out of control as she paced around, shifting forms every few seconds as she spoke, half to herself and half to Free. "You want me to be honest? Fine I'll be honest! *He won't like what you have to say.* He doesn't have to!" She looked at Free. "Do you know how many things can go wrong at any given time and wreck everything? I've been doing the math – so much math! Do you know that if the percentage of changeling and pony birth rates vary by more than a few percent, it becomes an unsustainable situation?" She shifted into her griffon form which looked a lot like Techbird but a slightly different coloration. "In order for society to continue, there has to be rules. I made *four* rules to guide my research. One – Harmony triumphs over all! Two – the Lunar and Solar Diarchy must never fall! Three – the Crystal Kingdom must always remain strong and independent of all other countries! Four – the Nightmare must never be allowed to take another host!" She shifted again to her changeling form. "Do you know how hard it is to calculate *everything* that might lead to one of those rules being broken!"

Path cringed. "She's having a Twilight-style freak out."

Free just sighed. "So you like absolute rules? I have one - absolutes fail absolutely." He walked over to Pif, wrapped a wing around her, and exerted a calming force that he hadn't had to use in a long while. "Let's have a look at those rules, shall we? Number one - Harmony is a balance, not an absolute. You must always work at keeping a balance, and be prepared to shift your stance. Number two - Both Celestia and Luna disagree with you, and they have vastly more experience than all of us put together. They are Aspects of Harmony, and know that the ultimate good of the world might be something other than the diarchy, even if it's the best thing right now. Number three - the Crystal Kingdom is the guardian of the Heart, not its keeper. If it sets itself apart from other countries, it might risk alienating them. A strong alliance might be the better solution. Number four - well, you really should check with Twilight about that one. Your mother probably knows best that even the worst can possibly be saved. The Nightmare is imbalanced, which is why Harmony can abolish it, but perhaps if it finds balance, it too can be a force for good. How can you be sure if you don't try?"

Pif was able to calm down a little as she was influenced by that soothing force, but she was still agitated and fretting. "I... I... know, but the balance needs to be maintained. There are ways to ensure that Harmony is maintained no matter what. If Celestia and Luna fall, then who would raise the moon and the sun? The resulting climate shift from their positions being frozen would be unsustainable." She was starting to panic again. "The Nightmare is the single largest cause of disharmony short of Discord pre-reformation. Nightmare cannot be destroyed." She squirmed in Free's embrace. "I need more data! I need more input! If I have enough information, I can think of every scenario!"

Path had watched and listened with concern. Now he approached and put a hoof on Epiphany's shoulder. "Pif, not even the gods can think of every scenario, and we're not gods. Worse still, you're trying to do everything by yourself, and that's not Harmony, so your premise is fundamentally flawed. Look at our herd - our family consists of ponies, griffons, changelings, a dragon, and even one of the divine Aspects. We've been pretty happy together because we respect and work with each other, not all trying to do our own thing. I suspect that you have some excellent ideas to improve everyone's lives, but darling, you can't and shouldn't try to do it by yourself. You like quoting odds? I predict a 100% chance of failure through any number of means if you don't work with everyone else and use their interests and talents to best effect."

Pif kept squirming but she was slowly becoming calmer. "Mmm... I should make you link to my network... copy the info you managed to get from the Green Hive... then do the same to Luna and Celestia. With centuries of information, I would be able to figure out everything. Dads – I *need* to know everything. It's... it's just a drive that I have." She was suddenly distracted by a new thought, and started muttering to herself, "Oh, but Discord is older than both of them. What would happen if I was able to connect *him* to the network. I would get a complete understanding of Chaos Theory."

Free rolled his eyes. "Yeah, and permanently corrupt the hive-mind. Hon – Discord is not evil, which is why he can be trusted to teach Chaos Theory to the House students. However, he is the Aspect of Chaos, and adding him to the hive-mind would make it an extension of him, not the other way around. Again, it would cause unbalance. Your thirst for knowledge will always have a price, and the greater the knowledge, the greater the price. However, I think you need to learn that lesson firsthand before you can comprehend the consequences of your actions, so I've decided that you will start taking new lessons. I'll let your little side project continue, but without your presence, and Techbird is off-limits for the moment. Instead, you're going to spend some time with Luna. I'll make arrangements with her to take you on sabbatical."

Pif was alarmed, but that calming aura was too much for her to resist. "I... but I don't want to. She's always busy with Destined and teaching him how to dream-walk. I just want to work with Techbird to make the world better!" She slumped against Free and yawned, becoming so calm she was dozing off. "Mmnhhh... Only way to move forward is to gather all the information from the past and move beyond it."

Free slowly eased off the calming aura. "Pif – we already know to learn from the past. What we need to do is to learn from the present. And I think it's about time you learned in a different way. I also think that Destined needs to broaden his viewpoint too, so I think we'll have him concentrate on other studies for a while, which should free up Luna." He watched as she drifted off to sleep. "Tell Luna I'd like to talk to her when she visits your dreams."

The Mistake

Despite her initial reluctance, Pif discovered that working with Luna had opened up new avenues of inquiry, and the alicorn was a font of information. The next few weeks saw her feverishly working on a revised grand scheme that she envisioned for the future of Equestria and its relationship with the Hives. The day came when she was ready to present the results with the House, and requested an audience with the Council of Queens.

Normally when it was time for the quarterly queen and princess meeting, they had to drag Free to the meeting. There had been times that Twilight even had to snap teleport him when he wasn't paying attention. Therefore all of the queens and two of the princesses were surprised and not a little consternated when Free not only showed up willingly, but also did so in his Queen Gossamer changeling form, accompanied by Path and Pif who was also in her changeling form. While the queen and princess were hard to read due to their changeling nature, Path on the other hoof, was like reading a book. He was worried, and stressed, while Gossamer looked neutral. Pif, however, seemed to be happy and was carrying several charts and an easel.

Gossamer took her place in the already assembled room as they looked at the young princess with curiosity. Pif walked to the front and centre of the room, and she started setting up her little easel with a whole stack of title boards. The first one read: '**Creating and Maintaining a Dynamic Equilibrium between Ponies and Changelings: A Mathematical Approach.**'

A few of them looked over at Path and Free with questioning looks. The former just sighed and said, "Just… please let our daughter do her presentation. She says it won't take very long. Then we can continue with the other business."

Pif cleared her throat to get their attention and smiled proudly. "Your Highnesses, I am delighted to be able to present my blueprint for a better future for the Hives and for all of Equestria…."

Five hours later, Pif stormed out of the meeting room, with Luna following close behind. Pif was angry – *very* angry. She had put so much work into her analysis! It had taken weeks to get it all just right and for the math to be sound! Then they had simply dismissed her! As they walked away from the meeting room, she very irritatingly buzzed her wings as she ranted on the unfairness of it all. She stopped stomping and started pacing with frantic determination as she often tended to do, displaying a trait she had gained from Twilight – the need to be right, the need to complete a project. She was torn between retreating to her room and sulking, and going back and *making* the queens listen.

"They had the nerve to kick me out! I mean, yeah, they *asked* me to leave and I did on my own, but I didn't *want* to! My parents just nodded for me to go! How fair is that?! It's not fair at all, Auntie! It's just not fair!" Pif circled around Luna as she talked, orbiting the patient alicorn as she grumbled and fumed. "I DO GOOD WORK!" she howled at a Royal Guard who had done nothing other than just pass by. "Why won't they just tell me it's good? The formulas are correct; the math is sound; I'm right and I am objectively correct! Dianthia is just mad that I told her she had to reduce egg production by ten percent over the next fifty years!" At this point she was half talking to herself and only half talking to Luna, losing herself to her thoughts.

Luna let the young queen run down until she could get a sentence out uninterrupted. "My dear Epiphany, dost thou truly think that everyone at the meeting has failed to comprehend thy data? Between them, they have centuries of experience and can tell the truth of thy words. So must there not be another reason for their recalcitrance?" Luna hoped that she could get Pif to think the problem through by herself rather than having it explained to her.

Pif's pacing continued though, as did her ranting. "I know you understand it, and I know Mama Twilight understands it! I don't think Dads do though, and I don't think that half of the queens do. I know that Celestia does because she was around when the math was invented." She again buzzed her wings in annoyance. "I NEED MORE INFORMATION!" She huffed. "I could make it more accurate and more persuasive if I had more information! I had my personal network read everything in every library that House Path has access to except for the books in the restricted wing of the Canterlot archives! Dads and Mom keep blocking me whenever I try to file a petition to access that!" She looked at Luna earnestly. "If I had more information I could be more precise!"

Luna sighed. "Pif, thou dost do some of the finest research in Equestria, and an objective view of data is extremely important for accurate conclusions, but thou art overlooking a significant factor. Thou art dealing with *people*, and people can never be quantified nor accurately predicted. Thou art striking at the very heart of who and what they are. House Path was founded upon the concept of learning to live in harmony with others by understanding their perspectives. This is something that thy parents understand quite well, which is why they support the queens who not only understand this, but also rely on it to manage their hives. Thou, on the other hoof, see them only as statistics."

Pif huffed again but started to calm down a bit. "Data is everything, Luna. I just... it's hard to explain. Nobody gets it when I talk to them. Papa Free doesn't even get it, and he's at the hub of the main hive network. Speaking about that, he's so mad at me already as it is. I took citizens for myself so that I could have them research libraries I couldn't get to, and I used a lot of love on my projects... a *very* large amount. As you already know, he screamed at me when I tore through nearly fifteen percent of the hive's love reserves for just one experiment, then I can't even tell him the results of it." She sighed. "Everything follows rules. Even you follow rules. Once I know and fully understand those rules and I know all factors, I can run simulations in my head. Between me and the ones that are under me, I can solve some really important things!" Her ears drooped. "I don't know why it's so hard for me to understand the House rules. Blue has his squad. Lucida is practically the leader. Destined and the others have their own thing too."

Luna pondered how she could get Pif to comprehend where she has gone wrong. She tried another tack. "Speaking of rules, let us talk about the scientific method of which thou art so fond. Let us say that an experiment has been set up with the same conditions for ten experimenters. They all run the experiment and all achieve the same result. However, while nine of them agree on a conclusion, one has a completely different one. What does the scientific method say about that? The likely correct conclusion is the one held by the nine, not the one. Epiphany, right now, thou art that one. Either the nine are completely wrong, or thou art ignoring an important factor. And no, if they all know what that factor doth be, then it is not hidden in some obscure hidden library book. So what can that factor be?"

Pif stopped and looked at Luna for a long moment, lost in thought. "Then my models must be wrong, all of them." Her eyes began to water. "Wait! My theories have been tested and they worked. I have done the impossible and reaped the richest tactical reward because of it!" She started pacing again. "The formulas I use are sound; they have been used for years. The variables? Is it the variables I'm not accounting for?" She kept pacing. "Data! I need more data to understand this. The formula is beginning to fail. I need to back it up somehow!" Pif was hyperventilating, but before it got out of hand she closed her eyes and started to whisper out the digits of pi. After the thirtieth digit she opened her eyes and looked at Luna with a smile. "Sorry, I almost started panicking again."

Luna facehoofed - she had been so close. Oh well, time to try another approach. "Thy formula was tested for a number of months, was it not? Yet thou dost propose a plan that would encompass two centuries. Statistical errors alone would invalidate it after such a period. Believe me, I have seen grand plans fail in far less time, and this was with the wholehearted support of the majority of ponies. The factor that thou art ignoring, and is the cause of failure for the vast majority of grandiose schemes, is that thou art dealing with people, not numbers. People make decisions based on other factors besides what might be optimum by thy reckoning, but yield results that bring them greater happiness. Stop thinking of them as data and start thinking of them as passionate beings, and thou might see where the difference of opinions may arise."

Pif stopped as she turned and looked to Luna. "Experience! That's what I'm missing – the pony experience! Well ponies, griffons, and dragons too. If I knew how they ticked, how they worked or at least had some credible sources on the topic, I could create a formula based on them. I could modify my own simulation, and then I could increase the accuracy by a few orders of magnitude! But where could I get such experience? I don't have the time to wait centuries and acquire it normally."

Luna snorted in amusement. "I believe that you just annoyed a vast reservoir of that experience."

Pif just looked at Luna for a moment, her expression changing as her eyes went wide, and her irises turned a very faint blue/silver. It was similar to Free's when he did magic, but her horn wasn't sparking, and no magic was happening. She wasn't actually casting anything, but this wasn't a look that Luna had seen on Pif before.

"A vast reservoir... of cultural knowledge." She licked her lips and took a step toward Luna. "Oh... I need to know this... I *really need* to." She took a step closer and whispered sadly, "I'm going to be a bad princess."

Luna frowned in concern at this odd reaction. She failed to understand Pif's latest change of direction, and asked, "Hast thou not understood what I have been telling you? Tis not data you need, but understanding of people of all races."

Pif's grin became wider and wider. "Understanding... understanding that only a person that has experienced centuries could possibly have." She pounced on the unsuspecting Luna with her fangs extended. She wasn't very strong – she didn't need to be. She was banking on the element of surprise, and she whispered in Luna's ear even as she sank her fangs into her neck, "I *need* information, Luna. If I don't keep getting more, the itching won't go away. I try to explain it but nobody understands." Pif began the process of linking Luna to her own network. However, with a mind that old and that large, she had to pull an astounding drain on the side network. That would be noticed by Free, and thus the timer had started. Apart from the blatant drain on the network to make the temporary connection, the energy needed to keep Luna connected might not be able to be sustained for too long, so she had to hurry.

Luna barely had a moment to realize what Pif intended to do, and she tried to yell a warning. "NO! WAIT...!" Abruptly her perceptions changed as she found herself in a vast repository of knowledge, with seemingly endless shelves of books. As an experienced dream-walker, she recognized the virtual world that she has been sent to, and she gasped in dismay. "Oh, Pif, what hast thou done? Thou hast no idea what horrors you have unleashed." Luna strained to break the connection while in the back of her mind she recalled a thousand years of Nightmare Moon in confinement, left to her anger, fear and utter loneliness.

The entire virtual library shook and shuddered violently as it strained under the weight of her connection. Luna watched as several empty book cases shakily appeared and then book after book

materialised to fill them, each having little moons on the lower part of the spine.

A few changelings appeared in the virtual world in a state of panic.

"Luna? How are you in here?" one asked.

"No! No! No!" another cried. "This is bad! This is so bad! Stay with her. I need to notify the others as to what is going on!"

The first changeling went to Luna and had her sit down while the second one disappeared.

"We thought she had this under control after Techbird!" It looked worriedly at the books being created. Almost all of them matched Luna's blue pelt with a crescent moon. However, Luna could see one jet black book with a darker full moon on the spine. The drone started running around trying to keep things organized, and Luna could feel the strain on her mind lessening as the changeling worked, but the world soon started shuddering again.

Luna grabbed the changeling by the shoulders in a painful grip. "If thou dost know a way to get through to Epiphany, thou must make her stop! The consequences might be dire if she does not. I am trying my hardest to withhold the dark knowledge, but this is something over which I have little power. Save thy princess, because I may not be able to!"

Four more changelings appeared and they all got to work. For a while it looked like they were able to keep the world stable, and the shaking went down by a sizable amount. However, books were still appearing on shelves, and for every ten normal books, another jet black book appeared in a random area. The latest one appeared on a nearby desk, and it looked like it melted into the surface partially. A black tar leaked onto the pristine surface.

A few moments later, there was a flash as Pif appeared in the virtual world, slamming into one of the old shelves and falling to the ground as books rained down on her. She pushed her head out of the pile with a groan. "It's too much! How can anyone... have this much? I can't... it's too much information too quickly!" She looked at Luna, or perhaps past her. Luna could tell when somebody was being pushed hard – far too hard in fact. "I'm stuck! Feedback loop.... too much information... can't disconnect! Mommy! Help me!"

As she spoke, she changed to changeling language which Luna was shocked to find that she now understood. Actually Luna was learning and understanding things she had no idea about previously, and she realized that the flow of information was not strictly one-way anymore. It did not seem to help her make sense of the chaos though, and it was getting worse again. The only constant in this virtual universe was a distressed child, and she embraced her. "Pif! Listen to me! You cannot keep this up and survive. Your connection must be broken. I cannot do it myself."

However, nothing she said seemed to have any effect. There was little that she could do except hope that one of Pif's minions alerted Free in time. Or was there? Another memory was forced to the surface, and she grasped it in desperation. "Tantabus - help me!"

The pitch blackness that was overtaking everything suddenly began to coalesce, and the chaos eased up. Soon the Tantabus was reformed, but it was different from when Luna used to torment herself for her failings. Now it was the embodiment of forgiveness of that failure, and hopefully it could contain the darkness for a while.

Luna's concept of time in the network was skewing things. The Tantabus was moving a lot faster than she expected it to. The mass was reaching out and grabbing the jet black books as they formed, at least partially resolving the issue of the dark information. However, more changelings were appearing, their horns glowing as they tried to stabilize the network. Luna was worried to see strange cracks forming in the false reality. Pif was now curled up helplessly around Luna, crying.

"Auntie... Auntie, I'm wrong... I'm so wrong! Mommy! I need her to help me!"

Luna felt a memory pushed onto her. It was a signal that Pif was losing all control of the network and she couldn't even control who received what information.

Luna murmured reassurances to Pif, hoping against hope to calm her down and regain some control, but the growing confusion showed it was not working. She started to lose track of what was happening as more or her memories were dragged to the surface. Suddenly she realized that she didn't recognize what was flashing through her mind. It seemed completely foreign to her. How could that be? She never forgot anything, so how could she not know what this... no these... There was another scene she could not recall experiencing. What in the name of the Moon was happening?

Luna's entire world changed as she now looked through the eyes of a small changeling, maybe one of the new chrome harvesters that Free bred? In the centre of the room there was Pif. She was looking more militant than usual as she poked the chalkboard with a stick several times.

"Everything adds up! The lack of a corpse, and the issue with Cogs a while back. The mad queen must still be alive but hiding! I need ideas as to how we can draw her out!" A changeling to the left commented. "Maybe if you leave enough love gel, she would come out of the woodwork to get it?"

A second changeling spoke up. "Maybe if you fake Luna or Celestia falling ill, she would try to take over again?"

Pif kept shaking her head as the suggestions came one after another.

"Why don't you give the impression that there is friction between you and the House? She would see it as a chance to get you on her side."

Pif stopped and looked at the changeling next to Luna. "Theta, you're a genius!"

As they talked, details of the memory faded. Luna was stunned. She realized that she must have experienced a random memory of that changeling that had been stored in the hive-mind. But that meant that there was no longer any control, no filters, no privacy. What would happen if more memories leaked over? That one seemed so real because it *had* been real once. It just wasn't *her* memory! Only it *was* hers now - she would not forget it any more than she did her genuine experiences. This was bad. If it continued, she could get lost in the memories and lose her sense of self. She was not a changeling that was adapted to being connected to a hive-mind.

Luna suddenly snapped back into the library scene. Things were getting much worse, and this time there were four changelings yelling.

"The network is beginning to collapse! Security be damned – contact the Queen and her consorts to get in here. We don't have the power for this!" The Tantabus was working overtime. When it had started, it was just working on taking the dark memories back, but now it was also working to help keep things held together. If all connections failed at once, it would be a disaster. Pif was wailing out in pain now. Luna desperately tried to think of a solution. Perhaps her dream-walking.... Before she could complete that thought, she felt herself getting pulled into a different memory.

This time Luna was sitting in a Ponyville cafe. By the sound of the thoughts in her head, she could tell that she experiencing the memories of Pif herself, and she was sipping tea. She relived the events of her clandestine conversation with Chrysalis, and when Pif hugged the disguised changeling queen, Luna felt a covert tracking spell being cast. As the mad queen walked off, she could tell that the spell had stuck. Luna now realized that she knew how to find Chrysalis... if she ever managed to get out of this situation with her mind intact. She was briefly side-tracked though as she experienced Pif's feelings for her grandmother as if they were her own. The dichotomy of the experience made her dizzy, but she recovered again as the memory ended. She gasped and tried to steady her thoughts... what had she been thinking? Oh, yes! Dream-walking. Perhaps this situation was akin to that, and she could approach this like a nightmare? But it needed concentration to slip into the dream-realm, and she didn't know if she could achieve it in this chaos. In fact it was still getting worse! She had to try though.

Luna did not get the chance. Abruptly she found herself being thrown into a cold pond and she gasped at the shock. She knew this memory, but from the opposite perspective. She saw herself standing at the edge of the pool, frowning in annoyance. This was a moment from her disastrous first attempt at foalsitting!

When Luna's perception was wrenched back to the virtual library, she found it to have degenerated into utter chaos. Whole pieces were missing, and both the changelings and the Tantabus were losing the battle against the collapse. Suddenly, two large plumes of white fire emerged in the centre of the library. It was Free and Path, and neither of them looked happy. Path's great inner calm and stability when transmitted across the network stopped further deterioration as Free directed the changelings. It looked like they were coming in, grabbing an armful of books then teleporting back out to the main network.

Free declared with great finality, "This mini-network is closed for business!"

Luna called out to Free, "Thou cannot close the network while our minds are linked to it! We could be lost permanently! Thou must find our bodies and disconnect Epiphany from me naturally!"

Path walked over to Luna and the still-crying Pif. "We are in the process of doing that. Right now both of you are in your tower chambers. Iridia is getting ready to disconnect both of you once we have shut down this side-network correctly. I am... disappointed in what has happened."

While Path talked with Luna, Free was instructing the drones to take various books from shelves. "Don't take any books that have a crescent or gibbous moon on the spine!" It looked like he was making sure not to copy any of Luna's memories to the network. "You did not ask to be connected, and we will not take memories not given freely," Free reassured Luna. As the shelves were emptied, they disappeared and the library shrunk. Pif, however, was still shaking, half crying, and half screaming as she clutched her head.

Luna looked at her distressed niece. "Right now is not the time for recriminations. What of Pif? We can clear the hive-mind, but what of her psyche? She may yet suffer from what she has witnessed of my memories."

Free shook his head. "She is going to be fine because of what we are going to be doing, but I imagine she will need you once she realizes what we did. She won't talk to us after that. Attacking you was the final straw though, and we have to use tough love or else we might lose her to the urge." Luna noticed that all the changeling assistants were disappearing, and even the Tantabus had withdrawn back into her. All that finally remained was the floor in a white void.

Path sighed as he walked up to them. "Everything that we needed to transfer over has been completed. Are you ready to close the network and initiate the disconnect?"

Free nodded as he looked back to Luna. "I hope you aren't too mad at her."

Luna shook her head sadly. "I have been too worried for her to be angry... yet."

Luna felt the ground behind her disappear and her vision went dark. When she opened her eyes again, she found herself staring at the ceiling of her bedroom. Path and Free looked down at her with a smile.

"So how was it like being in a hive-mind?" Path asked with a chuckle. "Was it as disorienting for you as it was for me the first time?"

Luna noticed Iridia slip out the door to leave the family by themselves. Twilight was curled around Pif who was whimpering and fretting, her eyes still closed and her legs kicking out weakly in random patterns.

"M-mommy," Pif whimpered before she opened her eyes. She looked around frantically. "Why is it so quiet?"

Luna shook her head as she reoriented herself. "It was a terrible mistake, but a learning experience. Did you know that Pif has a tracking spell on Chrysalis? Anyway, perhaps there might be merit in attempting something a *lot* more controlled, but I don't think I will partake until it is perfected. This could have been a real tragedy. A mortal mind cannot easily cope with an immortal's memories, especially the less savoury of mine."

Path sighed. "This is what I was initially worried about; your memory is vast, exceeding the current capacity of the network. When she pulled you into her smaller and weaker network, it crumbled under the pressure of your mind."

Free said, "Did you say that she knows where the mad queen is?"

Twilight was just watching the pair in shock. Pif slowly lifted her head up from where it had rested on Twilight's arm and she spoke quietly. "It... it's so much more than that. Everyone underestimates me." She mumbled more in half coherent speech, and Luna distinctly heard her say something about 'Tactical Sabotage', 'Lost Civilization', and the 'Total War Protocol'.

Twilight crooned and nuzzled Pif, making sure she was okay before the punishment hammer was dropped.

Luna shook her head sadly as she went over to Pif. "Young one, no amount of information nor intelligence can replace experience. We do not underestimate thee – it is thou who underestimates us. We have done our best to protect thee from thine ignorance, but today thou hast learned a bitter lesson. Let us hope that there will be no serious repercussions. I can say that I have been shaken by the experience, so how much worse must it have been for thee? Speak to me when thou art ready, but for now, it is thy parents that thou must pay heed to." Luna then addressed Free, Path and Twilight. "We must talk later. Epiphany's fate is yours to decide. I might be her Auntie, but I am not in a position to pass judgement right now."

Pif weakly grabbed Luna and pulled her into her growing cuddle pile. It was when they touched that Luna realized that Pif was shaking as if she was in a blizzard. She continued to weep from time to time as she began recovering. Free moved over to the left and Path to the right. Luna could practically feel the love radiating from them... Wait! Since when could she feel emotions?

Free noticed Luna's reactions and said, "There might be some lingering effects from your prolonged visit to the network. Anyway, Pif has already been punished by us. We all but severed her connection to the hive. She's only connected to me now, and she cannot ping the rest of the hive-mind for any information or communication. Giving her too much free rein too quickly caused this to happen, so now she has to earn it all back slowly."

Path looked over to Luna and spoke to her in the changeling tongue, which the night alicorn could now understand as easily as Equish. "We were planning on mixing the kids up a bit more. We were wondering if it was okay if Pif continued to stay here with you for a while. Destined needs to learn under Techbird for a lot longer too." Path chuckled softly and a little sadly. "It seems that the kids are taking a bit too much after their mentors."

Luna grimaced wryly. "Well, I do not think that she will attempt to mind-link with me again, and perhaps I would be an appropriate teacher as I know better than most the perils of the path she has been taking." She sighed. "Perhaps we have all been remiss in allowing the children so much freedom in their education. We have been guilty of not broadening it and tempering it with our own experience. I will take Pif as thou dost suggest."

Path nodded. "I wanted them to make their own paths, and in doing that I may have actually stunted their growth. I can't help but feel like I've failed, but I might be able to fix things. I will have Pif's stuff sent here while she recovers. Canterlot might do her some good."

Free however looked a little more frustrated than Path did but he was keeping it to himself.

Twilight finally spoke up. "At least my little girl will be okay. Is she shaking because of the shock of the experience?"

Free replied, "Partially, but also because she's trying to recover from being disconnected."

Twilight nodded in understanding. "I remember how Whirring Cogs described that. I never thought our daughter would ever have to endure that."

Free and Path wholeheartedly agreed.

A few days later, a Blue drone from the Canterlot team ran up to Chrysalis, interrupting what she was doing. "My queen, my queen! I have priority ten news! It's about your granddaughter!" the changeling said as it tried to catch its breath as it looked up to her.

That grabbed Chrysalis' attention immediately. "Speak! Has something happened to Epiphany?"

"She went to Canterlot, and after the queens' meeting she ambushed Luna and forced her to connect to her hive network!"

Chrysalis realized the implications of this fact. The network would either collapse under such a huge influx of information, or Pif would now have thousands of years of forgotten knowledge at her beck and call. "So, did my granddaughter survive the experience?" she asked with concern.

"We aren't sure. All of our spies are on it, but right now the only thing we know is that they were moved to Luna's room. Queen

Gossamer was frantic, Twilight Sparkle panicky, and Lord Path was quite distraught as they followed them in. Both Princess Epiphany and Luna were limp and non-responsive when we saw them disappear into the room."

"FOOL! What kind of useless information is that? You have told me nothing of value. I do not suffer failure gladly!"

It took two more days before Chrysalis was given another update. From further away on the network, barely within range of speech, she heard one of the drones report.

"She's alive, but her mini-network is gone. From what I can hear, Gossamer destroyed it herself. The princess is in the process of recovering in Luna's tower."

Chrysalis was relieved, but also frustrated and concerned. She had wanted to see her granddaughter again, but this made it difficult. "Find out if she revealed any information about us. If so, I may have to move up our plans."

The Fallout

Because Pif had lacked the foresight to corner Luna in the privacy of her tower but rather jumped her right in the open as soon as the urge had struck, she ended up causing the largest public relations disaster since the first changeling attack. Anti-changeling nobles used the incident to push their agendas and have sanctions levied against Epiphany. Free and Path fought against those sanctions, but they had to abstain from voting due to their biased point of view. Luna's speeches to appeal to reason were dismissed and only fed rumours that the princess was 'changed' by the incident.

The sanctions that were levied on Epiphany were banning her from shapeshifting, strictly limiting her ability to interact with Free's hive mind, and even limiting her opportunities to take in love. She now had to supplement her diet with emo-gel. They even tried to ban Pif from interacting with Luna, but the alicorn princess had vetoed that in no uncertain terms.

Nobody in the House Path herd was happy about this, but Celestia managed to talk them down from doing something rash, and convinced them that the outrage would fade away once the nobles found something else to focus on.

The negative PR came from both sides – the anti-changeling nobles who jumped on the chance to defame the emerging hive, as well as the other hives who were angry that Pif's actions had set them back a considerable amount.

Nothing is sourer than the taste of resentment, anger, and hate. Luna began to see the red flags as Pif began to hole herself up in the Lunar Tower, barely even coming out to eat. At least while she was recovering, she had gone with Luna to her nightly courts, but now she just hid away anytime Luna tried to talk to her about it. One night, Luna was able to convince her to go out to the theatre with her, but this proved to be a mistake. During the intermission, the spotlight was shone on Luna as the main actor, a thestral, dedicated the play to her. However, when everyone saw Luna, they also saw Pif, and the resulting wave of disgust, pity, anger, and hate was too much for her. She passed out before she was able to get out of the theatre.

That had been a few weeks ago. The young changeling had been rarely seen since, although she still kept up her private lessons with Luna. Every now and then though, she did slink out to one of the few late night places where she wasn't judged.

The latest clash between Pif and Blueblood had made things even worse for her. The very few times that she left the sanctuary of her room made her vulnerable to any number of unwanted contacts, and the insufferable and self-righteous noble was all too often found wandering the castle. This time he had been in the company of sycophants who had only egged him on while he mocked and berated the helpless changeling yet again. It took both an emotional and a physical toll on Pif, and late that night she had slipped out of the castle grounds to go to the one place that she was still treated decently by the proprietor.

Chrysalis' agents had to be very careful not to be identified by the other changelings, so they set themselves up inconspicuously to watch strategic places rather than actually hang about the palace. Despite the watch out for Blue Changelings, these agents were unsurpassed at subterfuge and eluded detection. That night about one in the morning, they detected emotional spikes of resentment, anger, and even hatred in a few cases, all leading toward Donut Joe's. Eventually one of the more forward-positioned drones made the announcement that the princess was wearing what looked like a hoodie to try to cover herself up, and she had taken a seat in one of the booths in Donut Joe's.

A short time later, Chrysalis pushed open the door of Donut Joe's, hearing the bell jingling as it announced her arrival. She was hit by a cloud of foul-tasting hate and contempt, but she wasn't the target of it.

She was in disguise, of course, but while she had taken unicorn form once more, she was wearing a more subtle guise this time due to the heightened distrust of changelings at the moment, and she had a friendly green coat and yellow mane. There were a few thestrals and a pegasus couple who were the source of negative emotions, and she spotted Pif in the booth at the back, trying to be inconspicuous in her hoodie but obviously not succeeding too well, judging by the distrustful glares cast her way. Rather than approach Pif immediately, she walked up to the counter first and ordered a hot chocolate and four chocolate eclairs from the only pony who was radiating any sympathy – Joe himself. When she had her food and drink, she took the tray and wandered over towards Pif. "Pardon me, but it looks like you could use some company. Mind if I join you, dear?" she asked without disguising her voice.

Pif looked up briefly with a dull flicker of recognition and shrugged.

Chrysalis smiled and said, "I'll take that as permission to sit with you." She did so and took a sip of her drink and then a bite from an eclair while studying the brooding child. "So, do you want to get things off your chest? I've got plenty of time on my hooves."

Pif laid her head on the table and let out a heavy sigh. "I... I don't even understand what happened. I went to the queens and demonstrated the way to logically and rationally run their hives at peak efficiency, and then I told Celestia and Twilight that they needed to encourage copulation to match pace with the Green and Red Queens' promiscuity, and then it somehow got warped into me trying to manipulate an entire city-state. Of course the thing with Luna didn't help." She let out a whine and bumped her head on the table. "I couldn't help it! I just... I just *needed to know* what was in her head! It was like Celestia and cake – I couldn't resist."

"I understand. It's always difficult for others to realize that we deserve to be respected and obeyed. Why else have we had to work in secret so that we can achieve our goals? Your only failure was to forget that part of your heritage and work behind the scenes. As for Luna... I must admit that you blundered there. No, don't object! I'm not saying that you didn't deserve to know what she knows, but you should have realized that it would be too much for you to cope with. If you had just called me to help, then we would both have been better off."

Pif looked up at Chrysalis with her dull eyes as she smiled weakly. "I knew that it was going to be difficult. Once I realized what I was doing, I set up several buffer steps between her consciousness and my mini network, but she tore through them like tissue paper. I had to focus everything I had on not losing myself to her memories; I was nearly lost to infinity. It took me almost a week to recover enough to be anything more than a shaking, whimpering mass." She sighed and rubbed her eyes. "What I could have known... But that was then and this is now. Dad ripped my mini-network apart after pillaging all the information on it. Then he all but tossed me from the Chrome Hive network. I can't even call upon any 'ling, not even my best assistants!" She groaned. "Oh, gods! The nobles had a field day with it, and it didn't help when I tried to punch Blueblood in the nose."

Chrysalis tried to conceal a snicker as she recalled that narcissistic buffoon whose self-love had tasted so curdled. "Did you at least give him a nosebleed? Anyway, while your network was stripped, surely you recall some information in your own head? They can't take that from you. Even a little bit of Luna's knowledge could be a big advantage."

Pif stuck out her long tongue out and snatched an éclair. "The real important stuff that I didn't want anyone else to know I put in my vault. It wasn't out on the network since I always considered the fact that Dad would do something to the network if it became too big. The downside was, as far as I can figure, that's why I was taken out by Luna's mind; it was a direct connection."

"Hmmm... so you have a lot of information but no means to use it, and now you are suffering under great restrictions; I would say that it's time for you to change your course of action. Obviously I was right when I previously urged you to join me. We both have so much in common except for your naive ideas about how ponies would accept your ideas. Now we can try things *my* way, and I assure you that you can have the resources of my hive... or should I say *our* hive... at your disposal."

Pif regarded Chrysalis for a few moments, and the older queen could tell that she was trying to read her. "I don't know, GramGram. I mean... while the only thing I can taste around here is hatred, disdain, and disappointment, Luna still helps me, which is amazing since she's the one I attacked. I have the information and you are right – I can't use it. I'm not even allowed to take my earth pony form due to the sanctions on me, although they haven't expelled me from Canterlot...."

It looked like Pif was on the fence about the idea, which was a massive improvement over the last time Chrysalis had asked the question. She pushed a little more. "What use is having Luna's support when nopony else will respect your efforts? You cannot thrive in this environment, and I certainly would not impose such a horrendous punishment as banning you from doing what comes naturally. You are a Princess, and the opinions of lesser beings should matter little to you. Come with me and be yourself, and receive the respect that you deserve!"

Pif sighed reluctantly and gave her GramGram a very slight smile.

"I have a few conditions."

Chrysalis raised her eyebrows in surprise. "Conditions? I open my heart and my hive to you, and you ask for conditions?" She smirked. "Very well, let me hear them."

The young changeling looked a little more happy and accepting of the idea with her grandmother's willingness to listen. "Could you please stop with the lesser beings talk? And can I have a say? I'm not asking that I get the final say; I just want to be able to give my opinion."

Chrysalis smiled indulgently. "As you wish, I will not call them that any more. As for having a say, my dear granddaughter, I have never wanted anything but your input! I have waited a long time and hoped that you could share this with me. We will be in this *together*!"

Pif's ears folded back slightly. She was still a bit wary, but the queen could tell that she made up her mind as she muttered, "At least I'll be where I'm not hated." She stood up. "I'm going to head back. I need to gather a few things first. Once I have them, I'll head out of the castle. I figure you'll be alerted to where I am."

"That won't be a problem," Chrysalis said with a satisfied smile. "You won't regret this. And Pif, you have made your grandmother very happy tonight."

Pif nodded, got up out of the booth, and left the shop to fly back to the Lunar Tower in the main castle.

Chrysalis watched her leave and then took her time finishing her drink and eclairs before leaving the shop, ignoring the hostile stares of the couple of customers who had seen her conversing with Pif. After all, they were still just lesser beings.

As Luna walked up to her tower suite, she heard the clip clop of somebody moving about the top floor, which meant it had to be Epiphany. Luna peered curiously into her room and observed the activity of her niece. She saw her packing things into a saddle-pack, several personal items, a family photo and a Return Crystal. The latter was an extremely sophisticated magical creation of Luna's that she had gifted to her herd members to enable them to travel instantly to their Griffonian home no matter where in Equus they were.

"What art thou doing, child?" she asked with concern.

Pif froze, then slowly turned towards Luna. The look on her face was guilt, pure and simple. "I... I was just going to go out to Donut Joe's again. I figured I would bring a few things to sketch with... since... nobody ever talks to me... or acknowledges me... They just sneer... and stare...." Pif was also a terrible liar.

Luna raised a sceptical eyebrow. "Dost thou need a photograph and school medals too?" She walked over and put a reassuring arm over Pif's shoulders. "I know that thy punishments seem harsh, but this too shall pass. Remember that mine lasted a thousand years. I know that to a child such as thee, thy punishment seems as bad, but things are not as bad as they seem right now."

Pif whimpered slightly as she leaned against Luna. "I know that yours lasted a thousand years, but you can't compare our situations; they are apples and oranges. Luna – except for you, all I can feel and taste is everyone's mistrust and anger, even hatred towards me."

"And what dost thou suppose that the first changelings to show themselves freely after the invasion had to endure? And *they* had done naught wrong! Respect and trust has to be earned, and thou didst ruin all of thine. Thou must work hard to restore it, and it will not be a quick recovery. It might not have been so bad if thou had been more circumspect and everypony had not learned that thou did 'attack' a princess. Thou dost pride thyself on thy logic, but thine emotions doth rule thee as much as other ponies. This is the lesson that thou must learn before things get better."

Pif leant in and hugged Luna tightly. "I can taste the disappointment, even from Moms and Dads, but I never tasted that from you. You were worried or sad or concerned, but never mad." She broke the hug as she sniffled slightly. "I... I'll just be a few hours at Donut Joe's... that's all." Her ears were flat against her head.

Luna knew that she was lying again, and her shaky hooves, also told Luna that she was begging her not to be called out on it. The Alicorn of the Moon nodded understandingly. "Think hard upon what I've said, and always remember that we love thee, no matter what doth occur."

Pif smiled gratefully at Luna. "You can always talk to me if I fall asleep... at Donut Joe's." She took a few steps back and pulled on her saddle-pack, and then jumped out the way she came in – through the window. She flew slowly and lazily toward the south, figuring that she had already been spotted, and Chrysalis would be joining her in due time.

Luna watched her go a little sadly. She hoped that she had made the right decision to let her niece leave, but it was something that she knew the young changeling needed to do to put her mistakes behind her and start afresh. "Good luck fly with thee, dear child. May thy new path take thee to happier places, and make no new stumbles getting there," she said softly.

Pif was not happy though. She felt like she was being ripped apart as she headed toward the outer suburbs of the city. She gave a heavy sigh. She *couldn't* go back now, even though she was already having second thoughts. As she moved lower to the ground, she shifted form, turning into a dark grey thestral. She didn't really know many thestrals, so she took the form of a feminized Leatherwing. She touched down on the ground, looking around. "Well... one more thing left to do, I guess."

Chrysalis got the word over the hive-mind that Epiphany had left the tower. Then came the follow-up message that she had changed to thestral form. Chrysalis nodded in approval and switched to thestral form also; it would look more natural for them to meet that way. She headed off to rendezvous with her grandchild.

It was only a few minutes before Pif saw a slightly taller thestral coming her way. Realizing that it was a changeling, she smiled slightly. "Hi, again."

Chrysalis smiled widely. "Shall we go, Pif? We have a long journey ahead of us, both physically and metaphorically."

"Yeah, let's go. There's one more thing I have to do first though." She searched in her mind for the last connection she had to the Chrome Hive-mind. She felt the nature of the connection for a long moment, appreciating it one last time before she severed it. In its place, Pif started to build a mental wall around her mind using both her own ability and a few tricks she remembered from Luna. She thought to herself, '*If I am to endure the quiet, I will make my home a fortress.*' The entire process took a few minutes, and Chrysalis could probably tell something was going, but it had to be done. However, her disconnection was neither covert nor subtle, and Free would know instantly. "That.... hurt." She gathered her strength and looked over to her grandmother. "Let's go."

Chrysalis nodded and gave her a reassuring hug. "Yes, let's go home."

Pif smiled a little more and she took off with Chrysalis to her new destiny, whatever it was.

Back in the castle, Luna's talkie-trottie was ringing insistently. Anticipating what it would be, she answered it reluctantly. "Luna speaking."

"**What happened?**" Rose's voice practically blasted from the phone. In the background, Luna could hear Free wailing, and then a few seconds later Path joined in on the borderline hysterical crying. "We were about to have herd time, and all of a sudden Free began freaking out."

Luna sighed sadly. "Roseclaw, Epiphany has chosen to leave Canterlot. I know not for sure, but I believe that she has turned her back on us for now. I suspect that Free doth suffer because she has severed her connection to him."

Rose was silent for a moment. "I see. Is there any way you can keep tabs on her while she's away? It might not be a permanent thing. Maybe she's waiting till the heat dies down? But now that I know what is going on, we can try to console Free, and once he calms down, so will Path."

"I can always find her in her dreams, but I cannot make her tell me anything that she doth not wish to tell me. However, at worst, I can assure you of her continued good health."

Rose sighed. "Please try your best. Let us know anything as soon as you can."

"I assure thee, I wish nothing less."

Some nights later when Luna located Pif's dreamscape, she found it highly guarded. Granted it was easy for her to get in since all of the wards and walls were of her own design, and Pif most likely had set it up that way. She found Pif's dream-self sitting in the House Path gardens, looking pensive. Without a word, she lied down besides the introspective child and nuzzled her.

Pif let out a surprised gasp and nuzzled Luna back with a soft sigh. "I miss you, Auntie."

"We all miss thee too, Pif." She looked around at the dreamscape. "And it would appear that thou might be a little homesick. It is still thy home and always will be, dost thou know?"

Pif nodded slowly. "I just can't go back yet."

Luna could feel something trying its best to leak into the dreamscape, but those wards were holding fast. Nothing would or could get past them.

"I think I can do some good where I am, even if the person I'm trying to help doesn't realize it yet."

"That person – it is Chrysalis, correct? I admire thine intentions, but I must remind thee of the consequences of thy previous good intentions."

Pif nodded slightly. "Which is why I'm also gathering intel." She leaned against Luna. "Just... don't tell them where I am or what I'm doing, promise?"

"Nay, child, I have already promised that I would keep an eye on thee. They worry so much for thy welfare. However, it was no difficult task for them to determine where thou didst go, and with whom. The exact details I cannot glean though, so I will not be able to tell them more than they already know unless thou dost tell me."

Pif hugged Luna tightly. "Best auntie ever."

Luna smiled lovingly and hugged her back. "Just remember though, Epiphany, I will continue to urge thee to come home whenever we meet. I, too, greatly miss my niece."

Chapter 14:
The Epiphany Gambit

Epiphany was confused; her grandmother's hive was not at all like she was expecting it to be. She looked about the luxurious royal chamber as she leaned back against Chrysalis. The queen pulled up a brush and began combing Pif's frazzled hair, smoothing it out as she chirred softly into her ear.

"You are going to love it here, my dear. Word has already gotten out in the hive that their princess has arrived and is here to stay. They are all so very happy and they want to meet you!" Chrysalis said with pride.

"Who wants to see me? I've only been here for a day; I didn't think it was really that big of a deal." Pif blushed a bit, but she was still loving the attention. She didn't notice her grandmother's horn light up faintly as she felt relaxed, so very relaxed. Soon she was asleep in the queen's arms, snoring softly.

The queen couldn't help but grin as she looked back down at her progeny and murmured, "Where I failed with Gossamer, I will succeed with Epiphany." Out of the corner of Chrysalis' eye, she saw her most loyal soldier slowly walk into the main room. "General Breezon – come to see the princess? How many are waiting for her?"

The large male changeling stood stiffly to attention as he saluted. "Almost all of the hive members that are not on active orders from you are waiting in the Great Hall to see her. They have their offerings to give her and wish her well."

Chrysalis nodded a few times in satisfaction as she smiled and looked down to Pif. She had only been asleep for a few moments, but it would have to enough. Soon she would become charged with love. She nudged her granddaughter awake and Pif's eyes snapped open. She looked around in confusion before getting back up to her hooves.

"Mmnhh... no, I'm up! I'm up! What's going on?" Pif asked Chrysalis and Breezon as she yawned softly.

"Everybody is waiting in the main hall; they want to see their new princess!" Chrysalis said cheerfully before standing up alongside Breezon.

All three of them walked to the Great Hall. Pif switched from her hybrid form to her pure changeling princess form before entering, and

then her eyes went wide. There were so many more than she was expecting, and they were all staring at *her*. So many changelings; so many eyes; she was starting to get nervous and moved to hide behind her grandmother – that was up until she felt their 'offerings'. The drones were feeding her gathered love? She hadn't had this feeling since she was a hatchling! But she didn't remember it being so sweet, so strong. It didn't take long before she was blushing and her wings were buzzing so hard it was producing a high pitched squeal.

Chrysalis grinned widely and her horn lit up slightly. Pif calmed down but she still had a silly grin on her face.

"All this love is just for me, GramGram?" Pif asked as she looked up at the queen, her wings still fully extended.

"But of course, my dear. They recognize that you have a right to rule them, only after me of course. To give tribute is in their nature. They are our drones after all." Her horn lit up slightly brighter as Pif looked up to her with a smile, the very edges of her eyes a pale green before she turned back to the crowd as she started to shift forms.

Pif's increasing arrogance showed as she grew a little taller and stronger-looking. She was now only a head shorter than Chrysalis, her horn was sharper than before, and it looked like she had armour plates. This change was of course fuelled by the overwhelming amounts of love being given to her.

"Hello! I am Princess Epiphany, granddaughter of Queen Chrysalis! I look forward to working with all of you in the future!" She waved as the 'lings all buzzed and cheered as Pif gazed over them all.

"I will be asking my grandmother if I can start my projects tomorrow. I might be calling on some of you to join my think tank!" Again she was met by cheers as she took a few steps back and headed out the way she had come. She was practically hovering as she left their sight.

Chrysalis just grinned as she looked at Breezon. "She was so starved for love and affection! This is going to be simpler than I thought. Oh Gossamer, you made it too easy."

The queen looked at the gathered 'lings and, with a mental command, they all scattered in fear before she turned back to Breezon.

"Shall we go feed? The royal family has brought their weekly tribute to me. A queen and her high general should always stay well-fed and battle ready."

Breezon nodded, and they walked toward the receiving room and their feast. All the while, Pif remained blissfully unaware as she rested in her royal chambers.

The next several days went by fast. Pif, for the most part, stayed out of the queen's hair. Every now and then, Pif would stop by and ask a few questions, request a few things, and of course the queen placated her. Much like the spider and the fly, she had to lure her in before she could strike, and so far it was working.

After the fifteenth day, Chrysalis woke up to find her network slightly altered. Twelve of her changelings' positions had been changed in the network, pulled from various locations and grouped into one place. She watched the one area intently to verify if she was correct and it was not long before she felt Pif on the network for a brief moment.

"My queen – is there something wrong?" Breezon asked as he looked at Chrysalis who seemed to have frozen for a moment.

She just looked at him and smiled. "She's taking her first steps deeper into the network. I can feel her; she's being very cautious. She's arranged a few of the drones so that she can access them easily. I wonder if her think-tank is taking off as well as she would like?"

Breezon just looked at her. "Do you think she will make a permanent connection?"

"Oh, she will. She *craves* attention and adoration, and the drones will give her more than she has ever felt before. For now let's go see what she's doing."

When they found Pif, she was in her 'Princess Chambers', the name that she had given the suite of rooms that Chrysalis had gifted her. However, it didn't have all of the luxury that the rooms were originally furnished with. The entire main room was lined with black chalkboards, all of which were covered with what looked like complex formulas. The twelve 'lings were in a circle around Pif as she lit her horn, and theirs lit in response, several times a second as she kept writing on the board.

"We did it?"

"WE DID IT!"

Her happy enthusiasm caused the other twelve to be happy too, and she started high-hoofing each and every one of them.

"Now that the theory is proven, we can begin construction!" She pointed at four of them and they hopped to their hooves, trotting in place from excitement. "Bring me the purest sand of type three that you can find!"

"Right!" Drones one, two, three, and four scurried off.

She then pointed out five others. "Bring me five barrels of the most highly concentrated love you can get your hooves on! If anyone asks, tell them that the Princess has requisitioned it."

They all saluted. "On it!" they said in unison and hastened away.

She pointed to the last three. "I need you three to rest up for at least a day. You're going to help me in the construction! Actually, why not just use my bed? It's large enough for the three of you with room to spare. And it's really soft and comfy."

The last three let out happy squees as they turned, only to bump into Chrysalis. They let out a scared chitter as they backed up and hid behind Pif.

"Granddaughter – what are you doing, and why did you just take love reserves and send my construction drones out?" she asked in an icy calm tone as the drones started to shake.

"You said that I could use hive resources to work on projects," Pif explained matter-of-factly. "I rearranged the twelve drones that were the smartest so I had easy access to them, and we began work. Project W is under way!"

Chrysalis just regarded her for a long moment while Breezon looked at the formulas on the wall. "Very well, but while you let the… *drones* sleep on *your* bed, you have royal duties to attend." Chrysalis smiled at the drones in a way that just made them fear her more as Pif nodded.

As Chrysalis walked down the hall with her granddaughter, she couldn't help but realize that in the few days that Pif had been in the hive, the drones had begun favouring her, calling her the 'Merciful Princess'. She hoped that the lenient attitude that she was showing Epiphany would not foster disobedience among her workers. Eventually Pif would have to make it clear that they needed to know their place.

"So what kind of royal duties do we have to do?" Pif asked as they entered the throne room.

"Right now, there are a few drones that need to be punished." Chrysalis lit her horn and four worker 'lings were herded in by the force of the queen's magic. "These four are guilty of stealing from our love reserves. Their actions, if they continued unchecked, could cause disaster in the hive. My granddaughter, I leave it up to you to punish them." Chrysalis took a few steps back and sat on her throne, with the general taking up position by her right side. She watched Pif carefully as the princess considered the offenders.

"This is your first time committing such an act?" Pif asked.

Out of the four cowering drones, one was brave enough to nod and reply. "We were just so hungry! We work in the lower levels, so we tend to get our rations of love last, if there is any left."

Pif frowned a bit, not realizing that Chrysalis and Breezon were reading her every move as she powered up her horn. The four offenders curled up into tight balls, expecting to be struck down, killed at best, or slowly tortured at worst. What actually happened surprised the offenders, confused Breezon, and enraged Chrysalis.

Pif's horn flared brightly to cover the four offenders, and their cries stopped as they stared at her, eyes widening in surprise. She was sharing her own love energy with them, feeding them when they were hungry, as well as mending the injuries that were sustained in their treatment prior to this point.

"I give you this gift, but be warned – if you do something like this again, I won't be able to be so merciful. You can feel my grandma's anger behind me; this is not what she would have done. Take advantage of your second chance and please don't do this again." Pif smiled as she walked over to the offenders and nuzzled each of them. "Off you go now."

The 'lings didn't waste any time and they hightailed it out of the throne room, thanking Epiphany profusely in passing. Pif smiled and turned to look at a very angry Chrysalis. Her ears folded back and she let out a soft squeak.

"You were supposed to *punish* them, granddaughter, not reward them and send them on their way!" She got louder and louder as Pif made herself look smaller.

"It was their first offense. I stressed the importance of their reformation. They won't do it again."

The queen sighed and shook her head as her anger deflated. "Still so young…. When they do it again, and they *will*, **you** will enact the punishment that I deem suitable. Are we clear?" The queen glared at Pif as she nodded a few times. "Good. Now go run along. That's your lesson for today." Chrysalis waved her off and Pif scampered back to her chambers.

Breezon looked at the queen. "How do you know that they will do it again?" he asked.

"Because I'm going to *make* them do it again," Chrysalis chuckled malevolently.

Nearly a fortnight passed before anything of significant interest happened. Chrysalis was at her position as the Saddle Arabian king's Royal Advisor. It was merely a front because she already had the entire royal family under her power, but this position kept eyes off of her and also kept her by the titular leader of the nation where she could monitor all information going in and out of the country. Therefore, she was more than a little confused when she heard the next petitioner to talk to the king and queen.

The herald looked at his scroll and announced, "My Lord, your next appointment is with Clip-Clop the Wise."

The king and queen looked just as puzzled as Chrysalis did. A large cart was wheeled out into the main hall, and once the small stallion came out from behind it, Chrysalis face-hoofed.

Pif was in stallion pony form, which didn't look all that much different from her natural changeling form, except for the lack of wings and her normal-looking eyes.

"My King, I have invented something which will revolutionize everything and improve the quality of life for all of your subjects!" Clip-Clop exclaimed as he pulled off a sheet that had been covering the cart to reveal a massively complicated system that neither the king nor Chrysalis understood. "If your guard would be so kind as to assist me?"

One of the guards walked over as Clip-Clop scooped a cup of water out of the main vat labelled 'INPUT'. "Now take a small sip – is it salty?"

The guard took a sip and licked before spitting it out again. "Yes. Yes it is!"

"As well it would be. Almost all of the available water in Saddle Arabia is contaminated with salt, but this machine can quickly and efficiently draw the salt out of the water, as well as other contaminants, and leave pure, clean drinking water!" She smiled, pressed a button on the side and the machine hummed into life. Clip-clop walked over to a tap labelled 'OUTPUT' and held a cup to the spout as crystal clear water poured into it. She shut the machine shut off when the cup was full and passed it to the guard who warily took a sip. His eyes widened and he drank the entire glass.

"It's so cold and clean! I have rarely tasted the like of it!" the guard exclaimed as Clip-Clop bowed to the king.

"This device is amazing. If this could be mass-produced, our water shortages would be solved!" the king exclaimed. "Talk to my royal accountant. We will see to it that you gain the resources needed to make this for large scale applications!"

Stallion Pif bowed again and then left, pushing the cart out with him, leaving the king with his advisor. Chrysalis was torn; she was very impressed that her granddaughter was able to create such a thing, but she was not at all happy that the device required love to function, and that she would waste the precious resource on lesser beings.

Several more weeks passed, and Pif had not wasted a moment of them. However, Chrysalis was getting frustrated because she still was not able to feel her granddaughter's presence in the hive-mind very often. Pif was only using a series of brief connections with the group of twelve she had picked to be her think-tank. This morning was different though, and the queen could feel a massive spike of energy coming from one particular section of the hive and that one particular group of 'lings.

For the first time, she could feel Pif directly connected to the network, but access to her was very difficult due to the amount of activity and energy being channelled. Maybe she should see what was going on?

Chrysalis made her way to Pif's room. Not bothering to knock, she entered and stopped in surprise, blinded by light and caught off-guard by a blast of wind. Gradually she made out a group of six of the 'lings each firing a solid beam of magic into a point in the centre of the room, while another three were offset and doing something similar. It looked like a star was forming in the centre of the room. Pif was on her hind hooves, standing next to *ten* now-empty barrels of love gel which they had apparently eaten, and she was channelling all of the energy that she had gained from them into the star-like point. Like the others, she was wearing black-tinted goggles and cackling with glee, perhaps more than she should be, although it was hardly surprising considering the amount of love she had consumed. She had the mad scientist thing down pat though.

"Yes! Yes! Keep going! We are at 94% fusion and 89% saturation! Don't let up, my friends!"

Every 'ling braced themselves and gave it all they had, and the queen could see something beginning to form out of the light. Although Chrysalis was irked at not only being confused but ignored, and even outright angry, she was concerned for Pif, and did not dare interrupt... whatever this was. The sheer amount of power being used could be disastrous if randomly released.

The light started to draw into the centre as the love permeating the air collapsed into it, and within a few more seconds, everything quieted down as the nine changelings collapsed to the ground, exhausted. The remaining three tended to them while Pif fell onto her belly, panting like she had just run a marathon. In the centre of the room for all to see was a strange floating sphere with a flawless mirror-like finish. The eerie thing was just how perfect it was, and that it floated there without anyone holding it up.

Pif looked over to Chrysalis with an almost drunken smile on her muzzle. "GramGram, we did it. For the first time, theory has been made reality."

Chrysalis frowned. Now that the fireworks were over, she wanted answers! "What theory is that? How best to consume the hive's energy reserves in one enormous indulgence? I've given you a lot of freedom, Epiphany, but I expect you to be a responsible member of the hive at the same time."

Pif slowly got up to her feet and hugged Chrysalis tightly. "I haven't wasted it, GramGram! I made it *better*!" She weakly reached out with her hoof, and that strange orb moved over to Chrysalis. "Don't try to drain it; just feel it. Trace the patterns and notice the flow, and you'll see what I mean. This is *big*, GramGram. It's the experiment that Mom wouldn't let me do because she thought I wasn't smart enough to get it right!" She lit up her horn, wrapping her magic around the queen's horn as she guided it through channels and vertices that the queen would not know existed, and even Pif wouldn't know if not for those walls upon walls of calculations. There were ten barrels of love energy inside that small hoof-sized perfect sphere, but when Chrysalis felt where Pif was leading her into the sphere, she could feel that there was a little more than should be there. It was a barely detectable amount of extra love energy, but a faint spark in the very core of the sphere that defied explanation.

Chrysalis' eyes widened in surprise. "The power – it's all still there and more! What is this? What purpose does this serve, child?"

"It's a way to improve lives."

"How can... *this*... improve our lives? The hive is already rich and powerful without extravagant toys. And what is this inexplicable thing that I'm feeling within?"

Pif just grinned with just one eye remaining open. "It's generating its own love, just like the Crystal Heart. A small, nearly imperceptible amount right now, but the theory is sound, and the concept worked. I think I might know how the Old Ones did it, Gram Gram...." Her voice trailed off as she leant forward slightly against Chrysalis and went still.

Chrysalis heard Pif start snoring, and she realized that her granddaughter had fallen asleep while her connection to the hive-mind was still active. Pif had needed the hive-mind's computing power to accomplish her task, but she had been too exhausted and left with too little energy to close it like she normally did. *'A love generator? Was such a thing truly possible? Yet it took ten barrels of stored love energy to create it – would it actually justify its creation?'*

It had been a week since Luna had last visited Pif's dreamscape, and as she phased in, she looked about her with an eyebrow raised in curiosity at the perfect sphere dominating the scene. This was new – perhaps this would be an interesting visit. She approached her recumbent niece.

"Good evening, Pif. If what I am seeing is any indication, thou hast been very busy. Do I sense a feeling of accomplishment?"

Pif nodded and smiled. "I did something I thought was virtually impossible, but my calculations held out! It worked, and I'm glad it finished when it did. My horn was getting red hot."

Luna smiled proudly at Pif as she lay down next to her to cuddle her with a wing. "I am glad for thee. I know thy desire to achieve great things, and I believe that thou shalt accomplish much. So... what didst thou accomplish that has so excited thee?"

"That!" Pif said as she pointed to the sphere with great pride.

Luna smirked. "That says so much, and yet so little. Need I ask thy parents to what thou art referring? A dream construction can tell me little."

"It was a project that Moms and Dads thought too dangerous for me to do at the Chrome Hive. It's a unification of Crystalmancy and Amouremancy. Basically I made a storage container for massive amounts of love energy, and once it reached a critical density, it began producing it on its own."

Luna was impressed. "I thought the secrets of generating love artificially were lost with the ancients. What powers this artefact? Thou cannot get something for nothing."

Pif scratched her head. "That's just it... I'm not completely sure, although of course I suspect it draws upon ambient mana in much the same manner that we believe the Crystal Heart does. I can't deconstruct the Heart, but my theory on how it works showed that when I factored in everything, there is still a net increase in love. My sphere's energy increase is very small, but it's definitely there, so it must be something that I have yet to even consider."

"Be careful, dear Pif. It is rare that the known quantities are the cause of the biggest problems. I could tell thee tales of overconfident mages who have created remarkable spells, only to discover too late that unforeseen side-effects caused undesired results ranging from unpleasant to disastrous."

Pif nodded slowly. "I'll be careful. Now that I am certain that I'm on the right track, I can start experimenting to quantify those unknowns. In other news..." She paused to figure out how to say what she said next. "I have made friends, and they like me a lot. They like working with me a lot more than their previous tasks, and I'm thinking about how I can work it to my advantage."

"I am very happy to hear that. So what is this advantage that thou dost mention?"

Pif's ears folded back slightly. "Oh, I just seem to work with them a lot better. They are... faster than my previous team if that makes sense."

"Perhaps it's the environment? Nevertheless, it means a lot to me that thou art happy again, and I can tell thee that thy parents will be reassured as well. They miss thee so much, and always eagerly await news of my visits with thee."

Pif looked at Luna and couldn't help but smile a bit at the mention of her parents. "They miss me? I thought they would be focused on Lucida or Blue Streak."

"Oh, Pif, just because thou didst make mistakes and they had to mete out punishment, dost not mean that they love thee any less. Of course they miss thee, but they also realize that thou must find thy balance and happiness once more. If thy work here accomplishes that, then they wish thee every success. And it would seem that there are factors here that have enabled thy greater success with thy new team, so that is a very positive beginning. Just remember, I beg thee, that thy goals might not always be Chrysalis' goals. Be wary, dear niece."

"I can tell that already. I can feel how angry she is when I pass down rulings when she lets me because I always side with compassion. She's been... more assertive as of late." Pif indicated the unwavering barrier that walled off her dreamscape. It looked like there was a thick green mist trying to get in, but it wasn't able to penetrate the wall. "She wants in, and I think her lack of progress is upsetting her."

"Thou dost play a dangerous game, Pif. Chrysalis is an old and experienced queen, and for all thy talent, thou art still an amateur. While I have no doubt that thy grandmother doth love thee, I also believe that she will not let that stand in the way of her mad ambitions. While she would prefer thee to stand by her side and share her dreams, thou art not her, and hopefully never will be, and therefore inevitably you will clash. Remember, Chrysalis didst first try to convert Free to her cause, but then attempted to kill her child when he rejected her. Do not tempt the same fate."

Pif sighed a bit. "I am starting to realize this, although I think I'm making some progress. However, that's why I have the return crystal close by me at all times. I just need to throw it at my hooves and I'll be sent to wherever you are, although I have no idea if it will be comfortable."

"That is a wise course of action. Do not be afraid to seek my counsel in the meantime. While I have my preferences, I will not seek to force them upon thee. I seek to guide, not lead. If thou dost return, it must be on thine own terms, not ours." Luna noticed that Pif was taller and her chitin plates bulkier and stronger than before, a reflection of her real self's growing defences. Despite her rather naïve hopes, Pif was not ignorant of the need to protect herself. She gave Pif a reassuring hug and said, "I am curious, Pif – this dream form of thine – it has grown muchly as of recent. Does it represent thy growth in spirit, or is it a reflection of thy true form?"

Pif looked at herself. "I... I never really noticed it before." She stood tall to show off herself to Luna as she walked around in a circle, and she looked a lot more muscular than before. "Huh! How about that? I think it must be like I really am; I sure didn't consciously try to change my dream-self this way." She settled down next to Luna once more. "Luna... I was wondering... when I had you in the mini-network, could some of your memories have been transferred to me by accident?"

Luna grimaced. "It is inevitable. While Free did remove the memories stored in thy network, some were impressed upon thy mind before thou didst lose control and try to shut down the torrent. What dost thou think that thou hast gained from me?"

"One name keeps coming to mind, but I have heard of it before."

"A name? Speak! Thou hast aroused my curiosity."

"I don't know old Equish, so it might be nothing. It was *Lune Unyielding*."

"Ah! An odd thing to recall. Let me give it form for thee." Luna concentrated and created a dream facsimile of an ebony blade which had her symbol embossed upon the handle. "Lune Unyielding is my sacred weapon, imbued with dozens of enchantments and a portion of my own power. Its edge is ever sharp, and its blade unbreakable. It is only drawn in times of war, and it last drew blood against thy grandmother's hordes. Does this disturb thee?"

Pif grew still and she seemed almost hypnotized by the blade. When Luna moved it, her eyes followed it intently. "It does not. It looks... it looks right. I feel like I've known it for a long time."

"As it is my memory that thou dost possess, that is hardly surprising. The memory is no less real for having been stolen. Nevertheless, feeling an affinity for it is not the same thing. A blade like this chooses its wielder as much as the inverse. It might indicate that it would consider thee a suitable wielder, but it also will only serve one master at a time, and I will not be relinquishing it."

Pif hummed slightly in thought as she nodded a few times. Then she smiled. "Hee! I'm not going to fight you for it. I'm pretty sure that the wielder of Lune Unyielding can't be decided by a tickle war." She snuggled up against Luna. "I'm glad you visit me from time to time. It's nice to know you still want to talk to me."

"Tsk! Didst thou ever doubt that I care for thee, and wish to look out for thy welfare? Our dream conversations are the least that I can do under the circumstances. How could I cuddle thee otherwise?" Luna then tickled Pif. "And thou art correct - I am the Tickle Queen!"

Pif let out a squeal as she flailed about while she was tickled. Her laughs got louder before the dream abruptly collapsed, sending Luna back into the space between dreams. Back in Saddle Arabia, Pif suddenly woke, curled up next to Chrysalis in her chambers. "Sneaky Auntie!" she murmured before going back to sleep.

Luna withdrew her consciousness back to her body and considered what had happened. She nodded in satisfaction before getting up and heading out to join the rest of the herd. She had a lot of news to relate – much of it good, but some a little disturbing. She realized that a crossroads might soon be reached, and they all needed to be prepared.

Pif was working on her latest device when she felt Chrysalis call for her over the network. She sighed a bit, regretting that her grandmother had managed to strengthen the link to her. The queen's figurative looking over the shoulder had become a lot more obtrusive lately, and was making her tasks significantly more difficult. Pif looked over to the twelve 'lings that had been working with her and making her goals possible despite the handicap. She had managed to get them clothes and they were all dressed up in lab coats, something that they treasured because it was a unique feature that showed that they had the Princess' favour. She instructed them to keep working as she walked out of her room and into the throne room where she froze. Chrysalis was looking at her with a large grin on her muzzle. Breezon was unreadable as always, but what worried her was that also present were the same four 'lings from last time. Her heart sank.

Chrysalis spoke up with a smirk. "Do you remember our agreement? What would happen if these four did it again? Come stand next to me child."

Pif slowly and very warily walked over to her, and she slowly turned to face the four that were looking even more frightened than the previous occasion.

Chrysalis scowled at the terrified 'lings and said, "Your punishment will be far more severe. The penalty for stealing from the hive not once but twice is **death**." The queen boomed out the last word for everyone in the hive to hear over the hive-link, and everyling turned their attention to what was going on in the room.

"GramGram, you *can't* be serious! I'm not going to kill them just for being hungry!" Pif screamed at Chrysalis, only to see the queen's horn glow in response.

"I do not believe that I was asking."

Everyone in the hive froze as they watched what was happening. The queen was overwhelming the comparatively weak mental defences of the princess as she forced her will on the queen-in-training. Pif looked back at the four with her eyes glowing a sickly green. A slightly sadistic grin grew on her face as Pif walked over to them, her horn charging up. "You four have been naughty 'lings, haven't you? I tried to help you, and you stabbed me in the back, so now I have to do the same to you." She started laughing, her normally smooth voice starting to mimic Chrysalis' tones. Her horn discharged twice and two of the 'lings fell to the ground, a hole where their hearts used to be. Pif continued to stalk the remaining two as they futilely tried to retreat. "What have you to say for yourself, my little drones?" Before they could speak, her horn discharged two more times, and the last two fell over in a heap, dead.

Pif's eyes cleared up and she blinked a few times before she looked down at the drones at her feet. Her eyes widened in horror and she turned to glare at Chrysalis. **"Why did you make me do that? They could have learned! They *could* have learned! They didn't have to die!"**

The queen smirked. "Child its time you learned that a quee–"

A loud smack rung out in the chamber and the entire hive froze up in shock. Pif had her hoof outstretched and the queen's head was turned to the side. She had struck the queen! Breezon was quick to respond, and he swung his hoof in a punch that connected with Pif's head *hard*. Before the princess knew it, she was on her back, completely exposed and a heavy hoof was on her neck keeping her in place.

"How dare you strike the queen?! Royalty or not, that is unforgivable!" the general roared out.

The queen just grinned. "Breezon – let her up. I think she needs to go back to her room and think about what she did."

The general slowly took his hoof off of Pif's neck and she scrambled to her hooves and galloped out of the royal chamber. He then turned to Chrysalis. "Why didn't you punish her for striking you, my queen?" he asked.

"Because, my dear general, I had been worried that she wasn't capable of violence. Now I know that all I need to do is push her hard enough." The queen laughed long and loud.

The next several days after Pif's outburst went very slowly. Chrysalis was monitoring how Pif was using the network but she found that she wasn't doing much of anything. The few times that she had connected to the hive network to go over things with her twelve, she was saturated with caution and fear. The queen started to wonder if she had pushed Pif too hard too fast. Her granddaughter was of no use to her if she was terrified and turning into a recluse. Although she was gradually working on projects, they seem to have been drastically reduced in scale.

A week after the 'punishment', Chrysalis was working on her plans in the throne room when she heard a knock on the door, and it slowly opened. She turned around to see Pif in her usual hybrid form pushed up against the door, making herself look small. She was already shaking as the still-fresh memories of this room came back to her.

"Hi, GramGram."

The queen smiled softly and patted the spot next to her. Pif was reluctant to come closer, but eventually she slowly walked over and sat next to Chrysalis as the queen put her arm around her gently.

"Epiphany, you know that I did not like being slapped, right?" Chrysalis asked softly.

What she said as well as her tone just made Pif start shaking again. "I'm sorry, GramGram. I really am. I just don't like killing. Nobody ever deserves to die." She nuzzled against Chrysalis, not noticing that the queen's horn was glowing.

"Oh Pif, you have such potential. I just need to push you to realize it. Fortunately, the tribute is tonight, and I have demanded that they bring double so that you and I can feast together." The queen smiled as she looked down at Pif who looked back up with eyes that were gradually being outlined by a ring of faint green.

"That sounds lovely," Pif said dully.

"I know it does. Come along now," Chrysalis said as she got up and headed toward the chamber behind the royal throne.

As Pif walked down the gilded hallway, she found herself getting more and more hungry, and her hooves shook with each step. "GramGram, why am I so hungry? Why am I so weak?" Pif asked as she looked toward the far end of the room. Whatever was there was getting tastier and tastier.

"Oh, Pif, you're hungry because I'm venting your love back into the network in order to make this next treat all the sweeter."

Pif was barely able to understand what she was saying as she lurched toward the room, and the two of them entered the strange chamber. There were two ponies standing there with wide smiles on their face. By the looks of their eyes, it was clear that they were under Chrysalis' thrall. Pif, however, was in no condition to tell as she walked right up to one of them, panting heavily.

The red earth pony mare giggled softly and did a little circle about Pif, running her tail under the changeling's chin. "You look so hungry," she said enticingly.

The other pony, an off-white pegasus, moved over to where he knew he had to go as Chrysalis sat down with a grin. The pegasus leaned over and Chrysalis licked her neck a few times, a haze going over the changeling's eyes as she viewed the pony's chi paths directly.

"Can you feel the love, Epiphany? All you need to do is bare your fangs, and your instincts will take over from that point on." The queen grinned as she looked at her tribute, and with a large hiss, she dug her fangs into the pegasus' neck, extracting the love as his eyes went wide and he went limp, occasionally convulsing.

Pif looked at the queen, then looked back to her 'tribute'. The earth pony was grinning as she leaned in and nuzzled Pif who was already shaking as she fought with herself. "Come on – just a bite will fill you up."

Pif panted softly as the haze covered her eyes. She looked back at the earth pony and she could see the varying channels swirling around her body: hate... love... ambition... magic... it was all there, and all she had to do was just give in. Her fangs slowly exposed themselves as she moved in, letting them graze the pony's neck, and she focused intently on the natural pulse of her body.

"Mmnhh... come on... just a little bite!" the earth pony moaned with a shudder as she bared her neck for Epiphany.

Pif could feel the love, but when she dived deeper, she could feel the pathways her love took to the rest of the hive network. She could feel *all* of it! Pif took a sip, but then her mind revolted and she stopped. Pif whispered just loud enough for Chrysalis to hear, "If it's not Free, it's the nobles. If it's not the nobles, then it's you. I'm always a pawn, and the only difference is who's moving the pieces."

The queen just chuckled as she tossed the corpse of her tribute to the side. "That's how life works – give it enough time and soon you'll become a puppet master as well."

Pif's eyes glowed a bright white as she shifted into her full changeling form and her wings flared out. She grabbed onto the network as completely as she could and in one hard tug she inverted the flow of the love energy, not only taking her own energy back, but also causing every nearby drone to collapse from exhaustion.

Breezon burst into the chamber just as Chrysalis started to snarl. "If you betray me, you'll have nobody else left to turn to! You will have nothing! **You will *be* nothing!**"

Pif had a moment of clarity, and in the vault of her mind, two books from her link with Luna remained seared permanently into her memory, and for the first time she saw them clearly. "I may be nothing, but I'll always be more than *you*." Her chitin turned a bright chrome and she disappeared along with the earth pony that she still held. The resulting flash and concussive wave sent the rapidly approaching Breezon and still-stunned Chrysalis slamming into the side of the chamber.

"How did she...?! GENERAL, GET TO HER CHAMBER NOW!" Chrysalis screamed.

Pif reappeared in her chamber and she tossed the earth pony onto the bed. All twelve of her think-tank were waiting for her in her room, and they looked at her with fright. "What's going on?!" one of them screamed as they began panicking.

"Find my special backpack! Get the Crystal! Evacuation protocol!" Pif ordered.

They all moved with orderly haste, gathering all that they needed and putting it onto the bed.

The locked double-doors to the large chamber suddenly blew off their hinges. General Breezon stood there with a smoking horn and his sword drawn. He sneered, "Little princesses should know when they have gone too far."

Pif looked at the general, her eyes wide as she scanned her mind in a panic for something –*anything* – she could use. That jet black book was still there unopened, and she had a deep sense of dread before she opened it. Her eyes turned into narrow slits as she screamed out, "MIDNIGHT UNENDING!" Her horn fired out an intense jet of energy as it solidified into what looked like an ebony scythe. She grabbed it in her magic and ran at the charging general. She slashed at him with the scythe, but she did not have his combat prowess, only the few lessons that she had learned from Warfist. However, it was like the blade was moving itself, and scythe and sword clashed over and over again.

"Hurry up!" Pif screamed as all of the drones got on the bed and surrounded the earth pony. Pif shoved Breezon back, dashed over to the bed, and grabbed the Return Crystal that one of her assistants held out for her. She smashed the crystal on the floor, and the area-of-effect spell activated. She turned back just in time to see the general jump into range of the spell, and he teleported with them.

It was Friday dinner at House Path, and everyone in the herd was there, as well as the usual horde. Today was extra special, however, as the Crystal Prince and Princess decided to pay them a visit along with their daughter, Flurry Heart, to see how their favourite sister/sister-in-law was doing. However, in the middle of the dinner, Luna suddenly stood up, her horn lighting up violently. Her eyes went wide and glowed with power, and then she ran outside, yelling, "Epiphany hath activated the Return Crystal, but many doth accompany her!"

Luna ran out into the clearing outside the house just as the teleport completed, and a few things happened all at once. The spherical spell shimmered into being and then burst. A large bed fell to the ground with several Blue Changelings and a red earth pony mare upon it, and Shining Armor immediately threw a restraining force field around them. More importantly though were the two larger changelings doing battle in the air. No longer constrained by her room, Pif took off with the general on her tail. She focused all the stolen love to augment her physical abilities to match the general, and as a result, they were blurs moving around in complex patterns, and every now and then the spectators heard the clash of metal on metal.

"I'LL KILL YOU! NOTHING WILL SURVIVE AND NOBODY WILL REMEMBER YOUR PITIFUL EXISTENCE!" Pif screeched out as she launched a series of slashes upon the general.

"What a pity. With this much tenacity, you would have made a fine Blue Queen," Breezon laughed as he dodged and parried most of the attacks, letting her slash and cut him occasionally, and making her become more and more enraged.

"STOP TALKING AND START DYING!" Pif screamed as she spun the scythe around to deflect his blasts, her eyes turning bright teal as the scythe became darker, absorbing all light.

The changeling General started to worry as he could not press the attack, and he remained on the defensive. Every time he tried to get close, he was pushed away by the overwhelming attack of the changeling princess.

However, while Pif was gaining power from rage and adrenaline, the corruptive nature of the summoning spell was also quickly starting to overcome her.

Path narrowed his eyes and he growled, "Luna, is Pif being consumed by the nightmare?"

The alicorn shook her head. "Nay. The scythe is just one of her weapons, and it's a pale imitation at best, but all things based in her magic are heavily corrupted. If we don't stop this fast, Pif will become tainted."

Path nodded and calmly started giving orders. "Shining, when Pif and Breezon near the ground, I need you to confine them in a one-way barrier. Luna, be ready to grab Pif. It's time for the ultimate gambit, so stand-by. Cadance – those twelve changelings in the coats must be Pif's assistants, and they'll need protection. Free will fill you in."

Pif and Breezon were at a stalemate. While her power continued to grow, it also got more wild and frenzied. She could not penetrate his defences, but neither could he get past hers. His focus was so totally upon her though that he failed to notice that they were now confined within a force-field until too late. The fight continued unabated though, but his attention was drawn by a yell of anger, and he looked around just in time to see Path passing unhindered through the shield, aiming a flying kick at his head. Path's hoof connected with a sickening crack of chitin, and the general was sent flying, losing his sword in the process.

As soon as Breezon was distracted, Shining dropped the shield and Luna snatched Pif away. The alicorn's magic then banished the ebon scythe even as she drew the young changeling to herself and hugged her tightly. At first, Pif struggled and beat at Luna with her hooves, screaming incoherently. Luna took it stoically while projecting her love at the young changeling. Gradually Pif felt the affection that her auntie was lavishing upon her, and she began calming down. It was not long before Pif was returning the hug, tears flowing down her cheeks.

Meanwhile, Breezon had gotten back onto his hooves, snarling in rage. A mere pony had hit him! That pony would die! He charged to the attack, but was shocked to be effortlessly countered. After throwing a flurry of blows that failed to land, he stepped back to take stock of his foe more carefully. The earth pony was large, although not exceptionally so, but what stood out was his musculature. Breezon had never seen such a powerfully muscled pony before, but this was no mere bodybuilder. His experienced eye could tell that his physique was a result of hard training, and the way the pony held himself told him that he knew how to use his strength.

Path smirked at him. "I'm not such an easy target as a child, am I, General? I've been waiting nearly two decades to get another crack at Chrysalis, and I've been preparing all that time. A pity she's not here, but I'll be delighted to take it out on you." Path's expression shifted to one of utter rage. **"Anybody who attacks my daughter will suffer the consequences!"** Without another word, he hurled himself at Breezon.

Although Breezon approached the new fight with caution and a greater emphasis on tactics, the battle was not going well for him. The vast majority of his attacks had been easily evaded or parried. Path on the other hoof had slowly chipped away at his defences and gradually flaws had started to appear, and each time Path had taken full advantage of them. An attempt to grapple him had instead resulted in the pony latching onto a wing, and he had screamed in agony as it was ripped out. It lay on the ground, still bleeding green blood from its stump. His horn had cracks running along the base due to the repeated strikes against it whenever he had tried to charge up a spell. The general panted heavily and was close to being exhausted, but the green-haired pony circled him relentlessly, his body low and his mane almost standing on end, growling like a timberwolf. "Ponies don't act like this! Ponies are food, not predators!" he screamed in frustration.

Path just grinned as he kept circling him. "Ponies are so much more than that, but it's too late for you to learn. I'm going to kill you myself."

The tired general blinked, opening up another hole in his shattering defences. Path pounced on that mistake in an instant, a flying kick sending the general sprawling onto his back. Path followed it up by jumping onto him, his hoof-stomp cracking the chitin on his chest. The general howled out in pain, but he managed to grab the pony's hoof and haul it towards his mouth. He sank his fangs into Path's leg. "Let's see how well you fight without your earth pony magic!" he gloated, only to realize a moment later that his ability to drain pony magic was achieving nothing.

Path grunted in pain as the fangs sunk in, but he resisted the instinct to just rip his leg free which would have caused more damage. Instead he sneered at the changeling and said, "Not having much luck, are you? I burned out all my magic fighting your mad queen in the Crystal Kingdom. I trained with one of the world's foremost unarmed combat specialists to compensate. You never stood a chance."

The changeling realized his mistake and tried to drain the pony's positive emotions instead, despite the less than ideal location of the contact. Before he could though, Path's other leg gave him an uppercut that knocked his fangs out of the muscle. Then the leg came back down on the general's neck, forcing his windpipe shut without quite crushing it. Breezon's eyes went wide and he started thrashing in an attempt to break free, but Path held on grimly. He began to panic, shifting into different forms over and over as he tried to slip out of the pony's grasp, but it was too late, and his fate was sealed. The transformations happened slower and slower before they stopped, and as the general's consciousness slipped away, Path let go of his neck, letting Breezon's head loll limply to the ground.

Path turned to Shining Armor and said, "Confine him, please. This isn't over yet."

Shining nodded and a force bubble appeared about the beaten changeling. "What about those Blues?" he asked with a nod in their direction.

"They might be just as much victims of Chrysalis as well, but they still pose a risk for the moment. Just continue confining them for now."

Roseclaw came up with a bandage to bind the bleeding wound on Path's leg. "That was a magnificent battle, my warrior. I am so proud of you."

"Thanks, Rose, but time for that later. We have a final task to complete." He gestured to Luna to bring Pif over, and she arrived just as Free and Twilight joined them.

Still sniffling a bit, Pif detached herself from Luna and looked up at her parents. "I'm sorry," she said in the smallest of voices.

Path shook his head. "It's we who are sorry, Pif. I should never have let the nobles get their way. The punishment was far too great for the offense."

"I'm sorry too, Pif," Free confessed. "I failed to accept my responsibility as the hive's queen, and I should never have pushed you so hard to be my replacement. We will talk about this more later to try to right this wrong."

Twilight stepped up to hug Pif. "As a Princess of Equestria, Lady of the House of Path, and most of all as your mother, I should never have allowed this situation to happen. I failed you, Pif, and I am so sorry."

Roseclaw stepped up next. "I did not approve of some of the things that my herd had done, but I allowed them to go ahead, and for that I am sorry also. However, you are strong of will and a fighter, and you have come through despite all of this. As your mother also, and on behalf of Herd Path, I ask if you will forgive us as we forgive you?"

Pif burst into tears again as she hurled herself into Roseclaw's embrace. Path, Free, Twilight and Luna all came in to join the hug, and the young changeling found herself nearly drowning in a flood of love. Pif eventually said, "I need to know where I fit in, what I'm supposed to do."

Free replied, "Let's find out together, okay?"

Pif buried her head in Free's chest feathers and sniffled. "Sounds good to me, Mother."

After several long minutes of this, they were finally pulled away when Shining Armor announced, "The prisoner is waking."

Breezon regained consciousness to find himself pinned to a garden wall by magic bonds, and the members of Herd Path gathered in front of him, radiating hostility. Epiphany stood with them, and he spat in her direction. "Traitor!"

Pif turned her head away sadly. "My grandmother betrayed me first. I wanted to make things better for her hive, and perhaps even bring peace between it and Equestria. Instead she sought to subvert me even as she claimed to love me. I was never anything more than a pawn to Chrysalis, and I wasted my love on her. Now I can't even be sorry for the consequences."

"Consequences? What are you babbling about? Do you think this minor setback will stop her plans? You have no idea what you're up against!"

Pif looked back at him with the smallest of smiles. "You're wrong. I know virtually *everything*. I even told GramGram so, but she thought I was exaggerating. It all started with my first successful long-distance communication, and from that moment, Chrysalis' fate was sealed. If she had been true to me, nothing more would have happened, just as I promised, but she betrayed me, and thus she released me from my promise. I am going to destroy you, GramGram."

"I'm not your grandmother," Breezon replied with a scowl.

Pif just chuckled. "Still not listening, I see. Goodbye, GramGram."

Free stepped up then, shifting to queen form. She sneered at Breezon. "What she means, General, is that we know that Chrysalis implemented Pif's superior communication system, and she's currently seeing and hearing every word we're saying. So, hello again, Mom. You tried to take my daughter, Maggot Queen, and I cannot forgive that. You are dead. Your hive is dead."

"Fool!" Breezon shouted. "You have no power over us!"

Path replied with deadly seriousness, "That is where you are wrong, and as head of the House of Path, and in accordance with our charter to protect those who cannot protect themselves, we have found you guilty of leading two invasions, planning others, and committing a myriad of crimes against the sapient species of this world. You are an intractable threat to all of Equus. You have only been permitted to live in peace up until now as an act of mercy that your granddaughter begged of us. Your complete and utter destruction is the only option that you have left us. As Queen Chrysalis is the de facto head of government of Saddle Arabia, we can declare a total war protocol against you. It starts now." Path motioned for Luna to step forward.

The alicorn's horn glowed brightly and Breezon could see a spell being constructed. Then Luna's eyes started glowing with the power of the spell, and he tried to look away, only to have telekinesis force his head back. Luna's eyes locked with his, and the spell was released. It shot through the enhanced connection and started spreading throughout the Blue's hive-mind at the speed of thought to all Blue Changelings irrespective of distance, activating the hidden commands that Pif had laboriously constructed even as she had seemed to be working on other projects for the benefit of the hive. The commands that she had implanted into all who were connected to the hive-mind affected every Blue Changeling, causing them to shift to their natural form and let out a high pitch screech, exposing their true nature wherever they were in the world. All across Equus, their enemies started culling them immediately. Those who weren't caught immediately soon discovered that their connection to the hive-mind had been permanently severed, leaving them virtually helpless. The screeching was also at the exact resonance frequency of the new love containment glass that Pif had designed and Chrysalis had been producing as fast as possible, shattering them and causing high-energy explosions, with the biggest in the areas with the greatest amount of love energy stored. The Blue Hive's nursery was utterly obliterated, and the multitude of explosions elsewhere killed many others and buried even more in collapsing tunnels.

The throne room was damaged, but it survived. When the smoke and dust cleared, Chrysalis found her mind chillingly quiet. Even the two special guards in the throne room with her were a blank to her. Debris fell from the roof, and she realized that this room could also collapse at any time. It was time to abandon the hive. She ordered the guards to follow her, and she headed for the surface. They had to make many detours due to the collapsed tunnels, but they eventually approached one of the exits. A pained cry from just outside made her pause though, and she sensed a trap. With stealth that only a changeling could manage, she got as close to the tunnel mouth as possible and spotted Blue Streak in his magitek wings patrolling the sky with his squad, and some Wonderbolts further away, covering other areas. They were eliminating all survivors without mercy as they escaped the destroyed hive.

Chrysalis realized that they would not stop until they had found her and made sure that she was dead. She debated sending out one of her special guards disguised as herself, but unless they completely obliterated the changeling, the ruse would be revealed as it reverted upon death. There was only one recourse now, but it was one that she had planned for and kept hidden even from Epiphany. The special guards had been bred to serve as vessels for her mind in an emergency, and would in time grow into a new queen, but first she had to make a connection with one of them. With the hive-link broken, she had to resort to sinking her fangs into one to make a new connection. She pushed aside the guard's mind, ruthlessly supplanting it, but she retained a link to her old body. She puppeted it out of the tunnel, made a show of resistance, and watched as it was blasted mere moments later. She did not stop to watch them come down to positively identify the corpse. She knew that they would flush out the tunnels next, rooting out the last of her changelings. She took her final guard and retreated, eventually finding one of her secret passageways. She collapsed the tunnel behind her and took shelter in a top-secret bunker that had been stocked with supplies. When her enemies left, she would emerge and start anew.

Chrysalis burned with hate. The first and only thing on her agenda was House Path's utter destruction.

Path's hoof slammed into the base of Breezon's horn, snapping it off at the base. The general screamed and his body convulsed for a moment before he went totally limp.

"Azon! Get a stasis pod now!"

The doctor quickly fetched a pod, and Path tossed the half-dead Blue Changeling into it. Azon sealed him inside and, with the help of a student, carried it away to be dealt with later.

"Are we going to do the same to those other Blues?" Shining asked.

"No!" Pif exclaimed. "They're my friends!"

Path went over to Cadance and asked, "Did you manage to protect them from the effects of the spell?"

Cadance nodded happily. "They should be able to re-link with Pif without a problem."

Path said to Shining, "You can drop the force field now."

As soon as the bubble of magic surrounding them disappeared, the twelve changelings rushed over to Pif, briefly alarming Path, but all they did was start profusely thanking her, some even hugging her. As she touched each one, she re-formed a link with them, and soon she had her own mini-network once more.

One of the changelings turned to Path and bowed. "Thank you, Lord Path. On behalf of my colleagues, I swear loyalty to our Princess Epiphany…" He bowed to her. "To Queen Gossamer…" he bowed to a rather surprised Free. "And to the House of Path." He bowed once more to Path and then Twilight, Roseclaw, and Luna.

"Because Pif vouches for you, I am happy to welcome you all to House Path." Path then smirked a little. "If nothing else, you won't be bored."

The changeling looked a little confused by that last statement, but was reassured by the good humour that he could taste coming from his new Lord.

Path then indicated the red earth pony. "What's her story?" he asked Pif.

"Unwilling victim. Looks like she's coming out from under Chrysalis' spell. She'll need a lot of emotional support and reorientation before we can arrange to send her back home."

Path nodded and said, "We'll make sure that happens. Free, I think our daughter needs to be cleaned up after her experiences." He looked over himself, noting the various cuts and bruises he had incurred during the fight. "I'm going to take a shower and get cleaned up too. After that…" His hoof swept in the direction of the crowd of spectators on the balcony who had watched the events unfold. "I think we've got a lot of explaining to do."

Path and the rest of the herd had been explaining the facts behind the evening's unusual events to a rapt audience.

"It was the riskiest gambit that I will probably ever play. If I had known what Pif had planned before it started, I would have put a stop to it immediately."

"Which is exactly why I didn't tell anyone," Pif said from where she was snuggled tiredly between Luna and Free. "I literally couldn't take any more of the hostility at Canterlot, so when Chrysalis approached me at Donut Joe's, I saw it as an opportunity to get away from it all, as well as the cold shoulder I was getting from my parents." She shrugged apologetically, but Free just hugged her reassuringly and Path waved it off. "I also saw it as a chance to put my ideas to the test and try to reform Gra– uh, Chrysalis. I know now that I was terribly naïve, but I don't regret trying. I wasn't completely stupid though. A short while after I arrived at the hive and had gotten a large dose of love energy and a good rest, I started looking into a way of taking Chrysalis out if I could not reform her."

Free jumped in then. "Her experiments were mostly a blind for her most important activity. She used the information that she had taken from Chrysalis when she did her first hive network probe experiment to mask the fact that she implanted her hidden commands in the hive-mind. When she communicated with Luna in her dreamscape, she passed on the activation spell. That was also when she gave us updates on her progress, or lack thereof. She gave Chrysalis the technology to create a very efficient way to store love, but made it intentionally difficult for Chrysalis to comprehend, therefore failing to see that it was deliberately flawed and how easily it could be disrupted to cause a massive explosion upon release of all the stored energy. All Pif had to do was return with at least one drone to act as a remote link, and it could all be triggered."

Path continued the explanation. "Of course we couldn't expect to get all of them in the explosions, but Chrysalis never did discover the tracking spell that Pif had put on her long ago, and we've known where her hive was located for some time now. We planned to execute our attack very soon, and two days ago, we sent Blue Streak and his squad, plus several Wonderbolt elite squads to stand by to do clean up and to recover Chrysalis' body. This time we had to make sure that she didn't get away again. Although Chrysalis jumped the gun on us slightly, fortunately they were in place and waiting when the action began. Blue has been reporting that all has been progressing smoothly." Path sighed. "I am not proud of having to initiate what could be considered extermination, but it had to be done."

King Glimfeather looked over at Epiphany who appeared to have fallen asleep while draped in Luna's lap. "I don't know if she's a mastermind or a sociopath. She's played everyone. She used the backlash for biting Luna to her advantage, and she even knew that if she joined Chrysalis, she could have access to the queen's thoughts. She also knew that Luna could securely pass on details of her plan. It was amazing for something that was conceived and executed on the fly."

Pif slowly opened her eyes, apparently still awake despite her tiredness. "I wasn't expecting Breezon. I didn't anticipate almost giving in to ripping love out of a pony. I wasn't expecting Luna being so terribly sad when I left. There were a lot of things I did not expect that could have gone wrong, but I just happened to plan out the most important things." She looked up at Luna and continued, "In fact I was very nearly a complete idiot, Auntie. I truly wanted to believe that I could do some good there, but instead Chrysalis made me do something horrible."

Luna smiled reassuringly. "We all have our regrets, dear child. Do not let thine torture thee as I didst torture myself. Remember the lesson and move on with thy life."

"I will, Auntie." She looked over to Free and asked, "What happens now?"

Free replied, "We'll have a long talk about that, but for now I think I had better stop shirking my queenly responsibilities, and leave you free to figure out what you want to achieve with your life. I promise that you will have my *reasonable* cooperation from now on. Just let me know when you think you're ready to take over the hive."

Pif giggled. "I suppose that's for the best. I've been so focused on being groomed as the new queen that I have never even stopped to think if I *wanted* to be queen as yet. I think you're going to be stuck with the job for a while, Dad."

Free shrugged. "I have my daughter back, and my family to support me; I can think of worse fates."

"Pardon me, Princess Cadance, but may I have a word with you?"

Cadance looked up from the book that she had been reading in the sunroom. She recognized the speaker standing in the doorway as one of the twelve changelings that Pif had brought with her, still proudly dressed in his lab coat, but with the addition of a badge marking him as the chief assistant which he earned by his leadership qualities.

"Come in," she said with a smile. "What is your name?"

"Zavak, Your Highness," he replied as he trotted over to her.

"What can I do for you, Zavak?"

The changeling's magic drew an object from the saddlebag he was wearing. It was a small sphere with a perfectly reflective surface, and he passed it to the alicorn. "This was one of the projects Princess Epiphany worked on while she was in the Blue Hive. We understand its importance, but also its risks. This device is within your realm of responsibility, so we would like your opinion about what should be done with it."

Cadance examined it with her magical senses, and was startled to feel the very small amount of love emanating from it. "Although it is tiny in comparison, this object is akin in nature to the Crystal Heart. And you say that Pif was responsible for creating this?"

Zavak nodded. "With our assistance, Epiphany was able to make her theories reality."

"You do realize that with a fully working version of this, the hives could be forever free of their need to harvest love? Free of the vagaries of pony attitudes, the changelings could grow to meet their full potential. However, there is also a possible dark side to this invention. Changelings would also be free of the need to live in Harmony with other sapient races. Would they continue to do so? Chrysalis showed us what just one hive could do to us. What if *all* the hives turned against pony-kind?"

"With respect, Your Highness, that assumes love is the *only* thing that we would want from pony-kind, and I think you already realize that is not true. However, to put this into perspective, this prototype took nearly a hundred kilocadance to create, but only generates a millicadance of extra love. It's barely anything, so far."

Cadance smiled knowingly. "That's not the entire story though, is it?"

"You are very perceptive. Although its output is *currently* miniscule, as long as the excess is not drawn off, the love energy is recycled into the generation process in a positive feedback loop."

"So what you're saying is that the output is exponential? If that's true, eventually this will become another Crystal Heart."

"Exactly, hence why we are so concerned. It is a double-edged weapon, capable of doing as much harm as it could do good. In short, it is dangerous. So what do you think we should do with it?"

"You are thinking that I should take it back to the Crystal Kingdom with me? While it's true that I could offer it the same protection as the Crystal Heart, I believe that when it reaches its full potential, it would focus too much love energy in one place, with possible undesirable side-effects. However, in my opinion, the potential benefits outweigh the risks, and there is one hive that I would trust to keep it safe and handle it responsibly."

"The Chrome Hive," Zavak confirmed. "Epiphany thought so too, but she felt that we needed a second opinion, and one with the greatest degree of expertise. I am happy to have you confirm our hopes for the device. I will not live to see it reach its full potential, but sometime in the future, changeling-kind might at least be freed from the shackles of our needs."

Cadance passed the sphere back to the drone. "This is not mine to keep. It belongs to your princess, and it will be her legacy. Take very good care of it, for someday I believe it will change *everything* for *all* changelings."

Chapter 15: Meetings

As Epiphany reached the primary meeting room in Twilight's castle, she started to get a sense of dread; she could hear yelling, squawking and angry whinnying coming from the room. In the many times she had been at the castle, she had never heard anything nearly as violent as this. With a heavy sigh she opened the door to the highly polarized room.

Although she was aware of the differences of opinion over how Chrysalis and her hive had been handled, Pif had not expected there to be such a heated argument before she even arrived at the meeting of the many Heads of State. They had literally taken stands on opposite sides of the table. On her left, her fathers, Path and Free, were joined by Princess Luna, Prince Shining Armor, King Glimfeather, Red Changeling Queen Carpacia, Violet Changeling Queen Lamina, and Orange Changeling Queen Polistae. On her right, they faced off against Princess Cadance, Yellow Changeling Queen Orlare, and Green Changeling Queen Dianthia. Her mothers, Roseclaw and Twilight, seemed to be staying neutral along with Princess Celestia. Lucida sighed as she realized that her Aunt Cadance and Uncle Shining Armor were likely to be arguing a lot more in private later. Hopefully she could ameliorate that.

She had her work cut out for her though. Orlare, of all 'lings, was half-standing with her front hooves on the table, her wings spread open and her ears pinned back, practically screaming, "You dare call me a coward?! It is you who are the cowards! Only an ignorant fool decides to take the life of thousands on a whim!" She pointed her hoof accusingly at Carpacia, which only served to raise the tension and the anger in the room even further.

Carpacia was about to stand up, but Long Path moved before she did. Letting out a loud changeling *skree* that made Orlare back up slightly. He then bellowed, "YOU DARE CALL US COWARDS?!" His eyes narrowed. "I am all for peace, but there was *no* other option! We defended all of Equus from this global threat! We lost ponies, thestrals, griffons, *and* changelings on that day! It took all that we had and still the Crystal Kingdom was nearly destroyed because of it!" He stomped his hooves on the table.

It was then that Shining Armor stood up and started talking to back up Path. "In fact I saw a lot of good people die, but none of them were Yellow Changelings. Where was your support? When did you to rise to the defence of an ally? It's so easy for you to claim to be the bigger 'ling when you refused to aid those you claim to have an alliance with! Argent lost a son! Carpacia lost a daughter! You speak of moral superiority but more than your chitin is yellow!" Shining huffed as he sat back down. Orlare did not have a response to that, and she was floored by the aggression in the two ponies.

Cadance and Lamina jumped to Orlare's defence, but just then Celestia interjected, "This is not about the Crystal Kingdom War. This is about the tactical strike that occurred one week ago. We should all limit our comments and criticisms to that operation *only*." The white alicorn sat down as did all of the others.

The room was tensely quiet for a while as Lucida walked into the room followed by Spike, both carrying trays with drinks for everyone. "Let us remember that we are here to learn the exact circumstances of what happened. Once we have learned what has occurred, we can create legislation so that such a situation can hopefully never happen again, or at least it's covered by law." Lucida spoke in a calm voice as she passed the cups to everyone who sipped them as they calmed down. She then took her place at the head of the table as the meeting's moderator. She banged her gavel and said, "I call this meeting to order. I believe that the first speaker is Cinder. As Strike Coordinator, she was the one to receive the order to mobilize Blue's squad from Herd Path." Lucida nodded to Cinder who was seated with Blue Streak.

Cinder lifted up her notes and said, "From the public record of House Path, the vote to mobilize Blue Streak's Fast Response Strike Team was passed three votes to two, with Princess Luna, Lord Long Path, and Lord Free Agent for the motion, and with Princess Twilight and Lady Roseclaw against. It was decided that for the quickest response, ultrahigh capacity mana-capacitors would be used and the squad's limiters removed. At 23:00, Blue Streak, Night Wing, Shattered Quartz and Ramona Axetalon took off. Expedient Trajectory was approved. Taking the northern route, they arrived approximately six hours later." She was interrupted by Dianthia.

"How could they travel that fast without teleportation?" she asked Cinder.

"Without going into too much detail, Blue's team is equipped with flight protection enhancements, high-altitude breathing enchantments, and supersonic flight systems that allow them to go so high that air resistance isn't an issue. Once they are at their target altitude, their trajectory allows them coast at high velocity the rest of the way. It allows them to reach any desired destination very quickly. I believe that Sir

Blue Streak can continue from this point."

Blue stood up as Cinder sat down. "Due to our enhancements, we were able to rest undetected on some cirrus clouds and establish a surveillance post. Axetalon's superior far-sight coupled with Twilight Sparkle's changeling detection spell enabled him to perceive details of the capital city from that height, and he was able to observe that roughly one in ten were Blue Changelings. The original fear that the city had indeed been taken over was verified. Sixteen hours later, we were joined by three wing formations from the Wonderbolt Corps. When Epiphany triggered the return crystal, the resulting ping on the crystal communicators was our signal to act. When the Blue Changelings reverted back to their base form, the population at large started to fight back. The Wonderbolts joined in while we combed the area for changelings fleeing the hive, especially the queen. She was spotted and we attempted to capture her. However, she chose to fight us and she was killed in the attempt. Her body was taken back to the House for analysis by Twilight, Azon and Techbird. After the remaining resistance was overcome, we investigated the hive to gather as much intelligence as possible. However, due to most of the significant data being present only in the hive-mind and extensive damage to the hive tunnels, that was only minor." Blue Streak sat back down.

Tempers were about to flare again when Lucida took control of the situation. "Again, we are here to get facts above all else. We now know the basics of what happened in Saddle Arabia directly after the gambit was executed." Lucida looked at Shining and Polistae, both of them looking like they were getting ready to launch into a verbal assault again. She hastened to forestall them. "Epiphany has some details to fill in the blanks for us."

Pif stood up, uncomfortable under the glare of several of those present. "As Blue Streak said, most of the relevant intelligence was only present in the hive-mind. In order to protect myself from Queen Chrysalis' influence, I severely restricted my access to it. However, I did recruit several of her brightest changelings as my assistants, and they had almost unfettered access. While there were still parts of it closed off to them, the records of the covert invasion of Saddle Arabia and its takeover were complete, and plans to do the same with more nations were also well under way. My grandmother made it plain that she intended to eventually subjugate Equestria, but it became clear to me that this was likely by pitting all her conquered nations against this country. Chrysalis was again taking the long view, and after learning the lessons of the Crystal Kingdom War, it's quite possible that her plans might have succeeded this time. I attempted to change her mind about her plans of conquest through various means, but not only did she rebuff them, she also tried to corrupt me. In my assessment, my grandmother, Queen Chrysalis, was an irredeemable and implacable enemy of all nations and all races."

There was quiet in the room as the listeners digested that information. Lucida gave them a few moments before announcing, "Next, we will hear from Queen Orlare about the recovery efforts in the country." Lucida made a motion for Orlare to begin.

The changeling queen cleared her throat before speaking. "As this was all unfolding, we received a high-priority message from Lord Path indicating that he needed some of our best trauma counsellors. Within a day, we had them at Friendship Castle. Joining them were General Diamondhard from the Crystal Kingdom and Technician Skytalon, one of Techbird's chief assistants. We are in the process of helping the Saddle Arabian royal family recover. My best counsellor is working on repairing the damage to the royal family, while others are working on the PR nightmare for changelings in the country. Diamondhard is working on increasing security and changing protocols, and Skytalon is working on changing the energy source of the distillation devices made by Pif to maintain the supply of water to key areas." Orlare sat down after giving her report.

It was then that Path raised his hoof. And Lucida nodded for him to speak.

"We have successfully changed the energy source from love gel to standard mana energy. We are also working on setting up a satellite campus to not only begin offering advanced education, but also to house the volunteers that we'll soon be asking for to help run the water treatment centre we are in the process of designing." Path leaned back in his chair with a smile.

Lucida nodded. "Princess Twilight Sparkle, we are now ready for your report."

Twilight stood up, levitating her notes in front of her. "Firstly, to ensure that we did indeed have Queen Chrysalis' body, we confirmed the presence of the tracking spell that Epiphany attached to her some time back when she visited her granddaughter in Ponyville. This tracking spell was what enabled us to find Chrysalis' new hive, and thus also ensured that we had the real Chrysalis and not a changeling fake. After a complete analysis of Chrysalis's body, some rather unique issues were discovered, and the implications are startling. You can read these in full in the complete reports that I have passed out to all of you, but I will bring up the top three irregularities." She flipped through the large report. "Her body has a strong taint of corruptive magic in it. This indicates exposure to dark or nightmare-class magic. We believe that this was in part due to the fact that while Pif was battling Breezon, she activated a certain spell. While we were able to banish the spell in Pif, we believe that the spell was festering in Chrysalis before she was killed."

Celestia and Luna perked up at the news and listened intently.

"There is another inconsistency that was noticed but cannot be explained. All changelings currently alive that were present during the invasion of Canterlot have a tell-tale signature as a result. When we gave Free Agent, a.k.a. Queen Gossamer, a thorough check-up, we found it, and we subsequently have found it on other Blue Changelings, and to a lesser degree on all the changelings from other hives who had been there at the time. It's a form of chitin strain caused by the love detonation generated by Princess Cadance and Shining Armor that is prevalent in a few key locations on the body and is non-reversible. Chrysalis was at ground zero, and as such we would expect her to have the same chitin strain patterns as all the others, but she does not. The fact that she is a queen does not affect the results because Free is one also."

Twilight turned a page and continued. "Then there's the final irregularity – the body isn't as old as it should be. According to information from the Chrome Hive-mind, it should be at least two hundred years old, but instead it's approximately seventeen. That means that she, or rather her body, was not in existence until after the invasion of the Crystal Kingdom, and definitely not present during the Canterlot invasion. This leads to a startling conclusion, one that neither I nor my team can disprove: either Chrysalis has found a way to completely regenerate her body, or this Chrysalis is not the same as the one who was defeated in the Crystal Kingdom, nor is it the same as the one expelled from Canterlot."

The rest of the participants started to talk amongst themselves until Lucida banged her gavel to quiet everyone so Twilight could talk again.

"I will not speculate on the implications of these facts at this time, but we are currently working on extrapolating several scenarios and how to deal with them. This is what we know for certain so far."

Lucida tapped the gavel a few more times.

"I believe that this concludes the meeting for today. I encourage everyone to read the detailed reports before we gather again tomorrow to discuss the ramifications." Lucida banged the gavel and stood, as did everyone else. The other parties left the main meeting room already starting to converse. Lucida was relieved that the tensions had eased and they were back to actually talking civilly. Hopefully the same could be said tomorrow when they reconvened.

Ponyville was practically buzzing with conversation and activity, with so many different races currently in Ponyville for the summit, they all started to talk.

Argent Glimfeather was wondering what he would do with his free time. For the most part, his kingdom had little to do with the situation, and with no other plans, he was left to himself. That was until Blue Streak and Luna walked up to him, smiling.

"King Glimfeather, we were hoping that thou wouldst be free tonight." Luna said. "Blue and I have found a good place to dine. It is an Eyrish restaurant owned by a griff-pony who is also a chef, and has an artiste caste griffon chef too. I hear 'tis *really* good."

Argent smiled. "You know what? I think that my schedule is open. Let's go." The king dismissed his guards, and the three of them left the castle and walked down the road. With the recent influx of griffons due to the summit, he was just another unknown face, and he was enjoying the anonymity. They soon walked into a place where they were shouted at in Griffish.

"Welcome!" both chefs yelled at once while a violet changeling walked over and guided them to a table.

Argent watched the cooks with interest. The place was somewhat crowded, but the conversations were quiet as they were all watching the chefs with fascination. A giant fire plume erupted in the centre of the room as they moved the large slabs of meat into the flames. This was typical of Eyrish cooking – large portions, hearty spices, rare to medium cooking. They offered all kinds of cuts on the menu which proudly proclaimed '*the finest meats from a variety of non-sapient species*'.

"So what kind of cut wouldst thou like, Argent?" Luna asked as she selected something from the menu. Blue had already picked out what he wanted. Argent raised an eyebrow as he saw Blue pass a pill box to Luna and they both took a pill.

"What was that?" he asked.

"Oh!" Luna said as she looked back to him. "As thou dost know, the number of ponies that like to eat meat is very small, although 'tis not because of biology but due to their moral choice. However, griff-ponies have in a few generations been able to handle meat a lot better than ponies from Equestria. House Path's medical wing examined them to determine how they manage to do so, and created this pill so that we could eat fattier kinds of food without getting sick."

"I see," the griffon said, and then chuckled as he picked a certain item on the menu named after him. It was called the Glimfeather Cut.

The waitress came back to take their orders. "You are going to like that cut," she told Argent. "The chefs themselves came up with it. It's a very large cut from the most flavourful area. They said it's the only cut that is worthy of royalty."

Luna snickered a bit, realizing the waitress did not know that she was actually speaking to the king after whom it was named. "How about we get three of the Glimfeather Cuts, then?"

Blue nodded in agreement and the waitress left.

"So, you just walk around, and everyone leaves you alone?" Argent asked Luna with a grin.

"Well, not really. Ponyville is something of an exception. Between my sister, Twilight and all the chaos that happens here, 'tis not too exciting when royalty shows up," Luna explained with amusement, and the king smirked a bit in return.

The trio continued to converse as their meal arrived. Argent looked at the steak and licked his beak while Blue and Luna gawked at theirs.

"I… was not expecting it to be so big," Blue commented.

"Neither did I," Luna agreed.

The waitress then decided to speak. "The Glimfeather Cut is also the largest steak we have. We have a challenge that if you can eat it and

all the sides in one sitting, it's free, and you get a T-shirt."

Blue looked over his cut. "This has to be, like, two kilos!"

The waitress just grinned. "Two and a quarter kilograms, to be exact."

Argent just laughed as his knife cut off a generous portion. "What? You can topple a mad changeling queen twice, but you can't eat a steak?"

Blue grinned. "Oh, you are so on!" Blue started in as well, and Luna immediately joined them.

Two hours later, the trio walked back into the castle. Argent was grinning, rather satisfied with his shirt. It was plain white and said, "I survived the Glimfeather cut!" and had a picture of a generic griffon with wide eyes staring at a huge steak. Behind him were Blue and Luna. They had T-shirts as well, but neither of them was smiling. Blue's stomach looked like it was double its normal size as he groaned, dragging his hooves along the ground, and Luna was not much better.

Eventually they ran into Roseclaw who just blinked and looked at the three of them. "What happened to you guys?!"

Argent just laughed. "I had a light lunch before dinner. These two, however, could not handle a royal appetite."

Luna and Blue just fell over onto their sides, groaning as Argent chuckled and continued down the hall, proudly proclaiming, "I have yet to meet a meal that I couldn't conquer!"

Rose looked down at the pair who had already passed out from the food coma. She faceclawed and mumbled, "The House Champions, everybody..."

Path walked out of the main room yawning slightly as he headed toward his private room. He was exhausted from the yelling and the debating; normally he had more control over his emotions. He was just glad that Lucida was able to keep everything under control and prevent the sides from becoming too polarized. He was proud of how well she employed the skills that he had taught her.

Path shut the door to his room and went over to his bed, flopping onto it with a groan. Soon the door opened up and Roseclaw slinked in. Shutting the door behind her, she then walked over to Path.

"You always work too hard, even when things get too intense for your own good." Roseclaw sighed as she leaned in, crooning slightly before she nuzzled him, Path just blinked a few times.

"Hmmm... I didn't know you were attracted to me, Carpacia." Path looked up at her with a tired grin.

Rose gasped and took a few steps back before she narrowed her eyes. "How did you know?" the fake griffon said calmly.

"Simple – I can always smell myself and my other herd mates on each other. It's what happens when you curl up in a pile every night to pass out. You, on the other hoof, smell lightly of sweat and iron. You actually emulated her scent well; you just forgot about the other scents," Path explained.

"So how do you know that I'm Carpacia and not another different harvester or queen?" Rose challenged him with a grin as she crossed her arms defiantly.

"Because when you didn't think I was looking, you were practically eye-humping me during the entire meeting." He chuckled a bit. "So what do you really want?"

The griffon rolled her eyes and transformed back into Carpacia. "I am acknowledging you as a suitable sire for one of my general princesses. I need another because of Iron Chitin's virtuous death during the Crystal Kingdom siege. There always needs to be an odd number of generals."

Path just blinked at her. "You want me to sire a queen? How did you plan to do that without assuming earth pony form?"

Carpacia smirked. "I wished to seduce you a little before I revealed myself, but you were too perceptive for me."

Path was a little annoyed at that, but then again he was dealing with a changeling, not a pony. "Don't get me wrong – I think that's a pretty high honour to even be considered, but before anything else, I need to discuss this with my herd. If all of them agree, then I will consider it along with our conditions."

She just grinned. "The Red Hive values strength and honour above all other things. You lead a powerful Griffonian House, and you not only beat the Mad Queen twice, but you also beat her top general in unarmed combat without the help of any of your allies or magic. Consider me very impressed, Lord Path. You should ask your herd what they think. The offer is on the table."

She shifted back into Roseclaw's form and very deliberately sashayed out of the room, leaving him more than a little aroused as he pondered her request.

Path couldn't help but chuckle. "Rose is going to be strutting around for days when she hears about this – a breeding request from a *second* queen. Status level will go sky-high just from the request alone!" He then blinked a few times in realisation. "Does this make me a prime breeding stud?"

Twilight and Celestia had chosen to relax after the meeting by wandering through Ponyville without any specific goal, and they found themselves walking through the budding artist district of Ponyville. A few studios were open, and they all wanted the patronage of the two princesses. Much like everyone else though, they waited in line and went into them one by one.

Some of them were... *interesting.*

Twilight couldn't help but snicker a bit as she looked at a highly romanticized painting of Celestia raising the sun. "Huh! This looks a lot like the romantic period of five hundred years ago. Notice how the shadowing doesn't quite match the ambient light? This gives it the trademark mismatched layered effect of the era. The background is in pleasant morning light, but you are in highly contrasting lights and shadows. I mean, clearly the image is meant to draw all attention to you and force the viewer to ignore the softer background."

Celestia just chuckled as she walked with Twilight. "Been reading up on your art history, have you?"

Twilight just rolled her eyes. "I can do more than just friendship and magic! I can be cultured and proper... I just don't like to be. It's boring and stuffy."

They stopped at a large statue in the middle of the gallery and gawked up at it. The sculpture was made of fine crystals of amethyst and garnet, with some emeralds and rubies. They were looking at a massive statue of Spike! However, this was very stylized since neither of the princesses could remember the last time Spike was nearly two meters tall and sculpted like a draconian god. He was posed standing proudly, blowing fire up into the air.

Celestia said, "I see that there are still crystal ponies that adore Spike. I guess this explains why he splits his time between head curator of the Ponyville Library and staying in the Crystal Kingdom. He is the Crystal Champion after all."

"Ever wonder why there are so many champions of everything?" Twilight asked. "I mean, if you want to get technical about it, everyone in my herd is a Lord or a Lady, Warforged, Champion of X, Y, or Z. Even Blue is "Forged by the Fires of Combat" if you ask the right warrior-caste griffon. There seems to be so much war even as we try to reduce it." Twilight sighed as they walked into a different wing.

"Civilizations go through cycles, Twilight. You might not know it, but concepts similar to House Path pop up every 750 years or so, last for one or two centuries, then crumble under their own size. Look back at the Roam Empire, or before that the Greeks. The only thing that makes me think House Path might be any different is that you do not seek to rule, you only seek to mediate, defend, and educate. Path has no desire to take over anything, nor any of your herd. I believe that is the critical difference, but we shall see what happens in a few generations. Usually, the further away the movement is from its progenitors, the more things start to drift." Celestia walked into the next wing, then faltered and blinked.

Twilight *oofed* as she bumped into her. "What's going on? Isn't this the section where Flix is supposed to be exhibiting?"

Celestia nodded as she looked at the scene in front of her. Discord and Flix were handing out what looked like sunglasses to various people.

Flix shouted, "Remember that my paintings are best seen with these shades. If you do not wear them, you won't get the full effect!"

Discord just laughed. "They will help you comprehend the wonderousness of his work!"

Twilight frowned. "Wonderousness isn't a word..."

Flix walked over to the two of them with a grin. "Hi, Mom! Hi, Celestia! Have some glasses!" He handed them both a pair with a grin and then walked back to the centre of the room with Discord, who was handing them out as well.

"Well... here goes nothing!" Twilight put on the glasses and proceeded to lose her grip on reality. The paintings looked like portals to worlds never before seen by ponykind. When she looked at Celestia, her mouth hung open. The two-dimensional caricature of Celestia that she beheld walked toward one of the portals. When she turned around, there was a brief moment when she was invisible while seen edge-on.

"Flix, how are you doing this?" Celestia asked.

"An artist never gives away his secrets, but I did have some help from the Professor," Flix grinned.

Discord puffed out his chest. "Am I not the best instructor ever?"

Celestia leaned closer to the nearest painting and was suddenly sucked into it. Twilight shrieked and went in after her.

The universe they were in looked like a kindergartener had painted it. Celestia looked like a giant golden stick-figure pony, and Twilight was a smaller purple stick-figure.

"How do we get out of here?!" Twilight wailed.

"We just need to find the right exit gate is all," Celestia calmly replied as she kept walking. They shifted into another painting, and this one was quite different.

Celestia was in her golden armour, and looked dramatic due to the lighting in the painting. Every part of her was detailed, showing off her every curve and muscle. Twilight blinked a few times and looked at herself.

"Is this the painting we were looking at before?" she asked.

"That it is. I have to admit, I do love how they painted my plot; I can bounce a bit off of it!" She laughed as she headed into a different painting, and Twilight followed after her.

They took a few moments to look at the scene and they sat down after only a few seconds.

Stairs! Everywhere was stairs! Celestia and Twilight looked around, trying to figure out where one started and the other ended. Twilight lit up her horn and teleported, only failing to factor how her perspective would change. Celestia tried to stifle a laugh as Twilight fell down the stairs, then up the stairs, then to the left, then upside down....

"Ow! Ow! Ow! Ow! Oof!" Twilight exclaimed as she finally collided with Celestia and they carefully moved into the next painting.

Two cans of soup fell from the top of the painting and landed in the white void. One can's label said 'Condensed Friendship' with Twilight's cutie mark on the side, while the other said 'Condensed Sunlight' and had Celestia's cutie mark.

"Why are we cans, Celestia?" Can-Twilight asked.

"I believe this is from the Pop Art movement about eighty years ago," Can-Celestia said.

"I don't like this," Can-Twilight whined.

"Follow me then," Can-Celestia said coolly.

Both of the cans flopped over to one side – first the Celestia can and then the Twilight can, and they slowly rolled out of frame.

The next painting was confusing. A series of gold and white slash strokes represented Celestia, and a few purple slash strokes represented Twilight, the idea of direction was beyond them at this point.

"Are we in some kind of abstract impressionistic piece?" Celestia asked.

"I think this is Flix's work," Twilight replied. "He was talking to Rose and I about it earlier. Which means that now I can grab onto his signature!" Twilight moved close to Celestia and they disappeared, only to reappear back where they had started in front of Discord and Flix.

"You have three seconds to explain before I ground you!" Twilight growled, and even Celestia looked cross.

"Final project, my student! Find a way out of this!" Discord laughed as he jumped into a painting and disappeared.

Flix watched him leave with wide eyes as he furiously tried to figure out what he could do. He backed away from his mother until he was stopped by an ornate desk which had a display of vases on it. Then he had an idea!

He stood up straight. "Did you know that a Pinkie Promise is forever?"

One of the drawers opened up and Pinkie Pie sprung out of it. "FOREVVEEERRR!" she proclaimed.

Flix grabbed onto her hoof when she popped out, and stuck out his tongue as he was pulled back into the drawer with Pinkie. Twilight ran over to the drawer and opened it up, only to find nothing in there.

Celestia, however, was laughing, amused by the fact that Twilight was outsmarted by her son.

"FLIX, YOU ARE SO GROUNDED!" Twilight yelled at the now-empty drawer.

Destined looked at Nox and Leatherwing, and they grinned back at him. "I don't know, guys – I have a project I'm working on, and it's kind of important."

"Destined, your mother is the Princess of Magic and Friendship; you of all ponies should know the value of balancing work and leisure. You owe it to yourself to go out with us tonight," Nox said, his grin getting wider as Leatherwing nodded in agreement.

"Well… I guess it wouldn't be too bad. I mean, it's not like we are going to be out all night, right?" Destined smiled as the two thestrals beamed at him.

"Get your pouch and let's go!" Leatherwing exclaimed as he headed out with Nox, and Destined ran out to join them. They walked toward the club where Vinyl Scratch was scheduled to play, although Destined was not to know that.

"So, I was wondering," Destined began, "I don't think I ever asked you, Leatherwing, but why are you so small in comparison to Nox?"

Nox laughed as Leatherwing sighed. "I asked Luna the same thing when I first met him. Long story short – I am what you would call a New World thestral, and Nox is an Old World thestral. His colony, a much larger one by the way, is clear on the other side of the world, and they have evolved differently from the New World breed over the centuries that we've been separated. They tend to be a lot stronger, but they aren't quite as manoeuvrable in flight due to all of the extra muscle that they have. I think when Nox first showed up, the Solar Guard called him a walking siege engine."

Nox smiled a bit. "Yeah, they did call me that. However, despite what you think, I am a rather good flier. I just think that the less those diurnal ponies know, the better. Let them think I fly like I have just one wing; it will just make the battle all the sweeter when I surprise them."

Destined laughed as he shared the big thestral's amusement, stopping as they reached the club door. Night was already well under way, and the steady beat of bass was vibrating Destined's chest. "So this is where we're going?"

Nox nodded enthusiastically. "This is one of the best things that I have learned about the New World since I've been here. For those that are especially receptive to sound vibrations, this is the best show in Ponyville, so let's get going!"

Nox pushed both of them inside with him using his strong wings. Upon entering the club, Destined started to have a small panic attack due to all the people and the pulsing beat. Leatherwing, however, was bobbing his head to the music as his ears kept swivelling around, picking up on the notes too low or too high for Destined to hear. Nox kept the increasingly panicky alicorn calm until Leatherwing came back with three giant mangoes with straws in them.

Destined just blinked and stared at the mango as he took it. "What is it?"

Leatherwing smiled. "They call it a mango slammer. Have a sip!"

Destined took a small sip, and his eyes went wide. "This is the best thing ever!" he declared, and he started taking large gulps through his straw as Leatherwing smiled.

"Let's go to the dance floor!"

The trio went to the dance floor as the Ponystep began playing. As more and more people went onto the floor, they got separated.

Nox and Leatherwing were able to find each other via clicks and whistles, but it wasn't until they saw fireworks that they knew where Destined was.

Destined was drunk. No, not drunk – he was *sloshed*. He was chatting up a unicorn who was grinning at him, half because he was making a show, and half because she was concerned. Nox pushed through the crowd and looked at the unicorn.

"How many mango slammers did he have?" he asked in a concerned voice.

"I saw him drink five. I think he's on his sixth right now." The unicorn giggled a bit as she took his hoof and a pen, writing down her mailing address for him. "Write me when you wake up tomorrow, hon." She smiled and walked off, swaying her hips for the teenage alicorn as she left. Destined started laughing.

"I'm so smooth!" Destined exclaimed, nearly falling off of the chair.

Leatherwing groaned. "Luna is going to kill us! Come on, let's get him home."

Destined stood up, his horn glowing brightly. "I AM A MASTER OF SPACE AND TIME! TELEPORTING IS BUT A PALTRY FEAT!"

Nox's eyes went wide. "WAIT! NO!"

The group teleported, not in a bang but more of a whimper as they blinked out of the club to who knew where.

That night, the herd was preparing for bed after a rather eventful day. Path was feeling a bit pensive and Free picked up on it almost instantly.

"Hey Path, what's wrong? You seem really wound up about something," Free queried as he yawned.

"Well… yeah… there is something – something I was not expecting came up, so now I feel kind of awkward about it." Path curled up a bit.

Luna just blinked in concern. "So what's wrong?"

Path slowly sat up and looked at them all. "The Red Queen, Carpacia, has asked me to mate with her in order to breed a new princess."

The four just looked at him for a moment, not saying anything while they took in that statement. Roseclaw was first to react. She got up, puffed out her feathers a bit, and grinned smugly as she strutted around the room. "Of course! It is only natural that those seeking to continue their line would find the strongest potential seed, and naturally our warrior is the strongest male in the land. It's obvious that she would want him. Who am I to deprive the world of such potency?" Her feathers poofed out more.

Free rolled his eyes. "If your ego gets any bigger, Twilight is gonna need to make another wing in the castle for it." He laughed as Roseclaw's grin just kept getting bigger. He turned to Path and said, "More to the point though, do you think that she would let me have some fun with her? I mean Queen on Queen action would be pretty hot."

Path chuckled. "I could ask, but I'm fairly certain that the answer would be no. I remember Dianthia talking about how queens do not ever mix, be it due to political or genetic reasons."

Free deflated slightly and he huffed. "Well, that's no fun, but then again I bet I could feel what you're experiencing via our link, so I guess I could rut vicariously through you."

Luna spoke up. "I do not understand why this is an issue. In the old days, it was common practice for noble mares to seek out worthy mates to sire strong heirs. Path *has* to mate to ensure that his strength is passed on. Actually, I am reminded of several cases in which warriors and knights were elevated to nobility so that their strength could be used to enhance the usually dwindling capacity of the old noble bloodlines." Luna's eyes grew distant as her recollections took her far into the past.

Twilight was the last to speak up as she hummed thoughtfully. "I think that this could be a good thing. I couldn't really do any research last time because I wasn't in any condition to do so, but now I am fairly certain that I could render myself invisible, take notes, and do some subtle scanning while the act is in process."

Path stared at Twilight for a long moment before raising an eyebrow and saying, "Seriously? Your herdmate would be banging a changeling queen that's *not* Free, and all you would think of is doing research?"

Twilight shrugged helplessly. "What can I say? It's not my fault if it's something that has never been researched before."

Free laughed uproariously. "Oh, Sparkles, just when I think that you couldn't get any more adorkable!"

Path smirked a bit. "Okay. I'm prepared to say no if even one of you objects, so it's time for a vote. Rose, what do you think?"

Roseclaw was still grinning. "Of course I'm okay with my warrior spreading his legacy to those who are worthy. And think of the boost in status that would give us! I would be annoyed if you didn't!"

Path chuckled. "Okay, that's one vote for yes. Free?"

"Since when have I ever objected to some guilt-free mutually agreeable banging? It's not like she's asking to join the herd or anything. As long as you get to see the foal, I'm okay with it."

Path nodded and turned to his next mate. "Twilight?"

Twilight tapped her chin thoughtfully. "I think this could be a win-win situation. As long as I can take notes and do passive scans, and I'm allowed to examine the offspring later, I'm okay with it!"

"I'll let her know that those are your conditions," Path replied before turning to the other alicorn snuggled up to him. "Luna?"

"I have already expressed my approval. I have seen Free's dreams of the time that thou mated with him. I hope that thou dost bring that kind of ... exuberance when it is time for thee to quench the fires of my heat."

Path's eyes went wide as saucers. Luna smirked, and the others joined in with laughter.

Path huffed a bit and grabbed the large blankets, pulling them over the group. "Oh, hush! I'll let her know the decision in the morn–"

The group was startled out of their love pile as several large bangs went off in their room. In the centre of the room, Destined appeared, five mangoes fell to the floor, and the aroma of booze wafted over the group. "I AM THE BUCKING GOD OF MANGOES!" Destined yelled, his eyes glowing a bright white as sparks came off his horn.

Nox appeared in mid-air and he did not have enough time to open his wings to gain lift before he slammed face-first into the floor. His body contorted backwards and he slumped to the carpet.

However, Leatherwing fared the worst. His back half was poking out of the ceiling, while his front half was poking out of a side wall. Instead of being frightened or passing out, he just looked at his rear with a dismal sigh, his tail still swaying back and forth in front of his nose. "This is why I can't have nice things."

Destined started screaming out lyrics to one of the songs at the bar: "I am immortal, I have inside me blood of kings! I have no rival, No pony can be my equal! Take me to the future of your world!"

Destined stumbled around a few more times before Luna and Twilight got out of bed. Twilight cast a null-magic spell to disrupt his channelling. Luna teleported Leatherwing out of his predicament, and he reappeared mercifully intact in front of her. She also levitated Nox to his hooves and placed him beside Leatherwing. She did *not* look happy.

"Thou didst interrupt me with my herd. I enjoy my herd time. Why didst thou disrupt my herd time?" she asked with a quietly dangerous edge to her voice, and her eyes started to glow.

Leatherwing stammered as he was frozen in mid-sentence. "I... I... I thought he would like mangoes!"

"Wrong answer!" Luna teleported Leatherwing away and then glared at Nox.

Nox had a stupid, slightly tipsy smile on his face. He knew that he was in trouble, and nothing he could say would fix that. "I've got nothing. We got the colt drunker than hell because it took that much motivation for him to not freak out at a club. It worked though!" he added with an ingratiating grin.

Luna glared at him and shouted, "TO THE MOON!"

Nox disappeared in a bright flash. Luna looked to the still softly singing Destined and she hit him with a sleep spell. She then teleported him into his room with a groan.

The others looked at Luna and blinked a few times. The dark alicorn walked back over with a pout on her muzzle, and dug herself back under the covers. "I like my herd time. I don't get enough opportunities, so I do *not* like disruptions! Cuddle time is now! I'll deal with it tomorrow."

They all laughed as they found their favourite positions together under the large blanket. Almost everyone fell asleep quite easily since the day had been long and tiring. Path, however, just lay there, thinking about how he was going to approach the new situation. He was certain that Carpacia would approach him again, and when she did, they would open negotiations.

Nox looked up at the blue marble in the black sky. "I never thought I'd see this view again. Maybe the grin was overdoing it a *bit* too much," he murmured morosely.

Chapter 16:
The Calm Before The Storm

Five in the morning.

Nobody should be up at five in the morning, but someone stirred in Blue Streak's room. A figure dimly seen in the pre-dawn gloom moved over to a set of shelves, pressed a hidden switch, and removed a small object. Moments later, the room was still once more as the door quietly closed.

Nobody in Blue Streak's room was awake, nor was due to be for several hours. His room stood out when compared to his siblings. All of the furniture in the room had been moved to the edges, leaving a massive space in the middle where there was a depression lined with soft pillows and pelts, with a rise along the edges. If somebody looked at it objectively, they might think it was a fusion of a pony, griffish, and draconic bedroom, and curled up in the centre of that sleeping nest there was a dreaming dragoness. As Cinder tended to sleep in, and Blue had changed his sleeping habits to match hers, normally nothing would be happening until much later, so one could imagine the chaos that erupted when the door nearly flew off its hinges only a few hours later, and an old griffon strutted inside.

"**Blue Streak! You are late for your encouragement!**"

Warfist's voice rolled through the room with enough force to even wake up Cinder, and she looked up with eyes barely able to focus on the ornery griffon. She held what she thought was Blue, but quickly became confused as she realized that she was holding a body pillow instead of a warm pony.

"W-what...?" Cinder groaned groggily.

"**Where is he, Cinder?!**" Warfist bellowed at the top of his lungs. "**His encouragement is not yet complete!**" Warfist walked into the room and started looking around as the dragoness slowly woke up, groaning as she rubbed her eyes. "**He has an obligation that can only be repaid in sweat and pain!**" He kept pacing around, his razor-sharp eyes taking in anything that might indicate a hiding pony.

Cinder had changed little in the years that had gone by since Blue Streak's first visit to the Dragon Lands. She was only a few inches taller, but her territorial and possessive nature had become more pronounced. Most other females knew never to stare at Blue Streak when he was training outside if there was even a possibility that Cinder was around. She was known to singe tails as a warning for staring at what she said was rightly hers. This was a quality that Roseclaw was proud of – if Blue was to even consider having another mate, she would have to prove herself to the dragon first. Twilight, on the other hoof, was always trying to get her to calm down, although admittedly Cinder had never raised a claw against a female since the incident with Moira Skytalon. Then again, that incident had scarcely been forgotten either, despite the intervening years.

But that was neither here nor there right now. The dragoness looked at Warfist before she sighed, rolled onto her feet, swung her tail around a few times, and flapped her wings, extending and retracting them as she stretched. With another large yawn, she looked back at Warfist. The old griffon looked just as powerful as he had fifteen years ago.

"When we went to asleep, he was curled up with me, which is why I'm wondering why I woke up to just a pillow." Cinder groaned, stood up, and walked over to Warfist who was looking around the room to try and find evidence of where Blue had gone. Something apparently caught his eye.

"What was in this small drawer?" Warfist pointed to what looked like a compartment that came out of a normal shelf.

When Cinder looked at the empty drawer, she blinked a few times in confusion. "I have slept here for I don't know how long, and I have never seen that open." She slowly pressed it shut, and they noticed that the drawer was created so expertly that when it closed, neither of them could see the seam. "Huh! Well, I can think of a few places that he could be. I think Path and Lucida should be in the main hall right now; we should go see if he went through there. I mean…" She groaned again and rubbed her head. "He's not scheduled to go out on another training run with Shining for a few more days. It's supposed to be his downtime, so I don't see why he would have left the estate. He already went to the pub a few days ago; he's really only a weekend kind of guy when it comes to that," Cinder said as she walked past Warfist and went toward the door.

Warfist followed, and then nearly bumped into her when she stopped abruptly. He huffed slightly, clearly impatient.

Cinder looked back to him and asked, "So... why are you trying to find him so badly, and what is with this talk about encouragement? You stopped that after he came back from his first visit to the Dragon Lands. He hasn't had any 'encouragement', as you call it, for nearly four years." She exited the room and walked down the hall with Warfist beside her.

"This time it is not encouragement per se. I'm really here so that I can train him just a little more before I give him a gift." Warfist sighed as they rounded the corner.

"Oh? What gift would that be?" Cinder asked casually.

"Cinder, I am not a young griffon. I am ancient by warrior standards; eighty five is unheard of for somegriff who routinely sees battle. I could have led a campaign to try take over Equestria, but after the passing of my chick son and my hen wife, I started to doubt power. You know, when you pass, you can't take any of it with you. So that's what I want to do. I want to pass all that I am on to Blue Streak. It's an old Griffonian rite; a way to pass one's honour to another not of your direct blood," Warfist said neutrally as he kept walking.

"Isn't such a thing common? I mean that's how Lord Path was able to get this entire estate, and then when you fought one of Ravenclaw's cronies, you acquired all of his possessions," Cinder pointed out as they made their way down the stairs.

"An honour duel doesn't give you the opponent's honour, achievements, or their being. It just gives you their material possessions, and such things don't matter to me. This ritual is one of the most gruesome, and it's usually not practiced. Actually, I can only think of one that happened in the last ten years. It's taxing on the body, mind, and soul. One who attempts the Rite rarely comes out the same, if at all. On top of that, it can only be sanctioned by the heads of the ruling and warrior caste in a completely unopposed decision. It is so rare and so brutal, only the strongest of hardliners and traditionalists will sanction it, but all will accept the results," Warfist spoke seriously.

"What is so intense about this trial? What would push Blue to his limits?" Cinder asked.

"In order for him to gain my glory and my honour, he has to *kill* all those who would seek it for themselves. With no other challengers in his path, he would then have to face me to the death. Only after drinking my heart's blood will he be known as High General Blue Streak Warfist XVI." Warfist looked at her, his eyes stone cold. "Can you tell me that would not shake him to his very foundation? Ponies, even warrior ones, are by nature pacific; could he overcome that to take what I willingly give him?" He glared at Cinder until she looked away.

"That does sound brutal. I guess that's why it's not done very often," Cinder whispered. "Why would you even ask him to do that when you know he idolizes you?"

"The time will come when I will no longer be fit to be House Path's War Leader – can you imagine a warrior like me retiring to rot away for the remainder of my days? Better to pass in honorable battle and bequeath all that I am to Blue. However, let's not dwell on it for now. That event still lies far in the future, if Blue Streak accepts it at all."

Warfist opened the door to the meeting room where Path and

Lucida did all of their negotiations. Aside from Blue who had been adopted into the family, Lucida was the oldest of the children, and she had been groomed for the position from an early age. It had really started with the test about two years back, but it set a precedent. As the months went on, Path had hit her with more tests and let her sit in on more meetings, advisory boards and official deliberations. She hadn't noticed it, but Path was actually becoming more auxiliary and was really only serving to set the pace for the meetings. Most of the decisions were being made by the hippogriff, although every now and then, Path did have to jump in to give her an 'emergency advisory' about certain topics.

This meeting, however, was trying the patience of both of them. Chief Scruffy of the Diamond Dog Cooperative and Granite Will of the Crystal Kingdom Trading Company were currently in a heated dispute, with Lucida and Path in the middle of it all.

Path was an interesting case – for a pony who was now approaching his forties, he looked no older than when he had met Twilight in a Canterlot café all those years ago. In fact, the rigorous exercise and training that he did most days had added to his musculature and toned his body to make him fitter than he had ever been. Ponies and griffons alike were beginning to wonder if maybe he was more than he claimed to be. The only physical change that indicated aging was the fact he was no longer dying and trimming his face scruff. Instead, his green mane now descended down the sides of his face and met up on his chin. The well-kept beard almost made him look regal if not for his generally laidback attitude most of the time.

Lucida however....

"When you both came to House Path for mediation, what were you expecting? Were you expecting favour, Granite Will, because my mother is related to your prince? Were you expecting me to be biased toward you, Chief Scruffy, because I ruled in your favour in one of my first deliberations? In House Path, we will *always* balance the arguments of all parties fairly. To act otherwise would undo the very tenets that we were founded upon. We will *always* bring an equitable, and unbiased approach to any negotiations, even if it does not fit your expectations." Lucida spoke eloquently but with enough gravity behind her words to make all parties fall silent.

'*The speech training with Celestia has certainly paid off,*' Path thought to himself from his seat to the left of Lucida.

"You both have come to us and asked us to mediate your situation after normal avenues have failed. To sum up, one large business is worried about another large business because both of your main exports happen to be stone products and crystals. You're both the same size and have about the same output capacity. If one of you tries to take the market from the other, the resulting undercutting and price gouging would cause the *entire* industry to suffer," Lucida said as she looked over some of the papers for a sixth time. She was always very thorough with her research. "Together, both of you have over 90% of the industry market share. So I am glad you have come to us for mediation, and I have come up with a solution if you would hear me out."

"**I will not settle for anything less than sanctions on the Austri Islands!**" Granite Will bellowed.

"**I will not idly stand by while he makes threats to my people!**" Chief Scruffy barked out.

Rather than screech and throw things like Lucida used to do, she kept her cool as the two parties descended back into barking and neighing angrily at each other. She idly tapped her claws on the table until they both calmed down and looked over to her.

"Are you both done?" Lucida asked softly, sounding like a mother disappointed with her quarrelling foals.

Path just grinned as he watched his little girl; the seventeen-year-old had come so far in her studies and diplomatic classes with the princesses, empathy and body language classes with Dianthia and Fleur, and history lessons with Roseclaw and Twilight. Everyone's efforts, especially Lucida's, had paid off.

Lucida continued once she had the abashed traders' attention again. "What I propose is this: instead of competing directly with each other, work together. Chief Scruffy, focus on stone and rock production, and leave your sale of crystals mainly to the local market for now. Granite Will, focus on crystal production while leaving your rock and stone products to your local market. The only exceptions should be any products that are unique to your businesses, and to fill customer requirements that exceed your competitor's ability to fill. Do this for five years and then switch. This way you can put your focus mostly in one area while your profits are maximized. You don't have to worry about corporate warfare ruining your bottom line, and both of you could cooperate instead of being in opposition. For example, you could act as the other's agent in your area, taking a small commission on each sale," Lucida suggested as she stared both of the two energetic parties down, effectively draining them of their previous aggression.

"You may even use the intervening time to develop new products to be released at the beginning of each five year cycle. Sales by the other could be used as reliable indicators of what to stockpile for yourselves. There are many benefits to be had by focusing on your core products and not wasting time, effort, and above all, money to unnecessary fighting. While competition is a driving factor, cooperation can be more profitable. However, I have one caveat – if one of you decides to use your current five-year dominance of the market to unreasonably drive up prices, I will authorize your competition to use their reserves to undercut you to bring those prices back down. My proposal is meant to benefit the consumers as well as yourselves, and I would be happy to mediate on their behalf also. As a final point, I will remind you that by agreeing to mediation by House Path, you will be legally bound to any agreements that are made here, and they are enforceable by House Path by authority of your governments, so think hard and carefully, and be honest in your dealings."

Path stood up and smiled at the business representatives. "I think this proposal has a lot of potential, and you should take the opportunity to consider its ramifications. If both of you would be so kind as to return to your quarters for the day, you can enjoy our hospitality while you mull it over. We will meet back here at nine tomorrow morning to hear any final thoughts, and then hopefully we can officially resolve the matter to your mutual satisfaction."

The two parties nodded and slowly filed out as Cinder and Warfist walked into the meeting room. When both the diamond dog and crystal pony were out of earshot, Lucida groaned and thumped her head onto the desk. "Meetings, meetings, meetings... I know they're important, but damn it! I don't want to do them anymore this week. D-a-a-a-d, take over for me, *please*?" Lucida whined.

Path chuckled. "You're doing fine, Lucida. You just need to build up your endurance a bit more. I'm afraid that this will always be the less exciting side of the House of Path."

Before Lucida could reply, Cinder finally spoke up. "Hey, has either of you two seen Blue Streak around? Warfist and I are looking for him, and I honestly have no clue where he could be. Do you have any ideas?"

Path looked thoughtful for a moment. "Hmm... I think I saw him really early this morning heading over to the R&D department with Techbird and Pif. I generally don't like going down to their levels because they sometimes look at me like I'm an experiment." Path shivered as memories of his latest body scan came back to him. "But Lucida would be more than happy to take you down there, wouldn't you, dear?" Path added slyly.

"You just don't want to go down there, do you, Dad?" Lucida snarked.

Path grinned. "And you want a break from meetings, so I figure this way we both win."

"Deal!" Lucida said as she stood back up and stretched, her muscles and bones sore from sitting in the stuffy room for so long.

The hippogriff, the dragoness and the old griffon walked out of the main office and headed toward the smaller R&D department.

Almost everyone knew that the military centre of the House was in Griffonia, but the research centre was in Equestria. The main House had a small satellite department though, and every now and then, Techbird and Pif ran back and forth between the two bases of operation to make sure things were going smoothly. They had arrived last night with Luna, not only for the Friday dinner, but also to make sure that things were still on track at the Griffonian branch of '*Equus Innovations Incorporated*', the official name of the think-tank created by Pif and Techbird.

When they arrived at what looked like just a small hut, Warfist raised an eyebrow as he assessed the unimpressive building with disbelief. "Really? This is it? This is the massive think-tank that Epiphany goes on and on about?"

Lucida tried to conceal a grin. "I can see why you would be puzzled, Warfist. While I'm sure you're aware of it for security purposes, I don't think I've ever seen you in this area of the compound. Come on, let's go inside and you can see just what the Griffonian branch has to offer." Lucida opened the door and motioned for them to go inside.

Once the door closed behind them, the small room lit up to reveal what looked like a slightly recessed platform in the centre of the stark white room. A changeling guard looked over at the group, nodded at Lucida, and then went back to reading his book.

"The security – it's overwhelming," Warfist said in a deadpan tone.

Lucida rolled her eyes. "The changeling guard is merely the first line of security. He's able to detect hostile or malicious intent. The rest of the security is far less obvious. There are both magical wards placed by Mama Twilight, and hidden technological devices monitoring everyone coming into the facility." She stepped onto the platform, indicating to the rest of them to follow suit. The platform lurched and sank into the ground, quickly picking up speed as the white room disappeared above them. Cinder made a small scream of surprise as she latched onto Lucida, confused as to what was going on.

Lucida smiled. "Pif and Techbird are very protective about their R&D department. It's why we have to go down this shaft to access the primary research room. After that, we can go see where they are."

"How far down are we going?" Cinder asked, uncomfortable with the thought of how deep below the earth they were traveling.

"They tell me that's classified. However, Free says that if you fell from the entrance to the floor of the main room, you would be falling for nearly five minutes. Judge for yourself if he's exaggerating," Lucida added with a chuckle.

After considerably less than five minutes, the platform slowed down and entered through the top of a much larger white room. It was rather difficult to judge scale until they stopped moving and a Chrome Changeling walked up to them.

"Hi, Lucida, Miss Cinder, Master Warfist. Looking for Techbird and Epiphany, I take it?" the 'ling asked in a happy tone. The tech changeling was dressed in a white lab coat, and it looked like he had a clipboard on his back. His horn lit up and he moved it around to look at it. "It appears that Tech and Pif are currently in the astro-science wing, working on a new kind of propulsion technique." He flipped through a few more pages. "Multi-purpose asymmetrical thrust vectoring using atypical magical sources." The changeling looked at the group with a smile. "Exciting stuff! I wish I got to work on awesome projects like that." He looked over a second sheet on the clipboard. "Okay, so you should be looking for room 7-12-3."

"Why does the room number sound so strange?" Cinder asked.

The 'ling replied, "Oh, it's because each number correlates to a designation on the X, Y, and Z axis, so it would be the seventh room down, the twelfth room to the left, and then the third room forward." His horn lit up. "Hold on tight – the platform can be kind of disorienting for the first-time user!"

"What do you mean disor-AAAHHHH!" Cinder screamed yet again as the platform moved once more, but this time going in one room and out the other, giving them brief glimpses of other projects that were being worked on. It was not long before the platform slowed to a stop in another white room, but this time it was lined with what looked like black chalkboards. All of them were covered in equations and design schematics, and off to the side there was a strange device with several cables going in and out of it. A few were connected to a crystal mana battery, and beyond that they were able to see the two whom they were looking for, talking and pointing at an equation on one of the chalkboards.

"HEY, PIFFY!" Lucida yelled as she walked over to them as Warfist and Cinder followed.

Pif was in her compromise ponyling form – mostly earth pony, but with her distinctive changeling horn glowing as it manipulated a stick of chalk. She turned to look at her sister with a smile. "What's up, Lucy? Did the meeting go okay?"

Lucida groaned when Pif brought up the meeting and she shrugged it off. "Let's not talk about it. Has Blue been around lately? I know you still sometimes make him come down here for some tests every now and then."

"Actually I think I saw him going toward the Zenith Dome. Hey, Tech, can we take a break?" Pif asked. "I think we've been at this all night."

"It's night-time? Or is it morning? Sometimes I forget what day it even is. Yes, yes! Go have fun with your family. I need to figure out why the vector system shuts down before it can reach max thrust." Techbird waved her off as her attention went back to the chalkboard.

Warfist, Cinder, Lucida, and Epiphany all went back to the platform. Cinder couldn't help but laugh this time as they took off in another random direction, heading back to the main entrance of the R&D department.

"You know, it's almost like we're assembling a party; at least that's how it tends to go when I play Oubliettes & Ogres with the gaming club." Cinder giggled as Warfist rolled his eyes.

Once the group left the small entry hut, they headed toward the Zenith Dome.

"We all have wings, so why don't we just fly there?" Cinder suddenly asked. Everyone looked abashed at not thinking of that sooner.

Warfist face-clawed with a groan, then opened his wings and took to the sky. Lucida followed suit as Pif switched to pegasus form and did the same. Cinder bounded for a few meters before taking to the sky, heading toward the dome.

Zenith Dome was a project that was created by the combined efforts of Destined Path and Luna. It was a large observatory, and also a planetarium when it wasn't being used by either the resident or visiting astronomers. However, when it wasn't night time, Luna and Destined used it as a place to meditate and enjoy tea.

The group circled around the large structure. Since the sun had risen, the main doors that allowed the telescope to peer out were now closed. They landed at the door and settled their wings before entering. They were greeted with the most pleasant of smells – vanilla, cinnamon, and lavender. The group walked in with soft smiles on their faces. In the centre of the room next to the telescope, there was a recessed area where the two alicorns were sitting. Some incense was burning, and it looked like they were in the middle of... something. Every now and then, their horns would spark to life only to fade out again. They were completely oblivious to the four who were standing next to them.

Lucida grinned, leaned over to Destined, and licked the side of his face. As she moved up, the younger alicorn's eyes opened slowly, and then once he realized what was happening, he started screaming as he flailed out of his meditative stance. His yelling jarred Luna out of her meditative trance, and she started scream also, only much louder. Eventually, everyone was screaming from the ear-piercing alicorn's voice, except for Warfist who'd had enough, and he slammed his talons into the ground and let out a war screech.

"**This has gone on long enough! Somebody tell me where Blue Streak is, or so help me, everyone is getting *encouragement*!**" He glared at them all with his wings spread as widely as he could open them.

Destined calmed down as Luna started laughing at the antics that she allowed herself to get wrapped up into.

"If thou really dost wish to know where he is, Warfist, thou should go talk to his Aunt Greenfield, as only she may tell thee where he went. Destined, thou should also go with them. We have been meditating for the past four hours, after all."

Destined nodded and stood up. "Let's go to the worker barracks. Around this time, I believe she would be getting ready to tend to the fields for her morning shift."

Warfist was looking more and more frustrated; what should have only taken a few minutes was now into its second hour. "Princess Luna, would you be so kind to teleport us to the barracks?" Warfist asked as politely as he could manage.

Luna smiled and nodded. The group moved close together as Luna's horn lit up, although it was hardly necessary. Such a short distance teleport with so few people was trivial for her. With a quiet pop, the group disappeared and then reappeared in front of the barracks.

The barracks were one of the most radically altered areas of the estate. The ramshackle shanties that Ravenclaw had forced the earth ponies to live in had been torn down after these had been built to replace them. They threw out the common Griffonian ideals when it came to housing construction, and instead approached them with Manehatten flair. There were three large main buildings, each of them three stories high and built to Tech's and Clue's specifications. The former slaves had been given well-appointed rooms as thanks for their previously unacknowledged hard work. They had also been given a stipend, and while it was not as much as a normal griff worker would make, it was all that House Path had been able to afford then without reducing the workers' numbers. As the wealth and power of the House had grown, that gap had continued to narrow, and the House made huge strides transitioning the former slaves towards a fully free and equal status in Griffonian society. The resulting morale boost made the staff appreciate House Path all the more, and few had left to seek more lucrative employment when it had eventually become available to ponies.

Pif led the group up to one of the rooms and knocked on the door.

"How do you know this is her room number?" Cinder asked.

"I overheard Blue talking about his aunt once, and he mentioned this room number," Pif replied. "Of course that's now stored in the hive-mind, so I can always recall it."

The door opened to reveal an earth pony mare. Blue's aunt was quite a bit older now, but she was still a strong, toned mare who was as stubborn as ever. She welcomed them in and offered them tea. "It's been a while since I've seen you all. You have grown so big, Miss Lucida, just like Blue Streak."

"Speaking of him, do you know where he is?" Cinder asked.

"Oh... oh, hon, he didn't tell you yet? Well, it's always hard for him to let people see that part of him. I'm not surprised that he keeps it to himself." She sighed sadly as she sipped her tea.

"Is Blue okay? Did something happen to him?" Cinder was beginning to get concerned.

"On this day when he was two, something did happen, yes. It was the death of his biological parents. It's a loss that still hurts him." She looked at Warfist. "Can you let him rest for just one day? It's not as if he is out merely enjoying himself," Greenfield said sorrowfully.

Warfist nodded gravely. "I won't do what I was planning on doing today." He looked at Blue's mate and siblings. "However, I believe that you four should go to him and console him. If you are all here, he is probably grieving alone."

"So, where is he?" Destined asked.

Greenfield replied, "Do you know the hill on the south-eastern edge of the estate? I believe the foals are calling it Blight Hill nowadays."

Destined nodded. "Oh, you mean that creepy small hill that can't seem to grow anything, not even grass?" Destined asked. "Actually, now that I think about it, quite a few ponies are afraid of going up there. All that's left is the corpse of a tree."

"That's the tree that fell on Blue's parents. The strange thing is that it used to be so full of blossoms, and the ground below it always erupted into bloom when the springtime rolled around, but once Blue came and fetched everyone, everything was dead... his parents... the tree... the grass.... We tried for nearly six years to get anything to grow on that land. Animals don't even tread there, and we never figured out how or why that is the case," Greenfield said sadly. The group could tell that she found the topic painful.

Warfist nodded in understanding, and he said gruffly, "You four go check on Blue. I'm going to go back to the training barracks after I finish talking with Ms. Greenfield. I don't intend to bring anything up with him for a couple of days, so just make sure that he's going to be okay. I know what loss can do to a person. Dwelling on tragedy can create the conditions for further misfortune."

The youths said their farewells and left, while Warfist continued to have tea and talk to Blue's aunt about him.

"Come on, it's only a few moments away," Cinder said as she ran out of the house, bounding and leaping to catch enough air to take to the skies. Lucida, Pif, and Destined followed quickly after. They sailed together, catching a breeze that pushed them over toward the hill. As they came closer, they saw a blue dot on the brown, barren hilltop. They landed right at the boundary where plants ceased to grow, and Cinder motioned for them to be quiet. They could hear Blue talking apparently to nobody. He was looking down at one hoof that was holding what looked like a picture frame.

"I could do it, so why don't I? I can hold enough power within myself, so that's not an issue. I can get access to a spell... it's in the Crystal Archives. I can program a tek-horn. One Aspect and two alicorns... I could do it... I would do all of it to see you two again. I can barely remember your faces without this picture. I can't even remember your voices.... It wouldn't be that bad... they would forgive me... eventually." He sighed softly and his shoulders slumped. "But you would not."

They watched the earth pony slowly set the picture frame down onto a linen cloth on the ground, wrap it up, and then put it in his pouch. His ears twitched with irritation.

"I really wish you wouldn't eavesdrop on me," Blue said a bit more loudly. "Normally I wouldn't care, but I can't deal with it today." Blue waved them over.

"How could you tell we were here?" Cinder asked.

Blue waved one of his hooves; it didn't have his specialized shoe on it. "When I have the shoes off, I can sense changes to the magic of the area I'm in. I felt you the moment you landed." He turned back to them with a sigh as he put the shoe back on.

"So what can I do for you guys?" Blue smiled weakly, but it was apparent that he had been crying for a while. There was no way his eyes would be that red and the fur under his eyes that matted otherwise.

Destined however looked deadly serious. "What would you do if they would forgive you?"

"It doesn't matter; I won't do it. Nothing can undo what has been done. I could lie to myself, but I have read enough to know that it's a path I can never go down if I wish to remain who I am." He wiped his nose slightly as he perked back up with a silly grin. "So, does anybody wanna go get a drink or something? I'll buy! It could be f-u-u-n-n."

Pif shook her head. "Brother, did I ever tell you how foul hollow feelings taste? You aren't fooling me."

Blue's ears drooped again. "Listen I–"

Blue Streak was cut off as the sky suddenly darkened and a strange vortex appeared in mid-air. Then, with a burst of unknown energy, a grey pegasus emerged from it, shooting straight at the group before she

slowed down and came to a halt by smacking into the dead tree and falling onto her rump.

"Hi!" the mare said brightly, apparently unaffected by her precipitous arrival.

"What...? **What?!**" Destined fretted as he felt a kind of magic – no a kind of *force* that he had never felt before as he looked up at the hole and the whirling pattern around it.

"Who the hell are you?!" Cinder asked.

"Oh, it's Derpy!" Lucida said with a smile of recognition as she helped the pegasus up. "She's the mailmare in Ponyville. I think she and Time Turner are special someponies."

The vortex disappeared as Derpy tapped a device strapped on her left foreleg above her hoof. "Oh! I need to take you to the Doctor right now! There isn't even time for muffins!" Derpy tapped on the strange device again.

Destined looked at the horizon. "What's that strange glow?" he asked. A band of something indescribable rushed towards them at an incredible rate.

"Oh, no! The timeline is already changing!" Derpy exclaimed. She hopped into the centre of the group and pressed a button just before the shockwave washed over the estate. Pif was alarmed as she felt the connection to her hive snap as the five of them were flung through a new vortex.

They came to rest in the middle of a strange chamber filled with arcane devices. The group groaned as they untangled themselves from each other and slowly stood up. Pif however was shaking; she had not been disconnected from the hive-mind since the incident with Chrysalis, and she was finding the silence in her head unnerving.

"Okay, what the hell just happened and where are we?" Blue asked with a growl as a tan earth pony with an hourglass cutie mark trotted up to him.

"Hi there, Blue Streak! Ready to save the world?" the Doctor asked cheerfully.

Blue was stunned. "**WHAT?!**" he yelped.

\##

To be continued in: *"QUANTUM GALLOP"*

\##

Art Credits

Cover art

GrayPaint
http://graypaint.deviantart.com

Interior illustrations

Kat Miller
http://www.furaffinity.net/user/foxenawolf

All art is copyright © 2016 to the respective artists and is used with their express permission.

If you would like to see the colour versions of Kat's illustrations, please visit my website:
http://www.chakatsden.com/chakat/Stories/GrowingYears.html

Made in the USA
Charleston, SC
29 June 2016